THIS IS WHERE I LEAVE YOU

What would you do if you crept into your house on your wife's birthday to find her in bed? Having sex? With your boss?

And what if you were holding a lighted birthday cake covered in hot melted wax?

Well? What would you do?

And things only get worse for Judd Foxman when the death of his father brings his entire family together for the first time in years. Conspicuously absent – Judd's wife, Jen, whose affair with his boss has recently become oh-so-excruciatingly public.

Our hero Judd joins his folks as they reluctantly submit to their father's dying request: to spend seven days mourning together. In the same house. Like a real family.

As the week spins out of control, grudges resurface, secrets are revealed and old passions reawakened. Judd tries to make sense of the mess his life has become while trying not to get sucked into the regressive dramas of his dysfunctional family...

In the end, **THIS IS WHERE I LEAVE YOU** shows what happens when life throws all its crap at you at the same time – losing a job, parent and spouse – not to mention fighting off the advances of an overwhelmingly broody sister-in-law. All of which would be hard enough without the bombshell Jen dropped the day Judd's father died: she's pregnant.

Riotously funny and emotionally raw, this is a novel about love, marriage, divorce, family, and the ties that bind – whether we like it or not.

Also by Jonathan Tropper

Plan B

The Book of Joe

Everything Changes

How to Talk to a Widower

THIS IS WHERE I LEAVE YOU

JONATHAN TROPPER

First published in Great Britain in 2010 by Orion Books,
an imprint of The Orion Publishing Group Ltd
Orion House, 5 Upper Saint Martin's Lane
London WC2H 9EA

An Hachette UK Company

3 5 7 9 10 8 6 4 2

A CIP catalogue record for this book is
available from the British Library.

ISBN (Hardback) 978 0 7528 8583 4
ISBN (Trade Paperback) 978 0 7528 8584 1

Printed in Great Britain by Clays Ltd, St Ives plc

The Orion Publishing Group's policy is to use papers that
are natural, renewable and recyclable products and made
from wood grown in sustainable forests. The logging and
manufacturing processes are expected to conform to the
environmental regulations of the country of origin.

www.orionbooks.co.uk

Mom and Dad

THIS IS
WHERE I
LEAVE YOU

Chapter 1

D ad's dead," Wendy says offhandedly, like it's happened before, like it happens every day. It can be grating, this act of hers, to be utterly unfazed at all times, even in the face of tragedy. "He died two hours ago."

"How's Mom doing?"

"She's Mom, you know? She wanted to know how much to tip the coroner."

I have to smile, even as I chafe, as always, at our family's patented inability to express emotion during watershed events. There is no occasion calling for sincerity that the Foxman family won't quickly diminish or pervert through our own genetically engineered brand of irony and evasion. We banter, quip, and insult our way through birthdays, holidays, weddings, illnesses. Now Dad is dead and Wendy is cracking wise. It serves him right, since he was something of a pioneer at the forefront of emotional repression.

"It gets better," Wendy says.

"Better? Jesus, Wendy, do you hear yourself?"

"Okay, that came out wrong."

"You think?"

"He asked us to sit shiva."

"Who did?"

"Who are we talking about? Dad! Dad wanted us to sit shiva."

"Dad's dead."

Wendy sighs, like it's positively exhausting having to navigate the dense forest of my obtuseness. "Yes, apparently, that's the optimal time to do it."

"But Dad's an atheist."

"Dad *was* an atheist."

"You're telling me he found God before he died?"

"No, I'm telling you he's dead and you should conjugate your tenses accordingly."

If we sound like a couple of callous assholes, it's because that's how we were raised. But in fairness, we'd been mourning for a while already, on and off since he was first diagnosed a year and a half earlier. He'd been having stomachaches, swatting away my mother's pleas that he see a doctor, choosing instead to increase the regimen of the same antacids he'd been taking for years. He popped them like Life Savers, dropping small squibs of foil wrapping wherever he went, so that the carpets glittered like wet pavement. Then his stool turned red.

"Your father's not feeling well," my mother understated over the phone.

"My shit's bleeding," he groused from somewhere behind her. In the fifteen years since I'd moved out of the house, Dad never came to the phone. It was always Mom, with Dad in the background, contributing the odd comment when it suited him. That's how it was in person too. Mom always took center stage. Marrying her was like joining the chorus.

On the CAT scan, tumors bloomed like flowers against the charcoal desert of his duodenal lining. Into the lore of Dad's legendary stoicism would be added the fact that he spent a year treating metastatic stomach cancer with Tums. There were the predictable surgeries, the radiation, and then the Hail Mary rounds of chemo meant to shrink the tumors but that instead shrank him, his once broad shoulders reduced to skeletal knobs that disappeared beneath the surface of his slack skin. Then came the withering of muscle and sinew and the sad, crumbling descent into extreme pain management, culminating with him slipping into a coma, the one we knew he'd never come out of. And why should he? Why wake up to the painful, execrable mess of end-stage stomach cancer? It took four months for him to die, three more than the oncologists had predicted. "Your dad's a fighter," they would say when we visited, which was a crock, because he'd already been soundly beaten. If he was at all aware, he had to be pissed at how long it was taking him to do something as simple as die. Dad didn't believe in God, but he was a lifelong member of the Church of Shit or Get Off the Can.

So his actual death itself was less an event than a final sad detail.

"The funeral is tomorrow morning," Wendy says. "I'm flying in with the kids tonight. Barry's at a meeting in San Francisco. He'll catch the red-eye."

Wendy's husband, Barry, is a portfolio manager for a large hedge fund. As far as I can tell, he gets paid to fly around the world on private jets and lose golf games to other richer men who might need his fund's money. A few years ago, they transferred him to the L.A. office, which makes no sense, since he travels constantly, and Wendy would no doubt prefer to live back on the East Coast, where her cankles and postpregnancy jiggle are less of a liability. On the other hand, she's being very well compensated for the inconvenience.

"You're bringing the kids?"

"Believe me, I'd rather not. But seven days is just too long to leave them alone with the nanny."

The kids are Ryan and Cole, six and three, towheaded, cherub-cheeked boys who never met a room they couldn't trash in two minutes flat, and Serena, Wendy's seven-month-old baby girl.

"Seven days?"

"That's how long it takes to sit shiva."

"We're not really going to do this, are we?"

"It was his dying wish," Wendy says, and in that single instant I think maybe I can hear the raw grief in the back of her throat.

"Paul's going along with this?"

"Paul's the one who told me about it."

"What did he say?"

"He said Dad wants us to sit shiva."

Paul is my older brother by sixteen months. Mom insisted I hadn't been a mistake, that she'd fully intended to get pregnant again just seven months after giving birth to Paul. But I never really bought it, especially after my father, buzzed on peach schnapps at Friday-night dinner, had acknowledged somberly that back then they believed you couldn't get pregnant when you were breast-feeding. As for Paul and me, we get along fine as long as we don't spend any time together.

"Has anyone spoken to Phillip?" I say.

"I've left messages at all his last known numbers. On the off chance he plays them, and he's not in jail, or stoned, or dead in a ditch, there's every reason to believe that there's a small possibility he'll show up."

Phillip is our youngest brother, born nine years after me. It's hard to understand my parents' procreational logic. Wendy, Paul, and me, all within four years, and then Phillip, almost a decade later, slapped on like an awkward coda. He is the Paul McCartney of our family: better-looking than the rest of us, always facing a different direction in pictures, and occasionally rumored to be dead. As the baby, he was alternately coddled and ignored, which may have been a significant factor in his becoming such a terminally screwed-up adult. He is currently living in Manhattan, where you'd have to wake up pretty early in the morning to find a drug he hasn't done or a model he hasn't fucked. He will drop off the radar for months at a time and then show up unannounced at your house for dinner, where he might or might not casually mention that he's been in jail, or Tibet, or has just broken up with a quasi-famous actress. I haven't seen him in over a year.

"I hope he makes it," I say. "He'll be devastated if he doesn't."

"And speaking of screwed-up little brothers, how's your own Greek tragedy coming along?"

Wendy can be funny, almost charming in her pointed tactlessness, but if there is a line between crass and cruel, she's never noticed it. Usually I can stomach her, but the last few months have left me ragged and raw, and my defenses have been depleted.

"I have to go now," I say, trying my best to sound like a guy not in the midst of an ongoing meltdown.

"Jesus, Judd. I was just expressing concern."

"I'm sure you thought so."

"Oh, don't get all passive-aggressive. I get enough of that from Barry."

"I'll see you at the house."

"Fine, be that way," she says, disgusted. "Good-bye."

I wait her out.

"Are you still there?" she finally says.

"No." I hang up and imagine her slamming her phone down while the expletives fly in a machine-gun spray from her lips.

Wednesday

Chapter 2

I'm packing up my car for the two-hour drive to Elmsbrook when Jen pulls up in her marshmallow-colored SUV. She gets out quickly, before I can escape. I haven't seen her in a while, haven't returned her calls or stopped thinking about her. And here she is looking immaculate as ever in her clinging gym clothes, her hair an expensive shade of honey blond, the corners of her mouth inching up ever so slightly into the tentative smile of a little girl. I know every one of Jen's smiles, what they mean and where they lead.

The problem is that every time I see Jen, it instantly reminds me of the first time I ever saw her, riding that crappy red bike across the quad, long legs pumping, hair flying out behind her, face flushed with excitement, and that's exactly what you don't want to think about when confronted with your soon-to-be ex-wife. Ex-wife in waiting. Ex-wife elect. The self-help books and websites haven't come up with a proper title for spouses living in the purgatory that exists before the courts have officially ratified your personal tragedy. As usual, seeing Jen, I am instantly chagrined, not because she's obviously found out that I'm living in a crappy rented basement, but because ever since I moved out, seeing her makes me feel like I've been caught in a private, embarrassing moment—watching porn with my hand in my pants, singing along to Air Supply while picking my nose at a red light.

"Hey," she says.

I toss my suitcase into the trunk. "Hey."

We were married for nine years. Now we say "Hey" and avert our eyes.

"I've been leaving you messages."

"I've been busy."

"I'm sure." Her ironic inflection fills me with the familiar impulse to simultaneously kiss her deeply and strangle her until she turns blue. Neither is an option at this juncture, so I have to content myself with slamming the trunk harder than necessary.

"We need to talk, Judd."

"Now's not a good time."

She beats me to the driver's-side door and leans against it, flashing me her most accomplished smile, the one I always told her made me fall in love with her all over again. But she's miscalculated, because now all it does is remind me of everything I've lost. "There's no reason this can't be amicable," she says.

"You're fucking my boss. That's a pretty solid reason."

She closes her eyes, summoning up the massive reserves of patience required to deal with me. I used to kiss those eyelids as we drifted off to sleep, feel the rough flutter of her lashes like butterfly wings between my lips, her light breath tickling my chin and neck. "You're right," she says, trying to look like someone trying not to look bored. "I am a flawed person. I was unhappy and I did something inexcusable. But as much as you might hate me for ruining your life, playing the victim isn't really working out for you."

"Hey, I'm doing fine."

"Yeah. You're doing great."

Jen looks pointedly at the crappy house in which I now live below street level. It looks like a house drawn by a child: a triangle perched on a square, with sloppily staggered lines for bricks, a lone casement window, and a front door. It's flanked by houses of equal decrepitude on either side, nothing at all like the small, handsome colonial we bought with my life's savings and where Jen still lives rent-free, sleeping with another man in the bed that used to be mine.

My landlords are the Lees, an inscrutable, middle-aged Chinese couple who live in a state of perpetual silence. I have never heard them speak. He performs acupuncture in the living room; she sweeps the sidewalk thrice daily with a handmade straw broom that looks like a theater prop. I wake up and fall asleep to the whisper of her frantic bristles on the pavement. Beyond that, they don't seem to exist, and I often wonder why they bothered immigrating. Surely there were plenty of pinched nerves and dust in China.

"You didn't show up to the mediator," Jen says.

"I don't like him. He's not impartial."

"Of course he's impartial."

"He's partial to your breasts."

"Oh, for God's sake, that's just ridiculous."

"Yes, well, there's no accounting for taste."

And so on. I could report the rest of the conversation, but it's just more of the same, two people whose love became toxic, lobbing regret grenades at each other.

"I can't talk to you when you're like this," she finally says, stepping away from the car, winded.

"I'm always like this. This is how I am."

My father is dead! I want to shout at her. But I won't because she'll cry, and if she does, I probably will, and then she'll have found a way in, and I will not let her pierce my walls in a Trojan horse of sympathy. I'm going home to bury my father and face my family, and she should be there with me, but she's not mine anymore. You get married to have an ally against your family, and now I'm heading into the trenches alone.

Jen shakes her head sadly and I can see her lower lip trembling, the tear that's starting to form in the corner of her eye. I can't touch her, kiss her, love her, or even, as it turns out, have a conversation that doesn't degenerate into angry recriminations in the first three minutes. But I can still make her sad, and for now, I'll have to be satisfied with that. And it would be easier, so much easier, if she didn't insist on being so goddamned beautiful, so gym-toned and honey-haired and wide-eyed and vulnerable. Because even now, even after all that she's done to me, there's still something in her eyes that makes me want to shelter her at any cost, even though I know it's really me who needs the protection. It would be so much easier if she wasn't Jen. But she is, and where there was once the purest kind of love, there is now a snake pit of fury and resentment and a new dark and twisted love that hurts more than all the rest of it put together.

"Judd."

"I have to go," I say, opening my car door.

"I'm pregnant."

I've never been shot, but this is probably what it feels like, that split second of nothingness right before the pain catches up to the bullet. She was pregnant once before. She cried and kissed me and we danced like idiots in the bathroom. But our baby died before it could be born, strangled by the umbilical cord three weeks before Jen's due date.

"Congratulations. I'm sure Wade will be a wonderful father."

"I know this is hard for you. I just thought you should hear it from me."

"And now I have."

I climb into the car. She steps in front of it, so I can't pull out.

"Say something. Please."

"Okay. Fuck you, Jen. Fuck you very much. I hope Wade's kid has better luck in there than mine did. Can I go now?"

"Judd," she says, her voice low and unsteady. "You can't really hate me that much, can you?"

I look directly at her with all the sincerity I can muster. "Yes. I can."

And maybe it's the complicated grief over my father that has finally begun plucking at my nerves, or maybe it's simply the way Jen draws back as if slapped, but either way, the intense hurt that flashes behind the wide pools of her eyes for that one unguarded instant is almost enough to make me love her again.

Chapter 3

My marriage ended the way these things do: with paramedics and cheesecake.

Marriages fall apart. Everyone has reasons, but no one really knows why. We got married young. Maybe that was our mistake. In New York State, you can legally get married before you can do a shot of tequila. We knew marriage could be difficult in the same way that we knew there were starving children in Africa. It was a tragic fact but worlds away from our reality. We were going to be different. We would keep the fire stoked; best friends who fucked each other senseless every night. We would avoid the pitfalls of complacency; stay young at heart and in shape, keep our kisses long and deep and our bellies flat, hold hands when we walked, conduct whispered conversations deep into the night, make out in movie theaters, and go down on each other with undimmed enthusiasm until the arthritic limitations of old age made it inadvisable.

"Will you still love me when I'm old?" Jen would say, usually when we were in bed in her dorm room, lying drowsily on her dented mattress in the thick musk of our evaporating sex. She'd be lying on her belly and I'd be on my side, running a lazy finger down the shallow canyon of her spine to where it met the rising curves of her outstanding ass. I was stupidly proud of her ass when we were dating. I would hold open doors for her just to watch it bounce ahead of me, high and tight and perfectly proportioned in her jeans, and I would think to myself, *That is an ass to grow old with.* I looked at Jen's ass as my own personal achievement, wanted to take her ass home to meet my parents.

"When my breasts sag and my teeth fall out, and I'm all dried up and wrinkled like a prune?" Jen would say.

"Of course I will."

"You won't trade me in for a younger woman?"

"Of course I will. But I'll feel bad about it."

And we would laugh at the impossibility of it all.

Love made us partners in narcissism, and we talked ceaselessly about how close we were, how perfect our connection was, like we were the first people in history to ever get it exactly right. We were that couple for a while, nauseatingly impervious assholes, busy staring into each other's eyes while everyone else was trying to have a good time. When I think about how stupid we were, how obstinately clueless about the realities that awaited us, I just want to go back to that skinny, cocksure kid with his bloated heart and perennial erection, and kick his teeth in.

I want to tell him how he and the love of his life will slowly fall into a routine, how the sex, while still perfectly fine, will become commonplace enough that it won't be unheard of to postpone it in favor of a television show, or a late-night snack. How they'll stop strategically smothering their farts and closing the door to urinate; how he'll feel himself growing self-conscious telling funny stories to their friends in front of her, because she's heard all his funny stories before; how she won't laugh at his jokes the way other people do; how she'll start to spend more and more time on the phone with her girlfriends at night. How they will get into raging fights over the most trivial issues: the failure to replace a roll of toilet paper, a cereal bowl caked with oatmeal left to harden in the sink, proper management of the checkbook. How an unspoken point system will come into play, with each side keeping score according to their own complicated set of rules. I want to materialize before that smug little shit like the Ghost of Christmas Past and scare

the matrimonial impulse right out of him. *Forget marriage,* I'll rail at
him. *Just go for the tequila.* Then I'll whisk him away to the future and
show him the look on his face . . .

. . . when I walked into my bedroom and found Jen in bed with another
man.

By that point, I probably should have suspected something.
Adultery, like any other crime, generates evidence as an inevitable by-
product, like plants and oxygen or humans and, well, shit. So there were
no doubt a handful of ways I could have figured it out that would have
spared me the eye-gouging trauma of actually having to witness it firsthand. The clues must have been piling up for a while already, like unread
e-mails, just a click away from being read. A strange number on her cell
phone bill, a call quickly ended when I entered the room, the odd unex-
plained receipt, a minor bite mark on the slope of her neck that I didn't
remember inflicting, her markedly depleted libido. In the days that followed, I would review the last year or so of our marriage like the security tapes after a robbery, wondering how the hell I could have been so
damn oblivious, how it took actually walking in on them to finally get
the picture. And even then, as I watched them humping and moaning
on my bed, it took me a little while to put it all together.

Because the thing of it is, no matter how much you enjoy sex, there's
something jolting and strangely disturbing about witnessing the sex of
others. Nature has taken great pains to lay out the fundamentals of copulation so that it's impossible to get a particularly good view of the sex
you're having. Because when you get right down to it, sex is a messy,
gritty, often grotesque business to behold: the hairs; the abraded, dimpled flesh; the wide-open orifices; the exposed, glistening organs. And
the violence of the coupling itself, primitive and elemental, reminding

us that we're all just dumb animals clinging to our spot on the food chain, eating, sleeping, and fucking as much as possible before something bigger comes along and devours us.

So when I came home early on Jen's thirty-third birthday to find her lying spread-eagle on the bed, with some guy's wide, doughy ass hovering above her, clenching and unclenching to the universal beat of procreation, his hands jammed under her ass, lifting her up into each thrust, her fingers leaving white marks where they pressed into his back, well, it took some time to process.

It hadn't yet sunk in that it was Jen in the bed. All I knew was that it was my bed, and the only man who had any business having sex in it was me. I briefly considered the possibility that I was in the wrong house, but that seemed like a long shot, and a quick glance over to the picture of Jen on my night table, young and luminous in her bridal gown, confirmed that I was in the right place. Which was something of a minor relief actually, because to make that kind of mistake, to actually let yourself into your neighbor's house and walk upstairs to their bedroom oblivious to your error, was probably cause to expect the worst from a brain scan. And if I had walked in on my neighbors rutting like dogs in the middle of the afternoon, I doubt that even the most heartfelt apology would have been accepted, and I'd never be able to make eye contact with them again, let alone ask them to get the mail when we went on vacation. Also, our neighbors, the Bowens, were in their late sixties and Mr. Bowen was eating his way toward his third heart attack. Even if he was still sexually active, which I highly doubted given the circumference of his gelatinous gut, the effect of such an untimely intrusion would probably have sent him into cardiac arrest. So, all things considered, it was probably a good thing that I was in my own house.

Except, that being the case, it posed a handful of troubling scenarios, the most obvious of which was that the woman writhing on the bed in a pool of her own sweat, inserting her French-manicured index finger like a dart into the bull's-eye of her lover's anus, was my wife, Jen.

Which, of course, I'd known the instant I stepped into the room. But my brain was shielding me from the realization, giving me little random thoughts to process, just to keep me distracted, really, while, behind the scenes, my subconscious scrambled to assemble the facts and prepare a strategy for damage control. So instead of thinking, right away, *Jen is fucking someone, my marriage is over,* or something along those lines, my next thought was actually this: *Jen never sticks her finger into my asshole during sex.* Not that I had any desire for her to do so, especially now that I was seeing firsthand, so to speak, where it had been. We did some fun, nasty stuff from time to time, Jen and I—positions, props, creamy desserts, et cetera—but I fell squarely into that category of men who simply never feel the desire to bring their asshole into the mix. Not that I was judging the men who did.

Except for the man who was currently impaled two knuckles deep on my wife's index finger, one digit away from the one she used to flip the bird at the guy who had cut us off in the HOV lane last week, two away from the diamond eternity band I'd bought her on our fifth anniversary. I was judging him pretty severely, actually. So much so that it took me an extra beat to realize that he was, in fact, Wade Boulanger, a popular radio personality who, in addition to screwing my wife and apparently enjoying the occasional bit of anal stimulation, was also my boss.

Wade is the host of a popular WIRX morning drive radio program called *Man Up with Wade Boulanger.* He talks about sex, cars, sports, and money. But mostly about sex. He consults on air with porn stars, strippers, and prostitutes. He takes calls from men and women who tell him, in graphic detail, about their sex lives. He announces and then rates his own farts. He tells lovelorn, sex-starved callers to "Man up already!" There are T-shirts and coffee mugs and bumper stickers with the catch-phrase. He is a professional asshole, syndicated in twelve markets. The advertisers line up like sheep.

I'm not knocking it. I was his producer. I booked the guests. I over-saw the interns screening the calls, the I.T. geeks who run the website. I met with the station bosses about format and sponsorship. I liaised with legal, H.R., and advertising. I ordered lunch and bleeped the curse words.

I'd been fresh out of college and working as an assistant at WRAD, a small local station, when Wade's career was just heating up, and for some reason he liked me. When his producer was fired over a flap with the FCC, Wade hired me. We took long lunches after the show, whole afternoons spent in restaurants on the station's dime, drinking dirty martinis and coming up with bits. He called me his voice of reason, valued my opinion, and took me with him when he moved from the lo-cal affiliate to WIRX. And when the show went into syndication, he threatened to walk when the station balked at my contract.

Wade is tall and beefy, with dark, wiry hair and a cleft that makes his chin look like a tiny ass. His teeth are a shade of white not found in nature. At forty, Wade still references his fraternity brothers like they matter, still evaluates passing breasts out loud, still calls them tits. He is that guy. It's easy to picture him in his frat-boy prime, chugging down beers to rounds of applause, humiliating pledges, slipping roofies into the red plastic cups of pretty freshman girls at keggers.

There's nothing in life, really, to prepare you for the experience of see-ing your wife have sex with another man. It's one of those surreal events that you've imagined at one point or another without any real clarity, like dying or winning the lottery. When it comes to knowing how to react, you're in uncharted territories. And so, in the absence of any reaction, I stood there frozen, watching Jen's face as Wade pumped away at her like the piston of a wide, hairy engine. Her head was arched back, chin pointed up to God, as she panted heavily through her wide-open mouth, eyes clamped shut with pleasure. I tried to recall if she'd ever looked so intensely committed, so beautifully dirty when we had sex, but it was hard to say. I'd never had this vantage point before. Also, it had been forever since we'd had sex during the day, and at night it's harder to make out the nuances of your partner's expression. Then Jen let out a long, urgent moan that started low before suddenly jumping up a few octaves into this kind of wounded puppy's yelp. I was pretty damn sure I'd never heard her make that sound before. And as she did it, her hands slid down Wade's back to grab his ass and pull him deeper into her.

I found myself wondering about Wade Boulanger's cock.

Specifically, was it bigger than mine? Thicker? Harder? Was it slightly curved, the way some cocks are, hitting places inside of her that mine had never hit, heretofore untapped bits of soft tissue that made her cry out like that? Was Wade a more skilled lover? Had he studied Tantric technique? He had certainly slept with enough hookers and porn stars to have gotten some hands-on instruction. From where I was standing, it certainly looked like Wade knew what he was doing, but, in fairness, I had never seen myself have sex. Jen and I never videotaped ourselves the way some couples did, and now I kind of regretted that. Reviewing the game tapes every now and then might have been helpful. For all I knew, I looked every bit as convincing. But that yelp . . . I'd been having every kind of sex with Jen for over ten years, and she had never yelped like that. I'd have remembered.

I realized that I was already thinking about how I would tell Jen—my Jen—about this later, how I would describe this insanity to her tonight when I got home. But I already was home. And my Jen didn't exist anymore, had dispersed into mist right before my eyes. And this new Jen, this squealing, sweating, anal-probing Jen, didn't need me to tell her. She could probably tell me a few things.

I experienced a smattering of microscopic pinpricks across my stomach, the first hint of the anguish being readied below in the darkest recesses of my churning guts. It was still forming, but I could already feel the intense heat of it rising up into my chest like a concentrated laser beam, and I knew that once the world started spinning again, it would blossom into a white-hot flash and incinerate me.

And still they fucked, in and out, up and down, grunt and yelp, like they were going for a record, and underneath it all, the sounds you don't think about, the slapping and slishing, the farting suction, the mechanical sounds of intercourse, the air thick with the pungent smell of their sex. And still I stood there, letting it happen, trembling like a weed. Then Wade lifted Jen's left leg over his head and brought it down onto her right one, turning her onto her side without missing a thrust. It was not an easy maneuver to accomplish without withdrawing, this little bit of stunt fuckery, but the ease with which he did it, and the way Jen turned and rolled on cue, made it clear that they'd been down this particular road before. And that's when it occurred to me to wonder how long this had been going on: a month? Six months? How many positions had they mastered? How much of my marriage was a lie? Jen was fucking Wade Boulanger sideways on my bed, on the rumpled Ralph Lauren duvet she'd bought at Nordstrom when we first moved into the house. My life, as I knew it, was over.

This is probably as good a time as any to mention that I was holding a large birthday cake.

* * *

I had left work early to pick up the cake, a chocolate-strawberry cheesecake, her favorite. Jen always called in sick on her birthday. We were going to go out for dinner later, but I'd come home early to surprise her with the cake. In the driveway, I opened the box and planted thirty-three candles and one for good luck. I stopped in the foyer to light the candles with a long-stemmed oven lighter bought specifically for this purpose. I could hear her moving around upstairs, so I discarded the box and headed up, treading slowly and evenly on the balls of my feet like a cat burglar, articulating each step the way you do to keep candles lit. Now the candles were already more than halfway melted, gobs of spent red wax splashed across the pristine white frosting like blood dripped on snow. If things had gone according to plan, Jen would have blown them out by now. Then she would have wiped a chunk of frosting off with her finger and licked it, kissed me with cream cheese lips, and we would have lived happily ever after. But I hadn't planned for this contingency and now the cake was ruined.

Later, I knew, there would be a slew of painful questions that re-solved nothing. How could she do it? When did it start? Why? Were they in love, or simply after the thrill of illicit sex? Which answer did I prefer?

I didn't really want to know the answers to any of these questions. When you've borne witness to your wife's illicit copulation, you'd prob-ably have a better chance at achieving some sort of closure with a .357 Magnum at close range than with the scientific method. But I knew I'd ask regardless, because that's what you did. I'd been forced into a movie, and there was nothing to do but follow the script. But right then, at that very moment, it came to me like a revelation, the single most important question to be asked, and I was pretty damn certain I was ready to know the answer. The question, in its simplest form, was this: How far up

Wade Boulanger's ass could I jam a chocolate-strawberry cheesecake with thirty-three burning candles and one for good luck?

Pretty damn far, as it turns out.

After that, many things happened, quickly and simultaneously.

The first thing that happened was that Wade screamed. Not because he suddenly had an asshole full of chocolate-strawberry cheesecake, although that certainly would have been reason enough. Wade screamed, I would find out later from an indiscreet paramedic, because, before entering Jen, he had applied a cream to his cock, a cream advertised on his radio program, formulated to enhance sexual performance, and a cream that, unbeknownst to him, was highly flammable, and now, thanks to the thirty-three birthday candles and one for good luck, his testicles were on fire. They hadn't put a warning on the label, probably because most men keep their privates away from open flames as a matter of routine. So Wade screamed as he flew off—and out—of Jen, and rolled across the bed onto his back, cupping his flaming scrotum as he went. To make matters worse, he'd been only seconds away from ejaculating when he caught fire, and now, even as he writhed in pain, he spurted tiny ribbons of baked ejaculate into the air.

As Wade screamed and burned and came hotly into his hands, Jen screamed as well, rolling as fast as she could in the other direction. Jen screamed first because Wade had pulled out of her with such force, knocking the bridge of her nose with his forehead hard enough to bring tears to her eyes. And then, through the kaleidoscopic prism of her tears, she saw me standing at the foot of the bed, my hands covered in red and brown cheese goop, and so her scream was one of surprise and shame, which turned to pain as she rolled off the bed, landing in a heap on the floor, the heel of Wade's overturned, four-hundred-dollar loafer digging painfully into her thigh.

And I screamed, because what I felt right then was so much worse than burned balls or a broken nose, which is what Jen would later find out she had suffered. This wrecked room had been my bedroom; this bed, smeared with cheesecake and bodily fluids, had been my bed; and this woman, this naked, cowering, crumpled woman on the floor, had been my wife, and now, in a matter of seconds, I had lost them all.

And then everyone stopped screaming and there followed one of those moments of dead silence where you just stand there feeling the planet spin beneath your feet until it makes you dizzy. The smells of sex and burnt scrotum filled the air like a gas leak, and I swear, if someone had lit a match the room would have exploded.

"Judd!" Jen cried out from the floor.

Still groaning in pain, his eyes lit with terror at the untold damage his testes might have sustained, Wade rolled clumsily off the bed and charged into the bathroom, slamming the door behind him. Naked men shouldn't run. From behind the door, the sound of running water could be heard, punctuated by Wade's guttural curses.

I looked at Jen, sitting naked on the floor, her back up against her night table, knees pulled up against her flattened breasts as she sobbed into her hands, and I felt the urge to get on my knees and pull her into my arms, the way I would have under pretty much any other circumstances. And I actually felt myself moving toward her, but then stopped. It had been only a minute or so since I'd walked through the bedroom door, and my brain had not yet adjusted to this suddenly transformed world where I no longer comforted Jen because I hated her. I was a whirling mass of outdated reflexes and violent impulses, and I had no idea what the hell I was supposed to do. The urge to flee was overwhelming, but leaving the two of them in my house seemed too much like unconditional surrender. I needed to lash out, hide, get out of there, weep, plant my thumbs in Wade's eye sockets to crush his eyeballs, hold

Jen, strangle Jen, kill myself, go to sleep, and wake up and be twenty again, all in the same instant. A complete nervous breakdown was not out of the question.

Jen looked up at me, stricken, her eyes red with tears, blood and snot running from her nose down her chin and onto her chest. I actually felt bad for her, and hated myself for it.

"I can't believe you did this," I heard myself say.

"I'm so sorry," she said, shivering into her arms.

"Get dressed, and get him out of my house."

That was the extent of our conversation. Nine years of marriage gone in a heartbeat, and not very much to say about it. I stepped out of the bedroom, slamming the door behind me hard enough to dislodge something in the drywall, which could be heard rattling inside as it fell. I stood in the hall for a moment, shaken and desolate, exhaled a breath I didn't realize I was holding, and headed downstairs to smash her grandmother's china to smithereens, which is what I was still doing when the police and the paramedics showed up.

"So what happens now?" Jen said. We were standing in the kitchen, attempting a conversation amidst the copious ruins of the shattered china.

"Shut up."

"I know this won't mean anything to you right now, but I am really sorrier than I'll ever be able to tell you."

"Stop talking."

It wasn't going very well.

"There's no excuse for what I've done. I'd been unhappy for so long, you know, just kind of lost, and—"

"Will you please just shut your goddamn mouth?!" I shouted at her, and she flinched as if she thought I might hit her. Her nose had already swelled considerably and was starting to turn a nasty shade of purple in the spot where Wade's forehead had smashed it earlier. When word of our troubles spread through the neighborhood, her bruised face would be the subject of tireless speculation among the housewives as they whispered over their nonfat lattes.

I closed my eyes and rubbed my temples. "I'm going to ask you some questions, and I need you to answer them in as few words as possible. Do you understand?"

She nodded.

"How long have you been fucking Wade?"

"Judd—"

"Answer the question!"

"A little over a year."

You'd have thought, after the events of the last half hour, that I was beyond shocking by now. A little over a year wasn't a fling, a random sexual indiscretion. It was a relationship. It meant that Jen and Wade had an anniversary. On our first anniversary, we had checked into a bed-and-breakfast in Newport. Jen wore a lavender negligee and I read her this goofy poem that made her cry so that later I could still taste the salt on her cheeks. How had Jen and Wade marked their first anniversary? And, now that you mention it, where did they count from? Their first flirtation? First kiss? First fuck? The first time someone said "I love you"? Jen was both sentimental and meticulous with her calendar and no doubt knew the exact dates of every one of those milestones.

For the last year or so, Jen had been running off at every possible opportunity to have sex with Wade Boulanger, my overly athletic, alpha male boss. It was inconceivable to me, no different than if I'd just found out that she was a serial killer, which would have been preferable actually. I'd have attended the trial, nodded somberly at the guilty verdict, told my story to *People* magazine, and gone about my business. At least I'd know where I was going to sleep that night.

"A little over a year," I repeated. "You're some kind of liar then, huh?"

"I've become one, yes." She held my gaze, almost defiantly.

"Do you love him?"

She looked away.

I wasn't expecting that, and it hurt.

Jen sighed, a long, dramatic, self-pitying sigh, as I considered the ramifications of slitting her throat with a shard of china. "We had our problems long before things started with Wade."

"Well, nothing like the ones we've got now."

She may have said something after that, but I had stopped hearing her. There was just the crunch of bone china underfoot as I walked across the kitchen, and the wailing hinge of the front door as I swung it open, and the sudden hiss of expelled air when my body finally remembered to start breathing again.

What the hell happens now?

I sat in my car, still in the driveway, gripping the wheel tight enough to turn my knuckles white, paralyzed with indecision. There is nothing sadder than sitting in a car and having absolutely nowhere to go. Unless, maybe, it's sitting in a car in the driveway of the home that is suddenly no longer your home. Because, generally, even when you have nowhere to go, you can at least go home. Jen hadn't just cheated on me, she'd made me homeless. A red-hot rage colored my fear like blood in the water, made me tremble. I wanted to throttle Jen, to feel her windpipe collapse under my thumbs. I wanted to stab Wade with one of those curved knives designed by aboriginal tribes for gutting humans, in through the sternum and up behind the chest plate to puncture vital organs, watch the dark blood, thick with dislodged bits of tissue, gurgle out of his mouth. I wanted to commit a dramatic suicide, drive through a guardrail into the Hudson River, leave Jen paralyzed with a guilt that would haunt her for the rest of her life, like I knew the sight of Wade humping her would now always haunt me. But she'd probably just go back into therapy, maybe even to that shrink she'd left because he made it a practice to hug her tightly after every session, a Freudian copping a feel. He would somehow convince her that she was the victim in all of this, that she owed it to herself to be happy again, and then my death would have been in vain. The best I could hope for was that she'd cheat on Wade by sleeping with her horny therapist, but was it actually cheating if you cheated on your illicit lover? I was new to all of this and didn't know the bylaws.

In the rearview mirror I could see the front of the house, the bottom corners of the living room picture window, the line where the stone foundation gave way to staggered red bricks. My entire life, the sum total of my existence, was contained behind that wall, and it seemed to me that I should be able to step out of the car, walk through the front door, and simply reclaim it. The door would stick; it always did in the warmer months and needed to be pressed down as the doorknob was turned while you leaned your shoulder into the heavy alder wood. I had the keys right there, jingling against the steering column that I had no idea which way to turn.

What the bloody motherfucking hell happens now?

I checked my watch, the white-gold Rolex Cosmograph Daytona Jen had bought me for my thirtieth birthday. I'd been fine with the Citizen I wore, missed it, actually, when she gave me this bulky piece of showy hardware, but things like that were important to Jen. She'd taken to the suburbs like an actress getting into character for a new role, and she was always determined that we both look the part.

"We could go on a great vacation for what this watch costs," I'd objected.

"We can go on a great vacation anyway," she said. "Vacations come and go. A watch like this is an heirloom."

I was too young to have an heirloom. The word conjured up images of bedridden old men with yellow, calcified toenails and skeletal wrists, wasting away in musty rooms that smelled of Lysol and decay. "It's five mortgage payments," I said.

"It's a gift," Jen said, getting all snippy like she sometimes did.

"A gift that I paid for."

I'd been married long enough to know that the remark was wrong and unkind and not remotely constructive, but I said it anyway. I did that sometimes. I couldn't begin to tell you why. You get married and patterns form. Jen was genetically incapable of rendering any kind of verbal apology. I sometimes said shitty things that I didn't quite mean. We accepted these foibles in ourselves and in each other, except at the moments they actually surfaced in real time, at which point we had to fight the urge to savagely bludgeon each other.

"So our money is your money?" Jen said, her eyes lighting up with the joy of indignation, and just like that, she had seamlessly transitioned us into a different fight. This was a skill she'd perfected over time, like a boxer who jabs and moves before the counterpunch can arrive. Arguing with her never failed to make me dizzy.

In the end, I kept the watch; there was never really any question. The Citizen was relegated to the little compartment in my sock drawer that held a set of keys to our old apartment, a couple of obsolete cell phones, my college I.D. card, a couple of Japanese throwing stars from my brief ninja phase in junior high, the foul ball I'd caught off Lee Mazzilli at Shea Stadium when I was a kid, and a handful of other artifacts from versions of myself long since dead and buried.

And now the Rolex said three o'clock in the afternoon. I needed some time to think, to consider the situation, figure out my next move. I fingered the buttons on my cell phone, flipped through my list of contacts, but I already knew I wouldn't call anyone. Maybe Jen and I could still fix this thing, and if we did, we wouldn't want anyone looking at us funny. I knew irrevocable damage had been done, innocence had been lost, trust slaughtered, but still, it was the age-old conundrum: If a wife sleeps with a boss, but no one finds out about it, did it actually happen? There was no one to call, no friends who weren't also connected to Jen. I thought about calling my mother, but my father was in a coma and she had enough to deal with. My life was in a free fall, and there was nowhere to turn. A cold sense of desolation lodged itself somewhere in the base of my throat, and suddenly I was no longer enraged or devastated, but terrified of the immense, throbbing loneliness that was only now closing like a vise on my internal organs.

I drove through Kingston's small business district, past the train station, to the I-87 overpass. I pulled over and watched the interstate for a while, the eighteen-wheelers and early commuters speeding past just ahead of the afternoon rush that would soon choke the northbound side. I considered getting on the highway and driving north, stopping only for gas and donuts until I reached Maine. I would find a small seaside town, rent a little house, and start over. The winters would be rough, but I'd trade in my Lexus for a rugged pickup truck with chains on the tires. I'd get a job, maybe something where I worked with my hands, drink at the local pub, adopt a one-eyed Labrador, and make friends with the fishermen. They'd tease me about my roots, maybe even affectionately refer to me as "New York." In time, I would develop the faintest down-east accent. There would be a woman there, also from somewhere else, also running from an ugly past. She would be pretty and vulnerable and we would know each other instantly, would love each other fiercely, the way only two damaged people can. Nothing else would matter. Everyone in town would come to the wedding, held in the gazebo on the lawn of the town square. We'd be congratulated on the marquee of the local diner, right above the blue-plate special.

But then reality reasserted itself. There would be no small house in Maine, no one-eyed Labrador, no pretty, dark-eyed woman to make me whole again, and for a moment I sat there and mourned them. Then I turned the car around, still trembling—I hadn't stopped since I'd left the house—and headed back into town, telling myself the interstate would still be there tomorrow, but for now, I was going to have to find something a little closer to home.

There's not very much I'm proud of when it comes to the weeks that followed. I went into hibernation in the Lees' dank, rented basement, growing roots on the sagging couch that the advertisement had called a "daybed." The room smelled of mildew and laundry detergent, and when it was quiet, I could hear the lone, bare lightbulb humming in its socket. I watched television pretty much nonstop. I rarely showered and grew a beard. I masturbated joylessly. I shaved the beard into a goatee and gained fifteen pounds. I composed long, humiliating e-mails to Jen, rage-filled diatribes and pathetic entreaties, tapping away furiously on my BlackBerry until my thumbs burned, cursing, excoriating, imploring, begging, and, ultimately, deleting. I lay there at night, staring at the ceiling as the house's ancient plumbing shook and clanged violently behind the thin drywall, picturing Jen and Wade going at it like porn stars to the rhythm of the banging pipes. *Bang! Bang! Bang!* And then climax, to the rumble of water through the walls every time one of the Lees flushed, which was pretty much every fifteen minutes or so. My God, it was like those two never stopped urinating. All night, at regular intervals I could hear them above me, Mrs. Lee's quick pitter-patter, the hiss of Mr. Lee dragging his slippers, the heavy plastic smack of the toilet seat, and then the flush, which sounded like white-water rapids behind the scraped gypsum walls of the basement. I was thirty-four years old and homeless, lying awake in the dead of night on a lumpy sofa bed in a rented basement, listening to my landlords piss and shit while my former wife and former boss sixty-nined in my head. Rock bottom rose up to meet me.

Chapter 4

12:15 p.m.

The gravedigger looks like Santa Claus, and I don't believe for a minute he doesn't know it. With his long white beard and stout build, he has to know the effect of wearing a red and white anorak and how inappropriate the whole getup looks in the Mount Zion Cemetery. When you spend your days putting corpses into the ground, I guess you have to find the fun where you can. But this morning, as we bury my father in a teeming downpour, Saint Nick is all business, even as his ridiculous raincoat makes him stand out like a bloodstain against a sky the color of a dead tooth. He quietly directs the pallbearers in the placement of the coffin onto the hydraulic frame rigged over the freshly dug grave. Paul and I are at the head of the coffin, and Wendy's husband, Barry, is in the middle, across from the empty spot where Phillip would have been if he'd shown up. My uncle Mickey and his son Julius, fresh off the plane from Miami, carry the foot of the coffin. We haven't seen Mickey in decades—he and Dad had a falling-out over some money Dad lent him—and Julius is all but a stranger to us. They look like suntanned gangsters, this uncle and cousin, in their unnecessary designer sunglasses, their slicked-back hair, their matching diamond pinky rings.

"To the right," Saint Nick says. "All together now. No one lower him yet. You in the back, come up about six inches . . . there you go. Now on my mark, we're going to lower him. Gentlemen at the feet, you're out first, and watch your fingers . . ."

Movie directors often shoot funerals in the rain. The mourners stand in their dark suits under large black umbrellas, the kind you never have handy in real life, while the rain falls symbolically all around them, on grass and tombstones and the roofs of cars, generating atmosphere. What they don't show you is how the legs of your suit, caked with grass clippings, cling soaked to your shins, how even under umbrellas the rain still manages to find your scalp, running down your skull and past your collar like wet slugs, so that while you're supposed to be meditating on the deceased, instead you're mentally tracking that trickle of water as it slides down your back. The movies don't convey how the soaked, muddy ground will swallow up the dress shoes of the pallbearers like quicksand, how the water, seeping into the pine of the coffin, will release the smell of death and decay, how the large mound of dirt meant to fill the grave will be transformed into an oozing pile of sludge that will splatter with each stab of the shovel and land on the coffin with an audible splat. And instead of a slow and dignified farewell, everyone just wants to get the deceased into the ground and get the hell back into their cars.

We, the pallbearers, step away soaked and muddy from the grave and melt back into the fair-sized crowd gathered graveside, where an ineffective canvas pop-up shelter has been erected to fend off the rain. Friends, neighbors, and business associates all jockey for position under the canvas, the less fortunate ones forced to the edges, where the pooled water pours down from the roof in thick, drenching rivulets. Paul stands beside his wife, Alice, who leans against him to warm him as he cries. Barry finds Wendy, who hands him back his BlackBerry, which he can't resist checking before sliding it into his belt holster like a gunslinger. I stand beside my mother, whose red eyes are dulled by the Valium she chose not to split today. Her hair, gray at the roots and auburn everywhere else, is pulled into a tight bun. Her black suit is formfitting and, as always, she's showing way too much surgically enhanced cleavage. The height of her stiletto heels, like the diameter of her breast implants, is inappropriate for both her age and the occasion. She squeezes my hand, avoiding direct eye contact, and I feel Jen's absence like a festering wound.

"It's okay to cry," Mom says quietly.

"I know."

"You can laugh too. There's no correct emotional response."

"Thanks, Mom."

Mom is a shrink, obviously. But she's more than that. Twenty-five years ago she wrote a book called *Cradle and All: A Mother's Guide to Enlightened Parenting.* The book was a national phenomenon and turned my mother into something of a celebrity expert on parenting. Predictably, my siblings and I were screwed up beyond repair.

You've seen *Cradle and All,* thick as an almanac, with red and black borders and cover art of a naked toddler morphing into a teenager. The book starts with breast-feeding and toilet training and goes all the way through puberty (defecation to masturbation, we used to say), advising mothers in the same frank, maternal, gratuitously shocking tone Mom often used with us. On the back cover is a photo of Mom striking a sex kitten pose on our living room couch. There's a tenth-anniversary edition, a fifteenth, a twentieth, and next year they will be releasing an updated twenty-fifth-anniversary edition, and Mom will do a twenty-city signing tour and all the major talk shows. There has been talk of an *Oprah* segment and the possibility of a face-lift before the book tour.

"Today we say good-bye to Morton Foxman, beloved husband and father, dear brother, and cherished friend."

The speaker is Boner Grodner. He was Paul's best friend when we were kids. Now he's Rabbi Charles Grodner of Temple Israel, but to those of us who grew up with him, who were invited to the back of the school bus, where he presided over private viewings of purloined pornography from his father's extensive collection, he will always be Boner. When Boner wasn't smoking pot with Paul and trying to discern the hidden messages in Led Zeppelin songs, he was holding forth shamelessly on the pros and cons of various sex acts.

"Mort was never a big fan of ritual . . . ," Boner says.

"Will you look at that," Wendy says, elbowing me in the ribs. I follow her gaze across the cemetery to the access road, where a black Porsche has noisily pulled up. And for a moment, I don't recognize him, this man attempting to knot his tie while running across the wet lawn in his rumpled suit pants and motorcycle jacket like he's finishing a marathon. And then I do, from the way he runs shamelessly toward us, without the slightest hint of decorum. He is wearing moccasins, of all things.

"Phillip," my mother says softly, and signals Boner to stop.

By this point Phillip's given up on the tie, which he leaves hanging unknotted around his neck. He comes running down the lawn and then slides the last few feet, like we used to do on the slight slope of our front lawn when it rained, coming to a stop right in front of my mother.

"Mom," he says, and throws his wet arms around her.

"You came," she says, overjoyed. Phillip is her baby, and he's spent his life reeling in the slack as fast as she can cut it for him.

"Of course I came," he says. He pulls back and looks up at me. "Judd."

"Hi, Phillip."

He grabs my arm and pulls me into a dramatic hug. Phillip, my baby brother, who used to climb into bed with me, smelling of lavender baby shampoo, and press his smooth, rounded cheek against mine, gently pulling at my arm hairs as I told him stories. He loved to guess the morals of Aesop's fables. Now he smells of cigarettes and mouthwash, and he's put on a good ten pounds or so since I last saw him, most of it in his face. I feel the familiar wave of loss and regret that always seems to accompany our infrequent reunions. I'd give anything for him to be five again, happy and unbroken.

He reaches past me to shake hands with Paul, who reciprocates quickly and self-consciously, trying to speed things along and get the funeral back on track. Phillip kisses Wendy's cheek.

"You got fat," she whispers.

"You got old," he responds in a stage whisper, loud enough for everyone to hear. Behind him, Boner clears his throat. Phillip turns around and straightens his jacket. "Sorry, Boner. Please continue." Wendy hits the back of his head. "Charlie! Sorry. Rabbi Grodner," he says quickly, but the chuckles have already rippled through the crowd and Boner looks momentarily homicidal.

"Before I call on Mort's eldest son, Paul, to remember his father for us, I'd like to read a short psalm . . ."

"I shouldn't have called him that," Phillip whispers to me, eyes wide. "Damn."

"It was an honest mistake."

"It was disrespectful."

I am tempted to point out that showing up a half hour late to his father's funeral might also be construed as disrespectful, but it would be pointless. Phillip has always been happily impervious to advice and criticism.

"Be quiet!" Paul hisses at us. Phillip winks at me. And here we stand at our father's grave, the three Foxman men, all roughed from the same template but put through different finishing processes. We each have our father's dark curly hair and square, dimpled chin, but there would be no mistaking us for twins. Paul looks like me, only bigger, broader, and angrier; me on steroids. Phillip looks like me, only slimmer and much better-looking, his features rendered more gracefully, his smile wide and effortlessly seductive.

When Boner finishes reading his psalm, Paul steps up to deliver what is meant to be a eulogy but instead seems to be an acceptance speech for the Most Dedicated Son award. He thanks Dad for teaching him how to run the business; he thanks his wife, Alice, for taking a leave of absence from her job as a dental hygienist to help out at the stores when Dad fell ill, he thanks Mom for taking care of Dad, and then he talks at length about what it was like working with his father, running Foxman Sporting Goods, the Hudson Valley's premiere sporting goods chain. He does not mention any of his siblings, all of whom are wet and cold and wishing for an orchestra to play him off the stage.

When he finally wraps up, he seems surprised that there is no applause. Saint Nick flips a switch on the hydraulics, and Dad's coffin slowly descends into the grave. Once he is down, Boner steps forward and solemnly hands a tall garden shovel to Paul. "It is customary for members of the immediate family to each shovel some dirt into the grave, fulfilling the obligation of burying a loved one," he says. "Our sages say burying someone is considered the truest form of kindness and respect, as the deceased will not be able to thank you for it."

That's kind of funny, actually, since Dad was not exactly prone to expressing gratitude to his children when he was alive. You were either screwing up, or you were invisible. He was quiet and stern in a way that led you to expect an Eastern European accent. He had soft blue eyes and unusually thick forearms, and when he made a fist it looked like he could punch through anything. He mowed his own lawn, washed his own car, and painted his own house. He did all these things capably, painstakingly, and in a way that silently passed judgment on anyone who paid for someone else to do it. He rarely laughed at jokes, just nodded his understanding, as if it was all pretty much what he'd expected. Of course, there was a lot more to him than that, it's just that none of it is coming to me right now. At some point you lose sight of your actual parents; you just see a basketful of history and unresolved issues.

Paul digs into the large mound and tosses a scoop of muddy earth into the grave. He hands the shovel to me, and I do the same, and when the dirt hits the coffin I can feel something in me start to shake. I close my eyes against the hot wetness, and I can see Dad, reclining on a lounge chair in our backyard, gripping the hose gun and shooting at the moving targets of his young children as we ran between bases, making a machine-gun noise with his lips. He liked us as young children. It was when we grew older that he didn't know what to make of us. Childhood feels so permanent, like it's the entire world, and then one day it's over and you're shoveling wet dirt onto your father's coffin, stunned at the impermanence of everything. I hand the shovel to Wendy, who digs up maybe a tablespoon or so of damp earth and who manages to miss the open grave entirely. Phillip, who is congenitally incapable of moderation, digs up a comically huge pile that turns out to have a stone in it. The stone hits the coffin like a gunshot, startling us all, and the gray silence is pierced by a long howl as Phillip falls to his knees, sobbing. "Daddy!" he cries, while the rest of us watch him unravel, standing by silently horrified and, probably, ever so slightly envious.

Chapter 5

1:55 p.m.

We all reconvene at Knob's End, the cul-de-sac where my parents' house stands. The house, a large white colonial, stands at the center of the dead end, where the blacktop blossoms into a wide circle, ideal for street hockey and bike riding. West Covington is a major thoroughfare through Elmsbrook, winding its way past strip malls and corporate parks before finally veering off into the residential area, where at the last rotary, it becomes Knob's End. When people give directions to any home or business on West Covington, they use our house as a negative landmark; if you see the big white house, then you've gone too far. Which is precisely what I'm thinking as I pull into the driveway.

Dad was obsessive about maintaining the house. He was a handy guy, always painting and staining, cleaning out the gutters, changing out pipes, power-washing the patio. He was an electrician by trade, but he gave it up to go into business, and he missed working with his hands, couldn't face the weekend without the prospect of manual labor. But now the paint is cracked and flaking off the window frames, there's an ugly brown water stain just below the roofline, the bluestones on the front walk rattle like loose teeth, and the rose trellises lean away from the house like they're trying to escape. The lawn hasn't been watered enough, and it's brown in patches, but the twin dogwoods we used to climb are in full bloom, their crimson leaves fanned out like an awning over the front walk. Consumed with Dad's slow death, Mom forgot to cancel the pool service, and so the swimming pool in the yard glistens with blue water, but the grass is starting to come up through the paving stones around it. The house is like a woman you find attractive at a distance. The closer you get, the more you wonder what you were thinking.

Linda Callen, our neighbor and my mother's closest friend, opens the door and hugs each one of us as we step into the house. She's a pear-shaped woman with an easy smile, and there's something vaguely rodent-like about her, not in a feral way, but more like a wise mother rat from a Disney cartoon, the sort that will sit in a tiny rocking chair and wear little rat glasses and be voiced by Judi Dench or Helen Mirren. A kindly, regal, Academy Award–winning rat. She's known us since birth and looks at us as her own children. Her son, Horry, stands behind her, staring at his feet as he takes our coats.

"Hey, Judd," he says to me.

"Hey, Horry."

He stiffens up when I pat his back. "I'm very sorry about Mort."

"Thanks."

When Horry was a toddler, his father, Ted, got drunk and somehow managed to drown himself in little Horry's inflatable wading pool while Linda was out shopping. She came home to find Horry shivering in the pool, crying hysterically over his partially submerged dead father. After that it was just the two of them, living up the block from us and, more often than not, in our house. A grade ahead of Paul and behind Wendy, Horry integrated seamlessly into our family. In high school, he fell for Wendy, like everyone else in Elmsbrook did at some point or another, but he had the inside track, and so for a year or so we would walk in on them making out in darkened rooms. Then, in his sophomore year of college, Horry got into a fight in a bar—details are sketchy—and the upshot was that someone took a sawed-off baseball bat to his head and now Horry is a thirty-six-year-old man who lives with his mother and cannot drive a car or focus on anything for more than a few seconds. Sometimes he has these mini seizures where he stiffens up and loses the ability to speak. Every day my dad would pick him up and take him with him to the store, where Horry helped out in the stockroom and took everyone's lunch orders. Now I guess he'll be working for Paul.

When Wendy sees Horry, she throws her arms around him without taking off her raincoat, and he drops the coats he's gathered to hug her back.

"Hey, Sunflower."

"Horry," she whispers into his neck.

His shirt is speckled with raindrops from her coat. He kisses her wet scalp, and when she pulls back, her eyes are red.

"Don't cry," he says.

"I'm not," she says, and then bursts into tears.

"Okay, okay," Horry says, blinking nervously as he bends down to pick up the coats he dropped.

2:07 p.m.

SERENA, WENDY'S BABY girl, screams like she's been stabbed. We can all hear her in amplified stereo as we eat lunch, thanks to the high-tech baby monitor Wendy has set up on the table in the front hall, but Wendy doesn't seem at all inclined to go upstairs and quiet the baby. "We're Letting Her Cry," she announces, like it's a movement they've joined. If they're letting her cry anyway, I don't really see the point of the baby monitor, but that's one of those questions I've learned not to ask, because I'll just get that condescending look all parents reserve for non-parents, to remind you that you're not yet a complete person.

And the screaming baby is the least of it. Ryan, Wendy's six-year-old, has discovered the living room piano, which hasn't been tuned in decades, and he's pounding out a throbbing cacophony with both fists. Barry, who has decided that now would be an optimal time to return some business calls, is pacing the hall between the dining room and the living room, loudly arguing the finer points of some deal that will no doubt add to his already grotesque fortune. Because he's wearing a wireless earpiece, he looks like a lunatic ranting to himself. "The Japanese will never go for that," he says, shaking his head. "We're ready to commit, but the paper price is unacceptable."

The thing about people who work in finance is that they consider their job infinitely more important than anything or anyone, and so it's perfectly legitimate to tell everyone else to fuck off because they have a conference call with Dubai. Billions of dollars are involved, so things like a kid's birthday or a wife's dead father are simply not at the top of the agenda. Barry is almost never around, and when he is, he's on the phone or scanning his BlackBerry with the furrowed brow of one who is dealing with shit that dwarfs your shit exponentially. If Barry was sitting next to the president of the United States during a nuclear attack, he'd still be staring down at his BlackBerry with his default expression, the one that says *You think you've got problems?* From what I can see he is not very good to Wendy, barely registers her existence, and leaves her to do all the heavy lifting with the kids. Wendy, though, has inherited our mother's genetic imperative to keep up appearances. Everything is wonderful. Period.

"Cut it out, Ryan!" Barry hisses in the direction of the piano, covering his earpiece with his palm. Not because it's annoying, not because the bereaved might want a little peace and quiet, but because "Daddy's on the phone." Ryan stops for a second and seems to earnestly consider his father's request, but fails to see the upside, and so the two-fisted sonata resumes.

"Wendy!" Barry calls, and the way it rolls off his tongue, fast and plaintive, it's less his wife's name than a tic to be politely ignored in company, which is what Wendy does.

Linda serves up a meal of poached salmon and mashed potatoes. She circles the table, doling out heaping servings wherever she sees the white of a dish, ducking around Barry, who is still pacing and cursing loudly into his earpiece. Alice helps Linda, because Alice is an in-law and technically not one of the bereaved. Barry doesn't help, because Barry is technically an asshole.

Alice and Paul have been trying to have a baby for a while now, without much success. She's taking fertility drugs that cause her to gain weight and hormones that cause her to cry about how fat she is. This according to Wendy, who also informed me that when Alice thinks she's ovulating, she stays in bed and makes Paul come home on his lunch breaks. "Can you imagine?" Wendy said. "Poor Paul has to get it up twice a day for that . . . ?"

Right now Alice is making a face as she stares at Ryan at the piano. It's a forced smile that says *I am so okay enjoying the cuteness of someone else's child, even though I can't seem to grow one of my own.* She flashes Paul a meaningful look that he doesn't catch, so focused is he on shoveling mashed potatoes into his mouth and avoiding eye contact with the rest of his siblings.

Ryan has apparently found something else to abuse, and the piano falls silent at exactly the same time that the baby monitor does, and the sudden quiet feels awkward, like we were all hiding behind the noise.

"Bitches ain't shit but hos and trix!" The rap song blares loudly across the table, and Phillip quickly reaches into his shirt pocket and sheepishly pulls out his flashing cell phone. "I keep meaning to change that ringtone," he says, flipping it open. "Hey . . . What? No, that's great! Perfect timing." He flips the phone closed and looks at all of us meaningfully. "She's here," he says, like we've all been waiting. Like we have any

idea what he's talking about. Then he strides out of the dining room and hits the front door running. We all run into the kitchen to peer out the bay window to the street, where a woman has just stepped out of the backseat of a dark Lincoln Town Car. The mystery woman has no visible tattoos, no obvious breast implants, no fuck-me pumps, no "bubble butt"—as Phillip generally refers to his ass of choice—straining against a short skirt under which no underwear is being worn. Even at a distance it's clear that this woman, in her well-tailored pantsuit, with her blond hair tied back in a neat, Grace Kelly bun, is someone who wears under-wear. Expensive underwear, I should think, maybe even sexy underwear, from Victoria's Secret or La Perla. She's definitely attractive, but sleek and finished, like brushed chrome. In other words, she is exactly the kind of woman you would expect not to have any association with Phil-lip. Sophisticated, refined, and, from what I can see, significantly older than him.

"Who is that?" my mother says.

"Maybe his lawyer," Wendy guesses.

"Phillip has a lawyer?" Alice says.

"Only when he's in trouble."

"Is he in trouble?"

"Odds are."

By now Phillip has reached her. They don't shake hands or kiss chastely, but attack each other with ravenous mouths and sloppy tongues.

"Well, I guess she's not his lawyer," Alice says, maybe just a tad snidely. You can never tell with Alice. She doesn't like Wendy. She's not crazy about any of us. Alice comes from a nice family, where the siblings and siblings-in-law kiss each other hello and good-bye and remember each other's birthdays and anniversaries and call their parents just to say hi, calls that end with breezy I-love-yous that are effortless and true. To

her, we Foxmans are a savage race, brutish aliens who don't express affection and shamelessly watch our baby brother grope the ass of a
stranger through the kitchen window.

"I'll e-mail you the ratios," Barry says behind us. "We've inverted
them twice already."

Having traded enough spit for the time being, Phillip and his mystery guest head up the front walk, and we move away from the window,
Wendy, as always, getting in the last word: "It would be so like Phillip to
be doing his lawyer."

2:30 p.m.

"THIS IS TRACY," Phillip announces proudly, standing at the head of the
table, where we are all once again seated, having scrambled back when
he finished tonguing and groping her and led her up the bluestone path.
"My fiancée." We are probably not all sitting there with our jaws on our
plates, but that's how it feels. Up close, it's clear she's a good fifteen or so
years older than him, a very well-preserved mid-fortysomething.

"Engaged to be engaged," Tracy corrects him fondly, in a manner
that suggests a long-standing familiarity with correcting Phillip. The
women Phillip usually dates aren't the sort to correct him. They are
strippers, actresses, waitresses, hairstylists, bridesmaids who hike up
their crinoline for him in the parking lot during the reception, and once,
memorably, the bride herself. "I couldn't help it," he told me through
cracked, swollen lips, from the hospital bed he'd subsequently landed in
when the groomsmen tracked him down. "It just happened." "It just
happened" was Phillip's go-to explanation for pretty much everything,
the perfect epitaph for a man who always seemed to be an innocent
bystander to his own life.

"Hello, everyone," Tracy says, confident and composed. "I'm sorry we're meeting under such sad circumstances." She doesn't giggle or crack her gum. Phillip throws his arm around her, grinning like he's just pulled off a great practical joke. No one says anything for a long moment, so Phillip performs a roll call.

"That's my sister, Wendy," he says, pointing.

"Great suit," Wendy says.

"Thank you."

"The guy talking to himself is her husband, Barry."

Barry looks right at Tracy and says, "I can maybe sell another eighth of a point to them. Maybe. But they'll want some pretty solid assurances. We've plowed this field before."

"Barry is something of an ass."

"Phillip!"

"It's okay, baby. He can't hear us. That's my brother Paul, and his wife, Alice. They don't like me very much."

"Only because you're such a douche," Paul says. It's the first thing he's said, I think, since he spoke at the funeral. There's no way to know what's pissing him off right now. In my family, we don't so much air our grievances as wallow in them. Anger and resentment are cumulative.

"Nice to meet you," Alice says, her overly sweet tone meant to apologize for Paul, for the rest of us, for being fifteen pounds overweight, for not being as elegant and composed as Tracy. *I was like you once,* her voice pleads. *A size two with perfect hair. Let's be best friends.*

"And that's my brother Judd. Actually, he does like me these days, if memory serves."

"Hi, Judd."

"Hey."

"Judd is recently cuckolded."

"Thanks for clarifying that, Phil," I say.

"Just looking to avoid any awkward faux pas later on," Phillip says. "Tracy's one of us now."

"Get out while you still can!" Alice jokes too loudly. Her agitated smile is a long, crooked fissure across her cheeks, widening painfully before faltering and then disappearing altogether.

"We've been down this road before," Barry says. "It's a nonstarter."

"And this is my mom," Phillip says, turning Tracy to face our mother, who is sitting beside Linda, forcing a smile.

"Hello, Tracy. I hope you won't judge our behavior too harshly. It's been a trying day."

"Please, Mrs. Foxman. I'm the one who should apologize, for arriving unannounced at such a difficult time."

"So why don't you?" Wendy says.

"Wendy!" Mom snaps.

"He called Barry an ass."

"I'm sorry," Phillip says. "It's been a while. It's entirely possible, though highly unlikely, that Barry is no longer an ass."

"Phillip." Tracy says his name sternly, with control and conviction, and Phillip clams up like a trained dog.

"Phillip is nervous," Tracy says. "This is hard for him. Obviously, he would have preferred to make the introductions under better circumstances, but in addition to being Phillip's fiancée, I am also his life coach, and we both felt, at this difficult time, that it would help him greatly if I were here."

"Define 'life coach,'" my mother says, her tone clipped and loaded.

"Tracy was my therapist," Phillip says proudly.

"You're his therapist and you're dating him?" Wendy says.

"As soon as we realized our feelings for each other, I referred Phillip to another colleague."

"Is that even ethical?"

"It's something we grappled with," Tracy says.

"It just happened," Phillip says in the same instant.

And then little Cole comes down the stairs, naked from the waist down, carrying the old white potty that's been sitting under the sink in the hall bathroom since Phillip was toilet trained. Cole is in what Wendy refers to as his E.T. stage, wherein he waddles around the house like E.T., exploring and trashing everything within reach, making strange little noises as he goes. He steps over to Barry, who has finally ended his call and sat down at the table, and proffers the potty for his inspection. "Look, Daddy," he says. "T!"

Barry looks down, uncomprehending. "What does he want?" Like he's never met his three-year-old son before.

"T!" Cole yells triumphantly. And indeed, the crap in the potty does seem to be shaped like a crude letter T. Then Cole bends down and heaves the potty up over his head in a high arc that brings it crashing down onto the dining room table, shattering glasses and sending silverware flying. Alice screams, Horry and I dive for cover, and the contents of Cole's overturned potty land on Paul's plate like a side dish. Paul jumps back like a grenade has landed, so violently that he somehow takes Alice down with him in a jumble of limbs and chair legs.

"Jesus Christ, Cole!" Barry screams. "What the hell is wrong with you!"

"Stop yelling!" Wendy yells.

Cole looks up at his frazzled, worthless parents and, with no preamble, bursts into a loud, fully realized crying fit. And since neither one of them seem inclined to comfort him, I exercise my uncle privileges and pick him up to blubber into my neck, his tiny kid butt sticky against my forearm. "Good job, little man," I say, "making in the potty like that." Positive reinforcement and all that. After this trauma, the kid will likely be in diapers until he's ten.

"I make a T," he says through subsiding tears, rubbing his snot on my collar, and there's nothing sweeter than a two-year-old speaking, with his high-pitched sincerity and his immigrant English. I've never really appreciated kids the way some people do, but I can listen to Cole talk all day. Of course, as an uncle, I'm not the one who has to scrape his crap off the table.

"That's right, Cole," I say, looking over at Paul's plate. "It is a T, and a nice one at that."

Paul and Alice climb to their feet shaken and nauseated. We are all standing now, posed around the table like a painting, the Foxman family minus one, contemplating the steaming, erudite turd on Paul's plate. It's utterly inconceivable that we will survive seven days together here, caroming off each other like spinning molecules in a chemical reaction. There's no way to know how it will all shake out, but as far as metaphors go, you can't do much better than shit on the good china.

Chapter 6

If you've ever been in a failed marriage, and statistically speaking, it's a safe bet that you have, or, if not, that you soon will be, then you'll know that the first thing you do at the end is reflect on the beginning. Maybe it's some form of reverse closure, or just the basic human impulse toward sentimentality, or masochism, but as you stand there shell-shocked in the charred ruins of your life, your mind will invariably go back to the time when it all started. And even if you didn't fall in love in the eighties, in your mind it will feel like the eighties, all innocent and airbrushed, with bright colors and shoulder pads and Pat Benatar or the Cure on the soundtrack. There you were, minding your own business, walking across campus to class, or stepping into a café for a cup of coffee, or dancing at a wedding, or drinking at a bar with some friends. And then you saw her, laughing at someone's joke, tucking her hair behind her ear, or taking the stage with a friend to sing a slightly drunken karaoke version of "Ninety-nine Red Balloons" (and she was just drunk enough to cop to knowing the German lyrics too), or she was leaning against the wall, eyebrows arched genially over her lite beer as she surveyed the scene, or she was strolling alone through the falling snow without a jacket, her sleeves pulled tightly over her hands in the absence of gloves, or she was . . .

. . . riding her bike across the quad, on her way to class. I had seen her around, with her small leather backpack, her blond ponytail flying in the slipstream behind her as she sailed past on her red Schwinn. We were both juniors, but we didn't have any classes together and were probably just a few weeks away from being on nodding terms. But on that day, as she pedaled past me, I called out to her, "Hey! Bike Girl!"

She braked too hard and skinned her shin on the pedal as she slid off the seat. "Ouch! Crap!"

"Oh, shit, I'm sorry," I said. "I didn't mean for you to actually stop."

She looked at me, perplexed. "But you called out to me." Her eyes were an incandescent green; I suspected tinted lenses, but I wanted to write a song about them right there anyway. I'd stand outside her dorm room with a guitar and serenade her, while her friends looked on, smiling approvingly in their skimpy pajamas.

"Yeah, I guess I did. Poor impulse control, I'm sorry. I didn't really have a plan beyond that."

Her laugh was rich and throaty. She did it like a girl who knew how to laugh, who had a long association with laughing. And she looked at me, this pretty blond girl, the kind of girl from whom I'd been conditioned to expect a smiling but no less firm rejection, and she said, "I'll give you five seconds to come up with one."

This was unprecedented, and the miracle emboldened me. "I just thought we'd have a lot to talk about," I said.

"Really."

"This bike, for instance. You're the only girl on campus who rides a bike."

"So?"

"I think you do it ironically."

"You're accusing me of ironic cycling?"

"It's a growing sport. There's an Olympic petition."

"Is your hair always like that?"

I had thick, curly hair like pulled springs, and back in college I kind of gave it the run of the place. "The higher the hair, the closer to God."

"I limp," she said.

"What?"

"That's why I ride the bike when I cross the quad. I was born with one leg shorter than the other."

"You're so full of shit."

"Afraid not."

So she got off the bike and showed me her custom sneaker. "You see how this sole is almost an inch thicker than the other?"

"Damn. I'm an asshole."

"It's okay. You didn't mean it."

"I'm Judd, by the way. Judd Foxman."

"I'm Jen."

"If it's all the same to you, I think I'll call you Bike Girl for a little while longer."

"Why would you do that?"

"I'm only going to call you Jen after I've kissed you."

She seemed accustomed to such bold repartee. "But what if you never do?"

"Then it won't matter anyway."

"You're ruling out the possibility of friendship."

"I'm guessing a girl like you has enough friends."

"And what kind of girl is that, exactly?"

"An ironic cycler."

That laugh again, from out of nowhere, like it had been percolating inside her waiting to be released. In the sixty seconds she'd known me, I'd already made her laugh twice, and I'd read enough *Playboy* by then to know that beautiful women want a man who can make them laugh. Of course, what they really meant was a man who could make them laugh after he'd delivered multiple orgasms on his private jet with his trusty nine-inch cock, but I was on a roll, and hope tentatively unfurled its wings in my chest, preparing to take flight.

I knew that she was much too pretty and well-adjusted for me. Over the last few years, I had carved out a niche for myself on campus among the screwed-up girls with dark lipstick and too many earrings, who worked through their mixed bag of childhood traumas by drinking excessively and having sex with unthreatening Jewish guys with ridiculous hair. This had actually happened exactly twice in as many years, but since it was all the action I'd seen, I liked to think of it as a niche. And I was not at all Jen's type, but her type, genetically gifted man-boys with expensive sports cars, hairless Abercrombie bodies, and entitlement issues, hadn't really been working for her as of late. Her last boyfriend, Everett—that was really his name, and he looked exactly how you're picturing him, only not as tall—had actually told her that her poor posture made her look unimpressive. This from a boy, she later railed to me, with a concave chest and a pencil-thin dick. The one before that, David, had returned from winter break to tell her he had gotten engaged and was getting married that spring. Jen was in turmoil; she was grappling with self-esteem issues and a failed attempt at anorexia. I was in the right place at the right time, and the gods were finally ready to cut me some slack.

But I didn't know any of that yet. All I knew was that a conversation that should have ended already seemed to have taken on a life of its own, and a girl who, according to the laws of the universe, shouldn't have given me a second glance was now leaning forward, her smiling mouth aimed unmistakably at mine. It was a quick, soft peck, but I felt the give in her lips, a hint of plush softness just beneath the surface, and I was in love. Seriously. Just like that.

"Poor impulse control," she said, proud of her daring.

"Jen." I exhaled slowly, running my tongue along the inside of my lips, savoring the waxy residue of her lip gloss.

"Judd."

"I think I'm going to call you Bike Girl until we have sex."

She laughed again, and that was three, for those keeping score at home, and I didn't stand a chance. Later on, Jen would swear that was the moment she knew she was going to marry me. That's the problem with college kids. I blame Hollywood for skewing their perspective. Life is just a big romantic comedy to them, and if you meet cute, happily-ever-after is a foregone conclusion. So there we were, the pretty blond girl milking her very slight congenital limp in order to seem damaged and more interesting, and the nervous boy with the ridiculous hair trying so hard to be clever, the two of us hypnotized by the syncopated rhythms of our furiously beating hearts and throbbing loins. That stupid, desperate, horny kid I was, standing obliviously on the fault line of his embryonic love, when really, what he should have been doing was running for his life.

Chapter 7

3:43 p.m.

Boner comes by with three volunteers from the Hebrew Burial Society to deliver the mourning supplies. They rearrange furniture and set things up with a hushed military precision, after which Boner gathers the four Foxman siblings in the living room. Five low folding chairs with thick wooden frames and faded vinyl upholstery are lined up in front of the fireplace. The mirror above the mantel has been clouded over with some kind of soapy white spray. The furniture has all been pushed to the perimeter of the room, and thirty or so white plastic catering chairs have been unfolded and placed in three rows facing the five low chairs. There are two silver collection plates placed on the piano. People paying their respects to the family can make dollar contributions to the burial society or to a local children's cancer society. A few lonely bills have been placed on each plate like tips. In the front hall, a thick candle formed in a tall glass is lit and placed on the table, next to Wendy's baby monitor. This is the shiva candle, and there is enough wax in the glass for the candle to burn for seven days.

Phillip nudges one of the low chairs with his toe. "It was nice of Yoda to lend us his chairs."

"They're shiva chairs," Boner says. "You sit low to the ground as a sign of mourning. Originally, the bereaved sat on the floor. Over time, the concept has evolved."

"It still has a ways to go," Phillip grumbles.

"What's with the mirror?" Wendy wants to know.

"It's customary to remove or cover all the mirrors in a house of mourning," Boner says. "We've fogged up all the bathroom mirrors as well. This is a time to avoid any and all impulses toward personal vanity and simply reflect on your father's life."

We all nod, the way you would at a self-indulgent museum tour guide, taking the path of least resistance to get to the snack bar.

"A little while ago, your father called me to the hospital," Boner says. He was a tense, chubby kid, and now he's a tense, beefy man, with rosy cheeks that make him look perpetually angry or embarrassed. I don't know exactly when Boner found God; I lost track of him after high school. Boner, not God. I lost track of God when I joined Little League and could no longer attend Hebrew school classes at Temple Israel, the synagogue we went to once a year for Rosh Hashanah services.

"Your father wasn't a religious man. But toward the end, he regretted the absence of tradition in his life, in the way he raised his children."

"That doesn't really sound like Dad," I say.

"It's actually somewhat common for people facing death to reach out to God," Boner says, in the exact same self-important, didactic tone he employed as a kid when explaining to us what a blow job was.

"Dad didn't believe in God," Phillip says. "Why would he reach out to something he didn't believe in?"

"I guess he changed his mind," Boner says, and I can tell he's still pissed at Phillip for the earlier nickname slip.

"Dad never changed his mind," I say.

"Your father's dying request was that his family sit shiva to mark his passing."

"He was on a lot of drugs," Wendy points out.

"He was perfectly lucid." Boner's face is starting to turn red.

"Did anyone else hear him say it?" Phillip.

"Phillip." Paul.

"What? I'm just saying. Maybe Bone—Charlie misunderstood."

"I didn't misunderstand," Boner says testily. "We discussed it at length."

"Don't some people sit shiva for just three days?" Me.

"Yes!" Wendy.

"No!" Boner shouts. "The word 'shiva' means 'seven.' It's seven days. That's why it's called shiva. Your father was very specific."

"Well, I can't be away from the business for seven days," Paul says. "Believe you me, Dad would never have gone for that."

"Listen, Charlie," I say, stepping forward. "You've delivered the message. You held up your end. We'll discuss it amongst ourselves now and come to a consensus. We'll call you if we have any questions."

"Stop it!"

We all turn to see my mother and Linda standing under the archway to the living room. "This is what your father wanted," Mom says sternly, stepping into the room. She has taken off her suit jacket, and her low-cut blouse reveals her infamous cleavage. "He was not a perfect man, and not a perfect father, but he was a good man, and he tried his best. And you all haven't exactly been model children lately."

"It's okay, Mom. Calm down," Paul says, reaching out for her.

"Stop interrupting me. Your father lay dying in his bed for the last half year or so. How many times did you visit him, any of you? Now I know, Wendy, Los Angeles isn't exactly next door, and, Judd, you've been going through a rough time, I understand that. And, Phillip . . . Well, God only knows what you've been up to. It's like having a son in Iraq. At least then I'd know where you were. But your father made his last wish known, and we will honor it. All of us. It's going to be crowded, and uncomfortable, and we'll all get on each other's nerves, but for the next seven days, you are all my children again." She takes a few steps into the room and smiles at us. "And you're all grounded."

My mother spins on one stiletto heel and plants herself like a child into one of the low seats. "Well," she says. "What are you waiting for?"

We all hunker down in the seats, silent and sullen, like a group of scolded schoolchildren.

"Um, Mrs. Foxman," Boner says, clearing his throat. "You're really not supposed to wear dress shoes when you're sitting shiva."

"I have bad arches," she says, flashing him a look sharp enough for a circumcision.

The one tattered remnant of Jewish observance that my parents had maintained was having the family stay over for Rosh Hashanah, the Jewish New Year. Every year, as summer bled into fall, the call would come, more a summons than an invitation, and we would all descend upon Knob's End, to argue over sleeping arrangements, grudgingly attend services at Temple Israel, and share an overwrought holiday meal during which, tradition had it, at least one person would theatrically storm out of the house in a huff. Usually, it would be Alice or Wendy, although a few years ago it was memorably Jen, after my father, already well into his peach schnapps, told her, apropos of nothing in particular, that our dead son wouldn't have been technically Jewish since she was a gentile. This was just a few months after she'd delivered our dead baby, and so no one blamed her for hurling her plate at him as she stormed out. "What got into her?" he said. On the plus side, she insisted we go home immediately, which got me out of having to attend the interminable services at Temple Israel the following morning, where Cantor Rothman's slow, operatic tenor makes you want to prostrate yourself on the spot and accept Jesus Christ as your Lord and Savior.

4:02 p.m.

ALICE AND TRACY are helping Linda in the kitchen. Horry, on Paul's orders, has gone back to the store to finish out the day. The Elmsbrook store is the flagship, and it stays open until nine every night. Barry is upstairs, watching a video with the boys. So it's just the four of us and Mom, sitting on low chairs, feeling sheepish and uncomfortable.

"So," Phillip says. "What happens now?"

"People will come," Mom says.

"How do they know when to come?"

"We are not the first people to ever sit shiva," Paul grumbles.

"People will come," Mom says.

"Oh, people will come, Ray," Phillip intones, doing his best James Earl Jones. "People will most definitely come." Phillip is a repository of random snatches of film dialogue and song lyrics. To make room for all of it in his brain, he apparently cleared out all the areas where things like reason and common sense are stored. When triggered, he will quote thoughtlessly, like some kind of savant.

Paul looks up to catch me staring at the scar on his right hand. It's a thick, pink line that runs up the meaty edge of his palm, crossing his wrist and ending in a splotchy cluster on the inside of his forearm. There's another, nastier one on his shoulder that radiates up toward his neck in raised tendrils the color of dead flesh, where the rottweiler missed his jugular by a few inches. Whenever I see him, I can't help but stare at the scars, looking for the teeth marks I know are there.

He twists his arm around self-consciously, hiding the scar, and flashes me a hard look. Paul has not addressed me directly since I arrived. He rarely addresses me if he doesn't have to. This is due to a combination of factors, most notably the rottweiler attack that ended his college baseball career before it started and for which he blames me. He's never come out and said that, of course. Other than Phillip, the men in my family never come out and say anything. So I don't know for sure if that's when Paul started hating me, or if that's just when Paul started hating everybody.

Another possible factor is that I lost my virginity to Alice back in high school, and she to me, which isn't as creepy as it sounds. Alice was my year in high school, not even on Paul's radar until many years later, when she cleaned his teeth and he picked her up with the always reliable "Didn't you used to go out with my kid brother?" By then I was long gone from Elmsbrook, already engaged to Jen, so if anyone is to blame for that one, it's Paul and not me. He knew going in that I'd been there first. For all I know, he may have even started sleeping with her to somehow get back at me for the dog attack, which would have been twisted and stupid and so very Paul. So now, every time Paul sees me, it's there in the back of his mind, that I deflowered his wife, that I've seen Alice naked, that I've kissed the wine-colored birthmark in the shape of a question mark that starts below her navel and ends at the junction of her legs. It was seventeen years ago, but men don't let go of things like that. And every time Alice and I see each other, we can't help but flash back to those four months we spent having sex in cars, basements, shrubs, and once, late at night, in the plastic tunnel above the slide in the elementary school playground. You never forget your first time, no matter how much you'd like to.

"How are things at the store?" I ask him.

He looks at me, considering the question. "Same old same old."

"Any plans to expand to any more locations?"

"Nope. No plans to expand. We're in a recession, or don't you read the paper?"

"I was just asking."

"Although I guess a recession is the least of your problems, huh, Judd?"

"What do you mean by that, Paul?" We are ending our sentences with names, which is the equivalent of fighters circling, looking to throw the first punch.

"Paul," Mom says.

"It's okay, Mom," I say. "We're just catching up."

"Forget it," Paul says.

"No. It's fine," I say. "What you meant was, between being unemployed and my wife screwing around, I have bigger things to worry about than the economic state of the country. Right?"

"That's certainly one way of looking at it."

"I was surprised I didn't hear from you when it happened," I say. "I moved out almost eight weeks ago. I mean, none of you called me. That's par for the course, I guess. If you didn't call when we lost the baby, I wouldn't expect you to call over something as trivial as the end of my marriage. But I figured you'd have called, Paul, just to rub it in a little. It's lucky Dad died when he did, or who knows when you may have gotten around to it?"

"I'm not happy about it. I always liked Jen."

"Thanks, Paul." I wait an extra beat for emphasis. "And I always liked Alice."

"What did you just say?" Paul says, clenching teeth, fists, and bowels.

"Which part didn't you hear?"

"All the young girls love Alice." Phillip sings out the Elton John lyrics, loud and off-key. *"Tender young Alice they say . . ."*

"So, Phillip," Wendy says. "How did you go about seducing your therapist?"

"Later," Phillip says. "It's just getting interesting."

"Oh, for crying out loud!" my mother says.

I look at the Rolex Jen bought for me with my own money that I haven't gotten around to selling on eBay yet. We've been sitting shiva for exactly one half hour. The doorbell rings, and God only knows to what depths of passive-aggressive sniping we might have descended if it hadn't. And as the room starts to fill with the first somber-faced neighbors coming to pay their respects, it becomes clear to me that the reason for filling the shiva house with visitors is most likely to prevent the mourners from tearing each other limb from limb.

When we were little kids, Dad took Paul and me fishing at a wide, shallow creek in the shadow of an overpass near some back roads a few miles north of the town limits. Paul and I pulled water-smoothed rocks from the creek bed and Dad knotted them into our fishing lines to serve as weights. Then, after slicing some inchworms with his pocket knife to bait our hooks, he taught us how to cast our lines out across the creek. For Paul and me, the casting was more fun than the fishing. We would reel our lines in, stretch the rods out behind us, and try to cast as far across the creek as we could. About an hour into this, Paul slung his rod back and managed to hook my ear just before he launched his rod forward. I felt a sudden, hot pain as my ear cartilage tore, the rock in his line flying back to slap my skull, and suddenly I was on my back in the dirt, looking up at a cloudless sky. Dad had to take off his T-shirt to stanch the flow of blood. Paul stood over me apologizing, but angrily, like it was all my fault. Flecks of my blood clung to Dad's curly chest hairs. I didn't feel a lot of pain, I just remember being amazed at how Dad's crumpled T-shirt went from white to completely red in a matter of minutes. The damage to my ear turned out to be minimal, but there's still the faint depression in the bone behind my ear where the rock hit me, like a fingerprint in hardened clay.

Chapter 8

7:45 p.m.

We've been at it for a few hours already, and the visitors keep coming, pouring through the door in an endless stream, as if busloads are being dropped off at the front door every half hour. Knob's End has become a parking lot, and my face is sore from smiling politely as my mother introduces and reintroduces everyone, my ass numb from the cheap foam underneath the crappy vinyl of the shiva chair. The plastic tips of the flimsy catering chairs set up around the room scrape the oak floor as the guests jockey for position, gradually working their way from the back of the room to the front, where they can ask the same questions as the guests who came before them, invoke the same platitudes, and squeeze my mother's forearm with theatrically pursed lips. We should have a handout at the door to speed things along, a brief summary of Dad's illness and all that transpired in the final days, maybe even a photocopy of his charts and a four-color printout of his last CAT scan, because that seems to be what all of his and Mom's peers want to talk about. And at the bottom of the handout a simple asterisked declaration would state that it's of absolutely no interest to us where you were when you found out our father/husband had died, like he was John F. Kennedy or Kurt Cobain.

Paul gets by without saying much, offering up a series of Rorschach grunts that people seem to hear as actual responses. Wendy shamelessly takes cell phone calls from her girlfriends back in L.A., and Phillip amuses himself by lying his ass off, seeing how far he can push the boundaries of credibility.

> Middle-Aged Woman: My God, Phillip! The last time I saw you, you were in high school. What do you do now?
> Phillip: I run a Middle East think tank in D.C.
> Phillip: I manage a private equity biotech fund.
> Phillip: I've been coordinating a freshwater project for UNICEF in Africa.
> Phillip: I'm working as a stuntman on the new Spielberg project.

And then there are the platters. Jews don't send flowers, they send food, in large quantities: fruit platters, assorted cookie platters, cold cuts, casseroles, cakes, wild rice salads, bagels and smoked salmon. Linda, who has effortlessly slipped back into her habitual role of supplemental caretaker for the Foxman clan, sets up the nonperishable items on the dining room table, along with a coffee samovar, which leads to an ad hoc buffet situation. The visitors work their way through the chairs, chat with the bereaved, and then gravitate into the dining room for coffee and nosh. It's like a wake, except it's going to last for seven days, and there's no booze. Who knows what kind of epic party this might become if someone popped the plastic lock on the whiskey bar?

The visitors are mostly senior citizens, friends and neighbors of my parents, coming to see and be seen, to pay their respects and contemplate their own impending mortality, their heart conditions and cancers still percolating below the surface, in livers and lungs and blood cells. Another of their number has fallen, and while they're here to console my mother, you can see in their staunch, pale faces the morbid thrill of having been passed over by death. They have raised their kids, paid off their mortgages, and they will spend their golden years burying each other, somberly keeping track of their relentlessly dwindling numbers over coffee and crumb cake in houses just like this one.

I'm supposed to be decades away from this, supposed to be just starting my own family, but there's been a setback, a calamitous detour, and you wouldn't think you could get any more depressed while sitting shiva for your father, but you'd be wrong. Suddenly, I can't stop seeing the footprints of time on everyone in the room. The liver spots, the multiple chins, the sagging necks, the jowls, the flaps of skin over eyes, the spotted scalps, the frown lines etched into permanence, the stooped shoulders, the sagging man breasts, the bowed legs. When does it all happen? In increments, so you can't watch out for it, you can't fix it. One day you just wake up and discover that you got old while you were sleeping.

There were so many things I thought I might become back in college, but then I fell for Jen and all my lofty aspirations evaporated in a lusty haze. I just never imagined a girl like that would want someone like me, and I had this idea that if I applied all of my energy toward keeping her happy, the future would sort itself out. And so I disappeared without a trace into the Bermuda Triangle of her creamy spread thighs, scraping through my classes with B's and C's, and when, shortly after graduation, she accepted my proposal, I remember feeling, more than anything, an overwhelming sense of relief, like I had just finished a marathon.

And now I have no wife, no child, no job, no home, or anything else that would point to a life being lived with any success. I may not be old, but I'm too old to have this much nothing. I've got the double chin of a stranger in photographs, the incipient swell of love handles just above my hips, and I'm pretty sure that my hairline, the one boundary I've always been able to count on, is starting to creep back on me when I'm not looking, because every so often my fingers discover some fresh topography on my upper forehead. To have nothing when you're twenty is cool, it's expected, but to have nothing when you're halfway to seventy, soft-ening and widening on a daily basis, is something altogether different. It's like setting out to drive cross-country without any gas money. I will look back at this time and see it as the start of a slow process that ends with me dying alone after living out my days in an empty apartment with only the television and a slow, waddling dog to keep me company, the kind of place that will smell stale to visitors, but not to me, since the stale thing will be me. And I can feel that miserable future hurtling to-ward me at high speed, thundering across the plains in a cloud of dust like a wildebeest stampede.

Before I know it, I'm on my feet, ducking and weaving through the crowd, intercepting random bits of conversation, keeping my eye on the sanctuary of the kitchen door.

". . . Paul, the older one. He spoke very nicely . . ."

". . . on a ventilator for three months . . . basically a vegetable . . ."

". . . a place down on Lake Winnipesaukee. We do it every year. It's beautiful. Maureen brings the kids . . ."

". . . recently separated. Apparently, there was a third party in-volved . . ."

That last one pierces me like a fishhook—but by then I'm at the door, and I'm not looking back. I step into the air-conditioned quiet of the kitchen and lean up against the wall, catching my breath. Linda is crouched at the fridge, absently chewing on the nub of a raw carrot like a cigar, trying to make room for all of the food that's been delivered.

"Hey there, Judd," she says, smiling at me. "What can I get you? And, bear in mind, we have pretty much everything now."

"How about a vanilla milkshake?"

She closes the fridge and looks at me. "That, we don't have."

"Well, then, I guess I'll have to run out and grab one."

Her smile is sweet and maternal. "Getting a little intense in there?"

"We passed intense a while ago."

"I heard the shouting."

"Yeah . . . sorry. And thank you, you know, for all of your help, for taking care of Mom and everything."

She looks startled for a second, seems on the verge of saying something, but then just pops the carrot back into her mouth and smiles. From the other room, we can hear my mother laughing.

"Well, Mom seems to be enjoying herself, at any rate."

"She's had a long time to prepare for this."

"I guess so."

We stand there for a minute, the well of small talk having run dry.

"Horry looks good," I say, and wish instantly that I hadn't.

Linda's smile is sad, ragged, and somehow beautiful, the aching smile of the long-suffering. "You learn not to think about what might have been, and to just appreciate what you have."

"Yeah. I'm probably not the right guy to hear that right about now."

She steps over to me and puts her arms on my shoulders. It's been forever since I've been touched, since I've even had any sustained eye contact, and I can see my tears reflected in her eyes. "You're going to be okay, Judd. I know you feel lost now, but you won't feel this way for long."

"How do you know?" I am suddenly inches away from a full-on crying jag. Linda diapered me, fed me, mothered me almost as much as my own mother, without ever being recognized for it. I should have sent her Mother's Day cards every year, should have called her every so often to see how she was doing. How is it that, in all these years, I never once spared so much as a thought for her? I feel a dark wave of regret for the kind of person I turned out to be.

"You're a romantic, Judd. You always were. And you'll find love again, or it will come find you."

"Did it ever find you again?"

Something changes in her expression, and she lets go of me.

"I'm sorry," I say. "That was a terrible thing to say."

She nods, accepting my apology. "It would be a terrible mistake to go through life thinking that people are the sum total of what you see."

"I know."

"No, you don't," Linda says, not unkindly. "And it's not the time or place to go into details, but rest assured, I have not spent the last thirty years sleeping alone."

"Of course not. I'm an asshole."

"Maybe, but you get a free pass this week." She offers up a friendly smirk. "Just don't abuse it." She looks out the window to the crowded street in front. "Looks like you're parked in by Jerry Lamb's Hummer. Why a retired doctor needs to drive a tank like that in Elmsbrook, New York, is a question for the ages. His penis can't be that small, can it?" She reaches into her apron and tosses me some keys. "It's the blue Camry. If you time it right, you can pick up Horry on your way back. I don't like him walking home this late."

8:30 p.m.

LINDA'S CAR SMELLS like yeast and flowers. Other than the small gold locket that hangs from her rearview mirror, the car is empty and clean in a way that strikes me as sad. Or maybe anything empty is just striking a chord with me these days. The earlier rain has tapered off into a light mist that dusts the windshield just enough to blur the headlights of on-coming cars. I drive down Centre Street and park at a meter in front of Foxman Sporting Goods' flagship store.

Dad worked as an electrician, but when Paul was born he decided he wanted a legacy for his children. He borrowed money from his father-in-law to buy a small sporting goods store out of bankruptcy, and over the years he expanded it into a chain of six stores across the Hudson Valley and into Connecticut. He was a firm believer in customer service and a knowledgeable staff, and proudly rebuffed the larger national chains who offered to buy him out every few years. Every Saturday he would visit the five satellite stores, to check their books and troubleshoot. When Paul and I were younger, he would wake us up at first light and hustle us into his car to come along. Dobbs Ferry, Tarrytown, Valhalla, Stamford, and Fairfield. I'd sit in the back, my eyes still glazed with sleep, watching the sun come up behind the trees along the highway through the tinted windows of his secondhand Cadillac. The car smelled of pipe tobacco and the tape deck played a steady rotation of Simon and Garfunkel, Neil Diamond, Jackson Browne, and Peggy Lee. Every so often I'll hear one of those songs, in an elevator or a waiting room, and it will take me right back to that car, lulled into semiconsciousness by the soft thrum of the road seams, my father humming along to the music in his gravelly voice.

Once a quarter he'd bring along Barney Cronish, his accountant. Paul hated it when Barney came, because he had to give up the front seat for him, and because Barney had to stop at every rest stop on the thruway, either to buy a coffee or piss out the last one. Barney also farted loudly and without shame, at which point Paul and I would crack our windows and stick our heads into the wind like a couple of dogs to escape the rancid, cabbage smell. Sometimes my father would press the window lock button in the front and play dumb while we suffocated, which was the closest he came to joking around.

Dad didn't seem to know how to be around us when he wasn't working. He was great with us when we were small, would cradle us in his massive forearms or bounce us on his knee while humming Mozart . . . As toddlers, we would cling to his sausage fingers as he walked us down the block, and he would lie down with us at bedtime, often falling asleep on the bed with us, until Mom came to get him. But he seemed hopelessly bewildered by us once we got a little bit older. He didn't understand our infatuation with television and video games, seemed bewildered by our able-bodied laziness, by our messy rooms and unmade beds, our longer hair and our silk-screened T-shirts. The older we got, the further he retreated into his work, his weekend papers, and his schnapps. Sometimes I think that having Phillip was my mother's last-ditch effort to find her husband again.

The hunter-green awnings of the shop, usually speckled with dried bird droppings and water stains, have recently been cleaned, and the windows, anticipating the fall season, are crammed with hockey, ski, and snowboard gear. The mannequin in the corner is wearing a goalie mask, and in the ominous flicker of the fluorescent light he looks like Jason, the serial killer from those *Friday the 13th* movies. Elmsbrook is the perfect town for a serial killer, and I mean that in the best possible way. It's always the picturesque towns, with clean sidewalks and clock towers, where Jason and Freddy come to slaughter oversexed teenagers. Centre Street has a cobblestone pedestrian walkway with benches and a fountain, the stores have matching awnings, and the overall vibe is pleasant and well kept.

And maybe because I'm thinking of serial killers, when Horry suddenly knocks on my window, I jump in my seat. Or maybe it's because he looks kind of scary. His long hair is held off his face by a white Nike headband with the price tag still attached, flapping against his forehead, and there's a good inch of ash suspended at the tip of the cigarette wedged between his lips.

"You scared me," I say.

"I have that effect on people."

I laugh, not because it's funny, but to be polite. You can't help but feel bad for Horry, but you're supposed to treat him like anyone else, because he's damaged but not an idiot, and he'll sniff out your pity like a dog sniffs out fear.

"Shouldn't you be at home, sitting Sheba?"

"Shiva."

"Shiva is an Indian god, the one with six arms. Or maybe it's four arms and two legs. I don't know. Six limbs, maybe."

"Well, it also means 'seven' in Hebrew."

"Six limbs, seven days . . ." He pauses to ponder the potential theological implications for a moment but reaches no conclusions other than now would be a good time to take another drag on his cigarette. "Well, shouldn't you be there?"

"Yes, I should," I say. "How are things inside?"

"Dead." He shrugs. "You coming in?"

"Nah. I just stopped by because your mom thought you'd want a lift home."

"She sent you?"

"She knew I was going out."

He shakes his head and grimaces. "I need to get my own place, like, yesterday."

"So why don't you?"

He taps his head. "Brain injury. There are things I can't do."

"Like what?"

"Like remembering what the fuck it is I can't do." He opens the passenger door and throws himself down in the seat. "You're not allowed to smoke in Mom's car," he says, blowing a ring.

"I'm not. You are."

"I have plausible deniability." He flicks his ash onto the floor mat. "You used to date Penelope Moore, didn't you?"

"Penny Moore. Yeah. We were friends. Whatever happened to her?"

"She teaches ice skating over at the rink. The indoor one, where we played hockey."

"Kelton's."

"Right. I still skate there sometimes."

"You were a pretty good hockey player."

"No, you were a pretty good hockey player. I was a great hockey player."

"I never would have thought she'd still be living here."

"Why, because she doesn't have a brain injury?"

"No! Horry. Jesus! I'm sorry. That's not what I meant."

But he's grinning at me through the haze of smoke that has filled the space between us. "I'm just messing with you, Judd. Lighten up."

"Fuck you."

"I am already good and fucked, my brother from another mother."

"Wow. Penny Moore. What in the world made you think of Penny Moore?"

"She's in the store."

"Right now?"

"Yeah. She works the register on weeknights. You should go in and say hello."

"Penny Moore," I say. The name alone conjures up her wicked smile, the taste of her kiss. We once made a pact, Penny and I. I wonder if she still remembers.

"She'd be happy to see you, I bet."

"Maybe some other time," I say, starting the car.

"I say something wrong?"

I shake my head. "It's just hard to see people from your past when your present is so cataclysmically fucked."

Horry nods sagely. "Welcome to my world." He fishes around in his pockets for a moment, spilling some loose change onto his seat before pulling out a sloppily rolled joint, which he lights from the dying embers of his cigarette. He inhales deeply and then offers me the joint, still holding his breath.

"None for me, thanks," I say.

He shrugs and lets the smoke dance around his open mouth. "Helps me keep my head right," he says. "Sometimes, when I feel a seizure coming on, this kind of heads it off at the pass."

"Won't your mom smell that?"

"What's she going to do, ground me?"

His voice is suddenly, uncharacteristically belligerent, and I get the sense that Linda asking me to pick him up was a salvo in a long-standing battle between mother and son.

"Everything okay with you, Horry?"

"Everything is swell."

He swings the blunt my way.

"I have to drive," I say.

He shrugs and takes another long drag. "More for me."

Chapter 9

9:05 p.m.

The shiva is still in full swing when I return to the living room. "Judd!" my mother shouts as I'm trying to slink quietly back to my seat. Every eye in the room finds me. "Where were you?"

"I just needed to get some air," I mutter, sliding back down into my shiva chair.

"You remember Betty Allison?" she says, indicating the birdlike woman sitting on the chair directly in front of me. The shiva chairs, by design, are lower than the chairs of the visitors, and so my view tends to be up the nostrils and skirts of the people seated directly in front of me.

"Sure," I say. "How are you, Mrs. Allison?"

"I'm so sorry about your father."

"Thanks."

"Betty's daughter Hannah was divorced last year," my mother says brightly, like she's delivering a nugget of particularly good news.

"I'm sorry to hear that," I say.

Betty nods. "He was addicted to Internet porn."

"It happens," I say.

"Judd's wife was cheating on him."

"Jesus Christ, Mom!"

"What? There's nothing to be ashamed of."

There are about twenty other people in the room, talking to my siblings or each other, and I can feel all their heads turning to us like a stadium wave. In the third grade, I briefly suffered from the paranoid delusion that when I went to the bathroom during class, the blackboard became a television screen and my entire class watched me piss. That's what this feels like.

"Hannah and her son are here visiting for the summer," Mom says, undeterred. "I thought it might be nice for you two to catch up, that's all."

In the first grade, Hannah Allison was immortalized in an inane jump-rope song the girls sang during recess to the tune of "Frère Jacques." *Hannah Allison, Hannah Allison / Two first names, two first names / You can call her Hannah / You can call her Allison / What a shame, two first names.* Hannah cried about the song, there was a meeting between her parents and the principal, and the song was banned from the school-yard. Like all banned songs, it became an instant underground classic and continued to haunt Hannah until her peers outgrew jump rope in favor of Run-Catch-Kiss. Beyond that, I remembered a small, mousy girl with bushy eyebrows and glasses.

"I'm sure Hannah has her own problems," I say, hoping my mother will see the murder in my eyes.

"Nonsense," Betty says. "I'm sure she'd love to hear from an old friend."

Betty and my mother smile conspiratorially at each other and I can hear the telepathy buzzing between them. Her husband was addicted to porn, his wife screwed around . . . it's perfect!

"I'm not ready to start dating anytime soon," I say.

"No one said anything about dating," my mother says.

"That's right," Betty agrees. "Just a friendly phone call. Maybe a cup of coffee."

They both look at me expectantly. I am conscious of Phillip's elbow in my ribs, his low, steady chuckle. I've got six more days of this, and if I don't nip it in the bud, my mother will be trumpeting my situation to the entire community.

"The thing is, I enjoy some good Internet porn myself, every now and then," I say.

"Judd!" my mother gasps, horrified.

"Some of it is done very tastefully. And especially now, being single and all. It's a great resource."

Phillip bursts out laughing. Betty Allison's face turns red, and my mother sits back in her chair, defeated. Hannah Allison and her two first names have been wiped off the board.

"He's just being funny," Mom says weakly.

"I would have to disagree," Betty says.

Phillip is laughing so hard that tears stream down his face as he slides down in his shiva chair. Everyone in the room looks at him, horrified by the sight of unfettered glee in a shiva house, but in a minute or so he'll be done laughing, and then, to anyone who sees him, his tear-streaked face and red eyes will seem entirely appropriate.

10:30 p.m.

THE LAST VISITORS have finally left. You can feel the house exhaling, returning to its normal proportions. After my shabby behavior toward Betty Allison, Linda began quietly shooing out the guests, her voice soft but unyielding as she told them that we'd been through a long and emotional day.

Unbeknownst to me, the sleeping arrangements were decided while I was out earlier. Wendy has pretty much taken over the upstairs, commandeering Phillip's room for the baby's Portacrib, her own old bedroom for Ryan and Cole, and the guest room for her and Barry. Phillip and Tracy are on the sofa bed in the den behind the kitchen. Paul and

Alice have unceremoniously taken my childhood bedroom, which is where I always stayed when I visited with Jen. But now, being the lone single sibling, I have been relegated to the basement, which seems to be the default for me these days.

As kids, Paul and I shared a room until he sprouted pubic hair and moved down to the basement, where the hiss and clank of the boiler would drown out his Led Zeppelin, his phone calls with girlfriends, and his ever busier masturbation schedule. Paul had been allowed to furnish the basement as he saw fit, which is why the sofa bed cannot be fully opened without hitting the corner of the Ping-Pong table, which is itself positioned against a support column, so whether it's a game of Ping-Pong or a good night's sleep you're after, you're going to be shit out of luck.

11:06 p.m.

DEATH IS EXHAUSTING. Whether it's from the trauma of burying my father or from spending the entire day in close proximity to my family, I barely have the energy to take my pants off before collapsing on the mostly opened sofa bed, my legs tilted upward toward the Ping-Pong table. There, beneath the house, in the oblong shadow cast by the single naked lightbulb, I can feel the panic rising, the sense that I'm disappearing. A few miles away, my father is buried in a grassy bluff overlooking the tangle of blacktop where the interstate and thruway intersect. We are both underground, both gone from the world. At least his legs are fully extended.

I turn on my cell phone. As expected, there's a new voice mail from Jen. She's been calling me every day for the last few weeks, determined to achieve some level of amicability and open communication to facilitate a quick and peaceful divorce and so that she can believe she's been forgiven. She always cared a little too much about being liked, and the guilt over her betrayal isn't nearly as upsetting to her as the fact that I now despise her. I've taken to keeping my phone off and not returning her calls. I am still perfecting the art of hating her, and until I've got it down, I don't feel ready to engage. This infuriates her, and so she tries every possible approach to draw me out: contrite, dispassionate, tearful, philosophical, plaintive, and witty. Sometimes I play her messages, left over the course of weeks, all in a row, listening to the erratic swing of her tone between each beep. Tonight she actually descends into something of a rage, telling me I can't keep avoiding her, threatening to empty our joint checking account if I don't return her call by tomorrow. No doubt she'd like to be divorced by the time she and Wade have their baby. I especially like today's voice mail, because she's shouting at me like I'm standing right there in front of her, like it's an actual conversation. Still, just to be safe, first thing tomorrow I'll run out to the bank and with-draw the bulk of what's left in our checking account. It was around twenty-two thousand dollars last time I checked, although the balance has probably fallen a bit since then. I have a feeling her next voice mail will break new ground.

Thursday

Chapter 10

I have a recurring dream in which I'm walking down the street, all foot-loose and fancy-free, when I look down and realize that beneath my pants, one of my legs is actually a prosthesis, molded plastic and rubber with a steel core. And then I remember, with a sinking feeling, that my leg had been amputated from the knee down a few years back. I had simply forgotten. The way you can forget in dreams. The way you wish you could forget in real life but, of course, can't. In real life, you don't get to choose what you forget. So I'm walking, usually out on Route 120 in Elmsbrook, past the crappy strip malls, the mini golf, the discount chains, and the themed restaurants, when I suddenly remember that I lost my leg a few years ago, maybe cancer, maybe a car accident, what-ever. The point is, I have this fake leg clamped to my thigh, chafing at my knee where my calf used to descend. And when I remember that I'm an amputee, I experience this moment of abject horror when I realize that when I get home I will have to take off the leg to go to sleep and I can't remember ever having done that before, but I must do it every night, and how do I pee, and who will ever want to have sex with me, and how the hell did this even happen anyway? And that's when I will myself awake, and I lie there in bed, sweaty and trembling, running my hands up and down both legs, just making sure. Then I get up to go to the bathroom, even if I don't have to, and the cold bathroom tiles against my heels are like finding fifty bucks in a jacket pocket from last fall.

These are the rare moments when it actually still feels good to be me.

And sometimes during my waking hours I think, wouldn't it be something if this life was just a dream too? And somewhere there's a more complete and happy and slimmer version of me sleeping in his bed, next to a wife who still loves him, the linens twisted up around their feet from their recent lovemaking, the sounds of their children's light snoring filling the dimly lit hallway. And that me, the one dreaming of this version, is about to shake himself awake from the nightmare of my life. I can feel his relief like it's my own.

7:43 a.m.

THERE IS NOTHING more pathetically optimistic than the morning erection. I am depressed, unemployed, unloved, basement-dwelling, and bereaved, but there it is, every morning like clockwork, rising up to greet the day, poking out of my fly cocksure and conspicuously useless. And every morning, I face the same choice: masturbate or urinate. It's the one time of the day where I feel like I have options.

But this morning I can hear the low groan of the floorboards above me, the rhythmic creak of the sofa bed in the den—Phillip and Tracy enjoying some early morning, pre-shiva coitus—and my options are whittled down to none. I can hear Tracy's muffled voice groaning something over and over again as they gather momentum. The first song that comes to mind is "The Star-Spangled Banner," and I hum it loudly to drown out the muffled cries and grunts seeping through the ceiling as I flee to the linoleum safety of the closet-sized bathroom. I'm still pissing when I reach the home of the brave, so I loudly hum the theme to *Star Trek* in a continuous loop until I've washed my hands and brushed my teeth. When I emerge, the noise has subsided, and my mother is sitting on the edge of my bed in the kind of short, satin bathrobe you'd want to see on your twenty-three-year-old girlfriend.

"Sleep well?" she says.

"Not really."

Upstairs the creaking begins again. Mom looks up at the ceiling and smiles at me. "That boy," she says, shaking her head fondly. "Tracy must be forty-five if she's a day. Obviously, he's working through some mother issues." She leans forward, and the satin lapels of her robe spread, revealing the large D cups she had installed about fifteen years ago. She'd discovered a lump that turned out to be benign and somehow converted the experience into an excuse to upgrade her breasts. She hasn't worn a bra since.

"Mom!" I say, looking away. "Cover up, will you?"

She looks down, lovingly surveying the promontories of her age-inappropriate breasts like she would an infant grandchild, before unhurriedly refastening her robe. "You were always something of a prude," she says.

"It's a mystery to me why anyone in this house might have mother issues."

"They're breasts, Judd. The same ones you suckled at."

"Those are something other than breasts."

"Your father didn't see it that way. When we made love, he used to love to—"

"Shut up, Mom!"

"Why is it so hard for you to accept that your mother is a sexual being? Do you think you were immaculately conceived? I should think it would make you happy that your father and I were still fucking."

Yes. That's what she said. My mother is a sixty-three-year-old bestselling author with a Ph.D. in clinical psychology and Pamela Anderson's breasts, who talks about fucking her late husband like she's discussing current events.

"Let's pretend, for the sake of argument, that that was a remotely normal thing to say to your son. It still doesn't mean I want to hear the intimate details of your sex life."

"Judd. I'm your mother, and I love you." That's what she always says, what she advises the millions of mothers who read *Cradle and All* to say, just before eviscerating or emasculating their offspring. The next word is always "but." According to Doctor Hillary Foxman, the patron saint of frustrated mothers, this is called softening, rendering the child receptive to correction. What I've learned, after nine years of marital spats, is that everything before the "but" is bullshit.

"But," she says, "your sorrow has become malignant."

I nod slowly, as if considering her words. "Thanks, Mom. That wasn't even the slightest bit helpful."

She shrugs and pulls herself up off the bed, stopping at the foot of the stairs to consider me. Dust mites dance in the sunlight pouring down from the opened door upstairs, and I can see the bags under her eyes, the gray roots at her scalp, and the acute sadness in her eyes as she looks at me. Somewhere in there, underneath those ridiculous breasts and the psychobabble, is a real mother, hurting for her child, and for reasons I probably couldn't begin to explain without years of therapy, her pain fills me with a quiet, relentless rage.

"I miss your father," she says.

"I miss him too."

"Do you?"

"I missed him while he was still alive."

She nods. "He was never comfortable expressing himself. But he loved you very much."

"Not like he loved you."

She smiles and massages the back of her neck. Upstairs, Phillip and Tracy have finally, mercifully finished, and a welcome quiet fills the room.

"I'm sorry you couldn't have your old room," she says. "I thought Paul and Alice could use some privacy. They've been trying to conceive, you know."

"Wendy mentioned something."

"That sofa bed is fine for sleeping, but it's simply not built for pro-creation. The springs creak like a couple of fighting cats. You can hear it throughout the house."

"I don't suppose I can stop you from telling me why you know that."

"Your father and I made love on every bed in this house."

"Of course."

"Anyway, I found an ovulation test kit in the wastebasket in the hall bathroom, so I'm thinking these are key nights for Alice."

Mom never had any use for discretion, never even had the sense to fake it. She habitually went through our drawers and coat pockets, in-spected our sheets, listened in on our phone calls, and read Wendy's diary so often that we started composing entries just for her to find.

> Mr. Jorgenson, my phys ed teacher, still says I can't call him Ed,
> even after I had a three-way with him and Mike Stedman, who
> swears the whole genital herpes thing was just a nasty rumor
> started by his ex-girlfriend who was pissed at him for sleeping with
> me and Ed.

> Liz Coltrane gave me these awesome pills that make you vomit
> after every meal, so I don't have to use my finger anymore. It's
> much more civilized, and I can finally grow my nails again. Thin
> and manicured! Win-win!

I know incest is wrong. I just figured I'd do it once to see what all the fuss was about. But now Paul wants to do it with me all the time and it's starting to get creepy. It would have been so much easier with Judd, if only he wasn't gay.

Mom believed that intrafamily secrets were unhealthy, and because of that, we spent the better part of our childhood lying our asses off to her.

When I was twelve years old, she unceremoniously handed me a tube of KY Jelly and said that she could tell from the laundry that I'd begun masturbating, and this would increase my pleasure and prevent chafing, and if I had any questions, I should feel free to come to her. My siblings did joyous spit takes into their bowls of chicken soup, and my father grunted disapprovingly and said, "Jesus, Hill!" He uttered those two words so often that for a long time I thought Jesus's last name was actually Hill. In this particular case, I was unsure if it was masturbation my father condemned or the relative merits of discussing it over Friday-night dinner. I fled upstairs to sulk and didn't stop hating her even after discovering, a short while later, to my eternal chagrin, that she'd been right about the lube.

Chapter 11

8:25 a.m.

A shower in the morning is an imperative for the Foxman men, whose bed-head is legendary in this region. Our pillow-bent curls, sculpted by scalp oils, stand up in large, coiled clumps, making us look like electrocuted cartoon characters. The problem is that the water boiler cannot accommodate so many showers at the same time, and within minutes, the water goes from hot, to lukewarm, to chilled. Adding to the confusion, Tracy and Alice are both blow-drying their hair while Wendy is microwaving frozen waffles for the kids, so the circuit breakers trip, knocking out half the power in the house, including the basement lights.

You would think the home of a former electrician would be wired better, but it's a classic case of the cobbler's children going barefoot. Having been in the "trade," as he called it, Dad was much too stubborn to spend money on electricians. He did everything himself, refusing to file any work he did with the city, which saved him the trouble of having to bring things up to code. Having spent years laboring under the restrictions of the power company, he took a certain pride in outwitting them in his own home. He was always fishing lines through the walls, splicing and rewiring, creating a dense maze of circuitry behind our walls to the point where even he lost track of where everything went. The house gradually became something of an electrical puzzle, with too many lines on overburdened fuses and patchwork wiring that doesn't always hold up. Slamming the doors of certain rooms can actually turn off the lights, and there are extra wall switches everywhere, some redundant and some that do nothing, so it always takes a few tries for the uninitiated to turn on or off the light they want. When he had central air installed a few years ago, he was supposed to upgrade the house from two hundred to four hundred amps, but that would have involved filing with the power company, so instead, he rewired the electric panels in the basement to make room for the compressor and air handlers. As a result, the house is more than a little electrically temperamental, and Mom always jokes that one day she'll flip a switch and the house will explode. Until then, the circuit breakers will bravely go on tripping to protect the overloaded wires.

I rush through my shower, cold and blind and cursing a blue streak, then step shivering into the basement, where I find Alice in a white bathrobe, fiddling with the electric panel in the sparse morning light filtering down from upstairs.

"Hey," she says when she sees me. "I'm sorry to invade your space like this."

It's the invading of my old bedroom upstairs that she should be apologizing for, but I just say it's fine, suddenly self-conscious. The last time Alice saw me undressed was in this very room, several lifetimes ago. I looked better shirtless then, although I'm sure she did too. Time hasn't necessarily been unkind to us, but it hasn't gone out of its way either. And for the last two months, I've been living on a diet of delivered pizza and fried Chinese takeout. I suck in my gut and fold my arms strategically below my chest.

"I can't find the switch," she says.

I stand dripping beside her, studying the circuit panel. It's too dark to see the little orange tab that shows on a tripped fuse, so I run my hand down the line of switches until I feel one that has more give than the others. "It's this one," I say, flipping the switch. The lights flicker back on at exactly the same instant my towel falls. "Whoops!" I say, doubling over to catch it and pull it back up to my waist. "Sorry about that."

Alice smiles as I fumble with my towel. "Nothing I haven't seen before," she says, heading back upstairs; a rare lighthearted moment for Alice, which, if nothing else, confirms for me that I'm the only Foxman brother who didn't get any last night.

10:00 a.m.

"IT WAS A Saturday morning," Wendy says, "and, Mom, you were on a lecture tour. Dad was up on the roof, hammering the rain gutters back on or something. He was making a racket, so I was down in the basement, watching TV. It was a Brady Bunch movie, I still remember. The one where they go to Hawaii."

"I remember that one," Phillip says. "Alice hurts her back having a hula lesson, because of Peter's bad luck charm."

"Right," Wendy says. "That's not really germane to my story."

"I remember thinking it was nice that Alice got to go on vacation with them," Phillip says. "I mean, she was the housekeeper. You got the feeling that she hadn't really gone anywhere before."

"Phillip remembers every show or movie he's ever seen," Tracy says proudly, like we might not know.

"Now if only that were a marketable skill," Wendy says.

Tracy looks miffed, but Phillip laughs. He and Wendy have a long history of insulting each other. They don't even hear it anymore.

Tracy and Alice are on the couch; Linda is in an armchair, her feet up on one of the plastic folding chairs; and Barry is reading the *Wall Street Journal* in the backyard while the boys run around. The rest of us are back in our low shiva chairs, steeling ourselves for another ass-numbing day of greeting visitors at crotch level. Mom has asked us all to remember personal stories about Dad, which she is scribbling into a large brown journal.

"So, anyway, that's where I was, watching television, when I got my first period."

"I have one daughter, and I wasn't here the day she became a woman," Mom says. "I'll never forgive myself for that."

"Hardly your worst offense," Wendy says with a smirk. "So I run upstairs and I scream out the window to Dad, but he can't hear me over the hammering. So I step outside and call up to him, but he still can't hear me. So I grab a baseball off the lawn—Paul was always leaving baseballs on the lawn—and I throw it up to the roof. I only meant for it to hit the roof and roll down, just to catch his attention, but I guess I didn't know my own strength, and the ball hits Dad square on the back of his head, and he loses his balance and falls off the roof, pulling the rain gutter off with him as he goes."

"I don't remember this at all," Phillip says.

"Because it didn't happen on a television show," Wendy says. She turns to Tracy. "Phillip was their last child. He was basically raised by the television. We don't hold it against him."

"Spiteful bitch," Mom says with a smile.

"So Dad's lying on the ground, flat on his back. His arm is broken, and he's got this big gash on his forehead, and his eyes are closed, and I'm sure I've just killed him. So I scream, 'Daddy, wake up!' And he opens his eyes and he says, very calmly, 'I spent all morning putting that gutter on.' Then he gets up, and we get in the car, and he drives one-armed to the emergency room. And the nurse at the desk looks him up and down and says, 'What in the world happened to you?' and he says, 'My daughter got her period.'"

Everyone laughs.

"That's such a perfect story," Mom says, scribbling. "That's so very Mort."

"Victoria—that was the nurse's name—took me to the bathroom and taught me how to put in a tampon while they set Dad's arm, and I still see her face every time I use a tampon. She was a big old Jamaican woman with little black freckles like Morgan Freeman, and she said, 'Just ease it in, child. Don't you be scared. Bigger tings dan dis goin to go in dere. And come out.' I had nightmares for weeks."

"That was great. Can you tell another story about your period?"

"Shut up, Judd. Why don't you tell your favorite memory now?"

"I'm still thinking."

"I've got one," Phillip says. "When I was in Little League, I had trouble catching. So they put me out in right field. And in the last inning, I dropped two balls that cost us the game. Our coach was this fat guy, I forgot his name. He got all crazy and started screaming at me. He called me worthless. So Dad stepped between us and I didn't see what he did, but next thing I know, the coach is on the ground, and Dad is stepping on his chest. And he says, 'Call my son worthless again.'"

"That's fantastic," Alice says, clapping. "I never heard that one."

"This might sound twisted, but I hope, when I have a kid, that someone calls him a name, just so I can do for him what Dad did for me."

"That's beautiful, Phillip," Mom says.

"Yes," Tracy says. "But why not just hope that no one calls your child a name?"

Phillip looks at her. "Don't do that."

"What?"

"You know damn well what."

"I was just saying that as long as you're being theoretical, why not aim higher?"

"My dad stood up for me. I want to stand up for my kid."

"And teach him that violence is a legitimate means of conflict resolution?"

"He's going to have to learn it sometime."

"A few well-chosen words might have shamed your coach into apologizing."

"But if he had, I wouldn't have had a story to remind me of how my father took care of me, and you wouldn't have been able to suck all the joy out of it, and where would we all be then?"

Tracy blinks repeatedly, blushing as she gets to her feet. "I'm sorry, you're right. I was being insensitive."

"Apology accepted," Phillip says without looking at her.

"I'm going to take a walk and return some calls."

"You meant well, honey," Linda says to her as she leaves.

Once she's gone, Phillip looks around at us sheepishly. "She takes a little getting used to."

"Well, you shouldn't have dressed her down like that, in front of your family," Linda says. "She's still a guest here."

"I thought you were completely justified," Mom says.

"We'll just have to agree to disagree then," Linda says.

Mom casts a dark look at Linda before turning to me. "So, Judd, what do you have for me?"

What I have is nothing. I've been wracking my brain, but every memory I have of my father is tied up with everyone else. I know there must have been times when it was just the two of us, but I can't remember any of them. I can only see him in the context of everyone else. Phillip's story, in particular, made me think of riding home in Dad's car after Paul's games.

Paul was a standout pitcher, the only one of us with true ability, and driving home from his games, Dad would relive the highlights out loud, shaking his head in disbelief that one of his children was capable of anything other than disappointing him. Having a brother who was the school's most acclaimed athlete was not without its perks. It may not have been enough to land me a girlfriend, but being Paul's untalented runt of a brother was still better than being just another pimply underclassman with bad hair and an ass to kick. Still, I hated those car rides after the games, the Cadillac littered with samples and torn packaging, the next month's sale signage shifting and grinding in the trunk like tectonic plates every time Dad braked, listening to him come out of his customary shell to praise Paul in a way he would never praise me. Wendy would sit directly behind Dad, lip-syncing to his soliloquy, trying to get me to laugh, while Phillip whined about always having to sit between us on the hump, and Mom looked out the window, humming along to the oldies station on the radio.

In his senior year, Paul was awarded a full baseball scholarship to UMass. Now, not only was he the talented son, he was also paying his own way. Paul was golden. He spent his summer celebrating with his buddies and having sex with a rotation of baseball groupies. It was a busy time for him, and on those rare occasions he was home, he was either passed out in his basement bedroom or hungover at the kitchen table, reading the sports pages and sipping at a black coffee.

Simmering with envy, I wondered what I could do to distinguish myself as anything other than a waste of space. Athletics were out—I played hockey in a local league, but there was no school team, and I wasn't particularly gifted anyway. I briefly considered joining the debate team, but I knew my father wouldn't see the point to a group of kids putting on striped red and blue ties to argue in public. As far as I could see, my best shot at gaining his approval was to get wounded while foiling an armed robbery at the 7-Eleven. Instead, I spent my summer in the 7-Eleven parking lot, smoking pot and wishing for something bad to happen to Paul.

And then something did.

Chapter 12

11:30 a.m.

Mr. Applebaum is all over Mom. He clasps her hand between his, he pats her arm, his fingers snaking around her wrist, his eyes darting back and forth across her chest like a tiny tennis match is being played across the line of her cleavage. He's pulled his folding chair up close to her, and with Mom down in the shiva chair, he is perfectly positioned to ogle.

"I've been through this, Hillary," he says. His dark, bushy eyebrows call to mind political cartoons as they arch compassionately under his wiry silver hair. "When I lost Adele, the community was very supportive. Mort was wonderful. You remember, he came over and fixed the air conditioner during my shiva? All those people in the house, and the air handler crapped out."

"He knew machines," Mom says.

"Look at that," Wendy whispers. "He's staring at her breasts, and her head is practically between his knees."

"It's just the angle," I say. "These low chairs."

"These chairs are a practical joke. And Mom should wear less revealing shirts."

"She doesn't own less revealing shirts."

"I feel like I'm watching the opening scene of an AARP porno," Phillip says.

Mr. Applebaum rubs Mom's wrist. He's the only visitor right now, and so he's got her cornered. Not that she seems to mind the attention. "If you ever need to talk, Hill. Day or night. Just call, and I'll be there."

"I bet he will," Wendy says.

"Just call my name," Phillip sings in a head voice. *"And I'll be there."*

"Thank you, Peter. I appreciate that."

"It can be very lonely."

"I don't doubt it."

Applebaum sighs and looks down at her, reluctant to let go of her hand. "I'll be back tomorrow to check on you."

"Okay."

He stands up and then pulls her up by her hand to clutch her in a full-bodied embrace. "You're going to be fine, Hillary."

Mom pats his back while he holds her tight.

"The old guy just copped a feel," Paul says, joining in.

"Give him a break," I say. "They've known each other for years."

I remember Applebaum's wife, Adele, a tall, vivacious woman with big teeth and a resounding laugh. She would grab my hair when I was a kid and say, "Oh, Hill, the girls are just going to go wild over this one!" Then she'd wink at me and say, "Look me up when you're legal. We'll run away together." She started having strokes a few years ago. I remember him pushing her around at Paul's wedding in a wheelchair. She could only smile with half her face and couldn't reach my hair with her withered arm. I thought she may have winked at me, but it was hard to tell.

Applebaum finally lets go of Mom and turns to face the rest of us. "You kids take care of your beautiful mother, okay?"

"I believe he had an erection," Wendy says once he's gone.

"Oh, stop it. He did not," Mom says.

"Pushing seventy and he's still getting it up," Phillip muses. "The man's a keeper."

"You're all being horrible. You've known Peter forever. He's a fine man."

"That fine man was hitting on you." Paul .

"He was totally hitting on you." Wendy.

"He was most definitely not hitting on me," Mom says, flushed with pleasure.

Linda sticks her head in from the kitchen. "Is that horny old goat gone yet?"

"Oh, for heaven's sake," Mom says. "He was being compassionate."

"Not as compassionate as he'd like, I'm sure."

"So, he's lonely. You and I, at least, should be sympathetic," Mom says. "At our age, loneliness can seem so permanent."

"Ah . . . Look at all the lonely people," Phillip sings.

"Well, he might have had the decency to wait until you were through sitting shiva before groping you like that, that's all."

"He's a tactile man. That's just his way."

That's just his way. Jen used to say that. Like the first time she met Wade, at the WIRX holiday party, where he couldn't seem to stop rubbing her arms and touching her back as they talked. "That's just his way," she said, which was how she excused all manner of bad behavior except for mine. Once, when she was pissed at me, I went so far as to try it out as an argument for the defense. *"That's just my way,"* I said. She smiled sweetly and told me to fuck off. God, I miss our fights.

Linda is looking at Mom, shaking her head. "You don't actually believe half the things you say, do you?"

"I don't know," Mom says, sitting back in her chair. "I can be pretty convincing."

Chapter 13

The bank teller has a great ass. I know this because she had to get up and go to her boss's office when I told her I wanted to withdraw sixteen of the just under twenty thousand dollars remaining in mine and Jen's joint checking account. When she returns, I see that she has nice lips too—full and pouty—and she has a dimple in one cheek, and something about her eyes and the way she chews her gum makes me think she's a very sexual person. Her name is Marianna, which I know because it's on the little badge she has affixed just beside her breasts, which aren't particularly large but come together nicely in her push-up bra to form a perfectly adequate suntanned cleavage in the V-neck of her blouse. My guess is that she didn't go to college, at least not a four-year college. Probably community college for her associate's degree, and then right into the bank's training program. She is the kind of girl who dates the kind of guys who will ultimately screw around on her, guys like her brothers, who work with their hands and drink too many beers while watching football, and have a stupid tattoo of a dragon or the Rolling Stones' lips on their scapulas, guys upon whom she projects more romance and ambition than is actually there, and then she asks her girl-friends, who are hairdressers and medical technicians and tanning salon clerks and secretaries, why she can't find a nice guy. And I'm dying to tell her that I'm a nice guy. I'm the last nice guy. And I haven't been kissed or rubbed in months, and I'm as horny as a high school kid, but I'm also dying to fall in love, and if you let me, I'll fall in love with you, and cherish you, and listen to your dreams and your hurts and I'll be faithful and funny and I'll never forget your birthday or make out with your girlfriend and blame it on too many shots, or come home from guys' night out drunk and smelling of strippers. That's what I want to tell her, but instead I say, "Can I have an envelope for that?" and if you want to know where all the good guys are, we're standing right in front of you, lacking the balls to actually make ourselves heard.

This is something that's been happening to me more and more lately. The world is suddenly brimming with young, nubile women, and I can't leave the house without falling in love. I intuit whole personalities from a single smile, live out entire relationships with the woman sitting in the next car at a red light. Legs and lips hypnotize me. I am smitten by skin and breasts and hair, by smiles and frowns, by the freedom of an unhurried gait, the grace of a shrug. I imagine myself not only having sex with these women, but living with them and meeting their parents and sharing the Sunday paper in bed. I am still raw and soft from losing Jen, still missing a level of detachment and discernment, undersexed and lonely and not yet fit for mixed company.

Marianna carefully loads sixteen thousand dollars into a large manila envelope for me, and she has a yellow sunset painted onto the red nail of each ring finger, and her skin is creamy and immaculate, and I know that I will never kiss those plump lips, never see her naked, never even make her smile. We are separated by three inches of bulletproof glass and a million other barriers that I can't articulate or overcome. So I take my envelope and file away her generic smile for further worthless review. I leave the bank more heartbroken and deflated than when I entered it, and that is saying something.

Chapter 14

Wade made it perfectly clear that he wasn't firing me.

"I want to make this perfectly clear," he said. "I am not firing you." It had been six or seven tear-fused panicky days since I'd walked in on him and Jen, days spent curled up in a ball in the Lees' basement, still ensconced in a hollow daze, alternately enraged, grief-stricken, terrified, and shitfaced.

Wade was sitting behind his large Asian desk in his large corner office. He didn't need a desk; he did no paperwork. He didn't need an office either. The running joke was that the sole reason for the office was so that he had a place to screw the hot interns. Ha ha.

He pulled his lips back into a thoughtful grimace, revealing a symmetrical wall of large, bleached white teeth. If you were to draw a caricature of Wade, you would emphasize those supernaturally perfect teeth, his ridiculously broad shoulders, and, of course, his unrepentant cock. "Obviously, this is a very difficult situation. You hate me right now. Of course you do. I'm sure you'd like nothing better than to bludgeon me to death with a blunt instrument. What I did was inexcusable, and I feel terrible about it. I know you probably don't believe that, but it's true."

He smiled sheepishly at me, as if he'd just admitted something mildly embarrassing about himself, like he suffers from constipation or gets regular pedicures. Then he shrugged those broad spherical shoulders that throbbed like organs beneath his expensive dress shirt. I guess I'd always been somewhat envious of Wade's shoulders, because when you get right down to it, mine are just your basic, stripped-down version, while Wade's are the fully loaded models that fill a shirt perfectly and look just as good out of one. I could hope they're obscenely hairy, the way some men's are, but it would be futile, because Wade is the kind of guy who would never stand for shoulder hair. He'd have it permanently removed by laser, and even though results vary, he'd be the guy for whom it worked. I'd probably get burned or develop a permanent discoloration. This stuff is all preordained.

Like most guys with genetically superior shoulders, Wade was an asshole, an alpha male who asserted his presence physically, through viselike handshakes and powerful backslaps, the kind of guy who needed to win at everything. His tone now was carefully apologetic, conciliatory even, but still, his expression radiated the smug satisfaction of having asserted his sexual dominance. *I fucked your woman,* his eyes said. *Better than you ever could.*

"Are you going to keep fucking her?" I said.

"What?"

"Are you going to keep fucking my wife?"

Wade looked over to Stuart Kaplan, who sat unobtrusively behind us on the couch. Stuart was the station manager and default head of human resources. It was something of a workplace irony that they couldn't seem to hire the right person to run H.R., and after the last woman quit, Stuart had simply absorbed the department. Wade made fun of him ceaselessly on the air, called him Stuart the Suit. They had clearly met in anticipation of this meeting, to discuss the hairy legal ramifications of the marquee radio host sleeping with the wife of one of his staff. And now Stuart was sitting in to serve as a witness that I wasn't being dismissed or subtly urged to resign in any way.

"Listen," Stuart interjected. "I don't think that's a constructive approach to take here—"

"You said you feel terrible about it," I said, staring at the small patch of stubble between Wade's eyes where he shaved his unibrow. "So, that being the case, do you think you're going to stop? I think it's a fair question, and not at all irrelevant to this discussion."

"I think we should confine this talk to our professional relationship."

"So you're going to keep fucking her."

Wade looked to Stuart for some help.

"I know this is hard," Stuart said.

"How do you know that, Stuart the Suit? Did he fuck your wife too?"

Stuart was sixty years old, had a closet full of identical pin-striped suits and a rattling chest full of phlegm from years of chain-smoking. His moods swung to whatever extent they did on the basis of his increasingly erratic bowel function. If he even had a wife, the odds of Wade or even Stuart himself wanting to sleep with her were probably quite low.

"Judd," Stuart said resignedly, which was how he said pretty much everything.

"Stuart," I said.

He slid a document in front of me. It was a contract, acknowledging a significant raise, provided that I would indemnify *Man Up with Wade Boulanger* and WIRX from any future legal proceedings.

"How are your testicles, Wade?"

"They're fine."

I hoped they were blistered and peeling, or at least caked in A&D Ointment and sticking uncomfortably to his underwear.

"Listen, Judd," Wade said, returning to his prepared script. "You're a fantastic producer. You're integral to the show. Regardless of how things shake out personally, we don't want to lose you."

I was being offered a consolation prize. Numbers had been crunched, risks assessed, and they had estimated the value of my broken marriage at another thirty thousand dollars a year before taxes. My life had just become inordinately expensive. I was going to have to pay alimony and keep up the mortgage on the house while renting my own apartment. Even with this raise, things would be tight, but it would certainly help. The only smart choice was to accept the offer and soldier on while I looked for another opportunity. The idea of working for Wade sickened me, but this was not a time to be unemployed on top of everything else.

I looked up at Wade, at his furrowed brow, his pursed lips, those goddamn shoulders. He met my gaze as he exhaled, long and slow. And then he said, "I love her, Judd."

"Wade!" Stuart shouted, making us both jump.

I jumped to my feet. "Fuck you."

"Judd," Stuart said.

"Stuart!" I shouted back, startling all three of us. And then I tore up the document. And then I grabbed my chair and hurled it across the desk at Wade, who jumped up and fell back in his own chair, knocking over magazines, souvenir beer mugs from sponsors, and the glass rectangle filled with neon blue liquid that, when turned on, created the soothing impression of waves. "You'll be hearing from my lawyers," I said, even though I didn't have a single lawyer, let alone lawyers, even though I had no idea where to get a lawyer or what kind of lawyer you needed when your boss climbed into bed with your wife. The good ones were probably not listed in the Yellow Pages. But I had just torn up a contract and hurled a chair across the room, and that sort of violence required punctuation with a coherent statement of some kind, and "You'll be hearing from my lawyers" is what came to mind.

I stepped out of Wade's office, into the large common area. Assistants and interns sat frozen at their desks, staring; ad sales executives hovered in cubicles, awakened from their corporate stupor by the commotion. I saw the truth in their averted gazes. They all knew. Everybody knew. Under their scrutiny, my rage dissolved almost instantly, replaced with the hot shame of public emasculation. My wife had slept with another man, so what did that make me? A limp, flaccid, inadequate lover, possibly a premature ejaculator, or maybe even gay. The array of possibilities was breathtaking.

"His balls caught fire," I announced in the quivering voice of a very small man. Then I walked down the corridor to the elevators as slowly and proudly as possible, which wasn't terribly slow or proud, when you got right down to it.

Chapter 15

7:00 p.m.

The house is filled again, thirty or forty visitors, sitting in the plastic chairs, crammed around the buffet in the dining room, spilling over into the front hall and kitchen. The smell of perfume and instant coffee fills the air. Random fragments of conversation fly back and forth across the room like shuttlecocks. Our shiva is quite the scene for the over-sixty set. Outside on the cul-de-sac, two men back out of opposing parking spots and lightly crash into each other. A small crowd gathers outside and everyone looks out the window as hands are wrung and fingers pointed, and a short while later the red swirl of police lights dances across the living room walls as reports are filed. And the visitors keep coming, old friends and distant relatives, the new seamlessly replacing the old, walking in somber and unsure, walking out satisfied and well fed. By now, we see them not as individuals, but as a single coffee-swilling, bagel-chomping, tearfully smiling mass of well-wishers and rubberneckers. We can all nod and smile and carry on our end of the conversation in an endless loop while our minds float somewhere outside our bodies. We are thinking about our kids, our lack of kids, about finances and fiancées and soon-to-be ex-wives, about the sex we're not having, the sex our soon-to-be ex-wives are having, about loneliness and love and death and Dad, and this constant crowd is like a fog on a dark road; you just keep driving and watch it dissipate in your low beams.

The energy changes a little when some girls show up to visit Phillip. There are three of them, in their early twenties, and they breeze into the room in a whirling miasma of bronzed legs and bouncing asses, trailing sexuality like fairy dust as they make their way to Phillip's chair. They instantly become the center of attention, and while other conversations are still going on, these girls, as they flex their smooth calves to go up on the tips of their high espadrilles to kiss Phillip's cheek, seem to be followed by their own spotlight. After the kisses, the hugs, the dramatic expressions of condolence punctuated by the flipping of hair and batting of lashes, three empty chairs magically materialize in front of Phillip's shiva chair, and the girls sit down. They are accustomed to seats appearing for them wherever they go; they assume it's probably like that for everyone. I recognize these girls, old high school friends of Phillip's, all of whom he slept with repeatedly, two of whom, it was rumored, he slept with together on more than one occasion.

"Oh my God, Phillip," Chelsea says. She is a long-legged redhead in a skirt that would be appropriate for tennis. She and Phillip were on and off for years. "I haven't seen you since that boat party, you remember? That Russian kid with the yacht? Oh my God, we got so messed up that night."

"I remember," Phillip says.

"I'm so sorry about your father," Janelle says. She has a pretty face underneath her spray-on tan and is slightly chunky, but in that way men like.

"Thank you."

"He was such a nice man," Kelly says. Kelly has a platinum pixie cut and a come-hither smile, and you can just picture her drinking too much and dancing on the pool table in the frat house.

"So, Philly," Chelsea says. "What have you been up to?"

"I've been doing A&R work for a record label."

"That's so cool!"

"It's a small, independent label, a boutique," Phillip says modestly. "Nothing too exciting. You guys remember my brother Judd?"

They turn to me as one and say hi. I say hi back and try to decide which one I would most want to sleep with. The answer is, all of them. Line them up and I'll knock them down. They are pretty and sexy and friendly and easy and exactly the kind of girls I never had a chance with back in the day. But now . . . now I'm divorced and damaged, and aren't these the kind of girls who like damaged men?

"So what have you all been up to?" Phillip says, and what follows is ten minutes of giggles and banter, repeatedly tossed hair, and some really bad grammar. They laugh at pretty much everything Phillip says, and Chelsea, in particular, seems to hang on his every word, her chair gradually inching closer until her ankles rest easily against his. And then Tracy comes back, having spent the afternoon out of the house after her argument with Phillip. I watch her enter the room, see her register these hot young things surrounding her man as she makes her way through the chairs to Phillip's side. "Hey, babe," she says, smiling first at him and then at the girls. I have never heard her say "babe," and it rolls clumsily off her tongue like a hasty lie. "How's it going?"

"Great," he says. "These are some old friends of mine from high school."

"And college," Chelsea reminds him with a smile.

"That's right. Chelsea and I were also in college together."

"I love the name Chelsea," Tracy says.

"Thanks."

"This is Tracy," Phillip says. He doesn't say "my fiancée," or any other designation, and the omission lands with a resounding thud in our midst. But Tracy clings admirably to her gracious smile, and for the first time since I've met her, I feel bad for her. She's a smart woman, and on some level, she has to know that this thing with Phillip will never work. Still, she leans forward to graciously shake hands and repeat each girl's name as she's introduced, like she's at a business meeting. The girls flash their whitened teeth and extend their hands, their French-manicured nails catching the light and slicing the air like razor blades.

8:15 p.m.

"LONG DAY, HUH?" Linda says to me. She's sitting on a stool at the center island in the kitchen, peering down through her bifocals at the *Times* crossword puzzle.

"I thought I might go pick up Horry again."

"I thought you might, too," she says, sliding her car keys across the marble countertop. "You're blocked in again."

"Thanks."

She takes off her reading glasses. "How does he seem to you?"

"Horry? I don't know. Fine I guess."

"He does not seem fine, Judd. Don't be diplomatic with me."

I nod and think about it. "He seems angry, maybe. Frustrated."

"He hates me."

"I'm sure he doesn't hate you. But he's a thirty-six-year-old man living with his mother. That can't be healthy."

"He's not healthy."

"He seems fine."

"He has seizures. He wets his bed. He forgets things, important things, like locking the door or turning off the oven or putting out his cigarette before he falls asleep, or, once in a while, putting on his pants before he goes out. Sometimes he goes into these trances where he just stands there staring at the wall. I can't bear the thought of him living alone and staring at the walls for hours on end, with no one there to snap him out of it."

"On the other hand, he might need some independence."

"What he needs is to get laid," Linda says sharply. "That boy always had a girlfriend, remember? I lived in fear that he'd call me from college to tell me he'd knocked up some twit." She leans forward and lowers her voice. "It's never easy for him, seeing Wendy like this."

"I hadn't thought of that."

"You think you're lonely now, Judd, but you've got nothing on that boy."

"No. I guess I don't."

"Which reminds me, you should go into the store when you pick him up and say hello to that Penelope Moore."

I stare at her, nonplussed. "You're just full of surprises, aren't you?"

She puts her glasses on and turns back to her puzzle, a small smile playing across her lips. "You have no idea," she says.

Chapter 16

8:42 p.m.

There was always something of a little girl about Penny Moore, with her pale skin and wide eyes, and that hasn't changed in the years since I last saw her. When she sees me, her face lights up, and she leaps athletically over the counter to hug me. She's dressed in jeans and a button-down oxford, her long dark hair tied loosely behind her head. From twenty feet away, she could pass for a college student. Only as she draws closer do you see the slightly looser flesh beneath her eyes, the soft commas at the corners of her mouth.

"Hey, Judd Foxman." She feels thin in my arms, less substantial than I remember.

"Hi, Penny."

She kisses my cheek and then steps back so we can look at each other. "I'm so sorry about Mort," she says.

"Thanks."

"I saw you at the funeral."

"Really? I didn't see you."

"I avoided you. I never know what to say at funerals."

"Fair enough."

Penny's honesty has always been like nudity in an action movie: gratuitous, but no less welcome for it.

"So, how long has it been?" she says. "Seven, eight years?"

"Something like that."

She gives me the once-over. "You look like hell."

"Thanks. You look great."

"Don't I, though?" she says, smiling.

What I'm thinking is that she looks fine, pretty even, but nothing like the ripe prom queen she was back in high school. I wanted her so badly then; everybody did. But she was out of my league so I settled for becoming her best friend, a form of masochism unique to underconfident teenage boys, our time together spent with her telling me about all the assholes she chose to have sex with instead of me. Time and troubles have sharpened her softer edges, and now her face is a knife, her breasts like two clenched fists under her tight blouse. She's a sexy street-fight of a woman, and I have been alone and untouched for a while now, and just watching her lips slide against her teeth as she smiles is enough to get me going.

"So, I heard about your wife," she says. "Or lack thereof."

"Good news travels fast."

"Well, your brother is my boss."

"And how's that working out for you?"

She shrugs. "He flirts a little, but he keeps his hands to himself."

Penny's plan was to get married and move to Connecticut when she grew up, have four kids and a golden retriever, and write children's books for a living. Now she's thirty-five, still living in Elmsbrook, and considers the fact that she doesn't get groped in the workplace a perk worth mentioning.

"You're feeling sorry for me," Penny says.

"No."

"You never were any good at covering up."

"I'm feeling much too sorry for me these days to worry about anyone else."

"Your wife left you, Judd. It happens every day."

"Jesus, Penny."

"I'm sorry. That was harsh, and totally uncalled for."

"And what's your story?"

She shrugs. "I don't have one. No great traumatic event to blame my small life on. No catastrophes, no divorce. Plenty of bad men, but plenty of good ones too, that simply didn't want me in the end. I tried to make something of myself and I failed. That happens every day too."

"Horry says you're still skating."

She nods. "I teach over at Kelton's."

"I used to love watching you skate."

"Yes, you did. Do you remember our pact?"

"I do."

We look at each other and then away. An awkward silence descends between us, which Penny fills by saying, "Awkward silence."

"Yeah."

"So, you're sitting shiva."

"Yes."

"I'll have to make it over there one of these days."

"You've got five left."

"You're really doing all seven days? That's hard-core."

"Tell me about it."

"Well, I still skate every morning at eleven, if you want to come by."

"They're open that early?"

"They open at one, but the owner lets me have a key in exchange for sexual favors."

"That's good."

"That was a joke, Judd."

"I know."

"You used to laugh at my jokes."

"You used to be funnier."

She laughs at that. "They all can't be gems." Penny looks at me for a long moment, and I wonder what she sees. I was plain-looking back in high school, when we were best friends and the sexual tension was mine alone. I'm still plain-looking, only now I'm older, thicker, and sadder.

"Listen, Judd," she says. "I think we've reached that point where this conversation runs the risk of devolving into small talk, and I don't think either of us wants that. So I'm going to give you a kiss and send you on your way." She leans forward and kisses my cheek, just grazing the corner of my lips. "I did that on purpose," she says with a grin. "Give you something other than your ex-wife to think about while you sit all day."

I smile. "You were always so good at not covering up."

Penny's smile is sad and a little off. "It's the antidepressants. They've obliterated whatever filters I have left."

We made the pact when we were twenty. We were on summer break from our respective colleges. Her boyfriend was backpacking through Europe, and my girlfriend was as of yet nonexistent, and miraculously, after years of seeing me as nothing more than a friendly ear and a sympathetic shoulder, Penny finally seemed ready to recognize other parts of my anatomy. I spent my days working in the flagship store and my nights coming up with places to almost but not quite have sex with Penny, who had arrived at a moral rationale concerning her boyfriend that grandfathered me in as long as there was no actual intercourse. One night, as we lay naked and sweaty in the darkness of my basement while my parents slept upstairs, she stopped her moaning and grinding against my erection to press her damp hands against the sides of my face. "You know you're my best friend," she said.

"I do." It was infinitely less painful to hear it then, with the full length of her hot skin pressed wetly against mine.

"This could be the last summer we ever spend together. The last time at all that we're even here."

"Why do you say that?"

"Real life, Judd," she said. "It's coming for us. Who knows where the hell we'll end up? So we should make a pact."

"What kind of pact?" We were still moving lightly against each other, maintaining our rhythm, like joggers at an intersection.

"Two-pronged. First: We always speak on our birthdays, no matter where we are, no matter what's happening. No exceptions."

"Okay."

"And second: If neither one of us has someone by the time we're forty, we get married. We don't date; we don't have long, annoying talks about it. We just find each other and get married."

"That's a serious pact."

"But it makes sense. We love each other, and we're clearly attracted to each other." She pressed her damp groin into mine for emphasis.

And what I wanted to say right then was, *If it makes so much sense, why do we have to wait until we're forty? Why can't we be together right now?* But there were backpacking boyfriends and separate colleges to consider. This was summer fun, sweet and loving, but if Penny thought I was falling for her, she'd have put an end to it right then and there, and that was unthinkable to me.

"Come on, Judd," she said with a grin, running two fingers down the groove of my slick spine. "Will you be my fail-safe?"

I smiled right back at her, like someone who totally got it. "Of course I will."

And then, to seal the pact, she spit onto her fingers and reached down between us, and for a while there was nothing but the soft wet sounds of lubricated skin on skin and thrashing tongues, until I shuddered and came violently across her soft, pale belly. She smiled at me as I finished, kissed my nose, and then grabbed my hand and pressed it between her spread thighs.

"Now you do me," she said.

8:50 p.m.

WHEN I STEP out of the store, Horry is sitting in the passenger seat, staring straight ahead, trembling. His hand is suspended out the window, the cigarette in it long burned down to the butt.

"Hey, man," I say.

He doesn't answer. His head bobs up and down on his neck, and his lips tremble with exertion, like weights are holding his mouth closed. "Unggh," he says.

His arm is dead weight as I maneuver it back through the window and onto his lap. I drive slowly, but on the first right turn he falls sideways, his head landing on my shoulder, so I pull over and we just sit there for a while, Horry's head resting on my shoulder as his body trembles like there's a small electrical current running through him.

Gradually, the trembling subsides, and then, after a little bit, Horry grunts and sits up, wiping the drool off of his chin with the back of his hand. He looks over at me and nods. "You see Penny?"

"Yeah."

He nods and clears his throat and I can hear the loose smoker's phlegm rattling around in his chest.

"Can you hear me when you're, you know, out of it like that?"

"Yeah. Usually. I just can't talk. It's like part of me blows a fuse, but the rest of me is there, waiting for the lights to go back on."

I start the car. "You ready?"

He looks out the window. "This is the block, isn't it? Where you and Paul got attacked."

I hadn't really been paying attention to the scenery, but now I can see we're on Ludlow, just a few driveways down from Tony Rusco's house. Paul and I ran for our lives down this sidewalk, the Christmas jingle of the rottweiler's tags coming up fast behind us. I close my eyes against the sidewalk, but I can still hear his screams, still feel the cold terror crushing my bowels.

Horry leans back in his seat and lights up a cigarette. "I hit Wendy once."

It takes me a minute to register what he's said. "I remember."

"I don't know if I ever even said I'm sorry for that."

"She forgave you."

"I really clocked her good."

Wendy had taken off a semester to help Linda and Mom care for Horry when he came home from the hospital. Back then they hadn't yet found the right dose to take the edge off his anger, and he would descend into fits of rage where he tried to destroy anything he could get his hands on. Wendy, who had seen too many movies, decided the best thing to do would be to throw her arms around him and hold on until her love calmed him, but he hurled her across the room, and then when she came back he landed a solid punch, hard enough to break two of her teeth. Wendy didn't hold it against him, but I think she became a little scared of him after that, and when Linda insisted she go back to school and get on with her life, she didn't object. The next time Wendy came back to Elmsbrook, it was with Barry in tow.

"That was a long time ago, Horry. You weren't yourself."

He nods and blows his smoke out into the night, watching it dissipate in the amber glow of the streetlight. "I'm still not," he says.

Friday

Chapter 17

2:00 a.m.

I am having sex with Jen. She bucks and writhes under me, her hips rising up hard against mine. Her nails slice my back; her fingers grab my ass and then slide down my thigh to where my leg ends at midcalf in a hard, creased stump. But it's not me, it's Wade lying on top of Jen, and I'm sitting on the reading chair by the window, watching them go at it while I pull at the worn straps of my prosthesis, trying to strap it on so that I can get the hell out of there. And now it's me again, lying in the smooth delta of Jen's opened thighs, but it's no longer Jen, it's Penny Moore, and I've got both of my legs again, and Penny's got her legs wrapped around me, and she's biting down on my earlobe as she moans, and it's actually feeling pretty good. Then, from behind me, a low guttural growl, and when I turn, I see the rottweiler, with the tattered threads of Paul's red T-shirt still hanging from his teeth, alongside a thick chain of white drool. And when I turn back to Penny, she's Chelsea, Phillip's old girlfriend, and I've got one leg again, and the dog is crouching, getting ready to attack, and no matter how much I try to pull out of Chelsea, she just keeps rocking her hips and licking her lips. And then the rottweiler is upon us, and I can smell his feral scent and feel the crush of his jaws on the back of my neck, and I'm sandwiched between Phillip's old girlfriend and a vicious rottweiler and I've got one and a half legs and this is not any way to die. And just as I feel the searing pain of the dog's teeth sinking into the skin of my neck, my shout fills the basement and I wake up shivering violently in my own sweat.

It's like Stephen King is writing my dreams in to *Penthouse Forum*.

Chapter 18

The lights go out again while I'm in the shower. When I step out into the basement, Alice is at the electrical panel again in her bathrobe. "We must stop meeting like this," she says.

"This house sucks," I say.

Alice smiles. "Which one is it, again?"

"I think it was number fourteen."

"I can't see the numbers."

I go over to her, holding my towel in place with one hand.

"You smell like a little boy."

"They've only got baby shampoo down here."

"I love that smell." She leans back against me, breathing deeply. "The smell of a clean baby."

"Yes. Well . . ." Her own hair is freshly shampooed and has that clean, blow-dried smell, like baked honey, and that, combined with the sheer fabric of her bathrobe and my highly sensitized libido, makes for an awkward family moment. "I'll have to find a new manly fragrance when I start dating again."

"Oh, right," she says, turning around to face me. "We haven't really talked about that. How are you doing, Judd?"

"I'm fine." I need to curtail this conversation for reasons both emotional and anatomical. "Here it is." I lean past her to flip a breaker. The lights don't go back on, but from upstairs, we can hear Paul yelling, "Who's dicking around with the damn lights?!"

Alice chuckles and turns around to flip it back. "Paul signs the payroll while he's on the toilet."

"Two turds with one stone."

She laughs and flips another switch. The lights come back on. "Let there be light."

"Amen."

"Anyway, Judd," she says, turning back to me. "I know you're going through a lot right now, and your family . . . well, they're not exactly famous for their emotional wherewithal. So, if you ever want to talk, just remember, we were friends long before we were family."

"Thanks, Alice. I'll keep that in mind."

She seems about to say something else, but after a moment she just nods and leans forward to kiss my cheek. I lean forward, not so much to accept the kiss, but to avoid any incidental lower-body contact. Things are hard enough already.

So to speak.

9:37 a.m.

BREAKFAST IS SERVED. On platters, of course. The pastries and bagels continue to arrive every day, courtesy of my parents' friends and set out by Linda, who quietly lets herself in every morning to see to things. Horry's here too this morning, sipping thoughtfully at his coffee, sneaking glances at Wendy over the rim of his mug. His T-shirt says, YOU'RE UGLY, BUT YOU INTRIGUE ME. Beneath the T-shirt, his compact muscles bulge in exactly the way mine never did. Tracy is buttering a bagel for Phillip, and Phillip is creaming her coffee, and they're smiling at each other in a way that makes it hard to look at them. I guess there was no

lasting fallout from the Chelsea/Janelle/Kelly visit. Wendy is giving the
baby a bottle while Barry chews a muffin and reads the *Wall Street Journal.* Ryan and Cole are watching cartoons on the small television in the
kitchen. Mom is in the kitchen with Linda, organizing the endless array
of catered platters. You could fill an airlift to Africa with all the food
generated by one dead Jew. Alice is spreading fat-free cream cheese on
a rice cake, and Paul is sitting next to her, chewing a glazed donut. He's
at the head of the table, but just to the side of Dad's chair, which sits
symbolically empty.

No one says anything. No one dares.

"Listen," Paul says. "We need to talk about the Place."

"The Place" was how Dad referred to the business. He never called
it the store, or the shop, or the company. "I'm heading out to the Place,"
he would say. "We hired a new girl at the Place." I guess Paul picked it up
somewhere along the way. Alice looks up from her rice cake, and you
can hear her ticking, the woman behind the man. Whatever he's going
to say, she knows all about it.

"What about it?" Phillip says.

"Barney will come by at some point to discuss Dad's will. But this is
the part I want to discuss. Dad left half of the business to me. The other
half is divided into three even shares for Wendy, Judd, and Phillip. So
together, each of you will own one-sixth of a business that has not shown
a profit in going on three years. The shares won't generate any cash for
you. Barney will have the bank valuate the shares, and then I'm going to
buy them back from you. Depending on the value, I may not have the
cash readily available, so I hope you'll all cut me a little slack until I come
up with it."

"What is each share worth, roughly?" Phillip says. "I mean, what are
we talking about here?"

"What about Mom?" Wendy asks. "Isn't the business hers too?"

"Between Mom's royalties and Dad's life insurance and pension, she's more than taken care of for the rest of her life," Paul says. "I know you all might have been expecting a little bit more from Dad's estate. Unfortunately, there's not much that isn't tied up in the business, which, like I said, isn't in the best shape. There is the house though. It's been assessed at upwards of a million dollars. Dad has it set up in a trust for us. When Mom sells it, we'll all make a nice profit."

"I'm not selling the house," Mom says from the kitchen doorway.

"Well, not right now."

"Not ever!" she says. "I'm only sixty-three years old, for God's sake."

"I just meant—"

"I know what you meant. You want to pull up the floorboards and look for money, you go right ahead. But make no mistake, I'm going to die in this house!"

"Okay, Mom," Paul says, turning red. He and Alice exchange a quick, guarded look. "Forget I said anything."

Mom starts to say something else, but Linda comes up behind her and puts a hand on her shoulder. "Hill," she says. "He didn't mean it like that."

"This is my home," Mom says, still irate.

"I know," Linda says, leading her back into the kitchen. "It's okay."

We all stare at Paul, pissed at him for implicating us.

"The point is," Paul says, "I've been working my ass off to try to save this business. I still don't know if I'm going to be able to. We're looking at closing one or possibly two stores—"

"I was actually thinking I'd like to join the company," Phillip says.

His statement is greeted with stunned silence. Alice looks at Paul, her eyes wide with alarm. Tracy looks at Phillip, proud and knowing. Even Barry puts down his paper to pay attention. Wendy looks at me, her eyes widening with glee. Her smile says, *This is about to get good.*

"What are you talking about?" Paul says.

Phillip wipes his mouth and clears his throat. "I talked to Dad about it a little while back. It's something he built for us, something he wanted to pass on. It's his legacy to us, and I'd like to be a part of it."

"Okay." Paul nods his head and puts down his coffee mug. "And what is it you'd like to do for the company, Phillip?"

"I want to help you grow it."

"The only thing you've ever grown was hemp."

"And I made a profit."

"Not nearly as much as we spent on your lawyers when you got busted."

"Listen, Paul. You don't believe in me. I get that. I never believed in myself either, really. But people can change. I've changed. And we complement each other. You're the brains of the operation, I know that. But what about advertising and promotion? What about personnel and PR? I'm a people person, Paul. That's who I am. And you're . . . not one. You're a good guy, but you're a hard-ass and, let's face it, you're a little scary. You're actually scaring me right now. Your face looks very red. Are you even breathing? Is he breathing?"

Paul brings his hand crashing down on the table. "This is my life!" he shouts. "I have given the last ten years of my life to this company, and it's barely supporting Alice and me. I'm in debt up to my ass, and the company is in trouble. I'm sorry, Phillip, but we just can't afford to be the next stop on your tour of professional self-destruction."

"I understand why you'd say that, I do," Phillip says. "But this is a family business, Paul. And I'm in the lucky sperm club, same as you."

Paul gets up and shoves his chair back. "We're not having this conversation."

Mom comes back into the room, looking concerned. "What conversation?"

"Fine," Phillip says. "I kind of dropped that like a bomb on you. It's a lot to absorb, and you need a little time."

"Absorb what?" Mom says. "Someone tell me what's going on."

"There's nothing to absorb, you dumb shit! You're not coming to work for me!"

"Well, technically speaking, we'd be partners. I'll buy out Judd and Wendy. Judd's not interested in the business, right, Judd? And Wendy, you're going to be richer than God."

I steal a glance at Barry to see if he's offended. He is not.

"Baby brother, you can't even buy a goddamn suit."

"People change, big brother."

Paul's eyes settle on Tracy for a long, uncomfortable beat, and a bitter smile slowly spreads across his face. "Oh. It all makes sense now. Engaged to be engaged." He shakes his head. "You're a whore."

"What did you just call her?" Phillip says, jumping to his feet.

"Not her, you. You've always been a whore."

"Why don't you come a little closer and say that?"

"Not in the house!" Mom says. She never broke up our fights, thought it was healthy for brothers to pound on each other every now and then, just not where they might break her things.

Paul steps right over to Phillip, where his height and weight advantage is more readily apparent. He's about two feet away when Tracy steps between them.

"Okay, men. This is good, really good," she says, her voice loud and clear, like she's running a seminar. "You've each expressed a valid point of view that the other now needs to consider and internalize in a non-confrontational manner. Nothing has to be resolved immediately. And nothing can be resolved until each of you has come to appreciate the other's position. So let's agree, shall we, to table this discussion until everyone has had time to assimilate the new information and reconsider his own position. Okay?"

We all stare at Tracy as if she just started jabbering in ancient tongues. We have always been a family of fighters and spectators. Intervening with reason and consideration demonstrates a dangerous cul--

tural ignorance. Paul looks her up and down as if he can't quite believe she's there. Then he nods and looks over at Phillip.

"Stupid. Little. Whore."

Phillip smiles like a movie star. "Infertile limp-dick."

Paul moves so fast that it's impossible to say whether Alice's shriek is in response to Phillip's remark or the sudden ensuing violence. His hands latch on to Phillip's neck and the two of them spin backward into the antique buffet, knocking over platters, candlesticks, and Tracy, who was still between them when Paul attacked.

"Not in the house!" Mom shrieks, smacking at their backs. "Take it outside!"

And who knows how much damage they might do, how badly Paul will beat Phillip's ass, if right then Jen doesn't appear like some kind of mirage, floating in from the front hall with an awkward smile. "Hi, everyone," she says.

At the sight of Jen, every person in the room freezes, along with most of my internal organs. Paul looks up at her in shock, his hand still cocked to punch Phillip, who has fallen to his knees against the wall.

"The door was open," Jen says. "I hope I'm not interrupting anything."

"Jen, dear," my mother says, suddenly composed. "What a nice surprise." These are the moments when you really have to wonder what reality my mother is living in. She can go from casually watching two of her sons pummeling each other to graciously welcoming the woman who ruined her other son's life without missing a beat.

As for me, I'm shocked and self-conscious that Jen is here, that our broken marriage is now, in effect, on display. But I also feel an unbidden rush of excitement at her arrival, wondering at the speed of light if this somehow means we'll be getting back together. In that instant, it doesn't seem so far-fetched; the pregnancy was a false alarm, she'll stay for the shiva, we'll have some hard talks, I'll yell and she'll cry, but she'll still bunk with me on that pitiful sofa bed in the basement. And when the shiva is over, we'll go home and start again. I won't even go back for my stuff at the Lees', just bequeath it to the next desperate tenant. I'll start fresh, all new things.

Jen looks at me. I look at her. And then I remember the money, sixteen thousand dollars sitting at the bottom of my duffel bag, the money she threatened me with in her voice mail. She's not here to get me back or even to pay her respects. She has Wade's baby in her belly and our money on her mind. And now the rage is back, along with a healthy measure of self-loathing for being the pathetic cuckold who wants his cheating wife back.

"I'm so sorry about Mort," Jen says, hugging my mother.

"Thank you, dear."

And before things can get any more surreal, Phillip, seeing his opening, hauls off from under Paul and sucker punches him right on the chin and Paul goes down hard. Phillip jumps to his feet and stands over Paul, wincing as he shakes off his fingers. Jen looks at me, eyebrows raised in surprise. I look back at her with a light shrug, and for that single instant, we are us again. And then I remember we're not and look away. Alice is on her knees, pulling up a dazed Paul, while Tracy hustles Phillip out of the room. "Who's the little whore now, bitch?" Phillip says, cradling his hand.

We should all just face reality and stop taking our meals together.

Chapter 19

10:00 a.m.

I'm so sorry about your father," Jen says to me once the room has cleared out. She moves to hug me, but I step back like she's contagious. She lowers her hands and nods sadly. She is wearing a navy dress that hangs effortlessly on her, stopping at midthigh. Her perfume reminds me of our bedroom, and it makes me homesick. "Why didn't you tell me?"

"Are you seriously asking me that?"

"No, I guess not," she says. "This must be hard for you."

"It's not like he died suddenly. I'll be fine."

"When will you be coming home?"

"I don't have a home."

"I mean, when will you be back in Kingston?"

"In about a week."

She gives me a funny look. "You're going to spend a week here? Every time you were here with me, you couldn't wait to be out that front door."

"We're sitting shiva."

"Oh. I didn't think—"

"Yeah. Dad wanted it."

She is momentarily distracted by a half-trashed platter of smoked salmon on the table. "Wow, that really reeks."

"It's lox. That's how it's supposed to smell."

"Well, could we go outside for a little bit? I can't handle the smell of fish ever since . . . you know."

"I don't mind it. And you won't be here for very long anyway."

"Judd, please. I know it's a bad time, but I really need to talk to you."

"What, Jen? What could you possibly have left to tell me? Are you and Wade getting married? Is that it?"

"No. It's nothing like that." She is looking around at the discarded food all over the dining room table, the half-eaten bagels and Danishes, the sliced vegetables, the maple syrup and waffle fragments smeared across the tablecloth by Ryan and Cole.

"Good, because, you know, adultery is probably not the best foundation upon which to build a marriage."

"Oh, crap."

"What?"

She looks at me and then covers her mouth and bolts from the room.

I find her in the powder room, vomiting into the toilet. When she's done, she flushes the toilet and sits on the floor with her back against the wall, wiping her mouth with a torn strand of toilet paper. "Jesus, I hate this part," she says.

She looks up at me, and there's something in her eyes that I don't like. When you've been married to someone for a while, you occasionally share these brief psychic moments, and right at that instant I know what she's going to say just before she says it, even while I'm thinking that it can't possibly be true.

The last time I had sex with Jen, as near as I can figure, was around three months ago. It was exactly the kind of rote, forgettable sex we'd been having at that time, the kind we'd sworn, back in the day, that we would never have. There was nothing technically wrong with it; tumescence and lubrication were both achieved on cue, his-and-hers orgasms distributed on schedule like party favors. It's just that after you've been married for a while, it becomes much harder to lose yourself in sex the way you used to. For one thing, you've become a bit too efficient, you've learned what works and what doesn't, and so foreplay, entry, and orgasm can often be condensed into a five-to-seven-minute span. Good sex requires many different things, but in most cases, efficiency isn't one of them.

Also, when you share all of the administrative headaches of life with someone else, small piles of unaddressed, quotidian resentments build up over time like plaque, lingering on the fringes of your consciousness even as you kiss, lick, and fondle each other. So even as Jen panted in my ear and rocked her hips beneath me, some part of her brain would be consumed with the basement lightbulb she'd been asking me to change for going on a week now, or how I never managed to fully close my dresser drawers in the morning, which didn't bother me but somehow threatened the delicate balance of her entire universe, or how I considered a cereal bowl washed even if all I did was rinse it with hot water and leave it in the sink, or how I never remembered to give her phone messages from friends who had called while she was out. And as I slid into Jen and felt her long smooth thighs clamp down on my hips, I might be thinking that she'd been a little bitchy tonight, that she had a tendency, at times, to react with a disproportionate amount of bitchiness, which only served to exacerbate things, digging whatever marital hole we were standing in a little deeper. Or maybe I'd be thinking about the latest American Express bill, how Jen had once again exceeded our budget by over a thousand dollars, and how I knew, if confronted, she'd have a rationale for every single line on the statement and then assure me that there had been returns made, that significant credits would appear on the next statement. I already knew from experience that these phantom credits would never materialize, or, if they did, Jen would use them to justify the next bill as well, effectively applying a single month's credit to two bills. When it came to profligate spending, Jen was a demon accountant, bending the laws of mathematics to her will. And even as she shuddered through her orgasm, Jen might have been thinking about how I couldn't, for the life of me, get my underwear from my body to the hamper without a stopover on the bedroom floor, or how I wasn't as warm as I should have been when her mother called, and maybe, as I came (after her—let the record show), I would probably be thinking about how much goddamn time she spent on the phone with her mother and girlfriends every night, or the way she spit large chunks of toothpaste out into the sink and left them there to harden into little winterfresh slugs that had to be scraped off the porcelain. She couldn't handle a slightly opened dresser drawer, but a sink full of crusty, expectorated toothpaste was apparently not an issue.

None of this was very serious, obviously, just the minor aches and pains of a living marriage. And every so often we'd get into a fight over something larger, and we'd scream and vent all of our gripes, tears would fall, hurts would be validated, and sex would get good again for a while, passionate and intense, and then the cycle would repeat.

So we lay there fucking through our resentment, our thoughts wandering as we rubbed mechanically against each other—for warmth, or intimacy, or maybe just base gratification, our minds a frenzy of disconnected thoughts and festering gripes, each of us too distracted to realize that the other was equally self-absorbed. And there was no hazy afterglow when we were finished, no lingering in each other's arms as the sweat slowly dried on our skin; just peeing, washing, and the donning of sleepwear, and then the warm, numbing glow of the television.

Chapter 20

S o, you're going to be a father," Jen says gingerly.

"How is that even possible?"

We are standing on the patio in the backyard, overlooking the pool, which is brimming from yesterday's rain. Today the skies are clear, and the August sun is burning through what's left of the morning fog.

"I'm almost three months. Think about it."

"You can't possibly know that it's mine."

"Yes, I can. Trust me."

"Trust is not my first impulse when it comes to you."

"It's your baby, Judd."

"Bullshit."

"It is."

"You can keep saying that, and I can keep saying 'bullshit,' or you can say something else."

She looks at me for a long moment and then shakes her head, giving in. "It turns out, Wade is sterile."

The sound of my laughter surprises me. There is nothing remotely funny about the wife who betrayed me, the wife who is no longer mine, with whom I have already buried one baby, telling me, after our marriage has been ruined, that she is carrying our baby. There are very serious, life-altering implications hovering in the air between us. But right at this moment, all I can think about is the fact that Wade Boulanger is all cock and no sperm. He may have destroyed my marriage and unseated me in my own home, but I'd unwittingly left behind a booby trap that just blew his legs off. So I laugh. Hard.

"I thought you might like that," Jen says wryly.

"You have to admit there's a certain karmic poetry to it."

"I'll only admit it if you stop laughing."

But I can't. It's the first time I've laughed in months, and it feels strange doing it, but I can't seem to stop. And soon Jen is laughing with me, while inside of her, cells replicate in an organized frenzy as the seed of our bad timing takes hold.

"Wade couldn't have been too happy about this."

"It was a blow. But we talked about it. He's okay with it. He supports me."

"Imagine my relief."

She closes her eyes, taking the hit, and then looks at me. "That was officially your last shot, okay? This is going to be tricky enough without you constantly punishing me."

"How exactly have you been punished? You have the house, you have Wade, and now you have the baby you've always wanted. I missed the part where life got so rough for you."

"People stare at me. I'm the town whore."

"If the shoe fits . . ."

"And now I'm a pregnant whore. You think this is easy for me?"

"I think it's a lot harder for me."

She looks at me for a moment, and then looks away, twirling her hair with her fingers. "Point taken."

Jen is allergic to the words "I'm sorry." She concedes with little expressions like "Point taken" or "Understood," or, my personal favorite, "Okay, let's drop it, then." But I know Jen, and I can tell she's feeling sorry, for me, for her, for the little fetus that will be unwittingly born into our broken lives.

"Please," she says. "Tell me what you're thinking."

It's an absurd request. Our minds, unedited by guilt or shame, are selfish and unkind, and the majority of our thoughts, at any given time, are not for public consumption, because they would either be hurtful or else just make us look like the selfish and unkind bastards we are. We don't share our thoughts, we share carefully sanitized, watered-down versions of them, Hollywood adaptations of those thoughts dumbed down for the PG-13 crowd.

What am I thinking?

I'm thinking I'm going to be a father, and I am not excited. I know I should be excited, and maybe at some point in the near future I will be excited, but at this moment, I feel numb, and if you were to peel away the numbness you'd find a thick mucous membrane of trepidation, and if you were to slice through that membrane, you would find a throbbing cluster of outrage and regret. We were supposed to be a family. We fell in love, our parents shook hands, we hired a band and a caterer and uttered vows, and now Jen will live in one place and I will live in another and this child of ours, this inconceivable progeny of our corrupted marriage, will live in a house with no siblings, thanks to his sterile, dipshit stepfather, and will be shuttled sadly between us, subject to the vagaries of our schedules, and he will be lonely and quiet and not quite sure of his place in the world. He will start dressing in black and experimenting with drugs and reading magazines devoted to firearms by the time he's thirteen. No matter how hard I try, he will prefer Jen to me, which hardly seems fair, given the circumstances. I've always wanted to be a father, but not like this, not with the deck already stacked so badly against me. If I marry someone else and we have a child, that will make sense, but this doesn't, this is a flesh-and-blood shackle that will keep Jen and

Wade in my life long after I should be free and clear of them. And if I do have children with someone else, this child will feel jealous and discarded and no doubt gravitate toward his sterile, dipshit stepfather, and Wade's already stolen my wife and home, I'll be damned if I'm going to let him walk off with my unborn child too, but he'll have the home-court advantage. Any thoughts of moving somewhere new and starting over will have to be shelved, because I don't know exactly what kind of father I'll be, but it won't be the kind who lives in another state and sends shitty cards with a ten-dollar bill in them. Now, in addition to alimony, I'll have to pay child support, which will be a neat trick considering the current state of my finances, and I'm going to be a father, I'm going to be a father, I'm going to be a father . . . I should be happy, should be thrilled, should be seeing the miracle in all of this, the silver lining, should be passing out cigars, should be hugging and kissing and thinking of names, but instead, thanks to my whore of a wife, the moment is marred by complication and despair and that's not fair to my child and it's not fair to me, and as soon as the kid is old enough, I'm going to sit him down and explain to him that none of this was my fault, that she did it to both of us.

And while I'm thinking all of that, another part of my brain is simultaneously thinking that Jen looks so damn beautiful right now, and she wore that little blue dress, and she knows how she looks in that dress, and I can't believe that she's not mine to touch anymore, because all I want to do is lift that dress up over her hips, slide into her, and stay in there until things change back, until we can once again be the family we were supposed to be.

And even as I'm thinking about her taste and her smell and her skin, I'm trying to figure Jen out, trying to glean if maybe she thinks this baby is a reason to rethink things, to maybe get rid of Wade and ask me to come back, and she's maybe here trying to get a read on me, to see how receptive I might be to that proposition. We lost something vital in our marriage after we lost the baby, after it became known that the odds of another pregnancy were long, and now here we are, expecting, but the damage cannot be undone. Wade cannot be unfucked, and neither, it seems, can we.

That is a quick distillation of the myriad random thoughts flashing through my mind, but all I say is, "I wish this had happened before . . . before you and Wade." Which I think is a pretty fair summation.

Without moving a muscle, Jen starts to silently cry, like those statues of the Virgin Mary that are always turning up in South American villages. "I know," she says, her voice low and trembling. "I do too."

I look at Jen. Jen looks at me. It's an electric moment, and later on I will wonder if that moment was a last chance blown by two people too tied up in their uncertainty and resentment to seize it. But as it happens, Tracy has picked this moment to step out into the yard, in leggings and a tank top, with a yoga mat slung over her shoulder. Her hair is back in a youthful ponytail, and maybe I'm reading into this, but it seems to me that, after seeing Phillip's ex-girlfriends last night, she is trying to look particularly youthful. "Hey, guys," she calls to us, all carefree and breezy, walking over to extend her hand to Jen. "We haven't been formally introduced. I'm Tracy."

"Jen," Jen says, shaking her hand.

"Don't mind me," Tracy says, scoping out a flat patch of yard and tossing down her mat. Then she bends over and starts to stretch.

"And who, exactly, is that?" Jen says.

"That's Tracy."

"So she says. Quite the firm grip, too."

"She's with Phillip."

"Oh. I won't get too attached, then."

"Don't do that."

"What?"

"Make fun of my family like you're still a part of it."

Jen looks stung. It's a good look for her. "Fair enough."

We stand there watching Tracy's rising ass as she descends into her Downward-Facing Dog, out of things to say. We are going to be parents. I'm going to be a father. I wonder if Wade will be in the delivery room, holding her hand while I sit off to the side like a spectator, waiting for my child to emerge from the spread legs that got us into this mess in the first place.

Phillip comes ambling out a moment later, in gym shorts and a tank top. "Namaste," he says to us with a wink and a little bow.

"Hey, Phillip," Jen says.

"Jen." Phillip considers her as he unrolls his yoga mat next to Tracy's. "I always suspected there might be something of the heartless slut in you."

"Takes one to know one, I guess."

Phillip nods and goes into a loose approximation of Tracy's pose. "True that. But know this, my profoundly disappointing sister-in-law. Your looks may be a matter of public record, but let's face it, your hottest years are behind you. As soon as we wrap this shiva, I am going to personally see to it that my brother here gets laid on a nightly basis by women ten years younger than you, ripe young honeys who will make him eternally grateful that you trashed your marriage."

Before Jen can respond, Tracy abruptly pulls out of her yoga pose and kicks Phillip's leg out from under him, causing him to fall on his ass.

"Prick!"

She yanks her mat up and storms disgustedly back toward the house while Phillip calls after her. "What the fuck, honey?!" Then, still sprawled on his ass, he turns to us. "She's usually very congenial. I don't know what bug crawled up her ass today."

"That remark about ripe young honeys," Jen says. "She may have taken that a bit personally."

"Huh," Phillip says, considering it. "In retrospect, that was probably insensitive of me."

"I mean, what is she, fifty?"

"She's forty-three and that was a cheap shot. I'd expect more, even from an adulteress." He rolls to his feet. "On the plus side, no yoga this morning." He reaches into his sock and pulls out a cigarette and lighter.

"You're not going to go after her?" I say.

"I'm gathering my wits about me," he says, flipping the cigarette into his mouth. "So, what were you guys talking about?"

"Nothing," I say.

"I'm pregnant," Jen says.

Phillip looks at Jen, then looks down at his freshly lit cigarette and pinches it out. "Mazel tov," he says, smiling widely.

I am going to be a father, just when I've lost my own. There are some who would see a certain divine balance in that, one soul departing to make room for another, but I'm not that guy. I don't believe in God when I'm in trouble, the way so many people do. But at times like this, when the irony seems too cruel and well crafted to be a coincidence, I can see God in the details. Due to some mental hiccup I can't explain, when I think of God, I picture Hugh Hefner: a thin, angular man with a prominent chin in a maroon smoking jacket. I don't know where that image came from or why it stuck the way it did. Maybe when I was a kid I was thinking about God and I happened upon a picture of Hef in a magazine and some neurons fired and a permanent association was made. But when your vision of God is America's horniest senior citizen in his pajamas, it's probably fair to say that you're not the kind of guy who sees miracles in the mundane coincidences fate lobs at your unsuspecting head like water balloons from a high terrace.

Chapter 21

I always imagined I'd be one of those cool dads, the ones you see with long hair and trendy clothing and a leather wrist cuff. One of those guys who change diapers and never yell and buy all the overpriced snacks at the ballpark and carry the kid on their shoulders all the way home. I spent a good deal more time picturing myself as a father than as a husband. I figured I'd be a husband first, and certainly, I imagined what sort of woman I might marry—a smart, sensitive, good-natured lingerie model—but I didn't picture myself as any particular type of husband. Just me, married, basically. A smarter man might have seen that as cause for concern, a big red flag flapping noisily in the wind.

Looking back, which is what you do when your life goes to shit, often and obsessively—I can't really say if Jen and I would have made it if we hadn't lost the baby. I know it's the zenith of stupidity to count on a baby to save a failing marriage. The kid can't even burp on his own, and you want him to repair a relationship that you've spent years twisting and tying into hard, salt-crusted sailor's knots. But still, I can't help wondering if that baby might have saved us, the same way that losing it accelerated our downward spiral into the thorny underbrush of marital decay. Losing *him.* Not *it.* "Losing it" is how you'd refer to your virginity or your wallet, but not your baby; even if you never did get to hold him, and smell his scalp, and wipe his white spittle off your shoulder. Yes, it was a boy. Baby Boy Foxman, it said, on his death certificate. He would have had untamable curly hair like me, and maybe Jen's luminous green eyes, and he and I would have gone to ball games and to the park, and I would have taught him to ride his bike and throw a curveball. I don't know how to throw a curveball, but you'd better believe I would have learned. And when he got older I'd have taught him to drive, and he wouldn't have felt the need to rebel, to do hard drugs or mutilate his smooth, handsome face (Jen's graceful cheekbones, my prominent chin) with studs and bolts, because there'd be nothing to rebel against, but if he had I would have given him his space, and then he'd have come back and we'd have bonded again, maybe over his first-ever beer—and who am I kidding, did I really believe he and his friends weren't scoring beer already from someone's older brother? But he was a smart kid with a good head on his shoulders and sometimes kids were going to act out, test their boundaries, but I trusted him to make the right decisions, and he knew he could always come to me, and . . . Damn. I'm off, just like that.

My point is that it would be too easy to say that losing the baby is where we went off the rails. People love to do that, to point to some single phenomenon, assign it all the blame, and wipe the slate clean, like when overeaters sue McDonald's for making them fat pigs. But the truth is always a lot fuzzier, hiding in soft focus on the periphery. When it comes down to it, you've either got the sort of marriage that will withstand trauma, or you don't. Jen and I had still loved each other, maybe not with the same hormonal ferocity that we did back when we'd first started dating, but no one really stays that way, do they? We still enjoyed each other's company, had enough in common, found each other suitably attractive. We were content enough on a daily basis. But there was no denying that certain colors had faded and levels had fallen, like when a plane loses one engine but still has another three to carry it across the ocean.

It took a long time for us to finally conceive. Jen had an asymmetrical

uterus that only the most nimble of sperm could navigate, but we perse-
vered. When Jen finally got an uncontestable blue line on her home
pregnancy test, we did a little dance in the bathroom doorway, Jen wav-
ing the pee stick above her head like a lighter at a concert. And for a
little while there, it was like new life had been breathed into us. We
would stay up late into the night, talking about neighborhoods, and
schools, and names, and how we wouldn't let it change us, while deep
down hoping to hell that it would, that this would be the thing that filled
the hole left by all the other unnamable things we had somehow lost
along the way. We started having sex more frequently, hotter, nastier sex
than we'd had in some time, especially in the later months, as the growing mound of her belly compelled us to seek out new positions—
sideways from behind, one hand wrapped greedily around Jen's
pornographically engorged breasts, the other sliding down below the
wide orb of her distended belly, where she would squeeze it tightly between her thighs and grind against it. I had become increasingly uncomfortable having missionary sex with her, convinced that with every
smack of our bellies I could actually feel the baby.

"I can't feel the baby," Jen said. She had called me at the station,
where I was simultaneously screening callers for Wade and looking at
pictures of Jessica Biel online.

"What do you mean?"

"He always kicks when I'm in the shower. Today he didn't."

"Maybe he's sleeping."

"I don't feel right. Something's wrong." She was in her eighth month,
and for the last few weeks her hormones were the inmates running the
asylum. I had learned the hard way that it was best to pretty much agree
with everything she said.

"Have you had any coffee? Maybe he just needs a little caffeine?"

"Just meet me at the doctor. I'm leaving now."

I sighed and closed out Jessica Biel, but not before I saw the silent judgment in her eyes.

I was late getting to the hospital. Late because there were no damn parking spots and how the hell do you build a major hospital and not think to include a single substantial parking lot? So I was a half hour late, on the one day in recorded history that Jen's doctor's office decided to run on time. Usually you stewed for an hour in the waiting room, reading parenting magazines and trading quick sympathetic looks with the other expectant fathers, wordlessly affirming that when you weren't sitting quietly whipped at the ob-gyn, you were out getting drunk at football games and hunting buffalo in a loincloth. But on that day, by the time I'd come in and identified myself and been led back to the examination room by the theatrically gay receptionist, Jen was already in tears, wiping the blue conducting goop from the sonogram off her belly. And as the room started to spin and my lungs started to contract, the doctor explained that our baby had been strangled in the womb by his umbilical cord. He'd already explained it all to Jen, so she had to hear it all again because I'd been late.

Jen stopped making eye contact with me after that. Our marriage had unwittingly become fused to that little ball of life growing in her belly, and when it died, so did we. And while she'd never admit to it and rationally knew that it was ridiculous, Jen simply couldn't handle the fact that I'd been late, that I'd let her go into that examination room by herself. People need someone to blame. I had failed her in some fundamental way, and she simply couldn't bring herself to forgive me. I think she may have tried to, but in the end, it just seemed easier for her to start sleeping with Wade instead. So now we've each done something unforgivable, and the universe is once again in perfect balance.

Chapter 22

11:25 a.m.

No visitors yet. The mornings are generally slow. Jen has left to go check into the Marriott over on Route 120. She's going to stay overnight, determined that we talk this through further. Phillip is still being yelled at by Tracy behind closed doors not thick enough to drown out her high-pitched, weepy admonishments. I feel bad for Tracy. I don't know much about her, but she seems to be a nice enough person. Dating Phillip brings out the slut or the shrew in a woman, and there would be no dignity in a woman her age playing the slut card. Paul has used the excuse of driving Horry to work to go check on things at the store. Alice is on the couch, balancing her coffee mug and some mini muffins on her plate. Barry's out in the backyard, trying to run a conference call while watching the kids in the pool. Mom, Wendy, and I are sitting on regular chairs, not willing to spend a moment longer than we have to in the shiva chairs.

"What did Jen have to say for herself?" Mom says.

"Nothing. The usual."

"She looked good," Wendy says. "Infidelity agrees with her." Jen's long limbs and slim build have always been viewed by Wendy with a mixture of resentment and awe.

"I think it's interesting that she came," Mom says. "I think it means something."

"What, Mom? What does it mean?"

"I'm just saying. Things may not be as finished as you think."

"Does it mean she wasn't screwing my boss for a year?"

"No, Judd, it doesn't mean that. She cheated on you, and I know that hurts. But it's only sex, Judd, scratching an itch. We've been programmed to attach far too much significance to it, to the point where we lose sight of everything else. It's just one tree in a thick forest."

"It's a pretty big damn tree."

"Over the course of a fifty-year marriage, one bad year isn't very significant. Your marriage might still be there to be saved. But you'll never know if you keep indulging your hate and anger like the world owes you reparations."

"Thanks, Mom. As always, your unsolicited advice, however useless, is greatly appreciated."

"You're welcome, sweetie."

Phillip emerges and lowers himself by his arms like a gymnast into an empty shiva chair, letting out a long, dejected sigh. "Apparently, I'm an irredeemable asshole."

"And yet, I have a feeling she's not done trying to redeem you," Mom says.

"Go figure."

"Why are you doing this, Philly?"

"Doing what?"

"Dating a cougar." Wendy.

"Dating your mother." Me.

"Jesus Christ." Phillip.

"I think she's nice," Alice says. "And very attractive."

"Yes, she's lovely," my mother says. "And closer to my age than yours."

"I'm not as young as you like to think, Mom. And neither are you."

"Don't be spiteful, Philly. It doesn't suit you."

"And that skirt doesn't suit you. You'll be giving everyone crotch shots from your shiva chair."

"I just want to make sure you've thought this through," Mom says. "Because there's no scenario in which this doesn't end badly."

"Much like this conversation," I say.

"Which ends right now," Phillip says.

"We are your family, Phillip. We love you."

We all say "But!" at the same instant.

Mom looks around, momentarily thrown. "That's right. But. *But* she's too old. *But* you're not going to start a family with her. *But* have you even thought about her in all of this?"

Phillip shakes his head, not taking the bait.

"What happens to Tracy when this runs its course, Philly? You'll have no trouble finding new lovers—knowing you, you already have. But the older she gets, the harder it will be for her to find someone. She has so much less time than you to find the right person, and you're wasting it for her."

"And why can't I be the right person?"

Mom smiles at him, sadly and with great tenderness. "Don't be an ass."

"That's it, I'm out of here," Phillip says, getting to his feet.

"I'll come with you," I say.

"You're not supposed to leave the house," Mom says. "We're sitting shiva."

"Ask Wendy about her marriage," I say. "We'll be back before the dust settles."

"Dick," Wendy says.

"Sorry, sis. It's every man for himself."

Paul, returned from the store, steps through the living room doorway just as Phillip reaches it. "Hey, Phillip," he says, smiles, and then punches him square in the jaw, sending him sprawling back into the room, knocking over a handful of chairs.

"Paul!" Alice shrieks.

"He sucker punched me before."

Phillip, flat on his back, props himself up on one elbow, wincing as he rubs his jaw. Tracy comes running out of her room, having heard the commotion. When she sees Phillip lying on the floor, she shakes her head in disgust and turns on her heel, disappearing back into the den. We won't be seeing her again anytime soon.

"If I stand up, are you going to hit me again?" Phillip says to Paul.

"No, I'm good," Paul says, rubbing his knuckles. He reaches over and offers Phillip his hand. Phillip takes it and Paul yanks him to his feet, and then, to everyone's surprise, pulls Phillip into a little hug and whispers something into his ear. Phillip nods and pats the back of Paul's head. Then he turns to me. "You coming?"

"Unless Paul wants to hit me too."

"What could I do to you that the universe hasn't already done?" Paul says.

"Oh," Phillip says, like he's just remembered something. "Jen's pregnant. It's Judd's."

Everyone in the room turns to stare at me.

"I think I speak for everyone when I say, holy shit!" Wendy says.

"How could you not tell me that?" Mom says.

"Now I'm going to hit you," I say to Phillip.

He shrugs. "Every man for himself."

Then Alice stands up and very deliberately lets her coffee mug and saucer fall to the floor, where they shatter into pieces. She looks around at all of us as tears form in her eyes. "Unbelievable," she says. And then, before anyone can say anything, can figure out what set her off, she turns and runs crying past us, up the stairs, and moments later we all jump as the door to my old bedroom slams shut and all the lights on the first floor go out.

Chapter 23

I've never been in a Porsche before. Phillip's rides low to the ground and I feel every seam in the road, every pebble, transmitted through the hard leather seat. The floor is strewn with plastic soda bottles and fast food wrappers, the ashtray spilling over with bent butts, and gas receipts.

"Nice car," I say.

He shifts into third and guns it. "I know what you're thinking," he says.

"What's that?"

"You're thinking I'm a fuckup and Tracy's rich, and I'm just with her because she pays my way and I get to drive cars like this."

"Why are you with her?"

Phillip sighs and shakes his head. "I've been trying to grow up, Judd. I know I've kind of cemented my place as the family fuckup, but believe it or not, that's not who I want to be. And having hit more than my share of brick walls, I figured maybe a better class of woman would be a good place to start."

"So you're not using her for her money. You're using her for her class."

"I'm not using her. Not any more than she's using me. Isn't that what love is? Two people who fulfill needs in each other?"

I shrug. "My wife spent the last year of our marriage sleeping with my boss. Don't ask me about love."

"Your pregnant wife."

"My pregnant wife."

Phillip grins. "Looks like I've got some competition in the family fuckup department."

"It appears that way."

"How are you dealing with that, by the way?"

"By trying really hard not to think about it."

"That's what I would do," he says approvingly. "So, where can I drop you?"

"What do you mean? I thought we would get lunch or something."

"There's something I have to go do."

"Something or someone?"

"Your faith in me is duly noted."

I look out the window at a flock of geese flying by in a V formation, getting out while the getting's good. "It's not you, Phillip. It's humanity in general."

"Well, cry me a river."

"Okay, drop me at Kelton's."

"The ice rink?"

"Yeah."

He gives me a quizzical look. "Going skating, are you?"

"There's something I want to see."

Phillip gives me a wry look. "Something or someone?"

Then, without warning, he swerves across the double yellow line to pass the minivan in front of us, and for a second we are faced with oncoming traffic and our own mortality. A second later he yanks us back across and, without downshifting, turns left through the intersection on what feels like two wheels, the centrifugal force throwing me against the door. "Jesus Christ, Phillip!"

The Porsche's tires gain traction and we rocket down the street to a chorus of angry horns from all the motorists he almost killed, and Phillip sighs. "Driving a Porsche is like fucking a model," he says, and he would know. "It will never feel as good as it looks."

12:20 p.m.

PENNY SKATES BACKWARD in circles to Huey Lewis and the News, her legs whipping and scissoring beneath her as she speeds across the ice, executing a leap and then a spin. She is wearing black leggings and a worn gray hoodie, her hair tucked into a black ski cap. She moves with grace and confidence, her face flushed from the cold, and she doesn't see me, shivering in my polo shirt on the lowest bleacher, falling briefly in love with her again . . . *If this ain't love, baby, just say so* . . . Huey Lewis and the News are done, and the Dream Academy comes on singing "Life in a Northern Town." Why are all skating rinks trapped in the eighties?

Penny picks up speed and then glides backward across the ice holding one leg up over her head with her hand. As she moves past, her eyes casually sweep up to the bleachers and she sees me. The surprise throws her balance off, and she goes down on her ass hard. I run through the opened door and out onto the ice, where she's already back on her skates, dusting the ice flakes off her leggings.

"You okay?" I say.

"You scared me," she says.

"I didn't mean to."

"You're not allowed on the ice without skates."

"Right. Sorry." I step back through the door onto the rubber matting.

Penny skates over to the door and gives me a long, measured look. Then she reaches into one of the pockets of her sweatshirt and tosses me a key chain. "There are hockey skates in the rental shack. Go grab yourself a pair and come on out."

"I wasn't planning on skating."

"And I wasn't planning on falling on my ass in front of an old boy-friend. Things happen. Just roll with it."

"I was never your boyfriend."

Penny grins. "Fuck-buddy, then."

"We never actually had sex."

"And we never will if you keep parsing words with me."

The hockey skates smell like something curled up and died in them. I'm laced up and on the ice in under five minutes.

I haven't skated in years, stopped playing pickup hockey around the time I got married, but it comes back fast. While I was putting on my skates, Penny dimmed the main lights and turned on the disco ef-fects, so we are skating to "Time After Time" through a dusky universe of spinning blue stars. It's like we've been transplanted into a romantic comedy, and all that's left to do is say something meaningful and kiss Penny at center ice while the music swells, and the happy ending is guar-anteed. *If you're lost you can look and you will find me, time after time.* Penny was always recklessly attracted to grand romantic gestures, to jumping into fountains fully clothed, to long, deep kisses in the rain. She dreamed of Richard Gere in his navy dress whites carrying her out of the factory, of telling Tom Cruise that he had her at hello. But we are hardly free and clear for a happy ending. After all this time, we are little more than strangers to each other, each of us pretending otherwise for our own sad reasons. I don't even know if I'm here because she's some-one I once loved, or because I'm just lonely and desperate and more than a little sexually frustrated and our past gives me something of a head start. And there's something off about Penny, something not quite there. I shouldn't be here. I should be back at home, mourning my father and adjusting to the reality of becoming one myself, continuing to put all my energies into falling out of love with Jen.

And yet . . . Penny's clear skin practically glows on the ice, and the piles of hair pouring out from beneath her cap fly behind her as she glides beside me, and there's something perfectly pretty about her. I watch her profile from the corner of my eye, her slightly bent nose, her sculpted cheekbones, her big hopeful eyes that always seem seconds away from welling up. *If you fall I will catch you I'll be waiting . . .*

"You want to hold hands?"

I look to see if she's joking. She's not. I consider telling Penny about the baby, but something stops me. I'd like to say it's just my not having adjusted to the reality yet, but the truth is probably a good deal more self-serving than that. I take her hand and we skate through the rotating constellations. Her hand is in a black knit glove and mine is a cold, raw claw. I can barely feel her. I could be holding on to anything.

12:55 p.m.

A FAT GUY with a walrus mustache and a jingling key ring shows up to open the rink for business. He waves to Penny, then disappears into a back room. A moment later the music stops, the lights come back on, and the stars disappear. As if by some unspoken agreement, Penny and I let go of each other. There will be no handholding under the harsh fluorescent lights. Walrus man reappears driving a beat-up Zamboni onto the ice.

"You know what would be nice?" Penny says as we step off.

"What's that?"

She considers me for a long moment. "Never mind, I withdraw."

"Come on. What were you going to say?"

"The moment's passed." She smiles and shrugs. I use my finger to free a thin strand of her hair where it's gotten caught in her mouth.

"Thanks for the skate," I say. "I needed that."

"I'm glad you came by," she says.

One or both of us may be lying.

1:00 p.m.

PENNY IS TEACHING her first lesson of the day, and Phillip is late, naturally. I sit on a bench in the parking lot, watching the other skating instructors show up, slender women in baby T's and black leggings that leave nothing to the imagination. They greet each other with waves and laughs. Their bodies, like Penny's, are lithe and toned, and they walk with a graceful athleticism as they make their way inside. I suck in my gut and return their perfunctory smiles as they pass, trying for all the world to look like a guy who isn't checking them out, even though, in their skintight leggings, you could spot those asses across a football field.

1:35 p.m.

PHILLIP DRIVES US back home, somewhat more subdued than earlier. The convertible top is down, and the afternoon sun is hitting us hard, burning off the lingering chill of the ice rink. He pulls up in front of the house and we sit there for a moment, steeling ourselves to go back inside. "If we didn't live on a dead end, I'd probably just keep on driving," he says.

"I know the feeling, little brother. But your problems will just follow you."

"I don't know, this is a pretty fast car. How was the ice rink?"

"It was a little strange, actually. How was your mystery errand?"

"No mystery," Phillip says. "I just needed some alone time to clear my head."

"And is it clear now?"

"No. That was just a figure of speech."

We smile sadly at each other. For some reason sitting here with my little brother, it suddenly occurs to me that we will never see our father again, and I feel a crushing desolation deep in my belly. We used to do this ventriloquist/dummy act for Dad. Phillip would sit on my lap and while I was trying to do the routine, he would suddenly spin and kiss my cheek, and then I'd yell at him and he'd say "sorry" in this high, hoarse cartoon voice, and Dad would laugh until his face turned purple. We didn't know why he found it so funny, but we relished the ability to make him laugh, and so we did it at every possible opportunity. And then, at some point, we didn't do it anymore. Maybe Dad stopped finding it funny, maybe I decided I was too old for it, maybe Phillip lost interest. You never know when it will be the last time you'll see your father, or kiss your wife, or play with your little brother, but there's always a last time. If you could remember every last time, you'd never stop grieving.

"Phillip," I say.

"Yeah."

"Your T-shirt is inside out."

"What? Shit." He pulls it up over his head. "I must have been wearing it wrong all morning."

I nod slowly, accepting the lie, feeling sad and old and not up to the conversation. "Stranger things have happened," I say.

Chapter 24

3:20 p.m.

Today's Inappropriately Self-Absorbed Shiva Caller award goes to Arlene Blinder, an obese, sour-faced neighbor with dark patches of varicose veins running up her thick, mottled legs. That's an unkind description, to be sure, but the view from down here in the chairs is not a pleasant one. All legs and crotch as far as the eye can see, and, if you look up, double chins and nasal hair. And Arlene Blinder is far from anyone's idea of a physical specimen. The small catering chair disappears into her massive bottom like it's been swallowed, and the thin metal legs creak and moan as she settles down. Arlene's husband, a rail of a man named Edward, sits beside her in silence, which is pretty much all anyone's ever seen him do. Somewhere there must be an office he goes to, a job he performs, but if he does, in fact, speak, no one but Arlene has ever been around to hear it.

"Oh, we're expanding the kitchen," she says, as if someone had asked. "It's been a nightmare. First they dig the foundation for the addition and discover a boulder the size of a car. They had to bring in all this equipment and it took them four days to get it out. And then, after they dig down, they tell me the existing foundation has crumbled, and they're going to have to underpin the rest of the house. I don't know what they're talking about, all I know is it's another fifteen thousand dollars out of the gate. If I'd known it was going to be like this, I never would have gotten started."

For the record, there are other visitors, a handful of pleasant-faced, middle-aged women, long-standing friends of my mother, attractive women in the early stages of disrepair, fighting to keep age at bay with facials, compression undergarments, and aggressively fashionable skirts bought off the rack at Neiman Marcus and Nordstrom. They run on treadmills, these women, work out with personal trainers and play tennis at the club, but still their hips widen, their legs thicken, their breasts sag. Genetics help some more than others, but they are all like melting ice cream bars, slowly sliding down the stick as they come apart. There is something in their expressions that is either wisdom or resignation as they sit quietly around my mother and Arlene relentlessly holds the floor like a dominant elephant bull.

"And then yesterday they knocked out the water line and I couldn't take my bath . . ."

"There's an image I didn't need," Wendy mutters.

"Look at her chair," Phillip hisses.

Indeed, the legs of the folding chair are visibly bowing, and whenever Arlene makes a hand gesture, the chair shudders and seems to sink a bit further.

"And the contractor is running two other jobs in the neighborhood. The Jacobsons, he's redoing their pool house, and he's doing a family room for the Duffs. So there are days when he doesn't even show up, and God forbid the man should answer his cell phone. So whenever there's a problem, which is pretty much always, I have to get in my car and go track him down."

"When will you be finished?" my mother asks, and for an instant I think she's asking when Arlene will be done boring us to tears.

"That's what I'd like to know," Arlene says. "At this rate, I won't have a kitchen for the holidays, and my Roger is supposed to be coming in with the grandchildren." Her Roger was in my class, a morbidly obese kid with crumbs on his shirt who wrote a computer program that he sold for millions, bought a mansion in Silicon Valley and a mail-order bride from the Philippines.

"It will be worth it when it's done," Mom says, trying to wrap things up.

"If it hasn't killed me by then," Arlene says, and then gasps at the potential offensiveness of her remark. But before the awkwardness of the moment can harden into something uncomfortable, there's a sharp cracking sound as Arlene's chair finally gives out, and she comes crashing down to the floor with a shriek. There follows a moment of stunned silence, the kind that stops time and pulls it like taffy. Everyone's inner child struggles to suppress a grade-school snicker. It takes a handful of women to help Arlene to her bloated feet. I look at Edward, who has gotten up from his own chair but has been pushed outside the circle of straining women, and our eyes meet. And maybe I'm projecting here, but I would swear, at that moment, that he's fighting back a smile that, unhindered, would split his face in two.

3:50 p.m.

ARLENE'S FALL EFFECTIVELY clears the house, which frees everyone else to weigh in on the news that I'm going to be a father.

> Mom: If it's a boy, I hope you'll consider naming him for your father.
> Linda: That's wonderful, Judd. I think you'll be a great father.
> Wendy: Jen is three months along? She doesn't even have a baby bump yet. You'd better make sure she's eating.
> Phillip: Wade may have won the battle, but you won the war. At least your boys can swim!

Tracy: That's wonderful, Judd. If you frame this with a positive attitude, it will be the greatest experience of your life.

Paul: This means I might have to rethink my theory that Jen left you
  because you're gay.

Phillip: I'm going to be an uncle.

Wendy: Dumb shit. You already are an uncle.

Phillip: I meant again.

Mom: Presumably, Jen's relationship with Wade is intensely sexual.
  This could very well be the end of them. Her priorities are going
  to change. You could start fresh.

Barry: New York is preparing the documents. We'll have to massage
  the interest rates a little bit, but we'll push it through. Believe me,
  in this economy, everyone wants this deal to happen.

Chapter 25

4:20 p.m.

Ryan and Cole are in the pool. Cole wears Spider-Man water wings on his arms to keep him afloat. He and Ryan are engaged in an endless cycle of jumping in off the side and then climbing out to jump in again. Wendy sits suspended over the water on the far edge of the diving board, flipping through a tabloid magazine, while I pick at a platter of pastries on one of the lounge chairs. Serena is asleep in her carriage under an umbrella. The sun is just receding beyond the perimeter of the yard, and the mosquitoes haven't yet emerged. It's the best time to be outside.

"My God, I'm fat," Wendy says, looking through pictures of starving starlets.

"You just had a baby, give yourself a break."

"I had a baby seven months ago. I've been dieting and running every day, and everything in my strike zone still feels like the blob. I won't even change in front of Barry."

"I feel like I've put on some weight myself," I say, biting into a marzipan-coated petit four.

She looks me over critically. "You are looking a little soft in the middle there. You may want to watch that. After all, you're going to be getting naked in front of new women now."

"From your mouth to God's ear."

Wendy laughs. "Jen had an incredible body. I would kill for her legs. And tits. And ass. I hope you're not holding out for another one like that. They're few and far between, and they generally don't put out for unemployed divorcees with no abs."

"Well, you know my motto. If at first you don't succeed, lower your standards."

"Mommy!" Ryan calls. "Watch me."

"Okay, honey," Wendy says absently, still looking down at the magazine. "Well, we can only hope that this pregnancy will leave Jen with stretch marks and a belly flap. No mother should have a stomach that flat. It's just unfair."

"I saw Penny today."

Wendy puts down the magazine. "Penny Moore? How'd she look?"

"I don't know. She looked good."

"Is she married? Divorced? Kids? What?"

"She's not married. She teaches skating and works evenings at the store."

"Our store? She worked for Dad?"

"Yup."

"So, Penny Moore is going to be your rebound. That's fantastic."

"No. I just ran into her."

"Serves her right after the way she led you on in high school."

"She didn't lead me on and she's not going to be my anything. She's just an old friend."

"She cock-teased you for your entire senior year. And if she didn't mean anything, then why did you mention it?"

"I'm just making conversation."

"I'm your sister, Judd. You don't make conversation with your sister. You wanted to say her name."

"And now I wish I hadn't."

"Oh, grow up. Your wife left you and you haven't had sex in forever.

You've got a kid coming, and God only knows what kind of mess that's going to be. That pregnancy may be the best thing that ever happened to you, but it's a ticking clock. You've got six months or so to get your shit together, to be ready to be a father and start caring for someone other than yourself. If I were you, I'd quit beating around the bush. You like Penny, admit you like her and go for it. Maybe you get somewhere with her, or maybe you get rejected. Either way, you get something."

"I've been married for almost ten years. I'm out of practice."

"No offense, little brother, but you didn't exactly have mad skills back in the day."

"Thanks for the confidence boost."

"I'm just being honest."

Horry emerges at the back door, sucking on an apple core. "Your uncle Stan is here. Your mom wants you back in your little chairs."

"Kill me now," Wendy says. "Please." She tries to stand up, but her foot slides on the magazine, and she lets out a startled shriek as she loses her balance and falls into the pool. I jump to my feet, but before I can get moving, Horry comes tearing down the lawn and, after just a few long strides, executes a long racing dive into the pool. He resurfaces and swims over to where Wendy is coughing and sputtering, her sundress pooling around her like a tent. Ryan stands on the side of the pool, terrified. Cole floats and sings to himself in the shallow end, oblivious.

"You okay?" Horry says.

"Yeah," Wendy says, somewhat nonplussed as he pulls her into a lifesaver's hold. He swims her over to the side so she can grab on to the ladder. "Oh, Horry, you jumped in with all your clothes."

"So did you," he says. "You okay?"

"Yeah. I can't believe I did that. I'm such a cow."

"You're not a cow," Horry says, pulling the hair off her face. "You're my sunflower."

She smiles tenderly at him and briefly touches his face. "I remember."

"You're not a cow," he says again, treading water slowly away from her. "And he should be better to you."

"Thank you," she says softly as Horry turns and swims toward the shallow end.

"You all wet," Cole says to him as he arrives at the stairs.

"That's right, little man."

"You play with me now?"

"Sure," Horry says, floating on his back. "I'll play."

The thing is that Wendy's in the pool, so it's impossible to tell if those are tears or just water that she's brushing off her cheeks.

Chapter 26

8:45 p.m.

The show goes on. We are all back in our shiva chairs, except for
Paul, who has begged off, claiming some kind of retail emergency
at the store. Alice has not been seen since the fit she threw this morning,
but Tracy has reappeared, sitting off to the side, smiling graciously. The
rest of us face the crowd like a rock band on tour, same set list, different
town. We perform our sad little shiva smiles on cue and repeat the same
inane conversations over and over again. *He just slipped away,* Mom
says. *Three kids now,* Wendy says. *I'm a photojournalist. I just got back
from a year in Iraq, embedded with a marine unit,* Phillip says. *We're
separated,* I say.

What happens is this. Every half hour or so, someone will ask me
where Jen is. And I will say that we are separated. Then, like a game of
telephone, word will quietly spread through the room, so that everyone
present will know not to ask. And then, invariably, new visitors will arrive, and someone uninformed will ask me again, and the cycle will repeat. I feel bad for the ones who ask, who bear the awkwardness for the
rest of the crowd.

My mother's closer friends have known for weeks. Millie Rosen
brings her daughter, Rochelle, who is twenty-seven, unmarried, and
pretty in a forgettable way. She positions her right in front of me and
makes painfully obvious attempts at engaging us in conversation. What

pretty much every person in Elmsbrook except Millie knows is that I am not Rochelle's type, being that I don't have breasts and a vagina.

Mom's older brother, Uncle Stan, has arrived with his latest senior citizen tramp, Trish, who wears her makeup like a drag queen, coloring way outside the lines with her lipstick and eyebrow pencils. Stan was an appellate court judge and married to my aunt Esther, a broad, sexless slab of a woman, for forty years. After Esther died of emphysema, Stan waited what he considered to be an appropriate mourning period, two weeks or so, and then began sleeping his way through all the willing widows in his retirement village down in Miami Beach. He's closing in on eighty and has his pick of the litter, being that he can still drive and screw. I know this because he's supremely gifted at working it into every conversation.

Uncle Stan is also highly accomplished in the field of flatulence, and he's been here long enough for the room to carry the stale stench of his geriatric farts. The other visitors look around, wrinkling up their noses, searching for the source or for an escape route, but they are too polite to say anything.

Phillip is not. "Christ, Uncle Stan! That's just brutal. How do you live with yourself?"

"It's all that coffee I drank on the airplane."

"He's also on a high-fiber diet. The combination is like jet fuel," Trish explains with a giggle. Women of a certain age shouldn't giggle.

"Trish is a nurse," Stan says proudly.

"Was," Trish says. "I'm retired."

"But she still has the uniform," Stan says, winking and kicking at my feet. "If you take my meaning."

"Stan!" Trish says, although she's not nearly as mortified as she should be, if you ask me. Stan shrugs, then leans forward in his chair to release some more deadly fumes.

"Lord have mercy," Wendy says under her breath.

8:54 p.m.

PAUL RETURNS FROM the store, but instead of joining us in the shiva chairs, he makes his way purposefully through the crowded hallway and disappears up the stairs, ostensibly to check on Alice. "Why is he off the hook?" Phillip grumbles, sounding ten years old.

Someone has gotten my mother started on the topic of toilet training, and the room falls silent as she holds forth. She is considered to be an expert on the topic, and the children of her friends still e-mail and call her to ask for guidance as they struggle to train their children. There is a long and celebrated chapter in *Cradle and All* in which she basically explains the psychology of crapping. She details the way she trained each of her children, the mistakes she made, and, sparing no scatology, the funny things that happened along the way. Mom draws heavily on her own maternal experience throughout the book, and we are all mentioned by name. There are two pages on Paul's undescended testicle, a section on Wendy's late-blooming breasts, and a full chapter on how Mom finally solved my bed-wetting problem when I was six years old. I used to shoplift copies from our local bookstore and toss them out in the Dumpsters behind the Getty station, in an effort to keep the books out of circulation. I was in the sixth grade when my classmates finally discovered the book, and I never heard the end of it. That was the year I learned how to fight.

As Mom warms to her topic, she becomes a lecturer again, enunciating, gesticulating, and inserting little canned jokes that her friends must have heard a thousand times already but still laugh at because she's in mourning. So Mom entertains the crowd with all the wisdom she's gleaned about children and their toilet habits, and it's so quiet that when another sound intrudes, we all hear it. It's indiscernible at first, a burst of static and what sounds like a child out of breath, but then Alice's voice can be heard loud and clear through Wendy's baby monitor in the front hall. And what Alice says is this:

Are you hard yet?

There is more panting and a low moan, and then Alice says, *Put it in me already.*

Then a moment of quiet, followed by Alice's short, high-pitched moans and Paul's grunts as they start to go at it. The visitors, all twenty or so of them, sit shell-shocked, their eyes wide, as Mom stops talking and turns toward the monitor.

Harder. Fuck me harder, Alice cries.

Quiet! Paul grunts.

Yes, baby. Come in me. Come now.

"I would not have figured Alice for a talker," Phillip says. "Nice."

"I put Serena in there to nap earlier," Wendy announces to the room. "I guess I forgot to take the monitor out. My bad."

Phillip leans back in his chair and grins widely. "This probably shouldn't be making me as happy as it is."

"Oh, for heaven's sake, people," Mom says sternly. "It's just sex. You've all had it. A few of you might even have some tonight."

"I know I will," Stan says, kicking my leg again. Dirty old man.

You could hear a pin drop in the living room. That is, if it weren't for Paul's escalating grunts and Alice urging him—*Come on, come on!*—over and over again.

"Sexual stamina runs in our family," Phillip explains to the crowd. "This could take a while."

Linda miraculously appears in the hall and unplugs the receiver. "Sorry about that, everybody." It's unclear if she's apologizing for what they've heard or what they'll now miss.

"Alice is ovulating," Mom explains.

Some of the women nod with understanding while their husbands grin stupidly and look up at the ceiling. The low buzz of hushed conversations slowly returns, like a machine powering up, but a short while later, Paul comes downstairs to sit in his shiva chair and the visitors fall silent, trying not to stare at him. Trying and failing. He looks around the room quizzically, then down at his shirt. He checks his fly. "What?" he says, looking over at me. "What's going on?"

Before I can answer, Uncle Stan stands up and begins to clap, his large, gnarled hands coming together with the mild clink of pinky rings, a doddering, bent standing ovation of one.

"Sit down before you fall down, old man," Mom says.

Paul looks around one more time, then shrugs and leans over to me, making a sour face.

"Who farted?" he says.

Chapter 27

9:30 p.m.

Penny shows up as the shiva is winding down for the night. "Hey," she says, taking the empty chair in front of my seat. She's wearing a black sundress and sandals, her skater's legs crossed tantalizingly at eye level. "I've never paid a shiva call before."

"You're doing great," I say.

"Some old perv pinched my butt on the stairs as I was coming in."

"That's my uncle Stan. He's harmless."

"Tell that to my butt cheek. It's like he wanted to take a piece with him."

"Hello, Penny," Mom says.

"Hi, Mrs. Foxman. I'm so sorry about Mort."

"Thank you. He was very fond of you."

"He was such a nice man. We all miss him down at the store."

"Well, it was very nice of you to come see us."

"I'm just sorry it's taken this long. You know we keep the store open until nine in the summer."

"Penny is the only one Dad trusted to close up and turn on the alarm," Paul says.

"It's not exactly rocket science," Penny says, blushing. Then, noticing Wendy, "Oh my God, Wendy! I didn't recognize you."

"That's because, unlike you, I've actually had the decency to age. Look at you. I bet they still card you in bars."

"Hardly," Penny says, shifting nervously under Wendy's unflinching scrutiny.

"I mean, Jesus," Wendy says, shaking her head. "What are you, a size two?"

9:50 p.m.

THE VISITORS ARE all gone, and the house has fallen quiet. Penny and I sit in the dark by the pool's edge with our feet in the water. The only light comes from two submerged pool lamps, so all we can see is a fine mist rising up off the heated water. "So, how are you doing?" she says.

"Fine, I guess. It's a lot of family time. I think we're going to need a year off from each other when this is over."

She nods, tracing little circles in the water with her toes. "I live around the corner from my parents. My mother has macular degeneration; she can't see well enough to drive anymore. So I take her grocery shopping every Tuesday and I have dinner with them every Sunday night."

"That's nice, isn't it?"

She shrugs. "It can be, with the right mix of meds. God, it's hot out here."

"Yeah. It's been like this all week. Muggy as hell."

"You'd think it would get cooler at night."

"Yeah. Not lately."

"Oh God, Judd. Listen to us. We're talking about the weather. Are we avoiding something, or do we simply have nothing to say to each other?"

"Conversation was never a problem for us."

"Well, then, let's put a moratorium on small talk, okay?"

"Deal."

"And for God's sake, let's get in the water already." She stands up, and I can't quite see her eyes, but I know they're daring me. "Turn around," she says.

I do, and a few seconds later I hear a light splash as she slides into the water. I turn around and see the dark pile of her dress on the ground. I pull off my polo shirt and my cargo pants. I hesitate for a moment when it comes to my boxer briefs. To doff or not to doff, that is the question. How did Penny answer it? In the dim light coming up from the depths of the pool, it's impossible to say. I slide into the pool with my underpants on. Better safe than sorry.

She holds on to a rung of the ladder while I tread water a foot or so in front of her. After a few moments, my eyes have adjusted enough that I can look into hers. I flash back to Horry and Wendy, looking at each other in this exact spot a few hours ago, this haunted pool that seems to pull dead and buried love to its surface.

"I've been thinking about you, Judd."

"Me too."

"Do you think you'd like to kiss me now?"

I glide over to her, my hand falling over hers on the ladder rung. Up close, I can make out the tantalizing outline of her breasts, wet and glistening, where they disappear into the water. "Listen," I say, but then, somehow we're already kissing, deep and slow, our tongues colliding softly, gathering speed. And her taste is exactly as I remember it, brings me back in an instant to those nights of sweaty dry-humping in my basement, and I can feel her nipples hard against my chest, her fingers gliding up my back to my neck, pressing against the spot where my spine becomes my skull.

I have kissed no one but Jen in over ten years, and we have not kissed like this in a very long time, with gaping mouths and frantic tongues, where kissing is its own kind of sex. I am kissing another woman, and the awareness of these lips opening against mine in wet surrender, these fingers snaking down my chest, these smooth, naked thighs wrapped around my hips, is both exhilarating and surreal. If one woman is willing to kiss me like this, it stands to reason that, in due time, others might be equally willing, and for the first time since I walked in on Jen and Wade, I feel something approaching optimism about my future.

After a while, Penny stops to catch her breath, gasping a little as she turns around to rest her arms against the edge of the pool. I swim up behind her and put my hands on either side of her arms, pressing my chest against her back. She leans her head back to press her cheek against mine. "That was so nice," she says.

My body falls against hers, and when my erection, straining underwater against my soaked underpants, falls lightly against the curve of her ass, she emits a low groan.

"Listen," I say. "There's something I want to tell you."

"Tell me tomorrow," she says, pressing herself hard against me. "Just do that now."

10:25 p.m.

Penny left a little while ago, after kissing me a few more times. Now I'm horny and throbbing and sleep is an impossibility, so, for some twisted reason, I dial Jen's cell.

"Hello?" Wade's voice. I should have realized he'd be there. Wade's not the sort of guy who would pass on the opportunity for some hotel sex. I hang up, wait a minute, and dial again. "Hello?" he says with a little more emphasis, like maybe the mystery caller hadn't understood him the first time. It's Jen's cell; why the hell is he picking up? I hang up and dial again. This time his voice is thin and clipped. "Judd," he says. I listen to his breathing for a long moment and then I hang up. On my next call, Jen picks up.

"Hey, Jen."

"Judd," she says, probably with a sardonic, knowing nod for Wade's benefit. I picture them lying in bed, him running his thick fingers up her naked thigh to the curve of her ass as she talks to me, his other hand fondling his thick, semi-erect cock, getting it ready for her. Wade could not get enough pancreatic cancer to satisfy me.

"So, we're going to be parents."

"It's late, Judd. Can we talk tomorrow?"

"Oh, I'm sorry. Am I interrupting something, again?"

"No. I'm just exhausted."

"Would you have left me?" I say, surprising both of us. "If you hadn't gotten caught, do you think you would have left me or left him?"

I can hear her breath catch on the phone. "I honestly don't know," she says.

It is one of those questions that can't possibly have a right answer, but hers still hurts.

"I'm sorry I disturbed you. Go back to sleep."

"Can we talk tomorrow?"

"Yeah. Maybe. I don't know."

"I hope we can."

"Bye."

I wait about three minutes and then dial Wade's cell phone.

"Hello?" he says.

I hang up. It's a small victory, but you learn to take them where you can get them.

*   *   *

Never marry a beautiful woman. Worship them if you must, go to bed with them if you can—by all means, everyone should have carnal knowledge of physical perfection at least once in their life—but when it comes to marriage, it's a losing proposition. You will never stop feeling like a gatecrasher at your own party. Instead of feeling lucky, you will spend your life on edge, waiting for the other stiletto to fall and puncture your heart like a bullet.

11:55 p.m.

I AM RUNNING through darkened halls. Behind me I hear the jingle of the rottweiler's tags, the scrabble of his paws on the floor, the low gurgle of his breath as he gains on me. I am sweating and panting, and no matter how hard I try, I can't seem to pick up any speed. And then I round a corner and my prosthetic leg falls off, clattering woodenly to the ground. I scream as I go down, and even though the dog is not yet upon me, I lurch awake knowing he will be soon.

Chapter 28

Alice Taylor was standing against the wall at Jeremy Borson's house party, sipping spiked punch from a plastic cup and smiling at something one of her friends was saying. We'd gotten friendly over the last few months; she had started touching my arms when we talked and walking closer to me in the halls, so that our hips occasionally bumped. Just a few days earlier, walking home from school, I had impulsively taken her hand when it grazed mine, and she had squeezed back and we'd stayed like that for the rest of the walk, never mentioning it. For the first time in my high school career, a girlfriend appeared to be within my reach. We'd be meeting tomorrow afternoon at the mall for burgers and a movie, and I fully intended to hold her hand again, maybe even try to kiss her during the movie.

And there she was, at Jeremy Borson's party, in cutoffs that showed off her smooth, tanned legs and a white V-neck sweater, her wavy brown hair pulled up off her forehead with a headband. Even as she laughed with her friends, I saw her eyes wandering over the rim of her cup to find mine, saw the little surreptitious smiles being aimed at me, the light dancing across the surface of her lip gloss. There was something new in those smiles, something bold and promising, and I began to make my way through the crowd, marshalling my resources and chugging down my spiked punch for courage. Maybe we'd go outside for a little while and I'd kiss her tonight. I was pretty sure she wanted me to.

The room was hot and throbbing; Tears for Fears blasting on the stereo system, girls dancing awkwardly in the square left by the prudent removal of a coffee table, kids pressed up against each other in the crowded living room, drinks held aloft at high angles to avoid spilling. Here and there couples made out against the walls, although the ones with any class went out to the yard to grope and suck in private. There were viral whispers of vomit in the powder room, of porno in the basement, of controlled substances in the garage.

I don't know exactly what happened. Someone bumped into someone across the room, maybe clowning around, maybe completely by accident, but we were a roomful of sweating dominoes, knocking one into another, until I was thrown forward into Tony Rusco, who had a beer bottle in his mouth right at that moment. The bottle banged audibly against his teeth, and he spewed his beer all over his shirt. He turned around, wiping his face on his arm, and, with no preamble, kicked me in the balls.

If you have no balls, or have some but have somehow made it through life thus far without ever having injured them, then you've missed out on one of the most exquisitely nuanced variations of agony known to man. It is the piano of pain, melody, harmony, bass, and percussion all in the same instrument.

First there's nothing. A surprising amount of nothing actually. No pain at all, just white noise and the shock of having been hit there, in your softest of places. And because the pain has yet to arrive, you dare to hope that it won't come at all, that the impact was less direct than you first thought. And then it comes, like thunder on the heels of lightning, at first just a faint rumble, a low, steady hum of discomfort. If it were a musical note, it would be one of those bottom bass notes they use in horror films to create an ominous sense of dread, of dark, fanged things hiding, poised to spring. It's a loaded hum, because you know a note that low only has one direction to go. And as you feel the dull, pulsating pain emanating from the center of your being, from your core, you think to yourself, *I can handle this, this is nothing, I can kick this pain's ass,* and that's the exact instant that you find yourself suddenly on your knees, doubled over and gasping, with no memory at all of how you got there. And now the pain is everywhere—in your groin, your gut, your kidneys, the tightly flexed muscles of your lower back where you didn't even think you had muscles. Your body is tensed too hard to breathe right so your lungs are constricted, and you're drooling because your head is hanging, and your heart can't pump your rushing blood fast enough, and you can feel yourself teetering, but you have no muscles left to correct with, so you end up collapsing onto your side, your nerves fusing together into knotted coils of anguish, your eyeballs turned up into your skull like you've grabbed hold of a live wire in the rain.

There's really nothing else like it.

Rusco didn't belong at this party. He had graduated two years ago, a small miracle considering the record of suspensions he'd racked up for fighting, drugs, and vandalism. Now he operated a forklift in the warehouse at one of the furniture outlets gathered in a cluster at the top of Route 9 and lifted free weights with his buddies in his front yard. He was rumored to have pulled a switchblade on Mr. Portis, our aging phys ed teacher, who had subsequently suffered a nervous breakdown; to have punched out the bouncer at the Dark Horse when they wouldn't serve him a beer; to have beat the shit out of his own father in the eighth grade.

So even if I could have gotten to my feet at that point to fight him, he'd have only knocked me down again, so I just curled up into the fetal position while the room spun around me and psychedelic colors swam across the insides of my eyelids, and Rusco put his boot on my head and said, "You want to watch where you're going, shithead."

And then he was gone, and Alice was hovering over me, helping me up, she and Jeremy taking me upstairs to Jeremy's parents' bedroom, where they lay me down on a paisley bedspread. "Are you okay?" she kept saying, while I tried my best not to cry. I was enjoying her concern and her proximity, her hair intimately brushing my face as she leaned over me, but I hadn't exactly kicked ass out there, and I would be damned if I was going to compound that by crying in front of her.

"He's such an asshole," Alice said.

I rolled away from her and closed my eyes. I think I might have dozed off because when I woke up she was gone, and a couple of seniors were making out in Jeremy's parents' bathroom, their quiet moans reverberating off the tiles.

I was limping home when Paul pulled up beside me in Dad's Cadillac. He'd been granted unlimited use of the car from the moment he was awarded his baseball scholarship, which was why, instead of being at the party, he'd been off somewhere getting laid in the backseat. "Hey!" he said. "What happened?"

"Nothing."

"I heard you got your ass kicked."

"It wasn't my ass."

I looked over at Paul and, to my surprise, saw that he was simmering with rage. "Get in," he said.

"It's past my curfew."

"Fuck curfew. Come with me."

"Where?"

Paul hit the wheel and looked straight ahead. "Just get in the car, will you?"

The Cadillac smelled of perfume and sex, and my balls throbbed with every bump and curve. "Fucking asshole," Paul muttered as he steered across Centre Street. "Let's see how he likes it when I stand on his head."

I was scared and still in considerable pain, but I felt safe next to Paul and touched that he was so angry that someone had hurt me. We had drifted apart in high school, but we were still brothers, and here he was, interrupting his own evening, which surely had involved some degree of female nudity, to stand up for his little brother.

"Quit crying," he said softly. "You can't let him see you like that."

It was a cloudless night and the neighborhood was bathed in the blue light of a low moon. Paul sped through the empty streets, and I fantasized that we were headed to the diner by the interstate, two brothers out for a late dinner to tell each other about their respective nights. We weren't those kinds of brothers anymore, but I often wished we were. A few minutes later, we pulled up in front of a dilapidated Victorian with a sagging porch. Rusco was out on the front lawn, perched on his weight bench, drinking a beer. The two guys he'd been with at the party were sitting on his front steps, each with a beer in hand. I watched as Rusco registered my presence in the passenger seat, watched him take in Paul's tall athletic frame as he strode angrily through the glow of the Cadillac's headlights and up the driveway, and, for one delicious moment, saw the fear that spread across his face as he realized what was happening.

"Hey, man," he said, getting to his feet. "You're on private property. Get the fuck off—"

Paul's fist hit his open mouth with a loud crack, and whatever euphoria I'd been feeling disappeared in an instant. Rusco went down hard as his two friends jumped up off the stairs, not sure what to make of Paul, who was now standing over Rusco and shouting, "Get up and fight, you little pussy!"

I jumped out of the car and ran up the sidewalk to where Rusco lay on his back, dazed. Blood spilled from his mouth, and my stomach turned when I saw that his two front teeth were gone. "Forget it, Paul," I pleaded, suddenly terrified. "Let's just go."

"Come here, Judd," he called to me. I came up and stood beside him as Rusco rolled over and tried to sit up. His chin looked like it had been dipped in red paint, and his eyes were rolling unfocused in their sockets. When he got to his knees, Paul kicked him in the stomach and he went down again. A light went on in an upstairs bedroom, and from in the house, I heard the sounds of barking.

"We have to get out of here, Paul."

"Kick him in the balls," Paul ordered me. His eyes were blazing, the cords on his neck standing out angrily against his skin.

"It's okay," I said. "We have to go."

The front porch light came on. I grabbed Paul's arm and started pulling him toward the car. "Come on!" I pleaded.

From the ground, Rusco lashed out with his leg, ineffectively hitting Paul's ankle. Paul grabbed the leg and lifted it, spreading Rusco's thighs. "Kick him in the nuts and then we'll go," he said.

The blood gathering on Rusco's chin started to run up his cheeks as Paul lifted his leg higher. When he opened his mouth to spit out some more blood, it looked like the very tip of his tongue was missing too. "I don't want to!" I shouted.

And then, behind us, the front door opened and a fat woman in green sweatpants and a large bra appeared, clutching the collar of an enraged rottweiler, who strained ferociously against her grip. She had the same jutting forehead as her son, the same small, humorless eyes. "What the hell is going on here?"

"We're leaving," I said, my voice cracking as Paul and I backed away.

"Tony, what happened? Oh my God! Is he okay?"

The rottweiler snarled and barked at us and I could see his spit flying in the yellow light of the porch as he fought to escape Mrs. Rusco's grip. We were almost at the curb when she said, "Get 'em, Max," and let go of the collar. The rottweiler flew off the stairs, and we turned and ran as fast as we could. I could hear his claws tearing at the concrete walk, his low growl vibrating deep within my bowels. Paul overtook me on the sidewalk and jumped through the open window into the passenger seat. I jumped onto the hood and then up onto the roof, feeling the aluminum bend under my weight. I turned just in time to see the dog leap through the window after Paul. The car shook under me as the dog snarled and growled, and Paul's screams changed from terror to agony. I screamed for help at the top of my lungs, screamed until my voice cracked and then refused to come. It would take three days before it returned, three days spent sitting in the hospital while they operated on Paul's shoulder and performed skin grafts onto his ruined arm. I screamed and cried and pissed my pants, helplessly stomping on the roof as Paul screamed and wept.

It was Rusco who ultimately got the dog out of the car. He came staggering down the walk, his chin and mouth caked with blood, and yanked open the door, yelling, "Down, Max!" as he went. By now the dog was in too much of a frenzy to heed his master, so Rusco pulled him out by his hind legs and tried to hold him back. The dog lurched out of his grip and tried to run back at the car, barking furiously, but Rusco stood in his way and yelled at him. The rottweiler danced around him, barking and snarling, and at first I thought it was blood dangling from its mouth, but then I realized it was a wet strip of Paul's red T-shirt. "Get out of here!" Rusco shouted. "He's going to get past me!"

"Hold him!" I yelled hysterically from the roof. Beneath me, the car was distressingly still.

"Just get in on the other side!"

I don't remember coming down off the car or opening the door. I remember Paul's head jammed under the steering wheel, his body spread across the bench at odd angles, the blood pooling up in the cracks between the vinyl seat cushions, the suffocating stench of blood and shit.

He didn't make a sound when I moved his head out from under the wheel so that I could sit down, but he groaned when I slammed the door, so I knew he was alive. So eager had Paul been to beat the shit out of Rusco, he hadn't even bothered to turn off the engine, so I was able to raise both windows immediately. A few seconds later, the rottweiler hit the side of the car with a thump, his teeth gnashing against the glass. I stared numbly past him at Rusco, who looked back at me expressionless, his face painted with blood like a savage, while the dog howled and threw himself repeatedly against the car. At some point I threw the car in gear and drove slowly away, not wanting to shake Paul. Through the rearview mirror, I watched the rottweiler chase us for a little bit, then stop in the middle of the street to bark furiously at us. I should have thrown the car into reverse and run him over, but I didn't, I just kept driving, and the ignored impulse became one more thing that would haunt me in the days and years to follow. If only I had backed over the dog. If only I had jumped off the roof of the car to help Paul. If only I had refused to get in the car with Paul to begin with.

At some point I managed to get my bearings and drive us to the emergency room, but I have no recollection of that. I vaguely recall a nurse sticking a needle in me because Paul had lost a lot of blood, and then my parents showed up and they stuck needles in them too. The police briefly impounded the Cadillac for evidence, which is why at some point I woke up in a panic in the back of the police car that was taking me home. My parents would be spending the night in the hospital. The cop driving me was an old guy whose face I couldn't quite make out from the backseat. He told me I'd saved my brother's life. It would soon become clear that Paul didn't see it that way. The silent consensus, evident in Paul's glare, my father's pained expression, and my mother's lack of intervention, was that the wrong brother had been mauled. I didn't know it at the time, but that was the night we broke, and in the years to follow, the jagged pieces of us would continue to drift further and further apart, small vital bits getting lost here and there, until there was no hope of ever putting us back together.

Animal Control put down Max two weeks later, after a hearing my father attended armed with grisly pictures of Paul's injuries. Suits and countersuits were filed, criminal charges leveled and dismissed. A few weeks later I finally kissed Alice Taylor in a darkened movie theater, and then surprised us both by crying like a baby.

Saturday

Chapter 29

5:06 a.m.

I wake up strangely energized, my stomach growling. Upstairs, the overstocked fridge offers me its bounty of sympathy food. I throw some cheese slices onto a soft bagel and then head up to the second floor. I haven't been up here since I got back. The bedroom doors are all closed, so there's really not much to see. I tiptoe up the attic stairs, which creak like a haunted house, and out the access window to the roof, climbing up the slate until I'm sitting at the highest point of the gable. When I was a kid I used to climb up here to look down at the block and gather my thoughts in private. Paul would climb up here with Boner to smoke weed and look at porn, and Wendy would come up to get a tan while her nails dried. I don't know if Phillip ever figured out the roof. By the time he was old enough, we were all out of the house.

Knob's End is on a high elevation, so you can see a lot from up here. You can see into backyards for blocks, swimming pools, swing sets, barbecues, discarded toys. You can see across the rooftops to where the early morning joggers are running on the track behind the baseball diamond in the county park over on Fenimore. You can watch the sun come up, coloring the sky white, then pink, then blue.

You can see your older sister, barefoot in boxer shorts and a T-shirt, walking hurriedly up the block from the direction of the Callens', tying her long, mussed hair back as she goes, and wonder what she might be doing coming from there at this hour. And then, just minutes after she's let herself in below, you can observe Linda Callen leaving your childhood home to quietly make her way down the block back to her house. It would probably help to see Linda's expression, but her back is to you, so you can only guess at it. You can ponder these two women, who miss each other by a matter of minutes, walking exactly opposite routes as quietly as the dew now dropping in a mist on the grass and on your face, and you can hazard any number of guesses as to what business they might be tending to in the soft focus of these hushed morning hours when the day is taking its first tentative breaths. You can sit up here, feeling above it all while knowing you're not, coming to the lonely conclusion that the only thing you can ever really know about anyone is that you don't know anything about them at all.

6:30 a.m.

I STEP OUT of the shower into pitch darkness. By now this has become routine. Wrapped in my towel, I walk across the basement to the circuit breaker. But this time, when I flip the switch, there is a crackle of electricity, a flash of blue light, and I am blown out of my towel and backward across the room, where I land flat on my back, poised on the precipice of unconsciousness. My body tingles with electricity, and I can feel every molecule in me, thrumming in harmony. I close my eyes and . . .

. . . I am three years old and riding my red plastic motorcycle in the park. It's cold out, I'm wearing my navy blue ski hat, and my nose is running copiously into my scarf. The plastic wheels of the motorcycle clatter loudly against the cracked asphalt as I push off with my feet to propel myself around an Olympic-sized sandbox. I don't know if I'm going clockwise or counterclockwise. I'm three years old; I don't know from clocks. Suddenly, a kid appears in my path, tall and fat, two lines of snot running equilaterally down from his nose to the corners of his mouth. He holds a gray milk crate over his head like the Ten Commandments being brought down from Sinai. "The Hulk!" he screams at me. I don't know what he means. I'm years away from Marvel comics, and even once I discover them, *The Incredible Hulk* will never make sense to me. Is he a good guy or a bad guy? You're never really sure, and moral ambivalence has no place in childhood. I'm three years old, and I have never heard of *The Incredible Hulk,* but this kid clearly relates to him intimately. And maybe he's pretending the milk crate is a car, or a house, or a large boulder, or an archenemy, I don't know. Whatever it's supposed to be, it hurts like hell when it hits my face. And then I'm off the motorcycle, lying on my side, the grit of the cold asphalt biting into my cheek. My nose and mouth are bleeding, and I'm coughing and spitting and crying, gagging on my own blood.

And then I'm borne up into the air by powerful arms, lifted high above the fat kid and my plastic motorcycle and the earth, really, my face pressed into my savior's large shoulder, which is somehow hard and soft at the same time. I bleed into the fuzz of his peacoat as he rubs my back and says, "It's okay, bubbie. You're okay. Everything's fine." And then he stands me up on a bench and pulls out a handkerchief to softly wipe away my blood. "That little bastard really nailed you," he says, gently picking me up again. I don't know what a little bastard is, I don't know who the Hulk is, I don't remember what exactly happened, but my father is holding me safely above the fray, and I'm burrowed hard into his powerful chest, and I'm aware of the fat kid somewhere down below, but I know the little bastard can't reach me up here.

6:32 a.m.

I COME TO with my mother's worried face hovering over me. "Judd," she says softly. "Just stay there for a moment." There are deep shadows under her eyes, and at this angle, the gray roots of her hair frame the upper half of her face. She looks tired and old, and I feel a surge of tenderness toward her. I'm still vibrating.

"He called me bubbie," I say.

"What, dear?"

"When I was little. Dad used to call me bubbie."

Mom looks at me and smiles. "I remember," she says, rubbing my chest.

"You're crying," I say.

"So are you."

And now I can feel the abundant wetness on my face, and she comes in and out of focus as I blink through fresh tears. "I miss him," I say, and something in me breaks.

And then Mom lets out an anguished cry and drops her head to sob into my chest while I cry into the brittle tangle of her hair, and we stay like that for a good long while.

Chapter 30

8:06 a.m.

This being Saturday, the laws of shiva are suspended, all outward signs of mourning put aside in honor of the Sabbath. Boner stops by to give us the news. He is dressed in a dark suit with a black shirt and looks ready to go out clubbing.

"You are still in mourning, of course," he says. "But there will be no visitors today, no outward observance of shiva."

"So, it's like a day off," I say.

"Not quite," he says. He looks at my mother, who nods, and then looks back at us. "This morning, you'll all come to temple to say Kaddish at morning services."

"Kaddish?"

"The prayer for the soul of the departed."

"Why can't we say it here?" Paul says.

"Kaddish is said responsively. It can only be said with a minyan, a quorum of at least ten men present to respond."

Paul looks at his childhood friend exasperatedly. *Give me a break!* But Boner just looks back and shrugs. *I don't make the rules.*

Paul blinks first. "When do services start?"

Boner checks his watch. "In twenty-five minutes. You'd better get dressed."

8:15 a.m.

THE SUIT I wore to the funeral has been lying on the basement floor in a crumpled heap ever since, so Mom brings me up to her bedroom and picks out one of Dad's suits for me. Dad only ever wore two kinds of suits: midnight blue and black. When I try on the black one Mom has chosen it fits perfectly, except for the slacks being an inch or so too short. I am somewhat surprised, because I've always seen him as taller than me. I never got close enough to know better.

Every so often, based on the tick of some internal clock, Dad would randomly decide to bring us all to temple on Saturday morning. "Get showered," he would say. "Sport jacket and tie." And Paul and I would grumble as we dressed. On these occasions Wendy was allowed to use Mom's makeup, so we'd all end up waiting in the living room while she fussed with her blush and rouge and Mom dolled up little Phillip in the androgynous sailor outfits that Dad worried would make him gay.

The yarmulkes in the olivewood box at the entrance to the sanctuary were black and constructed from nylon so insubstantial that a light draft from the air-conditioning vents was enough to launch them off our curly hair like hang gliders. Mom would fasten them to our hair with bobby pins while Dad threw a prayer shawl yellowed with age over his shoulders like a scarf. Then we'd follow him into the sanctuary, pausing every few feet as he stopped to shake someone's hand and say, "Good shabbos." We would follow suit, shaking the large cracked hands of these men, inhaling the clean scents of their aftershave and breath mints.

Rabbi Buxbaum would come down from his seat to greet us warmly, his smile obscured by his silver handlebar mustache. "Gentlemen," he would say with a wink, pressing hard butterscotch candies into our palms as he shook our hands, "and I use the term loosely."

Within ten minutes Mom would have to take Phillip outside to run through the halls of the Hebrew school we'd all sporadically attended, and Dad would close his eyes and rock lightly in his seat, humming along with the cantor to the liturgical melodies he recalled from his own loosely affiliated youth. Paul would make a goal out of two spread fingers at the edge of his prayer book, and I would attempt to flick my crumpled candy wrapper in. If Dad caught us he would smack the backs of our heads and tell us to knock it off. Wendy sat upright, crossing and uncrossing her legs, studying the women's dresses and mannerisms, scanning the rows for cute boys.

When services were over, there would be sacramental wine and light refreshments in the social hall. While my parents chatted with the other adults over creamed herring and pastries, Paul and I would sneak little plastic shot glasses of schnapps from the liquor table and try not to gag as it burned its way down our throats. Sometimes a kid would procure a tennis ball and we'd all go out to the lot behind the synagogue to play stickball in our shirtsleeves. By noon we'd be home again, suits hung up, our shirts piled on the dining room table for the dry cleaner, Mom and Dad holed up in their room for an afternoon "nap." All this happened two, maybe three times a year. There were years when it didn't happen at all, and then, one Saturday, apropos of nothing, Dad would once again wake us with "Sports jackets and ties, boys. Sports jackets and ties." It seemed to happen less and less as we got older, until, by the time I was a teenager, the only time we ever went to temple was for Rosh Hashanah and Yom Kippur.

Once, when I was old enough to ponder these things and young enough to think there might be credible answers, I whispered to Dad during Rosh Hashanah services, "Do you believe in God?"

"Not really," he said. "No."

"Then why do we come here?"

He sucked thoughtfully on his Tums tablet and put his arm around

me, draping me under his musty woolen prayer shawl, and then
shrugged. "I've been wrong before," he said.

And that pretty much summed up what theology there was to find
in the Foxman home.

9:40 a.m.

KADDISH IS ONLY said by the blood relatives of the deceased, so Barry,
Tracy, and Alice have all opted out of the trip, and who could blame
them? My siblings, Mom, and I arrive at temple an hour late, but Boner
has reserved a row of pews for us. I can feel all eyes in the cavernous
room on us as we make our way down the aisle, my brothers and I feeling awkward in our flimsy black yarmulkes and tattered prayer shawls
borrowed from the rack in the hall, which we wear slung over our shoulders like scarves. Boner wears a long white prayer shawl with bits of
silver trim around the collar that jingle like chain mail. He descends like
a spirit from his high seat on the front platform to dramatically hug each
one of us as we enter the pew. This seems gratuitous to me, as we all saw
each other an hour earlier, like when talk show hosts warmly greet their
guests even though they've obviously talked backstage before the show.

And Boner is definitely putting on a show. He strides the aisle like a
political candidate, shaking his congregants' hands, giving the younger
guys a quick hug with a fist to the back, leaning in to kiss the women on
the cheek, tousling the carefully brushed hair of the children, all the
while wishing everyone a good shabbos in a loud stage whisper meant
to be heard above the droning of the cantor. He is clearly aware that all
eyes are on him, and he basks in the attention of his captive audience.

Boner has become the kind of rabbi whose agenda seems to be
comprised solely of proving to the younger generations that Judaism is
cool, that rabbis can be hip, that he, Charlie Grodner, is a happening

guy. Hence the Armani suit, the abundance of product in his hair, the trendy sideburns, the diamond stud in his left ear. He's a rock star rabbi, and whether that's done to sell God to today's youth or simply as the sublimation of his unfulfilled Zeppelin fantasies is anyone's guess. I'd like to give him the benefit of the doubt, but it's hard to see divine purpose in the man who doodled anatomically correct images of anal sex in the back of his trigonometry notebook.

The temple hasn't changed since my childhood. The high stucco ceiling, the grand, bleached wood ark up front containing a handful of Torahs, each one colorfully adorned in a cloth cover and a silver crown. The *"In Memoriam"* plaques that line the walls, each name accompanied by a tiny orange bulb to be lit every year on the anniversary of their death. The older men, prayer shawls slung over stooped shoulders and weathered blazers, sucking on hard candies and humming along with the cantor. The younger men, with their better suits and creased yarmulkes; the women, dressed to the nines, their prayer books balanced on their laps atop designer handbags. The stained glass windows bending the sunlight, dedications handwritten on the glass in black calligraphy. And the large, raised platform up front, where the rabbi's lectern stands directly under the postmodern Eternal Light, a few feet in front of the ark, and where Boner now ascends to address the crowd.

"What's up, everyone?" he says. "Good shabbos, Elmsbrook!"

There is a low rumble of response.

"Oh, come on, I know you can do better than that. Good shabbos, Elmsbrook!"

The crowd responds with a *"Good shabbos,"* self-conscious and loud.

"That's what I'm talking about!" Boner says. "I'd like to take a moment to welcome the Foxman family back to our temple. As many of you know, Mort Foxman, one of our founding members, passed away a few days ago. His wife, Hillary, and his children, Paul, Judd, Wendy, and

Phillip, are here to say Kaddish for him and mark his passing before God
and before their community. Mort was a well-respected businessman
here in Elmsbrook; many of us grew up getting our sneakers and baseball gloves at Foxman's. On a personal note, I spent a good part of my
childhood in the Foxman home, playing ball with Paul and Judd—"

"Smoking weed," I whisper.

"Jerking off." Paul.

"Trying to touch my boobs." Wendy.

". . . and he leaves behind this legacy, his work ethic and his uncom-
promising values, for his children and grandchildren to carry on. May
the Lord comfort the family among the mourners of Zion."

"Amen," the crowd responds.

"I'd like to call Hillary and her children up to the bimah now, to say
Kaddish for their beloved husband and father, Morton Foxman."

Mom stands up first and strides down the aisle in her stiletto heels
like it's a runway, garnering appreciative glances from the older men in
the crowd, including Peter Applebaum, who shamelessly watches her
ass the entire way down.

"She couldn't find a longer skirt for temple?" Wendy mutters.

My siblings and I follow her up to the bimah, a raised table at the
front of the room, where the cantor hands each of us a laminated sheet
with the words of the Kaddish written in Hebrew and then transliter-
ated in English. "Just read it slowly and pause at the dashes for the responses," he says. "You'll be fine."

"Okay, everyone," Paul says. "On three?"

"*Yit'gadal v'yit'kadash sh'mei raba,*" we say.

"*Amen,*" says the congregation, all rising to their feet.

"*B'alma di v'ra khir'utei v'yam'likh mal'khutei . . .*"

We read off the ancient Hebrew words, with no idea of what they
might mean, and the congregation responds with more words that they

don't understand either. We are gathered together on a Saturday morning to speak gibberish to each other, and you would think, in these godless times, that the experience would be empty, but somehow it isn't. The five of us, huddled together shoulder to shoulder over the bimah, read the words aloud slowly, and the congregation, these old friends and acquaintances and strangers, all respond, and for reasons I can't begin to articulate, it feels like something is actually happening. It's got nothing to do with God or souls, just the palpable sense of goodwill and support emanating in waves from the pews around us, and I can't help but be moved by it. When we reach the end of the page, and the last "amen" has been said, I'm sorry that it's over. I could stay up here a while longer. And as we step down to make our way back to the pews, a quick survey of the sadness in my family's wet eyes tells me that I'm not the only one who feels that way. I don't feel any closer to my father than I did before, but for a moment there I was comforted, and that's more than I expected.

10:12 a.m.

As the cantor drones on, I stick my hand into the pocket of Dad's suit and discover what feels like an old, twisted tissue but turns out, upon further inspection, to be a very fat, bona fide, home-rolled joint. I palm the joint, hold it out over Phillip's lap, and discreetly show it to him. The only thing wider than his eyes is his smile. "I have to go to the bathroom," he says. He stands up and heads up the aisle. A few minutes later, I follow. The bathroom smells of powdered crotch, so we push open the double fire doors and head down the darkened hallways of the Temple Israel Hebrew School. Phillip finds an unlocked classroom and we sit down in miniature chairs, still wrapped in our prayer shawls.

"Where'd you get the doobage?" Phillip says.

"It was in Dad's suit."

"Dad was a stoner?" Phillip says. "So much about my life makes sense now."

"Shut up. It was probably medicinal. They prescribe it for cancer patients."

"I prefer to think that every once in a while Dad just liked to toke up and consider the universe."

"Think what you want, just light the fucker."

A few moments later, we're sprawled at our tiny attached desks, while the three-dimensional letters of the Hebrew alphabet taped above the blackboard float over us in a smoky haze.

"Can you still read Hebrew?" Phillip says.

"I doubt it," I say. "I know the letters, though."

"Aleph, beth, gimel, daleth . . . ," Phillip sings.

"He, vav, zayin, heth, teth, yod," I chime in.

We sing the rest of the Aleph-Bet together solemnly, like a funereal psalm, and when we're done, our voices echo briefly in the room.

"I miss Dad," Phillip says.

"I do too."

"I feel very alone. Like when I mess up now, he won't be there to help me."

"I guess we're officially adults now."

"Fuck that," Phillip says, taking an extra long pull on the joint. He blows out a perfect ring and then blows a jet of smoke through it. When it comes to worthless frat-boy skills, Phillip is second to none. He can light a match with his thumbnail, open a beer bottle with his teeth, flip a cigarette from the carton to his mouth with a flick of his wrist, play the *William Tell* overture by flicking his fingers against the soft underside of his jaw, burp the national anthem, fart on cue, and dislocate his shoulder upon request.

"Do you think maybe that's why you're with Tracy?" I say. "Because you want to know there's someone looking after you?"

Phillip lazily passes me the joint. "I don't know, but I like that theory much better than the one that postulates I'm trying to sleep with Mom."

The door to the classroom flies open. "What the hell?" Paul says. "Oh. Christ."

"In or out," I say.

"I should have known." He steps into the room, closing the door behind him.

"We learned from the master," Phillip says.

"Give it here." Paul takes a drag and sits down in one of the chairs. "Damn! That is some strong shit. Where'd you get it?"

"Dad," I say, indicating the blazer. "A gift from the beyond."

"I wouldn't have pegged Dad for a fan of the weed."

"People can change," Phillip says.

"People are who they are," Paul says, leaning back in his little chair to take another generous drag. "I really miss him," he says.

"Me too," I say.

"Me three." Phillip.

A ray of sunlight comes through the window, passing through the thick cloud of ganja smoke in a way that makes you think of God and heaven, and we sit there getting baked in our skullcaps and prayer shawls, three lost brothers in mourning, the full impact of their loss only now beginning to dawn on them.

"I love you guys," Phillip says, just as the smoke alarm goes off and the sprinklers come on.

10:25 a.m.

FORTUNATELY, THE SPRINKLERS in the sanctuary are in a different zone and must be set off independently, so the worshippers do not get soaked as they evacuate the building. In the classroom, though, the water rains down on us as Phillip grabs what's left of the joint, still lit, and swallows it whole, with the confidence of someone for whom joint swallowing is a routine practice. The sprinklers have also been activated in the hallway, and we run through the indoor storm, stopping at the fire doors that lead to the lobby area. Peering through the narrow vertical windows of the door, we can see the crowd moving through the lobby and out the glass doors to the synagogue's front lawn.

"Just act casual," Paul says. "Blend in."

It seems easy enough, only because we're too stoned to realize that three men dripping in their suits might stand out.

The air-conditioning is cold against my wet clothes. We discard our soaked prayer shawls and join the crowd moving out the doors and soon find ourselves standing in the parking lot, being warmed by the late-morning sun.

"What did you do!" my mother shouts, her heels clattering on the asphalt as she storms over to us. Wendy follows behind her, enjoying every second of it.

"Nothing," Phillip says. "It was a false alarm."

"Look at the three of you!"

"You guys smell like a dorm room," Wendy says, wrinkling up her nose.

"You got high at temple?" Mom says, outraged.

"Of course not." Paul.

"No." Me.

"Who's hungry?" Phillip.

In the distance, we can hear the wail of the fire trucks.

"Ah, shit," Paul says.

Mom leans against a car, exasperated. "I blame myself."

"That's a relief," I say. "Now can we get out of here?"

But just then Boner emerges from the crowd and comes striding purposefully over to us, brow furrowed, face flushed with anger. "What the hell, Paul?" he demands.

Paul shrugs. "False alarm, I guess."

"And you three are the only ones who got wet."

"It's been that kind of week," I say.

Boner steps right up into Paul's face. "I smell weed."

"You would know."

The two childhood friends stare each other down for a moment and then look away. The rules have changed. Boner sighs. "You guys should get out of here before the cops show up."

"That's a great idea," Wendy says. "Come on, Mom. I'll drive."

"Thanks, buddy," Paul says, smacking Boner's shoulder.

"Just go."

"Thanks for everything," I say, shaking his hand. "Good shabbos."

"Yeah, thanks, Boner," Phillip says.

Boner gives Phillip a withering look. "That was the last time you call me Boner, you hear me?"

Phillip looks at me, and I shake my head. *Don't do it.*

"I'm sorry, Boner."

Boner lunges at Phillip, but Paul catches him and turns him around, whispering in his ear, while I drag Phillip toward Mom's Jeep. "Jesus, Phillip. Grow up, would you?"

"I gotta be me," he says, snickering.

Wendy looks over the roof of Mom's car and smiles cheerfully at us. "You guys are so going to hell."

Chapter 31

1:05 p.m.

I wake up in the basement with a start to find Alice lying on her back beside me, looking up at the ceiling. "He stirs," she says.

I am momentarily disoriented. The last thing I can remember was coming downstairs to peel off my soaked suit. I haven't smoked weed in years, and my nap felt as deep as a night's sleep. "What time is it?"

"It's just after one." She turns onto her side to face me, resting her face on her hand. "You've been sleeping for almost two hours."

"Where is everyone?"

"Paul went to work. Everyone else is out at the pool."

"You're not."

"Neither are you." She stretches a bit, the tops of her breasts rising and spilling out of her low-cut dress.

"What's going on, Alice?"

"You seem to be staring at my breasts."

"Your breasts are in my face."

Alice props herself up on one elbow and pulls slowly at the neckline of her dress, stretching it down until her naked breasts emerge, round and whole. "You always liked my breasts."

"What's not to like?" I'm thinking that this is a dream, a strange, twisted, but not altogether unpleasant dream.

"I feel bad about how I reacted when I found out Jen was expecting. I should have been happy for you, and instead I just felt bad for me."

"A simple apology would have been fine," I say.

"There's nothing in the world I want more than to have a baby," she says. "You know that, right?"

"Yes."

She moves closer, so that her breasts are now dangerously close. The room starts to spin a little bit. *What was in that joint, Dad?* "Um, can you put those away?"

"In a minute," she says. "First I want you to listen to me."

"Okay."

Alice takes a deep breath and looks me dead in the eye. "I've been trying to get pregnant for almost two years. I don't ovulate regularly. My cycle never returned to normal when I came off the pill. I take a drug to make me ovulate, and my eggs have tested fine, but Paul won't get his sperm tested. I was thinking, maybe I would increase the odds and you'd give me some of yours."

"You want my sperm?"

"Yours seems to have what it takes."

"What does Paul think about that?"

"Paul will never know. It will be our secret. And you and I will never know if it was yours or Paul's sperm that did the trick. It's perfect, really. Any baby that resembles you will resemble Paul."

"There are so many things wrong with that idea, I don't even know where to start."

Alice rolls over, almost onto me, her face hovering inches above mine. "Won't you help me, Judd? Please? Forget Paul, forget everyone and everything else. We liked each other a lot once; we used to come to this basement and have sex right here where we're lying now. And maybe we were what we were then so you could help Paul and me with this now."

"If you and Paul need my sperm, you can have it. But not like this. We can go to a doctor. I mean, Jesus, Alice, look at what you're doing here."

She sits up on the bed, flushed and angry. "I've been going to doctors for two years, Judd. That's two years of needles and hormones and specialist after specialist. Do you have any idea how exhausting that is? I've been peeing on sticks and crying myself to sleep for two years. All Paul has to do is come home and screw me when I'm ovulating, and half the time he can't be bothered to do that. He actually smoked weed today." She starts to cry. "He knew I was ovulating and he came home stoned."

"Hey, it'll be okay." I could never resist a crying girl. I don't know what that says about me, but it's probably not something good. I reach out to touch her shoulder, and she takes my hand, cradling it against her breasts, which seem to be drawing all of the light in the dim basement. "Please, Judd," she whispers. Then, never taking her eyes from mine, she shimmies her way down the bed, dragging the waistband of my boxers down to my knees. Her tears are warm against my thighs. "Please."

She pulls up her dress, and I catch a glimpse of a dark thatch of pubic hair just before she grabs hold of my shamefully hard cock like a stick shift and straddles me.

"Alice. No."

And then she slides me into her, and she is drenched in there, probably from all that estrogen she's taking, and I haven't had sex in a very long time and as soon as her weight settles on me and she starts to move, I explode inside of her. She squeezes me between her thighs, rocking gently on me, her hand pressed down on my chest for support. After a moment, she tucks her breasts back into her dress and then leans forward to plant a quick, soft kiss on my lips. "Thank you," she says. "Our little secret."

Down below, I slide out of her with a soft, guilty plop.

2:00 p.m.

I FALL IN love twice on the way to meeting Jen over at the Marriott for a drink. The first time it's a girl walking her dog. She's wearing white shorts and a tank top that hangs just high enough to reveal a tan swatch of flat belly, and she's got mussed blond hair and great skin, but beyond that, she just seems cool and laid-back; a dog person, but not one of those intense dog people who French-kiss their dogs and have their pictures in their wallets and buy them birthday cards. Her dog is some kind of terrier, and if I asked her, she would tell me that he's a mutt, and how the minute she saw him at the shelter, she knew she would be taking him home. She's laughing into her cell phone, nice white teeth, and even though I can't hear the laugh, I know if I did, I'd like it. She looks like someone who doesn't sweat the small stuff, who would be happy going for pizza and a movie or just taking a long walk before going home and climbing into bed. The dog will not sleep with us, because the noise of our lovemaking riles him up—she may be just this side of reserved in a crowd, but in bed her sexuality flows uninhibited. And when we're done, lying sweaty and spent on the damp, twisted wreckage of our sheets, she entertains me with stories of her experimental lesbian phase in college, before padding naked into her studio to work on the latest book cover she's been commissioned to design, because she's a much sought-after graphic artist and she has deadlines to meet.

The second woman is in the car next to mine at a traffic light. She's dark-skinned, with long black hair and eyes the color of coal, and she's drumming on her steering wheel and singing along to whatever's on her radio. When she sees me watching, her sheepish grin is warm and direct, and I can tell that she's one of the nicest people you'll ever meet, fun and approachable and never a bad word to say about anyone. In fact, the only times we'll argue is when I'm trying to convince her that someone is a real asshole and she just won't see it. It will frustrate me, but then she'll smile and I'll remember why I'm with her, what a good and generous soul she has, and how she makes me a better person and how all of my friends are in love with her, and how good she is to my child, how she sings off-key in the shower, making up silly lyrics when she doesn't know the real ones, and how, when I'm feeling down, she wraps her arms around me from behind in bed and runs her lips over my shoulders, humming lightly into my skin until I've decompressed.

Then the light changes and she's gone, just like the dog-loving graphic artist before her, both of them headed back to sexy, softly lit, uncomplicated lives. And me? I'm mourning my father and having sex with my sister-in-law and falling in love with strangers on the way to see the wife who slept with my boss and is now simultaneously divorcing me and having my baby. I feel like the driver who spends that extra second fussing with his cell phone and looks up just in time to see the front of his car crash through the guardrail and drive off the cliff.

2:17 p.m.

THERE ARE DARK shadows under Jen's bloodshot eyes, and she nervously stirs her glass of ginger ale in the Clubhouse Grille, situated in a recessed portion of the hotel lobby. The only other patrons are a group of flight attendants a few tables over, laughing and drinking in their blue uniforms, their little suitcases lined up like sentries. There is a wedding this evening at the Marriott, and the lobby hums with industry as vendors scurry around in a state of controlled chaos. Party planners streak past, speaking urgently into headsets; flowers are carried through on trays; skinny kids dressed all in black tear silently across the floor in their sneakers like slacker ninjas, carrying bulky photographic equipment. Jen is nauseous and exhausted and wants to talk about our marriage.

"Yesterday was the first time you've asked me anything related to us," she says.

"We don't talk very often."

"I know. But we're going to be parents, Judd, and I think we're going to have to get better at talking to each other."

"So this baby is your free pass, is that it?"

She offers a wan grin. "I know it sucks, but yes. You're going to have to come to some kind of terms with me so that we can work together here."

"Maybe I don't want to work with you."

She puts down her glass and looks at me. "What does that mean, exactly?"

"I didn't want this baby. I once wanted a baby with you, but that was before I knew who you really were. Our dead baby was the one I wanted. This baby . . . doesn't feel real to me. It doesn't feel like mine any more than you do."

Jen studies her drink for a long time, and when she looks back up at me, her eyes are filled with tears. For an instant I flash to Alice's tears, dripping down her face and onto my belly, but I banish the memory before it can make me too queasy. One train wreck at a time, I always say.

"I think that may be the ugliest thing you've ever said to me."

"You wanted me to talk about it. I'm talking."

I don't remember what I just said, and I have no idea if I even meant it. I just know I wanted it to hurt. In the day or so I've known the baby is mine, I have managed to avoid doing any concrete thinking about it. It's still completely unreal to me, but if I said that to Jen, she would nod sympathetically and keep talking about being parents together, and I've got a splitting headache as it is. The fragments of my fractured life are spinning in my head like a buzz saw, and I feel moments away from coming apart in a very real and permanent way.

"Do you want to know why I started seeing Wade?" Jen says softly.

I consider it for a moment. "Not really, no."

"When our baby died, I was grieving. I needed to mourn him. You acted like everything was fine. Well, maybe not fine, but not so far from it. No big deal, Jen, we'll just make another one."

"You're exaggerating."

"Not by a lot."

"So you worked through your grief by having sex with Wade."

One of the ninjas drops a steel pole, which rolls thunderously across the marble floor. Jen jumps. The kid curses and picks up the pole. A party planner materializes to admonish him, somewhat severely, I think.

Jen looks intently at me. "You had stopped looking at me, stopped touching me. It was like I had failed you, failed to keep our baby safe, and until we had a new baby, I had nothing to offer you. You lost sight of me."

"That's not true."

"You wouldn't hold me, or cry with me. You just looked away and talked about how it would all be fine, how we'd try again when I was ready."

"I was trying to reassure you. I knew how much having a baby meant to you."

"You may not have meant to make me feel that way, but it was how I felt. And I guess, as wrong as it was—and I know it was wrong—Wade was someone I hadn't disappointed. He wanted me, and it had nothing to do with a baby. And that made him appealing."

I consider what she's saying, try to place myself back there, in those days after she'd delivered our strangled baby, but that time has become a dark blur, and I can't recall very much about it. "You never said anything to me."

"We were in such different places. I was grieving our dead child."

"So was I."

"You were looking at the calendar, asking the doctors when we could try again. You say you were trying to reassure me, and that's probably true. But to me, right then, it felt like you were moving on, leaving me behind. And somewhere along the way, you stopped seeing me as your wife; you just saw me as the mother of your dead and maybe future child." She clasps her hands together, shakes her head, and offers up a sad little smile. "It's tragic, really, when you think about it. I needed you to see me as your wife and all you could see was the failed mother. And now I need you to see me as the mother of your child, and all you can see is the failed wife."

"You've thought about this a lot."

"I don't get out much."

"You should have told me."

"I did. You didn't hear me."

"You should have kept telling me until I did. I would have eventually."

"Maybe you're right."

"We could have fixed this!" I am suddenly, violently furious. "We could have fixed it. But you gave up. You found someone else before I even knew anything was wrong. This could have been our baby."

"It's still our baby. You and me."

"There is no you and me," I say, getting up to leave. "We are strangers. And I don't see how I can raise a child with a stranger."

"Judd," she says, beseeching. "We're finally talking. Please sit down."

I can sense the flight attendants shutting up to tune in to the little drama playing out in their midst. I take a long, last look at Jen, at her tired eyes, her desperate expression.

"I can't do this."

"Please don't leave," she says, but I'm already moving, weaving through the tables to get out of there. The last thing I hear her say is "This isn't going to go away." And it's that very fact, obvious though it may be, that squeezes the air from my lungs and makes me run. Because, more than anything, what I want is for it to go away. I am not ready to be a father. I have nothing to offer: no wisdom, no expertise, no home, no job, no wife. If I wanted to adopt a child, I wouldn't even qualify. What I've got is a great big bag of nothing, and no kid will respect a father like that. This was my chance to start over, to find someone who would defy the odds and love me, to figure out the rest of my life. Now any chance of a clean break is gone, and as a single father I have become, by default, even more pathetic.

I'm heading down a wide, carpeted hallway toward the parking lot when my legs give out on me. I stumble against the wall and slide down until I'm sitting on the floor. A group of tuxedoed guys in their early twenties emerge from a conference room, bustling with nervous energy. They pass around a silver flask and smack each other a lot; the groom and his groomsmen. The groom is differentiated with tails and a white tie. He's in his early twenties, handsome in an almost pretty way, his face scrubbed, his hair gelled. The groomsmen file into another room at the behest of the photographer, who is ready to shoot the wedding party, and for a moment it's just the groom and me in the hall. Our eyes meet and he smiles a greeting.

"You okay, bro?" he says, brimming with benevolence and goodwill.

"Yeah," I say. "Good luck."

"Thanks. I'm going to need it."

"You have no idea."

I am not real to him. This is his wedding day, and nothing is real to him. And I am in mourning, and in shock, and he is not real to me. We are ghosts, passing each other in a haunted house, and it's hard to say who pities whom more. He straightens his tie and heads back into the conference room to record his cocky naïveté for posterity, and I get up on shaky feet and walk out to the parking lot.

4:40 p.m.

I MAKE THE two-hour drive back to Kingston, to the house Jen and I used to share. I let myself in through the front door, like I do from time to time when I know she and Wade aren't around. If I had a shrink, he would ask me why I feel the need to burglarize my former home, and I would tell him the same thing I'm telling you: I have no idea. I just know that sometimes, without any premeditation, I go there and poke around. Technically, the house is still half-mine, and if Jen truly didn't want me there, she'd have changed the locks, or at least the alarm code.

I let myself into the front hall, taking note of the mail table that no longer has the picture of Jen and me on it. The kitchen is unchanged, except for the fridge door, which no longer has the pictures of Jen and me at Martha's Vineyard or the old black and white of me from college that she always loved, sitting on a railing in my Bob Marley hat, smiling at her as she snapped the photo. There are no photos anywhere of her and Wade, which I'd like to read as a sign that she's not that invested yet, but when you've been carrying on a yearlong illicit affair, there just aren't a lot of photo ops.

I climb the stairs and swing open the door to our bedroom, the scene of the crime. There's the bed, there's the reading chair, there's the dresser, the mirror, nothing to indicate that this was any kind of marital ground zero. I walk over to my old dresser and pull open a random drawer. Inside are a handful of Wade's boxer shorts and undershirts and a pile of dark socks. The drawer beneath it has a selection of polo shirts and T-shirts. In the closet, there are a few pairs of jeans and two suits. From what I can tell, Wade has moved in the essentials, but not everything. He's still keeping his own place. I pull out the trousers from his suits and then go into the medicine chest for a pair of tweezers. I grab a six-pack of his beer from the fridge and take it with me to the den, where I watch *Mad Max* without sound on the plasma television while gently pulling the stitches out of his pant seams, leaving just enough to hold the pants together, so that they won't fall apart until he moves around in them a little, preferably at work, in front of a large crowd. After I put the pants back, I open the night table drawer. There's a bill-fold with a few hundred-dollar bills, a prescription bottle that says naproxen but that I know from past visits contains his Viagra stash, a checkbook, some loose change, receipts, a *Sports Illustrated*, a cell phone charger, and the spare key to his Maserati. I pocket the Viagra and three hundred dollars.

Down in the basement there's a carton full of our old photo albums. I pull one out and flip through it. Our trip to the Caribbean a few years ago, in the aftermath of our dead baby; a two-week consolation prize. We splurged on a private villa. There was the beach, a pool, a water slide, and a casino. We made a rule: no talking about the baby, about home, about anything of consequence. We lay on the sand for hours, baking in the sun, staring out at the blue water until we could see it with our eyes closed. We read our novels and retained nothing. The sun turned our brains to Jell-O. Jen bought some new bikinis that showed off her tan and let a fat native woman braid her hair in cornrows like Bo Derek's. In the evenings, we would have sex before dinner, urgently and desper-ately, bruising our groins, kissing our lips raw.

There was another couple, Ray and Tina from Chicago, on honey-moon for their second marriage. Ray had a Chrysler dealership. Tina had big hair, a pierced navel, and store-bought fingernails. She'd been his secretary for years. You didn't need much of an imagination to guess what had ended his first marriage. We all went on a midnight cruise, getting drunk on red rum drinks. There was a reggae band and we tried to dance but it's hard to dance to reggae unless you're very stoned. Ray stared at Jen's tight ass. Tina was shorter and a little bottom heavy, but she had these sexy bee-stung lips and she grazed my arms with her fake nails when she talked. Ray and I got drunk and he confided in me that he'd give anything to have sex with someone who looked like Jen. We joked about swapping for the night. Back in our villa, Jen and I made fun—but not in a mean way—of Ray's Tom Selleck mustache and thick gold necklace, of Tina's nails and that she wore heels to the beach.

After they went back to Chicago, we felt the silence between us even more. We read, we swam, we lay out on the beach, watching happier people. I went parasailing one day, and Jen rode in the speedboat, taking pictures of me in the sky. A day later, Jen was bitten by something in the ocean and her knee swelled up like a balloon. By the time we flew home, we could barely look at each other. Was she already seeing him then? Or maybe not yet seeing him, but flirting with him? Already redrafting the boundaries of her life? When, exactly, did she cross that line and stop being mine? The only thing more painful than not knowing would be knowing. Having to go back to every picture in every album and stamp it real or a lie. I don't have the stomach for it.

In the back of the album there's a single orphaned photo out of its sleeve, and I recognize it from our honeymoon in Anguilla: Jen in a pool—looking seductively at the camera while, in the background, whitecaps dapple the blue ocean. It's one of those accidentally perfect pictures you take, when the sun is just where it needs to be, and the focus is perfect, and you've caught your subject at her absolute best. I look at the photo for a long time, at Jen when she was still Jen, when we were still us. I put the album back in the box and make it as far as the second stair before turning around and pulling it back out.

Back in the car, I place the photo faceup on the passenger seat, where it stays for the drive back to Elmsbrook. I couldn't begin to tell you why.

7:45 p.m.

HOME, FOR LACK of a better word, or option. Fireflies flicker and glow in front of my windshield as dusk thickens into another humid summer night on Knob's End. I can smell barbecue. I follow the sounds of voices around to the backyard. Everyone is gathered on the patio eating, while Barry mans the grill. Wendy is sprawled on a lounge chair with Cole asleep on her chest. Everyone else is at the table, eating burgers and minute steaks, dipping chips and washing them down with Diet Coke. Paul is pitching a wiffle ball to Ryan, who whacks every third pitch or so. Horry plays the field while Phillip stands off to the side, providing the play-by-play through cupped hands. *"The pitch . . . Oh, he got a piece of that one, it's going deep, sending Callen to the warning track. That ball is out of here! Ryan Hollis's two thousandth career home run. The crowd goes wild. You know he'll be getting some tonight, Bill . . ."*

Mom and Linda are at the head of the table, sipping chardonnay out of plastic wineglasses and playing Rummykub. Alice sits with them, idly reading the weekend paper. I stand around the corner of the house, watching these people, these strangers, this family of mine, and I have never felt more lost and alone. My cell phone vibrates softly in my pocket, and I step back around the house to answer it.

"Hey," Penny says. "Want to go to a movie?"

My last trip to the movies didn't work out so well. It was a few weeks after I'd moved into the Lees' basement, and I could feel the walls closing in. So I took myself to the movies. Back when I lived with Jen, I had some friends. In the aftermath of our separation, Allan and Mike had met me for drinks and we'd all raised our glasses in agreement that Jen was a cheating bitch and I was the good guy here. I didn't know it at the time, but that night was actually my good-bye party. Jen would retain custody of our friends and I'd be wordlessly discarded. A few weeks later, as I circled the multiplex parking lot, I saw Allan and Mike with their wives, leaving the theater along with Jen and Wade, all walking in standard formation, talking and laughing in the cinematic afterglow, like it had always been just so. I tried to tell myself it was simply a chance encounter, but it was clear from their body language that they were all together, and probably not for the first time. It's a sad moment when you come to understand how truly replaceable you are. Friendship in the suburbs is wife-driven, and my friends were essentially those husbands of Jen's friends that I could most tolerate. Now that I'd been sidelined, Wade had stepped in for me like an understudy, a small note was inserted into the program, and the show went on without missing a beat.

8:30 p.m.

THE WRITER IS pretty, beautiful even, but in a toned-down way; neurotic and accessible. She kisses her fiancé good-bye in their beautifully cluttered apartment and travels to a comically unpronounceable seaside village in Scotland to do a story for the travel magazine she writes for. There she falls for a local widower who trains sheepdogs. The townsfolk are kindly eccentrics, the widower is rugged and built like an Olympic swimmer, and we forgive the ingénue her dalliance, since her eyes well up so beautifully when she talks about her recently deceased sister, and also because her fiancé is a cad who flirted with his sexpot secretary in the opening scene and likes his red sports car a little too much.

Penny and I sit in the back row, holding hands. She softly runs the fingers of her free hand up and down the inside of my forearm, playing with the short hairs on my wrist. I lean my head against hers, and we're seventeen again. We make out for a while, our tongues cool and sugary from the soda, and I never want the movie to end, not because it feels so good, although it certainly does—Penny kisses with passion and depth and just the right amount of tongue—but because when the movie ends the house lights will come back up, and real life will materialize around us like hidden creatures in the horror movie we should have gone to instead.

And even as we kiss, my hand now under the hem of her short skirt, rubbing her smooth thighs, her fingers in my hair as her tongue dances across my lower lip, I am aware of the on-screen plot resolving itself. The fiancé has shown up unannounced, there's some kind of sheepdog festival, a chase through a crowded farmers' market on motor scooters. The fiancé rides his scooter off an embankment and into the duck pond. Happily-ever-after is just a dramatic gesture and a heartfelt speech away. We stop making out and tune in for the last ten minutes. The girl is at the airport, alone, having broken it off with the fiancé, but too late to save her relationship with the widower. But here he comes, zipping through the airport on a stolen luggage cart. He delivers a loud speech about what he's learned about grief and love and second chances, proclaiming his love even as the cops handcuff him. Somehow, his trusty dog is there too, along with half the village, who have all had a hand in bringing him here to stop her from leaving. She kisses him while he's still handcuffed, and so he falls over and they kiss some more on the floor. Next to me, Penny sniffles at the happy ending. Then she leans over, takes my earlobe between her teeth, and says, "Take me home."

10:45 p.m.

PENNY LIVES IN a ground-floor apartment in a complex downtown, just a few blocks from Dad's store. There are framed movie posters on the walls—Audrey Hepburn, Marilyn Monroe, Julia Roberts—and not very much in the way of furniture: a mucous-green leather couch that she must have gotten a deal on because no one would choose that color in a vacuum. There's no matching love seat, which I find somewhat symbolic. A fat cat with yellow demon eyes is curled up on the couch, and the potpourri scattered in little bowls around the room almost manages to cover the smell of the unseen litter-box.

I'm nervous, the kind of nervous that leads to flop sweat and flaccidity. Too late I remember the Viagra I stole from Wade, now sitting worthlessly in my glove compartment. I have not had sex with a woman other than Jen in over ten years, if you don't count my bizarre sixty seconds with Alice earlier today, and you'd better believe I'm not counting it. I'm treating it like a dream or a UFO sighting, something maybe you'll talk about one day when you're drunk and among friends, but nothing that has any bearing on your actual life. But when your wife spent the last year of your marriage going elsewhere for her sexual gratification, it's only natural to have some performance anxiety.

Penny steps into the apartment, tossing keys and flipping off lights. I stand uncertainly in the doorway, my thighs trembling a little. I can feel all the crap I ate at the theater burrowing through my intestines, making me feel bloated and queasy. "Should I come in?" I say. My voice sounds hollow and scared.

She gives me a sharp, knowing smile. "If I were you, I would."

The bedroom is a mess, clothes everywhere, towels draped over an armchair to dry. Penny undresses in the light of the desk lamp, not sultry, not like a stripper, but the same way she would if I wasn't here, letting her clothing fall where she stands. She presents herself to me, her body lithe and smooth, breasts full and buoyant on her too-thin frame. I am self-conscious about my own soft body, with its budding love handles and lack of abdominal definition, but she doesn't seem to mind, kissing my thighs as she pulls down my pants and then falling down onto the bed with me, licking her way up my belly to my chin and then into my mouth. "You taste good," she murmurs. I worry that I have bad breath, that my ass will feel flabby in her hands when she grabs it, that I'm rubbing her breasts like a high school kid, that my dick won't get hard enough, that it won't measure up to other dicks she's seen, that I'll come too soon, that she won't come at all. I should go down on her, just to make sure she gets something out of the deal, but I'm intimidated by the thought of an uncharted vagina, terrified that after a few minutes of fruitless exploration she'll gently pull me back up by my ears and tell me it's okay when we both know it's not, that it felt good anyway when we both know it didn't.

The sex is as good and bad as first times tend to be, like a play rehearsal full of missed marks, botched lines, bad lighting, and no calls for an encore. We don't do it up against the wall, on the kitchen sink, in the shower, from behind while she's bent over the bed. It's just paint-by-numbers missionary sex: kiss, rub, lick, stroke, enter, rock, moan, and come, all at the proper time. I'm playing scared, letting her set the rhythm, trying my best to banish the image of Wade humping Jen that hovers in the background of my mind. Thanks in part to my earlier release with Alice, I'm able to hold out until Penny finishes, gasping and digging her teeth into my chin hard enough to leave a mark. And it occurs to me, as I surrender to my own somewhat subdued orgasm, that I've come twice today, and as sad and twisted as each occasion was, both involved actual, live women, one on top of me, and one beneath me, and maybe that's a cause for some small measure of optimism, even if we're not counting Alice. Which we're not.

When we're done, I roll off of Penny, feeling ridiculously accomplished and wondering how soon I can leave.

"That was nice," Penny says drowsily, throwing a leg over mine, splaying out her fingers against my chest.

"Okay. Give it to me straight," I say. "I can take it."

"What are you talking about?"

"Why did my wife need to have sex with someone else?"

"Because she's an evil bitch."

"Come on. Really."

Penny lies back on her pillow and removes her leg from mine. I grab it and put it back. I like it there. "In my limited experience, women rarely leave because the sex is bad. The sex becomes bad because something else has gone wrong."

"Really?"

"Nah. He probably just has a world-class schlong."

"Yeah, that's what I was thinking."

Penny laughs. "Judd Foxman. Naked in my bed. This is beyond surreal."

"Surreal is my new reality."

She kisses both my eyes and wraps her arms around me in a way that brings me dangerously close to tears. I should tell her about the baby. It's on the tip of my tongue.

"Judd Foxman."

"What?"

"Nothing. I just like to say your name."

Penny pulls me closer and burrows her head into the hollow of my neck, lazily repeating my name a few more times as she drifts off to sleep. I open my mouth to say any number of things, but in the end I just lie there, telling myself that no one can feel this disconnected forever.

11:30 p.m.

WENDY AND BARRY are standing on the front walk, having an argument. Wendy gesticulates wildly while Barry stands there absorbing it, swatting away gnats as he waits her out. I wonder, as I often do, why they stay together, what it is they offer each other that keeps them locked in this bloodless stalemate. But I suppose if I understood anything about marriage, I'd have understood my own a little bit better.

"I'm sorry, babe, it's the eleventh hour," Barry is saying. "I need to be there to close this deal now, or it's all going to go up in smoke."

"You've had a death in the family. Can't they understand that?"

"Yes, but I can't be gone for seven days. They need me there."

"And what about your family? We need you too."

"I'm doing this for my family."

"Right. That old load of crap."

They fall silent when I step out of the car.

"Where the hell have you been?" Wendy says.

"Clearing my head."

"You didn't tell anyone where you were going."

"There's actually a good reason for that."

"What?"

"I didn't want to."

Barry snickers. Dumb move. Wendy turns on him with a baleful stare, and I use the distraction to slide past them and into the house.

Mom and Linda are in the living room, playing Scrabble at the coffee table and drinking tea. Paul, Alice, and Tracy are on the couch watching Jon Stewart, while Phillip sits on the floor, thumbing through a shoebox of old photos. They all look up at me. Alice smiles, but I can't look at her, can't be anywhere near her. The monitor in the hall is broadcasting Serena's cries in stereo. No one seems terribly concerned.

"Where have you been?" Mom says.

"Out and about."

"Don't be evasive. Just say you'd rather not tell me."

"I'd rather not tell you."

"But now you have me curious. Did you see Jen today?"

"Yeah."

"And . . . ?"

"And now I'm going to bed."

Alice flashes me a meaningful look, and I try to remember if there's a lock on the basement door.

"Look at this picture," Phillip says.

I squat down to see the photo he's holding. I'm around eleven, Paul twelve, and Phillip is two years old. Paul and I are throwing him to each other, playing catch with our little brother in this very living room, twentysomething years ago. Phillip loved that, would laugh hysterically, his eyes wide with excitement as we launched him airborne at each other. *Pay catch, Yudd. Pay catch, Pole.* We are all smiling in the picture, three brothers having a grand old time just playing around in the living room, no agendas, no buried resentments or permanent scars. Even under the best of circumstances, there's just something so damn tragic about growing up.

"Look here," Phillip says, pointing to the corner of the photo. "In the breakfront."

The breakfront has two sets of glass doors, behind which Mom keeps her crystal glasses and the good china.

"I don't see anything."

"Look at the glass on the last door."

I stare at the picture and then, just as I'm about to give up, I see it, a reflection in the glass, a face and arms. Dad, watching us from off camera, smiling widely as Phillip flies between us. The breakfront still stands against the living room wall, and I look into the glass doors a moment. When I look back down Phillip is smiling at me.

"I did the same thing."

"He's like a ghost," I say.

"Last night I woke up and thought I saw him walking out of the study," Phillip says. When Phillip was little, he would put on his toy tool belt and stand beside Dad as he fixed things in the house. "The compressor is shot," he would repeat solemnly, brimming with self-importance. He was a very cute kid, and I can remember how much we all adored him, how even then, I hated the fact that he had to grow older.

The baby is still crying her little lungs out upstairs. I lean forward to tousle Phillip's hair. "I'm going to go check on that baby."

"They're letting her cry," Mom says.

"That doesn't make it right."

Phillip watches me as I stand back up and head for the stairs.

"Judd."

"Yeah."

He grins. "You smell like pussy."

11:40 p.m.

Serena stops crying the instant I pick her up. Her head is bald like an old man's, with just a ring of dark hair around the perimeter. She feels almost weightless against my chest in her little pink pajamas. "It's okay," I say softly, and make other idiotic sounds like you do when you're holding a baby. Her tiny fingers find my chin and she latches on with a surprisingly strong grip, like my chin will save her life, like my chin is exactly what she was crying out for. I sit down on the bed, cradling her little head against my shoulder, inhaling her sweet baby scent. Someday she'll get older, and the world will start having its way with her. She'll throw temper tantrums, she'll need speech therapy, she'll grow breasts and have pimples, she'll fight with her parents, she'll worry about her weight, she'll put out, she'll have her heart broken, she'll be happy, she'll be lonely, she'll be complicated, she'll be confused, she'll be depressed, she'll fall in love and get married, and she'll have a baby of her own. But right now she is pure and undiminished and beautiful. I lie back on the bed as she sleeps on my chest, listening to her tiny little snores, admiring the soft nub of her unformed nose, the sucking blister on her upturned lip. After a few minutes, when her breathing becomes almost imperceptible, I gently lay her down in the crib and head back downstairs. I crawl under my covers and drift off to sleep, still feeling the warm spot where she lay on my chest.

Sunday

Chapter 32

5:20 a.m.

Dad is bent over me, fixing my wooden leg with a socket wrench. I'm on a chair and he's on his knees in front of me, turning the wrench and humming Simon and Garfunkel. *I'd rather be a hammer than a nail. Yes I would.* I can see through his curly, gray hair to where it's thinning at his pink scalp, can smell the grease on him, can smell the detergent coming off his favorite blue work shirt. The socket wrench clicks noisily as it spins, and I can see the long muscles in his forearms flex and move as he turns it. He has spent his life working with tools, and they fit naturally into his hands. I'm staring down at him, knowing that I can't tell him that he's dead, that if I do he'll disappear. I want him to look up at me, want to see his face, but he is focused on the leg and he doesn't look up. "Almost there," he says. Then he puts down the socket wrench and grabs on to my knee with both hands. "Here we go," he says. He pulls on the prosthesis, which slides off my knee and splits down the middle, and his hands come away with one half of it in each, and there is my real leg again, hairless and pink, but whole and unharmed. Then he looks up at me and smiles widely, like he might have smiled at me when I was a little boy, like he never did once I was older, a warm and loving smile, uncomplicated by my own encroaching manhood, and the love surging between us is electric and palpable. When I wake up I squeeze my eyes shut, trying to escape the dim silence of the basement to find him again, but there's only darkness and the sad, steady whisper of the central air handler behind the wall, telling its mechanical secrets in the dark.

Chapter 33

5:38 a.m.

Up on top of the house. Looking over miles of roof; slate, concrete, copper, clay, all bathed in the pink glow of the sun rising over Elmsbrook. There's a bird, maybe a cardinal, maybe a robin, I don't know, it has a red chest. It's chirping in the branch of a tree of equally uncertain nomenclature. Elm, or oak, or ash. I think I used to know things like that, the names of birds and trees. Now it feels like I don't know much about anything. I don't know why planes fly, and what causes lightning, and what it means to short a stock, and the difference between the Shiites and Sunnis, and who's slaughtering whom in Darfur, and why the U.S. dollar is so weak, and why the American League is so much better than the National League. I don't know how Jen and I became strangers in our own marriage, how we let something that should have brought us closer derail us like a couple of amateurs. We were two reasonably smart people in love with each other, and then, one day we were less so, and maybe we were headed here anyway, maybe she just got there first, because she felt the loss of our baby more acutely. For a moment, a feeling circles me, something approaching clarity, maybe even acceptance, but it fails to settle and ultimately dissipates.

I think about Jen. I think about Penny. I could probably have something with Penny, but I'd still be thinking of Jen. I could maybe try to win

Jen back, but I'd still be thinking of Wade. And so would she. He'd be a ghost, haunting our bed every time we touched. So what do I do?

There are just too many things I don't know.

The girl in last night's movie saw the way the sheepdog trainer carried his injured daughter and she just knew, beyond a shadow of a doubt, that nothing mattered more than being with him. She knew. But she wasn't a real person, that girl, she was an actress with an eating disorder who was charged with DUI last year and who slept with her married director just long enough to wreck his life before falling out of love and off the wagon. That's love in real life: messy and corrupt and completely unreliable. I like Penny, and I still love Jen, and I hate Jen and I couldn't leave Penny's sad little apartment fast enough. I want someone who will love me and touch me and understand me and let me take care of them, but beyond that, I don't know.

I just don't know.

There's a scraping sound behind me, and Wendy climbs onto the roof, still groggy with sleep.

"Hey there."

"Good morning."

She stands beside me and reaches into the chimney for a second, her hand emerging with a box of Marlboros and a lighter. "Want one?"

"No, thanks."

"Mind if I do?"

I don't answer because it wouldn't matter. You can't let your dog crap on the sidewalk, but it's perfectly acceptable to blow carcinogens down other people's throats. Somewhere along the way, smokers exempted themselves from the social contract.

Wendy lights up, inhaling so deeply that I can picture her lungs inflating and darkening with smoke. "So, Barry's getting the hell out of Dodge."

"Where to?"

"Everywhere. California, Chicago, London. His fund took a big hit last year with the whole subprime thing, and I say that with no actual concept of what the whole subprime thing actually is. But apparently everything depends on getting this deal done."

"Are you worried?"

She shrugs. "It's Barry. This is what he does. If I worried, that would defeat the whole purpose of being married to him." She takes another drag on her cigarette. "So, you slept with Jen last night?"

"Penny."

"Oh! Good for you. Right?"

"I feel like I'll never be able to have sex with someone new without thinking the whole time about the fact that I'm having sex with someone new."

Wendy shrugs. "You'll get over it."

From below comes the sound of the front door closing, and a moment later Linda crosses the front yard. She stops on the sidewalk and turns her face up to the sky, letting the morning breeze kiss her face, before heading down the block toward her house.

"She's here early," Wendy muses.

"She's here late," I say.

"Oh," Wendy says. Then, "Oh! No!"

"Exactly."

"No way! You think?"

"Nothing surprises me anymore."

A quiet moment while Wendy processes the new information.

"It kind of makes sense, a little," she says.

"Kind of."

"If so, how do we feel about it?"

"We are numb."

Wendy considers that for a moment, tapping her lip with the end of her cigarette. "Yes. That's a perfect description of what we are."

The bird that may or may not be a cardinal or a robin takes flight, swooping down toward the backyard to catch the air pocket that will take her to the next tree. It would be nice to be able to do that, I think. To just pick up from wherever you were that wasn't working out for you and ride the winds to a better place. I'd be in Australia by now.

"You slept with Horry."

"He told you?"

"I was up here yesterday morning too. Saw you do the walk of shame."

She shrugs. "It's no big deal."

"It's adultery."

Wendy raises her eyebrows at me, biting back whatever it was she was prepared to say, a rare display of restraint. We are perched on a roof and you can't be too careful.

"Horry is grandfathered in."

"Is that how it works?"

"That's how it works."

"That makes half of your graduating class eligible."

She laughs and stubs out her cigarette on a roof shingle. "In an alternate universe where Horry didn't get his brains bashed in, he and I are married. Once in a blue moon I get to visit that universe."

"And it's really that simple."

"My alternate universe, my rules."

Behind and below us, the back door slams. We turn around to look down into the backyard. Tracy is standing at the head of the pool in a black one-piece bathing suit. Her dive is flawless, her stroke strong and graceful. She swims back and forth with machinelike precision, doing those little somersaults against the wall at each end like she's in the Olympics. I get tired just looking at her.

"Poor thing," Wendy says.

Tracy slices through the water like a shark, and Wendy and I watch her from our perch above the world, unaccustomed to such grace and discipline. I think, not for the first time, that she deserves better than Phillip, better than this family of ours. Someone should save her from us while there's still time.

Chapter 34

10:13 a.m.

There are tricks to paying a shiva call. You don't want to come during off-peak hours, or you risk being the only one there, face-to-face with five surly mourners who, but for your presence, would be off their low chairs, stretching their legs and their compressed spines, taking a bathroom break, or having a snack. Evenings are your safest bet, after seven, when everyone's eaten and the room is full. Weekday afternoons are a dead zone. Sunday is a crapshoot. Do a drive-by and count the parked cars before you stop. If you're lucky, there will already be a conversation going on when you come in, so you won't have to sit there trying to start one of your own. It's hard to talk to the bereft. You never know what's off-limits.

And speaking of limits, there apparently aren't any when it comes to Mom's slinky wardrobe. The old expression goes, a good speech is like a woman's skirt: short enough to hold your attention, long enough to cover the subject. Mom's short denim skirt isn't a speech, it's more like a quick, dirty joke, the kind people are always e-mailing to you. And she's wearing a tight black camisole with spaghetti straps. She looks like a retired stripper.

You would think everyone we know has already been over, but apparently not. The shiva calls start bright and early, people wanting to get their obligations over with in time to enjoy one of the last warm Sundays of the season. They sit visiting with us like they've got all the time in the world, while their golf clubs, tennis rackets, and swimsuits lie waiting for them in the trunks of their cars.

Boner shows up with a group of Paul's old buddies, all ex-jocks. They talk about the Yankees and the Mets and their fantasy baseball league, while their wives sit quietly beside them with looks of bored indulgence. *Better baseball than mistresses and hookers*, their expressions say. Boner is in jeans, a T-shirt, and flip-flops, every inch the cool rabbi off duty. His wife, Emily, is pretty and quiet, with nervous eyes and a flickering smile that never quite achieves ignition. The other guys have this running joke of apologizing to him every time they swear or say something off-color, which is pretty much every other minute. You can tell he'd like to swear a blue streak right back at them, but he is surrounded by his congregants, and it would be bad for business.

"Hey, Judd," Dan Reiss says to me. "How are things with Wade Boulanger?"

"What?"

"*Man Up*. Don't you work on the show?"

"Not anymore."

"That's too bad. I love that guy." He contorts his face and says, "Man up already!" in a hoarse, nasal voice.

"That's a good impression."

"You think?"

"Sure."

"What's he like off the air?"

"He's an asshole."

"Well, yeah. But is he a good guy?"

They talk about high school, relive their greatest triumphs on the baseball field. Everyone is careful not to mention college, but the specter of Paul's injury looms large over the conversation. Their very avoidance of the topic is reminder enough, like the puffy scar that snakes up the

side of his neck. You can see the muscles tightening in his face, the taut-
ness of his lips in their neutral position. His life is a daily reminder of the
life he might have had. I feel a surge of pity and tenderness toward him.
I want to tell him that I understand, that I forgive him for being such a
total prick to me.

I think about making a list of all the things I need to tell people before it's too late.

10:32 a.m.

GREG POLLAN, AN old friend of mine from high school, comes by. Our
friendship was based almost entirely on our mutual admiration of Clint
Eastwood. We would talk to each other in Clint's tough-guy rasp, and if
we passed each other in the halls, we would squint and draw imagi-
nary .357 Magnums. *I know what you're thinking; did he fire six shots,
or only five? Go ahead, make my day.* At some point we moved on to
Sylvester Stallone. In high school, if you can find a girl who will kiss you
and maybe let you touch her breasts and a guy who likes the same movies as you, your world is pretty much complete. Now Greg is fat and
married and his eyes bulge in their sockets, threatening to pop out and
shoot across the room. Triplets, he tells me. A goiter. He is unshaven
and tired and he heard an old friend was sitting shiva in the neighborhood and made it his business to come. Even though he's exhausted and
probably could have used the time better just turning up the A.C. in his
car and closing his eyes. I try to imagine a situation in which I'd have
been equally decent.

"So, I hear you produce the Wade Boulanger show."

"Yeah."

"He's very funny."

"Sometimes."

"I could do without all the farting though."

"You and me both."

"My wife hates him."

"Mine loves him."

"She thinks he's a misogynist blowhard, calls him Rush Limbaugh with a boner."

"That's pretty accurate, I guess. What are you up to?"

"Well, I was doing risk assessment for a while, and now I'm kind of consulting, by which I mean I got laid off."

"I'm sorry to hear that."

"So now I take care of the girls—they're four—and Debbie sells medical supplies. Also, we have an Amway website. I'll leave you my card."

I wonder how he gets up in the morning.

He tells me about some of the other kids from our class he's kept tabs on. Mike Salerno is divorced and drives a Ferrari. Jared Mathers is gay, to the surprise of absolutely no one. Randy Sawyer owns a string of bowling alleys. Julie Mehler is a state senator. Sandy Flynn's house burned down, but they all got out. Gary Daley was arrested for having kiddie porn on his office computer. And so on. Judd Foxman's pregnant wife left him for a popular misogynist blowhard radio personality. As a one-line update, I fit in quite nicely, actually. Better than I ever did back in the day.

Greg gets up from his chair. His skin is cratered and sallow. There are sweat marks on his polo shirt, under his flouncing man-breasts. One or two other visitors have to move their chairs to accommodate his exit. At some point in time, Greg gave up on things and accepted his fate to spend the rest of his life fat and exhausted and dull as a butter knife.

"Great to see you," he says. His hand is thick and clammy.

"Thanks for coming, man. I appreciate it."

"You bet."

He lumbers out of the room with the unhurried gait of a circus elephant. He was once a funny kid, pleasant-faced and not repulsive. A certain type of girl liked him. I wonder if he remembers our Clint Eastwood and Stallone impressions, if he watches *Rambo* like I do when I come across it flipping through the cable channels late at night, when the world is spinning much too fast for me to sleep.

Chapter 35

11:22 a.m.

It's a day for reunions. Some old girlfriends of Wendy's show up. She hides her diamond rings and sits up straighter. She trots out her boys for a command performance of cuteness. Ryan sulks, but Cole obliges, letting the women lift him up, pointing out their ears and eyes. Ryan picks his nose and wipes it on his shorts. Everyone coos. Snapshots of children are passed around and exclaimed over. Everyone is adorable. Everyone is perfect. No one here has ever produced an ugly or even ordinary baby.

The women look each other over as they chat, measuring thighs, bellies, hips, and asses, taking into account body types and recent pregnancies. They silently evaluate and pass judgment, realigning themselves in the pecking order. It's a brutal business, being a woman. Wendy sucks in her gut and crosses her legs, pointing her toes like a ballerina in a last-ditch effort to coax her calf muscle out of hiding. She has our mother's legs, sheathed in thick, smooth skin that defies definition.

Someone procures an old yearbook and they all shriek like hyenas.

11:35 a.m.

PETER APPLEBAUM IS back to comfort my mother at close range. There are other people over, attempting to visit with her, but he doesn't register them. He is a hammer, she is a nail, and the rest of them are screws. He's had a haircut since we last saw him, almost military in its closeness, and he has shaved the dark, gangrenous fuzz off his earlobes. His cologne fills the room like bad news. He is pulling out all the stops, Applebaum is. He has not many more years of sexual function ahead of him, and there is no time for the subtlety of a slow flirtation. He pats Mom's arms, takes her hand in both of his, and strokes it relentlessly. That's just his way. Mom tries to draw some of the other visitors into the conversation, tries to retrieve her hand, but Applebaum holds the line, talking and stroking, his bushy eyebrows unfurling like caterpillars.

Linda steps out from the kitchen, her expression grim, and makes her way through the visitors. She whispers something into Applebaum's ear, and his expression falls, his face turning red. He follows Linda back into the kitchen while Mom looks on, somewhat concerned. Behind the swinging door, slightly raised voices are drowned out by the sound of the Cuisinart. A few moments later, Applebaum shuffles down the front hall, stooped and deflated, pausing just long enough to leave a few bills on the tip plate next to the memorial candle. I feel sorry for him. There is some basis for comparison between us, I think.

Linda reemerges at the kitchen door and she and my mother exchange a long, dense look over the heads of the shiva callers, decimating whatever lingering doubts I might have had. Wendy looks over at me, raising a drawn eyebrow into something like a question mark, but she's not really asking.

11:45 a.m.

SOME DISTANT RELATIVES have driven up from Long Island to pay their respects: my mother's first cousin Sandra, her husband, Calvin, and their twin teenage sex-kitten daughters. The girls are vacant and beautiful and wield their budding sexuality with a certain lack of control, like a toddler with a power tool. They stretch their long, ripe bodies out on the couch and look around the room with the dismayed air of the recently conned. It was a long way to come for a room full of irrelevant relatives.

There is an air of striving perfection about this family, evident in Sandra's expensive-looking haircut and pedicure, Cal's—for that's what they call him—diamond-encrusted watch and expensive polo shirt with a golf club logo, in the girls' smooth, tanned legs dipped into white canvas tennis shoes, their blown hair, their flawless complexions. This isn't a family, it's a Christmas card. You can picture the plush carpets of their home in Long Island with views of the Sound, the stonework around the front door, the marble and mirrors in the foyer, the perfectly manicured lawn, the sixty-inch plasma television and leather furniture in the den, the art deco living room that no one is allowed into with shoes, the two-year leases on their matching Lexuses.

I don't like Cal. Cal's friends, if he has any, probably don't like him either. He has hairy forearms, showy biceps, a store-bought tan, and predatory eyes that seem to be looking for a conversation to interrupt, an argument to have. But Mom seems genuinely fond of Sandra, whose mother died when she was a young girl. Mom's parents took her in for a few years. There's a bond there.

"Cindy's on the swim team, All-American," Sandra tells mom. "And Dana's captain of the lacrosse team."

"We should send them equipment," Mom says. "Paul, you'll send them a package?"

"Sure, Mom."

"I can't believe Mort's gone," Sandra says, and then, unbelievably, starts to cry.

"He was a tough old guy," Cal says. If I didn't know this was his crude way of showing respect, I'd throw something at him. And then he'd probably beat the shit out of me.

"He was always very fond of you," Mom says, taking Sandra's hand, and I'm thinking, *If he was so fond of her, why is this only the third time in my life I've seen these people?*

"Wendy, where's the wedding album?"

Wendy pulls out the album, which creaks like a rusty hinge, and Mom and Sandra start playing a game where they identify dead relatives I've never heard of: aunts and uncles, a cousin with polio, a family friend who went to jail for armed robbery. "Come here, girls," Sandra says. The two girls slink over like cats. Phillip watches them a little too closely. Wendy smacks the back of his head.

"What?"

"You know what."

Mom shows us all pictures of her wedding—the washed-out colors, the men with their mustaches, the cigarettes during dinner, the bad toupees, the black plastic spectacle frames that make every man look like he works for the CIA. "You see how pretty I was," Mom says to the bored twins. She's not bragging. She's just looking at their dewy perfection and realizing that she's so much older than she ever believed she'd be. In most of the photos, Dad looks worried in his borrowed tuxedo, like there might be all sorts of trouble brewing right outside the frame. But there's one of the two of them, on the stairs of the catering hall; he's carrying her in his arms and they're laughing, at the photographer, at themselves in their ridiculous gown and tux, at the idea that they can do this thing, start a family. A lump forms in my throat and lodges there. You can kind of see who they were back then, innocent and in love; long before kids and a mortgage and rottweilers and cancer and possible (probable) lesbianism.

"He looks so handsome there," Sandra says.

"I could barely walk the next morning," Mom says.

The girls giggle loudly and shake like wind chimes. Wendy smacks Phillip's head again. This time he doesn't ask why.

12:10 p.m.

PAUL AND HIS friends have stepped outside into the side yard, where Paul's old batting cage still stands. Boner, who played shortstop in high school, wonders if he can still hit Paul's fastball. Paul wonders if he can still throw it. Horry, who lettered in football and played hockey in the county league, will don the musty catcher's gear, and Dan, who played outfield, will call balls and strikes. The other guys will stand around spinning bats like swords and making asinine comments, and Phillip and I will watch to see who makes a fool of himself first. There's simply no way to calculate the odds.

Paul pulls out his old glove and starts warming up, throwing lightly to Horry, rolling his shoulder around in its socket to loosen up. Even after all this time, his motion is graceful and assured, his body uncoiling precisely from his windup to launch each pitch. Boner tries out a few bats—we have no shortage of gear—and then steps into the netting, digging his flip-flops into the grass, settling down into his stance. He works the bat around for a little bit, and then Dan steps behind Horry, a cigarette dangling from his mouth, and says, "Batter up!"

Paul's first pitch goes a little wide and Boner holds his swing in check. Dan calls it a ball. The second pitch is low, but Boner swings anyway and misses.

"Strike one! One and one."

Paul shakes his head, not pleased with the pitch. He rolls his head around on his neck and shrugs his shoulders a few times. Then he settles and stares down the batter. He winds up and unleashes a straight fastball that lands in Horry's glove before Boner's swing has even crossed the plate.

"Strike two!"

The other guys applaud and cheer. They are all meatheads, their best years behind them. Tracy and Alice join us in the yard, along with Boner's wife and a few random shiva callers who are happy for the diversion. Paul bangs his mitt against his shoulder and grimaces a little, like it's tender. His next pitch is a changeup, and Boner manages to catch the edge of it, fouling it up into the net.

"Strike two!"

"Come on," Boner says. "Now I got you."

Paul removes his mitt to rub his pitching shoulder for a minute, trying to mask the pain he's feeling.

"Paul," Alice says. "It's enough."

His ligaments were shredded like cheese, the muscle ripped right off the bone. They did what they could to reassemble the working parts, but the lumpy patchwork mess of surgically spliced tissue beneath his skin cannot support the strain he's putting on it with these pitches.

"It's fine. I just need one more pitch."

"The hell you do," Boner says.

Alice shakes her head sadly.

That's the thing about jocks. They're wired to compete, regardless of angry wives or busted shoulders. They will not back down. If Paul strikes him out, Boner will leave here bruised and bitter. If Boner hits off Paul, Paul will brood about it for days. Whoever wins will gloat and talk some supposedly good-natured trash to rub it in. There can be no draw. Someone's going down.

Paul steps back onto the rubber mound, shaking his shoulder and rolling his neck. He leans forward onto his front knee and takes a deep, measured breath. Horry pounds his mitt. Boner swings his bat, squares up his stance, and settles down. Everyone is sweating and deadly serious, the fact of the shiva completely forgotten. "If it reaches the point where I think you're being a fucking idiot," Phillip says under his breath, "then you're probably being a fucking idiot."

Paul winds up and something goes wrong on his release. Three-quarters of the way through, he lets out an anguished cry and prematurely releases the ball, which flies hard and fast and right into Boner's face. Both men fall to their knees at the same time, Paul clutching his shoulder in pain, Boner's nose bleeding through his fingers, staining his white batting gloves. Boner's wife shrieks and runs to his side. Alice stands her ground outside the cage, willing herself to be unmoved, but then caves and runs to Paul, helping him to his feet, asking him whispered questions. It occurs to me that there's a deep and genuine love between them, and I wonder why I should find that so surprising. Dan and Emily help Boner to his feet, and Horry pulls off his mask and says, "Whose bright idea was this anyway?"

Paul walks gingerly over to Boner to apologize. They say some macho things to each other, bang fists, and slap asses, and in this manner, all is forgiven. Someone procures an ice pack from the freezer to press on Boner's bruised face. They may be over-the-hill idiot jocks, but you have to admire their code. If only all our conflicts could be resolved with a few grunts and a smack on the ass.

Chapter 36

12:45 p.m.

The parade of weathered flesh continues. Sitting in our shiva chairs, we develop a sad infatuation with the bared legs of our visitors. Some of the men wear pants, and for that we are eternally grateful. But this being late August, we get our fair share of men in shorts, showing off pale, hairless legs with withered calves and thick, raised veins like earthworms trapped beneath their flesh who died burrowing their way out. The more genetically gifted men still show some musculature in the calf and thigh areas, but it is more often than not marred by the surgical scars of multiple knee operations or heart bypasses that appropriated veins from the leg. And there's a special place in shiva hell reserved for men in sandals, their cracked, hardened toenails, dark with fungus, proudly on display. The women are more of a mixed bag. Some of them have managed to hold it together, but on others, skin hangs loosely off the bone, crinkled like cellophane; ankles disappear beneath mounds of flesh; and spider veins stretch out like bruises just below the skin. There really should be a dress code.

Two friends of mine from the radio show come by. Jeff is one of the writers, short and hairy in a way that makes him look dirty at all times. Kenny is an engineer, a former musician and roadie, with colorful tattoo

sleeves up both of his arms and long blond hair that he wears like a guitar god from the eighties. We were work buddies, hanging out in the
break room, bonding over television shows and playlists, and sympa-
thizing with Jeff, who bitched about Wade bungling all his best bits.
Sometimes, when the show was over, Kenny would roll a joint and we'd
sit in the control room unwinding while he played the guitar. I haven't
seen either one of them since I quit. They come in looking scared out of
their minds. It's touching, really.

"Hey," Jeff says as they sit down. "I'm really sorry about your dad."

"Condolences, man," Kenny says.

"Thanks. How are things at the station?"

"Oh, you know, same shit, different day." Jeff.

"It's not the same without you." Kenny.

"Who's producing?"

An awkward look passes between them.

"Um, I am," Kenny says.

"Congratulations," I say. "Good for you."

"I feel bad about it, man."

"Hey, it's fine. I quit."

"They were going to bring someone new in," Jeff explains.

"No," I say. "That's great. I'm glad it's you."

"Doesn't mean I think he's any less of a dipshit." Kenny.

"He's been more of a bastard ever since you left. You really kept him
in line." Jeff.

"Apparently not enough." Me.

They aren't sure whether it's okay to laugh at my little joke. Jeff
changes the subject, updating me on the soap-opera lives of the rest of
the staff. Kenny stares wide-eyed at my mother's breasts, like they might
come to life at any moment and attack him. I affect an air of cool detachment, reminding myself to be touched that they came, while I count
down the minutes until they leave. Ryan and Cole come in to stare at

Kenny's tattoos, and Kenny gives them the tour, showing them each one and explaining what it is.

"That's my Harley," he says.

"Harley," Cole repeats.

"That there is the queen of hearts and over here is the album cover of *The Wall*, by Pink Floyd."

"Pink Boy."

"And that little bird smoking the doobie is Woodstock. You know, Snoopy's friend?"

"Big Bird."

"Close enough. And that there is some spiritual Japanese writing, but I forgot what it means."

I walk them to the door and shake both of their hands. "Thanks for coming."

"Yeah. See you soon."

"Take care, man."

I watch them climb into Kenny's restored Camaro. They'll probably stop for lunch at TGI Friday's and talk about me in deeply sympathetic tones. Then they'll pull onto the interstate, crank up the classic rock, and resume their lives. It's quite likely that I will never see either one of them again, and the thought saddens me. They were daily fixtures in my life for the last seven years or so, and now they are gone. Or, more accurately, I am. Just like that. That's the thing about life; everything feels so permanent, but you can disappear in an instant.

I step through the crowd and slide wearily back into my seat, instantly depressed. Phillip throws his arms around me and pats my back. He's always had the ability to hone in on a mood.

"It was really nice of Bon Jovi to come," he says.

1:30 p.m.

AND STILL THEY come. Everyone we ever knew in our lives, pouring through the doors out of a sense of friendship, duty, community, or simply to secure reciprocation when it comes their turn to mourn.

Because more time has elapsed since the funeral and people are less worried about the appropriateness of it all, because there are apparently a lot of single women out there, because Mom has clearly put the word out, because I'm sitting here on display for all to see, because there is a premium placed on a divorced man without kids and no one here knows any better yet, and because some women of a certain age seem to think it's their God-given right to act as brokers in affairs of the heart, the matchmakers are out in full force today.

Lois Braun wants to set me up with her daughter Lucy, who—and Lois is emphatic on this point—could have married any number of the many boyfriends she had, if only she weren't so driven in her career. Lucy is now a vice president at PepsiCo, makes more money than she knows what to do with, and is finally ready to consider appropriate suitors. And for all I know, Lucy Braun might be my soul mate, or at least a bright, attractive woman with the body of a centerfold. But Lois's hair is dyed a different shade of blond than her eyebrows, and her skin hangs off her jaw in loose jowls with the texture of an orange peel, and when she speaks of Lucy in her hoarse smoker's voice, she sucks all traces of potential sexuality right out of her. Right out of the world, actually.

Barbara Lang's ex-husband has a stepdaughter who is a catalog model. She is divorced once and widowed once, but you'd never know it from her great attitude. She's currently writing a book on what to do when you're beautiful but your life sucks anyway, and she lives in Boston, but the world is so much smaller these days.

Renee Harper is a certified matchmaker and she wants me to avoid the dangerous pitfalls of online dating by hiring her to find and screen potential dates. I wonder what organization certifies matchmakers, what the criteria are, and, more immediately, how a sixtysomething woman who wears leopard-print spandex pants and bubblegum-pink lipstick to a Sunday-afternoon shiva call can possibly expect to be taken seriously as an arbiter of good taste.

"So, you'll call me?" Renee says, pressing her card into my palm.

"Sure."

"Really?"

"No. Not really."

Renee looks at me uncertainly.

"He's kidding." Mom.

"No, I'm not."

"He's not." Wendy.

"He's serious as a heart attack." Phillip.

"I'm sorry," Renee says, sounding more pissed than contrite. "I was just trying to help."

I look at Renee Harper, and Barbara Lang, and Lois Braun. They are smug and clueless and riding my last nerve. "I am still legally married," I say, raising my voice to the point that all the other hushed conversations going on around the room die instantly. "I'm still married and I have a baby on the way and I'm dealing with the death of my father, and this pathological need you all have to throw every sad lonely woman you know at me is not helping."

"Okay, Judd," Mom says.

"Do I really look so pathetic to all of you? Like I couldn't possibly meet someone on my own? Half the people in the world are women. Odds are that at least a few of them would be willing to go out with me."

"Damn right," Phillip chimes in. "And it's not like he's been celibate since he moved out. He had sex last night, FYI."

"Don't help me, Phillip."

"Right. Sorry."

Lois, Barbara, and Renee rise to their feet as one, lips pursed, faces burning with humiliation. They offer a chorus of mortified apologies in low, strained voices as they make their way out of the room. I estimate it will take them roughly three minutes to convert their shame to indignation. They'll blame the whole thing on my bad manners, benevolently excuse me on the grounds of my grief, and live to meddle another day. They couldn't have made it this far without developing some fairly foolproof defense mechanisms.

"Don't worry about it, girls," Mom calls after them. "You were just being kind. It's not you he's angry at."

"No, I'm pretty sure it is them."

Mom fixes me with a hard look, then leans back in her chair. "Well, I can see you're beginning to vent all that anger you have locked up in you, and that's healthy. I just think you could be a little more judicious in choosing your venue. There are a lot of innocent bystanders here."

"You always encouraged us to express ourselves in the moment. To let it out."

"That's right, honey. I also encouraged you to move your bowels twice a day. That doesn't mean I want to be there when you do." She nods to herself for a moment. "That was good, the whole venting-your-waste metaphor. I need to write that down." She pulls herself up off the chair, making a quick apology to what's left of her audience, and exits stage left, through the kitchen to her office.

Chapter 37

After my little outburst, I am deemed unfit for shiva, so I load Ryan and Cole into Wendy's rented minivan to drive them over to Wonderland, a second-rate amusement park a few miles down the interstate. I figure Wendy could use the break, as she's been offhandedly remarking, more than usual, about smothering them in their sleep. Wendy also told me to keep a close eye on Ryan, as he tends to wander, so I call for reinforcements.

"I'm taking my nephews to Wonderland. Want to come?" I say when Penny picks up.

"I don't know if I'm ready for that kind of commitment," she says.

She is waiting in front of her building when we pull up, looking edible in a T-shirt, short shorts, and tennis shoes. She could be nineteen. She could be my girlfriend. We could be going out to the amusement park, where we'd kiss on the lines, hold hands on the rides, and share cotton candy. I'd win her one of those giant stuffed animals and we'd carry it around the park with us like a badge of honor. Afterward it would take up permanent residence on her pink bedspread, where she'd lie across it while we spoke for hours on the phone.

Seeing her fills me up and breaks my heart all at once.

"I'm glad you called," she says, climbing into the minivan.

"So am I."

Her smile fills the car. Her feet go up on the dash, and she plays the drums on her raised thighs. The legs on this girl are really something else, smooth and toned and pretty damn flawless. If I look any longer, I will crash the van. We ride to the park, singing along to Cole's *Sesame Street* disc. Penny still remembers most of the words.

At the entrance, I buy the premium package and goofy hats for all of us. The kids love the hats, which are baseball hats with built-in dog ears on the top. I have the three hundred dollars I stole from Wade's billfold burning a hole in my pocket, and my goal is to leave here broke. A kid with a name tag and a digital camera asks us to pose for a picture with the cheesy plaster palace behind us. There are countless pictures of my family at various ages in just this spot. If we pulled them out of all the messy albums in the living room bookcases, you could probably track the steady growth of our family, like annual pencil marks on the wall to show how tall you've grown. Dad isn't in any of the Wonderland pictures, because he was always the one taking them, with this old Yaschika he'd bought when he first got married, because why the hell would he pay for a picture he could take better himself? As a matter of fact, you'd have to turn a lot of pages to find Dad in any of our albums. The inadvertent result of being the default photographer is that he was relegated to the role of a bit player in the actual recorded history of our family. There are entire years of our lives where he doesn't appear at all.

Penny puts her arm around me and we put our hands on the boys' shoulders. She pinches my ass when the camera flashes. The kid gives me a claim ticket and points out the booth where I can buy the photo later. I pocket the ticket, but I know I won't claim the photo. A photo of the four of us doesn't make any sense.

The sky is gray but not threatening yet. Hired teenagers walk around in ratty medieval costumes, looking hungover and bored as they pose for pictures with their aluminum swords. We take the boys on the carousel, the balloon race, the scrambler, and an airplane ride, everything that goes around in circles. Then Ryan announces he's too big for the kiddie rides, so I take him out to the larger park, leaving Penny to ride the mini coaster with Cole. Ryan and I ride the Buccaneer, the Tilt-a-Whirl, the Spider, and the Dragon, a wooden coaster famous for being the first ever built on the East Coast. Someone in an office somewhere actually thinks this is a valid selling point for a thrill ride. Ryan clings tightly to my arm, and I pretend for a moment that he's my son, that later we will fall asleep together reading stories in his bed. Then we find Penny and Cole and we all sit down for a late lunch of pizza and fries at one of the concessions. Ketchup and Cole are a deadly combination, and by the time we're done, his stained T-shirt makes it look like he's been in a knife fight. I buy him a Wonderland shirt, and then Ryan, who is no idiot, purposely drips ketchup on his own shirt. Kids are transparent, but they get the job done.

Later we get fake tattoos. Ryan gets the Superman logo on his tiny bicep. Cole gets Scooby-Doo. Penny gets a heart with an arrow through it on the back of her hand. I get a yellow and red firebird on the inside of my forearm. Cole falls asleep in his stroller and I push him across the park to the bandstand, while Ryan runs ahead of us. Penny wordlessly wraps her fingers around my elbow as we walk, and when I look at her she looks right back at me, daring me. There has been no time in your life that you wouldn't have killed for a girl like this to look at you like that. Then she does, and something in you doesn't respond and you realize that you don't understand yourself any better than you understand anyone else.

There's a local rock band playing loud covers at the bandstand. We find a bench and buy some cotton candy. Ryan nods off on the bench, his head on Penny's lap. I sit next to her, watching the band while she feeds me wisps of cotton candy. I lean over and kiss her sticky lips. She rests her head on my shoulder. "Can we stay until it gets dark?" she says.

Penny is beautiful. Not smoldering, like Jen, but pretty and sexy and

witty and fun. And she has the added distinction of seeming to genuinely like me. Sometimes, contentment is a matter of will. You have to
look at what you have right in front of you, at what it could be, and stop
measuring it against what you've lost. I know this to be wise and true,
just as I know that pretty much no one can do it.

A few minutes later my cell phone rings and it's Jen. "Something's
wrong," she says.

"What?"

"The baby. Judd . . . I'm bleeding."

"What, spotting?"

"More than that."

"Did you call an ambulance?"

"I called you. Judd, I'm going to lose this one too, aren't I?"

"Just try to take it easy. Are you still at the hotel?"

"Yes."

"Okay. Lie down. I'm calling an ambulance."

I hang up and dial 911. I'm conscious of Penny listening to me as I
give them the salient details. The lady on the other end sounds fat and
bored, but I appreciate her gruff efficiency. When I hang up, I look at
Penny, still beside me, looking pretty and lost. "I'm sorry. We have to go."

"So I gathered," she says, not quite looking at me.

I stand up and fuss with Cole's stroller while Penny softly wakes up
Ryan and stands him up.

"So, your wife is pregnant. It's yours?"

"Yeah."

"That seems like a pretty important piece of information to have
shared, maybe."

"I know. I'm sorry. I'm still processing it myself." I turn to head toward the park exit, but Penny stays where she is.

"I think I'll stay," she says.

"What?"

She shrugs. "Unless you need my help getting them to the car."

"What? No. That's fine, but I mean, how will you get home?"

"I'll call a car service later. It's fine."

"Are you sure?"

"Yes. There's nowhere I need to be."

"Okay. I'll call you later."

She shakes her head and smiles sadly. "I don't think you will, Judd Foxman." She steps forward and kisses my cheek. "I hope everything turns out okay."

I look at her, wondering what it is about her that makes me want to simultaneously devote my life to her and get as far away from her as I can possibly get.

"Penny."

"You have to go."

Ryan grabs on to the side of the stroller and we start making our way down the wide fairway toward the exit. When I turn around, Penny's back on the bench, listening to the band, tapping her foot to the beat and looking off toward the bandstand, or maybe past it. I look back every so often to watch her fade into the distance, which, I realize now, is what I'd been doing all along.

Chapter 38

4:10 p.m.

I drop the kids back at Knob's End, and then Phillip drives me over to the hospital in the Porsche. He drops me off at the emergency room and then goes to find parking. Jen is lying on a gurney behind some curtains, while a resident runs a probe over her belly. I remember this like it was yesterday, the last one to arrive, the tears in Jen's eyes, her gel-coated stomach bloated with our dead baby. *Not again. Please.*

"There's no heartbeat," she says, and starts to cry.

"The baby's in a tough spot to get a read," the resident says. She is a rotund woman with bulging eyes and no discernible lips. "Let's not get ahead of ourselves."

"I'm sorry, Judd," Jen sobs, reaching out for me. She grabs my hand before I can avoid her and pulls it over her mouth, crying onto it. "I'm so sorry."

"It's okay. Just try to relax." I find myself stroking her hair with my free hand. I go to this place where I'm totally present, but I'm also thinking that forty minutes ago I was walking through an amusement park with Penny, holding her hand, kissing the cotton candy off her lips. I'm living in separate universes, and I have no idea where I actually belong.

"I can't believe this is happening again," Jen gurgles. Her tears are hot on my fingertips. The resident continues to move the probe around.

I can't believe we're here doing this again, losing another baby. Fate already warned us to pack it in. We just didn't hear it in time.

"I deserve this," Jen says. "I do."

"Don't talk like that."

"What I did to you . . ." She looks up at me, her features slashed with regret. "I ruined us."

"Listen!" the resident says sharply. We turn to her, and then we hear it through the static, a fast, rhythmic, robotic swish.

"What's that?" I say, but of course I know. I've done this before.

"It's your baby's heartbeat."

"It sounds so fast," Jen says.

"To you, maybe," the resident says. "It sounds just fine to me."

On the gurney, Jen closes her eyes and cries with relief, still clinging to my hand. With my free hand, I wipe away my own tears before she can see them.

"So why was she bleeding?" I say.

"It could be any number of benign reasons. I've paged the ob-gyn on call. Someone will be down in a minute. But the baby doesn't seem to be in any distress."

"Wait," I say when she lifts the probe off Jen. "Can we listen for another minute?"

The resident flashes a kind, lipless smile and pulls out some kind of canvas belt gadget from a drawer and wraps it around Jen's belly. Then she leaves, and it's just Jen and me, listening to the frantic, throbbing heartbeat of our unborn child. She looks at me with shining wet eyes and smiles. "That's our baby," she says, beaming.

"He sounds nervous."

She laughs. "Wouldn't you be?"

We listen for a little longer. *Beat, swish, beat, swish, beat, swish.*

"Judd," Jen says, not quite looking at me. "We can do this, right?"

And this is where I stop regretting the way things should have been the first time I heard my baby's heartbeat. This is where I surrender to the magic of it all, the karmic appropriateness of becoming a father right now, when I've just lost my own. And maybe I do feel something; it's hard to say, because we've only just begun to try the moment on for size when the curtains fly open and Wade steps in, effectively murdering the moment and all the ones to follow.

4:45 p.m.

THE LAST TIME I saw Wade, I attacked him with an office chair. The time before that, I jammed a lit cheesecake up his ass and almost burned his balls off. So it's understandable that his first reaction upon seeing me is to flinch and assume a defensive posture. He stands in the doorway looking uncertainly at me, then moves past me self-consciously to approach Jen on the gurney. "You okay, babe?" he says. There are guys who can pull off "babe." I'm not one of them. Wade is, and I mean that in the worst possible way. I start scanning the shelves for sharp objects. "I got here as fast as I could. My GPS messed me up."

"I'm fine," Jen says.

"Good. Good." He rubs her shoulder lightly and then stops, too aware of me in the room. There's no choice but to turn and face me.

"Hey, Judd. How's it going?"

"It's going swell, Wade."

There's a knock on the door, and a bearded doctor enters the room, carrying Jen's chart.

"Jennifer Foxman?"

"Yes," she says.

My last name, still attached to her, is a kick in the crotch.

"I'm Doctor Rausch, from ob-gyn." He turns to Wade. "Mr. Foxman?"

"No," Wade says.

"I'm Mr. Foxman," I say.

"Nice to meet you," Doctor Rausch says perfunctorily, before looking at Wade. "And you are?"

"He's my wife's lover."

"Shit, Judd," Jen says, covering her eyes. "Not now."

"Wade Boulanger," Wade says, extending his hand. "It's complicated."

"Not the radio jock."

"I'm afraid so."

Doctor Rausch smiles. "My wife hates you."

"The wives generally do."

"Not mine, unfortunately," I say.

Doctor Rausch looks at me like I'm spoiling his good time. "Okay," he says, pulling some latex gloves out of his pocket. "I've got an ulcer and a long shift to get through. Whatever's going on here, you're not going to make it my problem. You two can wait outside."

"But I'm the father," I say.

"Congratulations. Now get the hell out of my exam room."

4:55 p.m.

"So, THIS IS some predicament we find ourselves in," Wade says.

We are standing against the wall in the crowded waiting room. There is what appears to be an entire Little League team and their parents sitting around, waiting for an injured teammate. Two construction workers prop up a third whose foot is wrapped in a blood-soaked towel. On a small television mounted too high for effective viewing, someone is cooking a soufflé.

"This predicament, as you call it, is my life. My family."

"Jen is my family too now."

"Jen is where you're presently parking your cock."

"Don't talk about her like that."

"I'm not, you dumb shit. I'm talking about you."

"You don't know anything about me."

"I know you're shooting blanks."

"Fuck you."

"Um, excuse me, guys," one of the Little League dads says, indicating the children present. But this train has already left the station.

"I know you pretty much fuck anyone who will have you. You fuck the interns, you fuck the sales reps, you fuck the sponsors, or, in one case that I know of, the sponsor's daughter, who at the time was not quite eighteen yet, was she? I know you won't last with Jen, because the last thing you want is to be saddled with someone else's kid. I know you've been praying for a miscarriage ever since you got the call and that now you're weighing your options, looking for the fastest way out of this mess. I know you want to think that underneath it all you're really a decent guy, but you're not so sure, are you, and for what it's worth I can pretty much confirm for you that underneath it all, you're not a decent guy at all. You're just an empty soul, devoid of any real substance. So you'll keep getting laid and getting paid to be the voice of the lowest common denominator, until, as inconceivable as it seems, someone even lower then you comes along, and then you'll get old and obscure, and you'll die alone."

It's safe to say we've got everyone's attention now. The Little League parents are horrified. The kids can barely contain their exhilaration that a grown-up said "fuck" so many times in one sentence. The construction guys are unimpressed.

"You feel better now?" Wade says with a shit-eating grin.

"Not even a little."

"That's too bad. It was a good speech."

"Let's just not talk, okay? Can we do that?"

"I didn't turn her, Judd," Wade says. "I didn't seduce her or come on to her, or anything."

"And by not talking I meant exactly what you're doing right now."

"She was lonely and angry and lost, and I didn't do that to her. You did that, all by yourself."

"And you saw an opening."

"Yes, I did. I'll admit it. She's beautiful, and I'm human. I crossed the line. But I didn't fuck her any more than she fucked me. It takes two, my friend. And believe me, no one was more surprised than me when it became something more. So you can go on hating me for it; I certainly would if I were you. But she came after me, Judd. Not the other way around. She came after me. You know that's true, and that's the thing you can't get past."

"That doesn't make me want you any less dead."

"Yeah, well, get in line."

And that's when I decide to hit him. I've already assaulted him twice before, but neither time was really that satisfying. I need the intimacy of direct violence, the blunt force of bone on bone. But moving from conversation to violence is just as hard as moving from flirting to kissing. There's that leap you have to take, to shed your inhibitions and expose your naked impulses.

This is how I do it. I bridge the distance between us by pointing at him and saying, "You don't get it, you dumb bastard," until my finger is inches from his eye. He swats the finger away, as expected, and that's my trigger. But I've used my right hand to point, so it's my weaker, less reliable left hand that swings around with the punch, and Wade reflexively turns away, so that my fist glances impotently off his goddamn shoulder. "Asshole!" he shouts, and shoves me back against the wall, not attacking back, just kind of getting me off of him. But that's when Phillip finally shows up, and all Phillip sees is Wade shoving me, so he steps in and coldcocks Wade with a high arcing punch he learned from watching mixed martial arts matches on television. The punch hits Wade in the nose and he goes down hard. Phillip stands over him with one foot on his chest and says, "Call my brother an asshole again."

A fat security guard materializes and pins Phillip's arms behind him. A second one comes up behind me, grabbing my arm tightly. "Let's go," he says, and they hustle us toward the exit.

"My wife is in there."

"We'll deal with it outside."

It's raining outside, a hard rain that makes a racket against the fiberglass awning of the emergency room. The guards release us beside a parked ambulance. They hold a quick, whispered conversation, and then one of them heads back inside. The other, a large black man with a shaved head and thirty-inch forearms, turns back to us. "Is that the *Man Up* guy in there?"

"That's him," I say.

"Which one of y'all hit him?"

"Nobody hit him, he just fell," Phillip says.

The guard smiles widely and extends his hand. "Shake my hand, man. I hate that loudmouth motherfucker."

Phillip shrugs and shakes his hand. "And if you hadn't pulled me off of him when you did, I'd have really kicked his ass."

5:20 p.m.

PHILLIP DOESN'T QUITE remember where he parked, so we get soaked walking around the lot. When he finally locates the Porsche, it's parked a few cars away from Wade's silver Maserati, with its MAN UP vanity plate. Before I have time to talk myself out of it, I climb up onto the roof of the car and jump up and down on it, screaming obscenities into the rain like a madman. I jump up and land hard on my knees, feeling the metal crumple satisfyingly beneath me. Phillip pops the trunk of the Porsche and pulls out an L-shaped tire iron. "Here," he says, tossing it up to me. "Go crazy."

But I'm suddenly out of steam. I slide down the front windshield and sit on the hood. Phillip joins me, and we sit there in silence for a few seconds as the rain pummels us.

"I miss Dad," I say.

"Me too."

"Why didn't I miss him more when he was alive? He was dying for two years, and I only visited him a handful of times. What could have been more important than spending time with your father?"

"He didn't want us around. He told me so. He didn't want us to remember him like that."

"Well, that was probably our time to step up and say 'Tough shit, Dad.'"

Phillip nods soberly. "Dad was always much tougher than us."

"I guess. How did we become such wimps?"

"Hey," Phillip says. "Did I or did I not just take out Wade Boulanger with one punch?"

"You did."

"Damn straight." He winces a little as he rubs his hand. "I think I broke my knuckle. Can you even break a knuckle? I should go back in and get it X-rayed."

"I heard the baby's heartbeat."

Phillip looks at me. "That's great. Right?"

"Yeah." I'm quiet for a moment. "I told Wade he was hoping for a miscarriage, but the truth is, I think part of me might have been. And how terrible is that, for a baby to be growing in the womb and for the father to be hoping it won't make it?"

"It's pretty terrible," Phillip says, lying back against the windshield to join me.

"Did you think Dad was a good father?"

Phillip ponders this for a moment. "I think he did his best. He was pretty old-school, I guess. He didn't always get us, didn't always appreciate us, but come on, look at us, right?"

"I think I could be a pretty good father, actually."

"I think you'll be great."

Raindrops land in small explosions on the Maserati's gleaming hood. "But I'll have to forgive her, won't I? I'll have to learn to live with the fact of Jen and Wade. I mean, for the sake of the kid."

"I don't know anything about parenting, but my guess is that there will be much larger sacrifices to be made."

I look over at Phillip, who is catching raindrops on his tongue. "You almost sounded wise right there."

Phillip grins. "In the land of the blind, the one-eyed man is king."

I smile and lean back on the windshield, looking up into the rain. "I'm going to be a dad," I say.

"Congratulations, big brother."

"Thank you."

"You ready to go home?"

"Okay."

He grabs the tire iron from me, and as he slides off the hood, he swings it to the side, noisily shattering the driver's-side window. The car alarm goes off instantly, a muted, almost apologetic wail. Phillip looks at me and smiles. "Whoops."

"You're an idiot."

"You just said I was wise."

"I'm seeing things more clearly now."

"Glad to hear it." He offers me the tire iron. "One for the road?"

"I'm trying to rise above here. To forgive and move on."

"And you will. In exactly thirty seconds." He tosses me the tire iron. The cold metal feels almost alive in my hands. I shouldn't be having this conversation. What I should be doing is climbing down off of Wade's car and talking my way past the security guards so that I can make sure Jen is okay. We are going to be parents together, and there's no place in that arrangement for juvenile acts of vandalism, no matter how satisfying. But Wade is already in there, probably back on his feet by now, taking charge, charming the doctors, asking all the right questions. I'm the extraneous one, the temperamental biological father who had to be forcibly restrained and removed. I realize now that this is how it will be: Wade on the inside, and me out here in the rain, and no magical heartbeat can change that. I will always be the odd man out, the guy everyone secretly hopes won't show up to the party and put everyone on edge. And right now, that seems like more injustice than any man should rightfully be asked to swallow. If that's what I have to look forward to, I'm not sure I'm going to be up for it after all. This is a crucial moment, I know that, but that's never stopped me before.

And thirty seconds is really all you need with a good tire iron in your hand.

Chapter 39

6:10 p.m.

Back at home, Mom and Linda are having a fight. They are in the kitchen, arguing in hushed tones. I can't be sure, but it sounds like Linda's crying. A fist pounds the counter. A cabinet door slams. There are no visitors right now, this being the dinner hour, but there is no dinner right now, since none of us will dare enter the kitchen. More low voices. Then Linda storms down the hall and out the front door, slamming it behind her hard enough to rattle the lightbulbs in their sconces. A minute later Mom comes out, still composing herself, and sinks down into her shiva chair. We all look at her expectantly. "What?" she says. "We had an argument."

"What about?" Wendy says.

"About none of your business." She stands up and heads for the stairs. "I think I feel a migraine coming on. I'm going to go lie down for a bit."

"Hey," Wendy shouts, stopping her at the foot of the stairs. "What happened to a family with no secrets?"

Mom nods to herself, holding on to the banister for support. When she turns to us, there are tears in her eyes. "It's been such a long time since we were really a family," she says.

7:50 p.m.

IT'S A NIGHT for lovers' tiffs. Alice is pissed at Paul for injuring his shoulder. She is berating him upstairs but is coming in loud and clear through the baby monitor. Back in the den, Tracy is furious with Phillip for hitting Wade. I sit in the kitchen eating dinner, listening to these two very similar arguments play out on different sides of the house. There are perks to being single.

Underneath it all, Alice is really angry at Paul because she's still not pregnant, and Tracy is angry at Phillip for having sex with Chelsea, which he probably has, or, if not, probably will. He's definitely been thinking about it. Tracy is angry at herself for letting Phillip make a fool of her, for blinding herself to certain obvious realities, for being in her forties. But this is not the time or place for such thorny issues, so in their frustration they overreact to sprained shoulders and bruised knuckles, and harmony is not in the cards at Knob's End tonight.

On the plus side, fresh new platters have been delivered. Teriyaki chicken wraps, pasta salad, deviled eggs, and a tray of black-and-white cookies. I don't know when I'll eat this well again. Wendy's boys sit across from me on stools at the kitchen island, freshly scrubbed and dressed in tight pajamas that cling to them like superhero costumes. Their damp hair, perfectly combed, gleams under the recessed lighting. They are like an advertisement for children's shampoo, or for children in general. Wendy tries to get them to eat, but their tiny stomachs are still bloated and churning from all the sugared crap they ingested at the amusement park today. I experience a clenching pang as I think of Penny. It's the feeling of having behaved poorly, of having hurt her. I would call her if I had any idea at all what I could possibly say besides "I'm sorry."

A hard rain pounds at the windows, looking for a way in. On the monitor, Alice yells at Paul. *"You could have done permanent damage. And for what? To strike out Boner Grodner?"*

"If she wakes the baby, I'm going to kick her fat ass," Wendy says as she assembles a plate for Mom.

"Mommy, you said a bad word," Ryan says.

"No, I didn't, honey."

"You said 'ass.'"

"'Ass' is just another word for a donkey."

"So it's not a bad word?"

"It is when children say it."

"Why?"

"I don't know," Wendy says, exasperated. "Those are just the rules, Ryan. Deal with it."

"We've been here for less than a week, and you've been in two fist-fights!" Tracy shouts at Phillip. *"This is clearly not a healthy place for you."*

We cannot make out the other half of either conversation because, in true Foxman form, Paul's and Phillip's responses are low and mono-syllabic. Under attack, we retreat into stoic fortresses built for one. It drove Jen crazy. The more she yelled, the quieter I got, sometimes not uttering a word for hours. Maybe if I had yelled back at her, things would be different now. Maybe yelling back is a kind of marital diplomacy I never learned.

Eventually someone slams the den door and the lights in the kitchen flicker and then go out. Phillip comes stomping into the dim room and opens up the freezer. He grabs an ice pack and sits down across from me, wincing as he presses it against his swollen hand.

"For a guy who punches people so often, I would think you'd know how to do it better," Wendy says.

"I think I may have broken something."

"Besides Tracy's heart?"

Phillip gives Wendy a dirty look. "Don't you ever get tired of being the thorn in everyone's side?"

Upstairs another door slams and the lights come back on. On the monitor, Serena starts to scream.

"Fat bitch!" Wendy mutters.

"You said a curse word!" Ryan shouts, gleefully horrified.

"A bitch is a female dog," Wendy says.

"Bitch!" Cole repeats happily.

The first time I heard my father curse, I was helping him install a timer in the garage for the lawn sprinklers. He had a screwdriver in his mouth, some screws in his hands, and he dropped a key washer, which rolled across the garage and down through the grate of the catch basin. "Ah, shit," he said. I was eight. I laughed until my ribs ached.

Paul enters the kitchen wordlessly and opens the freezer. Phillip has the only ice pack, so he grabs a slab of frozen meat and slips it under his shirt to press against his shoulder. He leans back against the fridge and closes his eyes for a second. Seated between him and Phillip, I feel conspicuously uninjured.

"I have to get out of here," Paul says, and heads for the door.

"You're in no condition to drive with that shoulder," Phillip says, getting to his feet. "I'll take you."

"Lucky me," Paul says, disappearing into the front hall.

"Asshole," Phillip says.

"An asshole is a donkey," Ryan says.

"Asshole," Cole says. "Bitch. Asshole. Elmo."

Phillip considers our nephews gravely. "It's good to see our influence on the next generation. We should seriously consider getting neutered."

"It's too late for me," I say.

"Yes it is. I forgot." He stands up and fumbles for his car keys. "Okay, then. Have a good night, everyone."

"Wait!" I say, following him out to the front hall, where Paul is already halfway out the door. "What about the shiva?"

We look into the living room at the five empty shiva chairs lined up in front of the fireplace. "You'll be fine," Paul says. "Just nod and smile."

"You can't leave me here alone."

Phillip flips a cigarette into his mouth and leans into the shiva candle to light it, which strikes me as somewhat sacrilegious, but I guess Dad wouldn't mind. "It's like a monsoon out there right now. I bet no one will even come tonight. So why don't you come with?"

"What if people come?"

Phillip grabs a legal pad and pen from a compartment in the hall table and draws up a quick sign:

SHIVA CANCELED ON ACCOUNT OF RAIN. TRY AGAIN TOMORROW. —THE MANAGEMENT.

He jams the paper under the knocker on the front door. "Problem solved," he says.

Chapter 40

9:15 p.m.

Sticky Fingers is in one of the last strip malls on Route 120, just about a mile down the road from the Marriott where Jen is staying. Or was staying. She is no doubt gone by now, hightailing it back to Kingston, with Wade grumbling about revenge scenarios as he drives.

Sticky Fingers. Famous for its spicy buffalo wings and nubile waitresses in their tight black T-shirts with the V-necks cut out jaggedly by scissors. The place is filled with women in short skirts or jeans, and tight sleeveless shirts. These women, with their hair and their bodies, their smiling lips, glossed to a shine. I am acutely conscious of every one of them, of every smooth thigh and creamy neck. I am dealing with major life issues here, death, divorce, fatherhood, and yet here, in this bar, I am all cock. I don't know why this is, what makes it so, but I'd be lying if I said otherwise. I sit with my brothers at a high round table, licking hot sauce off my fingers, trying to moderate my roving eye. There's a brunette with the kind of bee-stung lips you want to suck like candy. There's a blond girl in a short skirt with smooth, perfect legs and the kind of smile you feel in your chest. There's another blonde, a real one this time, with laughing eyes, and you just know she'd be fun and tender in bed. I want them all, slowly and softly, want to kiss them in the rain, save them from bad men, win their hearts, build a life. I'm probably too old for most of them. Maybe. I don't know. I haven't been single in over ten years; I can't tell how old anyone is anymore, including me.

I would kill to be in love again. I loved being in love—the deep kisses, the urgent sex, the passionate declarations, the late-night phone calls, the private language and inside jokes, the way her fingers rest possessively on your forearm during dinner with her friends.

"Boys' night out," Phillip says appreciatively. "Why don't we do this more?"

"Because we don't like each other very much," Paul says.

"That's crap, Paul. You're too angry at the world to know who you like and who you don't. I like you, Paul. I love you. Both of you. I was always too young to go anywhere with you guys. I always wished we'd hung out more as brothers."

"Well then, this must be a big moment for you."

"*The boys are back in town,*" Phillip sings.

A waitress comes to bring us our drinks. "Hey, Philly," she says. "How've you been?"

"Hey, Tammy. Looking good."

We cannot help but watch her as she leaves. God himself stops what he's doing to watch her ass as she crosses the crowded room. It's that kind of ass. The kind of ass that fills you with equal parts lust and regret, and then, almost instantly, chagrin, because, for Christ's sake, it's just an ass.

"Is there anyone in this town you haven't fucked?" Paul grumbles.

"Just because she was glad to see me doesn't mean I fucked her."

"So you didn't?"

Phillip shrugs. "It's not a fair test case. Everyone fucked Tammy Burns."

"I didn't," I say sadly.

"The night's young. Just be charming and tip well."

Someone has selected "Sweet Home Alabama" on the jukebox. Phillip sings along, tapping his hands on the table to the little piano riff between verses. Take a hundred jukeboxes from a hundred bars in a hundred cities and they'll all have "Sweet Home Alabama" in them. I don't know why that should be the case, but it is. And every one of those bars has two or three assholes who will sing along at the top of their lungs, especially when they get to the part that trashes Neil Young, and then look around like they should get a prize for knowing the words, like everyone doesn't know the words, like everyone didn't have that classic rock friend who put it on every mix he ever made, like everyone isn't sick to death already of "Sweet Home Alabama."

Lately, I get inexplicably angry around pretty girls.

The girls around the bar shake themselves lightly in time to the music, pouting the way girls do when they dance, like they're experts in something we'll never understand. I need to stop looking at these girls. No good will come from it. You keep looking at girls like this and then one day you catch a glimpse of yourself in the mirror behind the bar, and if you're not yet too old, you're on the borderline, and the last thing you ever want to be is the old guy in the bar. There's no dignity in it.

"Isn't that Horry?" I say, looking over to a corner table. Horry is there, chatting up some hot young thing. I catch his eye and he waves uncertainly. When I look back a few minutes later, he and the girl are gone. I guess I can't really blame him. I wouldn't feel comfortable hitting on women in front of the brothers of the married woman I recently slept with. You need GPS to follow the sex lives of this family. I wonder if love is this twisted for everyone or if our family is uniquely talented at making such a mess of it.

Paul slams a dollar bill down on the table. "I'd like to perform a demonstration," he says. "Phillip. Please go over to the jukebox and choose a song."

"You get two for a dollar."

"Then go crazy."

"Anything in particular you're in the mood for?"

"Surprise me."

Phillip hops off his stool and makes his way across the crowded room. "Watch," Paul says.

"What?"

"He won't be able to get there and back without touching at least three women."

There's a girl at the jukebox, in a little black halter top, her jeans doing that thing where they ride so low on her hips that you wonder what's holding them up. He leans over and whispers something to her. She looks up at him and laughs. And then she teeters a little bit, maybe because of her high heels, or possibly it's the free Jell-O shots for women between eight and ten o'clock. I don't know what makes women teeter. She grabs Phillip's arm to right herself. It's simple, effortless even, and the kind of thing that never happens to me. Her fingers continue to clutch his elbow as they chat. How does a simple wisecrack turn into bodily contact?

On his way back he is stopped by two girls who seem to know him. He leans in to accept a kiss from each one, his hands resting lightly on their exposed hips, just above the waist of their jeans, as he chats briefly. He's about ten feet away from us when he bumps into another girl, graciously guiding her past him with his hand on the small of her back as they trade smiles.

"Four," Paul says.

"Four what?" Phillip says.

"Nothing."

Phillip looks mildly irked and then shrugs. When the world is your sexual buffet, you don't sweat the small stuff. He takes a generous swig of beer. "So, Paul. I think it's great you and Alice want to have a kid."

Paul looks up at him and then down at the dwindling foam of his beer. "She's driving me crazy with it. We've burned through our savings on her quest for fertility."

"I find it interesting that you call it 'her' quest and not 'our' quest."

"And I find it interesting that you're sleeping with a woman in spitting distance of menopause, but I figure that's your own business."

Phillip puts down his beer, looking hurt. "You're an asshole, Paul. You're an asshole to me, you're an asshole to Judd. I hope to hell you turn out to be a better father than you are a brother."

"I'm the lousy brother?" Paul says, raising his voice. "You think it was just Dad who paid to keep you out of jail when you decided to take up marijuana farming? I didn't take profits for three years so that we could pay off your legal fees. And, Judd? Don't get me started on you."

"No need," I say. "I know all about your great sacrifice. You'll never let me forget it."

"What did you just say to me?" Paul says, getting to his feet. His stool clatters to the floor behind him.

I stand up to face him. "It was your own damn fault, Paul. You dragged me to Rusco's house. I kept telling you I didn't want to go, but you were going to show everyone what a tough bastard you were. I didn't ask you to do it, and I'm sick and tired of paying for it. The price is just too damn high."

"I think we should all just take a beat here," Phillip says, but it's too late.

Paul brings his beer mug crashing down on the table. He is seething now, his face red, his fists clenched. Around us, people move away quickly, anticipating a brawl. "I lost my scholarship. I lost everything. You went off to college and never looked back." He sinks his teeth into every word, and they come out chewed. "And now you want to tell me that you paid a price? You ungrateful prick!"

"You could have gone to college. You chose to stay home and get drunk for two years. Should I have done that with you, pissed away my future out of gratitude?"

"Okay, this is good. We're all talking here, getting everything out on the table." Phillip.

The bouncer is suddenly standing behind Paul, giving us a hard look with his one real eye. He's a retired boxer. There are framed clippings of his fights behind the bar. It's anyone's guess what kind of punch the guy might pack today, but he's got presence, and his expression carries a certain tired wisdom unique to people who have known violence intimately. He places a hand like a meat hook on Paul's shoulder. "Paul," he says in a hoarse, surprisingly gentle voice. "You either need to sit down or take this outside."

Paul nods, still looking at me, and then pats the bouncer's belly. "It's fine, Rod. I'm leaving anyway."

Rod the prizefighter looks pointedly at Phil and then me, visualizing the cataclysmic damage he'll do to us if it comes to that, before heading back across the bar. Paul throws a few bills down on the table.

"Paul," I say, feeling remorseful. "I've always felt bad about what happened."

"Just tell me this," he says, his voice low, his anger spent. "How many surgeries have I had?"

"What?"

"I don't mean when it happened. I mean since you moved out. How many operations?"

I think about it for a moment. "Three, I guess. Or four if you count the one you had right after I got married. The skin graft thing."

Paul shakes his head slowly. "Eight."

"What?"

"I've had eight surgeries. Skin and nerve grafts, tissue grafts, surgical pins. And how many times did you visit me in the hospital, or even call the house to see how I was doing?"

"I don't know. A bunch?"

He holds up two fingers. "Twice. You came to see me twice. That's it."

"That can't be right."

"It's not right, but it's the truth." He starts heading for the door.

"Paul," I say. "Wait a minute."

He turns to face me, and I'm shocked to see a tear running down his cheek. "Going to Rusco's house was stupid," he says. "Believe me, I spend time every day wishing I could go back there and stop myself, picturing the world I'd be living in now if I hadn't gone. But stupid or not, I went there for you. You want to call me a lousy brother? I guess maybe I am. I'll own up to it. But maybe you are too."

I sit back on my stool, watching him leave. I should call out to him, stop him, now that we're finally talking. But we are not a family of communicators. It took five shots and a decade's worth of repressed anger just to say this much tonight. I'm tapped out, and so is he.

"Well, I think you two had a real breakthrough there," Phillip says.

"Yeah? Then why do I feel so shitty?"

Phillip pats my back and messes up my hair. "Emotional growth hurts. It's nothing a few more shots won't fix."

He disappears into the crowd at the bar. I am left alone at the table to lick the bottom of my shot glasses and assimilate the new information. You think you have all the time in the world, and then your father dies. You think you're happily married, and then your wife fucks your boss. You think your brother is an asshole, and then you discover that it's been you all along. If nothing else, it's been educational.

10:30 p.m.

PHILLIP RETURNS WITH eight shot glasses jammed between every finger of both hands, another of his worthless skills. Somehow we do them all. The night takes on a kind of kaleidoscopic translucence, and I lose my sense of time and, occasionally, balance. When I come back from a trip to the bathroom, we've been joined by Phillip's old girlfriend, Chelsea. "Look who I bumped into," Phillip says. Chelsea is dressed for the hunt in a short denim skirt and a tank top that grants a generous view of her lightly freckled cleavage as she leans forward to kiss my cheek. "Fancy running into you guys here," she says, in case I haven't properly registered the complete randomness of this encounter from Phillip's remark. Chelsea's fingers dance up Phillip's arms like he's an instrument she's playing. I try to catch his eye, but he looks away every time. I want to tell him that he can't behave like this on my watch, but the shots have warmed my blood and toasted my veins, and someone has turned up the music, and to be heard I'd have to put my mouth close to his ear, like Chelsea is doing right now.

On my next bathroom trip, I see Horry making out with a skinny girl in the little nook between the men's room and the kitchen. She's a sloppy kisser, her tongue sliding out of her mouth to lick his lips when they separate, but he doesn't seem to mind. *Good for you, Horry,* I think. I am drunk and lost and would very much like to be making out with someone of no consequence right now, mashing tequila tongues, sliding my fingertips over smooth, booze-warmed skin. Instead, I urinate for a half hour, reading the stall graffiti, still smelling Chelsea's shampoo from when she kissed me hello.

When I get back to the table, Chelsea and Phillip are gone. The jukebox is playing goddamned "Sweet Home Alabama" again, and I think I'm going to be sick. The bathroom has a line, so I stumble out to the parking lot and puke behind one of the Dumpsters. I feel a little better after that, halfway to sober. The rain has finally stopped, or not really stopped, but dwindled to a fine, foggy mist that cools my burning skin. I wonder how I'm going to get home.

Chapter 41

11:15 p.m.

I can't recall if I settled the tab or not, but no one's come running out after me, and just the thought of going back inside starts my stomach acid frothing, so I'll just assume it's all good. I decide to take a walk. The neon lights of Route 120 spread out ahead of me like the Vegas Strip. P.F. Chang's, the Cheesecake Factory, the Pitch & Putt, Sushi Palace, Applebee's, Rock & Bowl, Szechuan Gardens, and the digital marquee of the AMC multiplex, all flashing and blinking, burning pink and red streaks into my eyelids when I close them. Generations of broken glass twinkle like glitter in the pavement. Teenagers rove in loud packs that form and disperse as they move down the sidewalk. Cell phones ring, obscenities fly. Blow jobs are administered in throbbing cars in the darkest corners of abandoned parking lots. They've been laying pipe beneath the blacktop forever now, and they don't bother taking down the barricades on the weekends anymore, so every few stoplights, traffic slows to a crawl, cars ejaculated out of the bottlenecks one by one, burning rubber just to make a point, since there's really nowhere here worth rushing to. They whiz by like missiles, these cars crammed with kids exactly like the one I used to be. Once in a while you can make out their laughter above the hollow din of tires scorching the blacktop like fighter jets on a runway.

There's a fountain in front of Sushi Palace, spraying a high illuminated geyser that changes colors every few seconds. Red, yellow, green, and violet. I stop to watch it for a little bit. A couple of kids sit on the edge of the fountain, kissing with such unabashed fervor that I have to look away.

As I walk, a silver car passes me and then quickly brakes, causing the cars behind it to swerve left and honk angrily. You don't see many Maseratis in Elmsbrook. The car pulls onto the shoulder and Wade climbs out. He's wearing the same suit he wore earlier and has a bandage across the bridge of his nose, a smear of purple bruising spreading out from under it. He frowns as he approaches me, picking up speed as he goes.

"What are you doing?" I say.

His punch arrives well before my worthless block can get there, landing squarely on my chin and lower lip, and down I go. There is a version of this fight in which a crowd of pedestrians grows around us as we grapple and trade punches, until I tackle Wade and we fall over into the sushi fountain, where I pummel him into submission, standing over him in victorious disgust, casually spitting some blood into the fountain. But I'm too drunk and tired to fight, so I curl up and close my eyes, prepared to absorb the kicks that will follow. After a few seconds I look up to see Wade standing above me, combing his hair with his fingers. "That was for my car," he says.

I get up on one knee and taste the salt and copper of blood on my lips. "Fair enough." I wipe my mouth with my sleeve and get to my feet.

"You're drunk."

"And you're an asshole. Are we going to just stand here stating the obvious?"

He shakes his head and smiles fondly at me. "You never could hold your liquor."

He reaches through the shattered passenger window to his glove compartment and comes out with a white towel, which he tosses to me. We lean against the car and I press the towel against my lips. It comes away bloody.

Rowdy, hopped-up college kids pass us in an endless, noisy blur like they're being mass produced or squeezed out of a tube—guys skulking in their T-shirts and cargo shorts, girls in low-slung jeans and flip-flops, pimples and breasts and tattoos and lipstick and legs and bra straps, and cigarettes; a colorful, sexy mélange. I feel old and tired and I just want to be them again, want to be young and stupid, filled with angst and attitude and unbridled lust. *Can I have a do-over, please? I swear to God I'll make a real go of it this time.*

"You were right, what you said about me," Wade says.

"What do you mean?"

He shakes his head and looks over his shoulder. "I'm not a decent guy. Not really." He pulls out a cigarette and lights it. "I think I always just told myself I was, that at some point I'd grow up and start behaving." He rubs the back of his neck as he blows smoke into the mist. "I always figured I could stop anytime I wanted to."

"What do you want, Wade?"

He peers down his nose at the glowing ember of his cigarette. "I don't know. Nothing, really. I just saw you as I was driving past, and I realized that I never actually apologized to you."

"So you hit me."

"Yeah. I didn't actually know I was going to do that until I did it."

"Got it."

"I know it won't change anything, but I just figured it was better said than not." He looks across the parking lot. "You want your job back?"

"Fuck you."

"I just thought I'd ask." He tosses the cigarette into a puddle and nods at me. "I'm really very sorry for everything. You were my only real friend, and it sucks that we're not friends anymore. I deserve it, but it still sucks. And whether you believe it or not, I really hope you guys will be able to put things back together, man. Sincerely."

The planet lurches beneath my feet. "What the hell are you talking about?"

Wade takes a deep breath and shakes his head. "I was kidding myself. I'm not going to be any kid's stepfather."

"You broke up with Jen?"

He shrugs, then turns and steps off the curb, walking around to the driver's side of the Maserati. "I think it's what's best for everyone."

I stare at him, incredulous, as the rage in me builds. "It's what's best for you."

"I know it looks that way."

"It is that way. You had a good thing going as long as she stayed married to me, as long as you didn't have to take any responsibility."

"It wasn't like that, Judd. I really did love her."

"And now you don't."

"Love isn't enough."

"She walked out on her marriage for you."

He looks at me over the scraped, dented roof of his car. His smile is sad and broken. "I'm a professional bastard, Judd. That's why they pay me the big bucks." He pushes a button on his key chain and opens the door.

It would be so perfect right now if a passing eighteen-wheeler lost control on the rain-slicked road and just plowed into him, irreversibly embedding his crushed corpse into the steel and leather of his Maserati. They'd have to bury the car with him and justice would be served with poetic flair. But this is real life, and in real life Wade gets to fuck my wife, to fuck my life, bloody my mouth, and then flash me a last rueful grin before speeding away on twelve Italian cylinders. His tires spin briefly on the slick blacktop before catching and hurtling him out into the traffic, just another set of red lights disappearing into the horizon.

If nothing else, I am now completely sober.

I sit down on the retaining wall of a parking lot, my mind racing. Jen has been left. Jen is alone in the world for the first time in her adult life—alone and pregnant and vulnerable and contrite and probably scared out of her mind. I don't know what it is I'm planning to do, or maybe I do, maybe I know exactly what I'm planning to do. Whichever it is, I like my chances.

11:45 p.m.

MY CAB DRIVER is Mr. Ruffalo, who taught English and driver's ed when I was in high school, until he fell for one of his students, Lily Tedesco. They would set off every Tuesday in the driver's ed car, Lily's hands positioned firmly at ten and two, and then pull over behind the county park, where they would discuss their plans to run away together after she graduated, and where she would crouch down between his legs, balancing herself on the training break to prove her love. They must have been spotted at some point because one day Mrs. Ruffalo showed up outside the school and tried to stab her husband with a steak knife hidden in the pocket of her red velour housecoat. No charges were ever filed, but the school board voted unanimously in favor of termination. Now he's divorced and driving the graveyard shift, and probably never gets to see the two kids who are now much older than they are in the bent and faded pictures he has taped to the sun visor of his cab. Life is huge, but it can turn on a dime.

"You're Foxman, right?" he says.

"Yeah."

"I teach you to drive?"

"Yes. I had you for freshman English too."

"Really?"

"*Romeo and Juliet. Silas Marner. The Catcher in the Rye.*"

"That's pretty good."

"You made us each memorize one of the *Canterbury Tales* in Middle English."

He laughs. "I was some kind of asshole, huh? It's funny what we remember." He cracks his window to light a cigarette. "You mind?"

The lights of Route 120 turn into a streak of colors in the grimy window of the cab. "Wonderful Tonight" is playing on the radio, and we stop talking to listen in silence. I have to believe it makes Ruffalo feel as sad and lost as it does me. He pulls up to the house just as the song is ending.

"You the ball player?"

"No, that's my brother, Paul."

He nods as I hand him a twenty. "That boy had a gift. It was a real shame what happened to him."

"Thanks."

"Death from above," he says ominously. "No one is safe."

"Tell me about it." I overtip, although I suspect the extra seven bucks won't make much of a difference in whatever it is that now passes for Mr. Ruffalo's life.

11:55 p.m.

DOWN IN THE basement, I wash some of Boner's foam spray off the mirror to better study my reflection. My bottom lip is split and swollen, my eyes bleary, my cheeks pale and puffy. I look like a corpse pulled from the river a week after the suicide. It's time for a gut check. I mean that literally. I pull off my shirt, which is caked with just enough blood and vomit to represent a much wilder night than the one I've had, and step back to study my torso. The overall effect does not match the image I cling to in my head. My belly is not yet what you'd call a gut, but you can see where the inevitable expansion will happen. I have no real chest to speak of; you'd miss it altogether if it weren't for the two hairless nipples pressed on like decals. Broader shoulders would create the illusion of fitness, but I am sorely lacking in that department as well. The overall impression is lean but soft, and getting softer. This is the package, ladies. Come and get it.

I lie down on the floor to do some sit-ups and promptly fall asleep.

Monday

Chapter 42

6:10 a.m.

I am sitting shiva naked. The cheap vinyl of the shiva chair sticks
to my ass like duct tape. Everyone I know is here, milling about,
lost in conversation, but at any moment someone is going to notice.
I can't get up to leave, can't really hide. I am utterly exposed. I turn
to Phillip, but it's not Phillip, it's my uncle Stan sitting next to me,
smacking his lips and farting a mile a minute. I ask him for his blazer.
He flashes a toothless grin and tells me he can see my balls. Over
the bowed heads of faceless visitors I see Penny, in the back, looking
strangely at me, and it makes me feel sad and embarrassed. And then
Jen arrives, looking nine months pregnant, full-faced and radiant. I
cannot let her see me like this. People greet her warmly, remark on
her belly, touch it with casual reverence. She moves across the back
of the room and then, just in front of her, I see him. He's seated in the
back row, cradling a baby in the crook of his arm. He looks like he
did when I was much younger, large and broad, with thick forearms
and a barrel chest. Our eyes meet and he winks at me, then gets up
to leave. *Wait! Dad!* But he can't hear me. He's heading to the door,
the baby pressed to his shoulder, chewing on the seam of his shirt. I
jump up to follow him, my nakedness forgotten, but only once I try
to walk do I realize that I've only got one leg, and I'm not wearing

my prosthesis. I fall down hard, my flesh hitting the oak floor with a resounding slap. Everyone turns to look at me, mouths agape, while through the crowd I see my father's head descend down the front stairs and disappear.

I wake up in pieces, still calling out for him to wait for me.

Chapter 43

6:40 a.m.

I climb up onto the roof and find Tracy already there, smoking one of Wendy's cigarettes. She turns around, surprised, and then offers me a weak smile. "Did I take your spot?"

"It's fine," I say, crawling out to sit next to her. "Always room for one more."

She offers me the pack. I take one and light it with hers. Then we sit there for a little while, staring out over the rooftops.

"What happened to your mouth?" she says.

"Someone apologized to me."

She grins. "Does it hurt?"

"Only when I smile."

"I don't think I've ever actually seen you smile."

"You're not really catching me at my best."

"I know." She turns to look at me. "Phillip has been sleeping with that girl, Chelsea, hasn't he?" There's no anger in her voice, just sad resignation.

"I don't know."

"But if you had to guess."

"He's my brother, Tracy."

"I understand." She takes a slow, tentative drag on the cigarette. Smoking doesn't come naturally to her. "I'm all alone here, Judd. I need a friend, someone to tell me if I'm crazy or not. Between you and me and the sunrise." She leans forward and pulls the cigarette from my mouth. She holds it up with hers, watching the wisps of smoke float off of them and mingle, and then crushes them both out on the slate. She is dangerously close to tears. "We're neither of us smokers," she says.

"No."

I look at her for a long time. She is older than me, but there's something of a frightened child in her, some ancient, lingering pain that has never been soothed. "Between you, me, and the sunrise," I say.

"Yes."

"I don't know for a fact that he slept with her. But my guess is that he did. And if he didn't, he will. And if it's not her, it will be, or has been, someone like her. The Chelseas of the world are drawn to him."

The tears slide quietly down her cheeks and she wraps her arms around her knees. "Thank you."

"I'm sorry," I say. "I know how badly it hurts."

She wipes her eyes and exhales slowly. "It's my own damn fault, really. Whatever lies he's told me, they pale in comparison to the lies I've been telling myself."

"You deserve better than him. I love him, but that's the truth."

"You know what's sad?"

"What?"

She smiles a little and turns her face up to the sky. "He really does love me. In his heart, he wants to be the man I need. It's just not in him."

"So, what are you going to do?"

She thinks about it for a moment and then shrugs. "I'll wait until the shiva ends. That seems only right. Then I'll gather up the tattered remnants of my dignity and say good-bye."

"He'll be crushed. You know that, right?"

"I'll let him keep the Porsche."

"Wow," I say. "Parting gifts."

"He meant well. I'm forty-four years old. I don't have time for anger anymore."

"You may be the best person I've ever known."

She smiles and pats my knee. "I talk a big game."

"Where were you when my life was going to shit?"

"I'm always available." She fumbles around in her pockets and comes up with an embossed business card. It says her name, followed by a slew of acronyms. Below that it says BOARD-CERTIFIED PSYCHOTHERAPIST, and below that it says LIFE COACH. And right below that, in boldfaced type, it says this: HAVE A PLAN.

"Have a plan," I say.

"Do you?"

"Whatever the opposite of a plan is, that's what I've got."

"Can I offer you a piece of unsolicited advice?"

"Sure."

Tracy turns to face me. "You got married right out of college. You're terrified of being alone. Anything you do now will be motivated by that fear. You have to stop worrying about finding love again. It will come when it comes. Get comfortable with being alone. It will empower you."

"Empower me to do what?"

"To be the father you want to be, the man you want to be. And then you'll be ready to make a plan."

I nod. I'm picturing Jen, trembling in her empty bed, shredded with regret. She's alone. I'm alone. I've never felt closer to her.

"Being alone isn't for everybody," I say.

6:55 a.m.

TRACY'S GONE BACK inside. I'm still sitting on the roof, watching the town come alive, when I see a girl step out the front door of the Callens' house. She's wearing a little black dress and high heels, and her hair is a mess, her face smudged with last night's makeup. It's the girl Horry was making out with at the bar last night. She squints in the emerging sunlight and looks around, somewhat disoriented. She's not sure where she is. But the advantage of a cul-de-sac is that there's only one direction to go. She heads hurriedly down the street. It's too early to be late for work. She's rushing from something, not toward it.

I haven't been in the Callens' house in years. The action was always at our house. The front hall smells of Pledge and potpourri. The oak flooring creaks beneath my feet. The wall by the staircase is adorned with framed photos of sunsets and forests taken by Linda in her travels.

I find Horry in his basement apartment, lying naked on the floor, in the last convulsive throes of his seizure. His mouth is filled with white foam, which drips down his chin like soap suds. The cloying smell of sex and sweat fills the dark bedroom. I grab a damp pillow off the bed and jam it under the back of his head, which is tapping out a staccato rhythm on the oak floor. Then I throw a blanket on him and press my hands against his chest and shoulders to let him know I'm there. He shakes beneath me like a dying animal, his rhythm slowing, his muscles unknotting as he comes to a gradual stop. I wipe the tears and sweat from his face, and after a short while, I see in the dim light that his eyes are now open.

"You there?" I say.

"Yeah," he grunts, his voice thick with spit. His eyes roam the room in quick, nervous jerks.

"She's gone," I say.

He closes his eyes. "And with a great story for her friends."

"We should page your doctor," I say.

Horry shakes his head. "I'll be fine. Sex can bring it on. Elevated heart rate, endorphins, adrenaline. Something."

"Aren't there meds you can take?"

"You can't get hard on the meds."

"Well then, I hope she was worth it."

He looks up at me. The whites of his eyes are vaguely pink, like something ran in the wash. "I wish I could remember."

After another few minutes, he rolls over and onto his knees. He ignores my proffered hand and stands up on his own, the blanket falling away from him.

"Well, you have some nice fingernail scratches on your ass," I say. "Always a good sign."

He smiles weakly and bends down to wrap the blanket around his waist. Horry's got the kind of abs you want, the kind that ripple and flex effortlessly under his skin. Looking at him, you can't help but be reminded of who he used to be, who he should be now. We all start out so damn sure, thinking we've got the world on a string. If we ever stopped to think about the infinite number of ways we could be undone, we'd never leave our bedrooms.

"Don't say anything to Wendy, okay?"

"You got it." It's not clear to me which part of this he wants kept from her, but it's not a talk I'd want to have with her anyway.

"Thanks." He rolls his head around on his neck, stretching out the kinks, and breathes deeply. "I can still smell her on me."

For some reason, I don't think he means the girl who just left.

7:40 a.m.

ALICE IS PERCHED on the edge of my bed when I come out of the shower. She's wearing sweatpants, a T-shirt, and the forlorn expression of an abandoned puppy.

"Alice . . . ," I say.

"I know."

Water drips down my legs to my heels, leaving a trail of wet foot-prints behind me.

She furrows her brow and looks away from me. "I just wanted to apologize for . . . the other day."

"It's okay." It isn't, but it's what you say, right?

"I got a little crazy. I'm sorry." She offers up a lame, hollow grin. "It's all these hormones I'm taking."

"Okay."

"Things don't have to get all weird between us."

"Okay."

"Can you say something besides 'okay'?"

"Fine."

"Come on, Judd. Throw me a bone."

"Get out of here, Alice."

"Please, Judd. You won't even look at me."

"Can you blame me?"

"No. I guess not." Alice looks down at her clasped fingers like she's kneeling in prayer and then back up at me. "The thing is, you're having a baby by accident. Wendy squirts her kids out at will and doesn't even seem to particularly like them. I've been trying for so long, and it just doesn't seem fair."

She sits there on the edge of the bed, pretty, sad, and tragically re-signed. I remember how she ran to help Paul when he hurt his shoulder yesterday, and I feel a powerful urge to kick her teeth in.

"You have a good marriage," I say.

"What?"

"You and Paul. You love each other, don't you?"

Her face turns red, and her eyes grow wide, like she's about to cry. "Yes. We do."

"That's a lot harder than having a baby. It's damn near impossible, really. And you're putting it at risk."

Alice thinks about that for a moment and then nods her head. "You're right. I know you're right."

"I mean, any asshole can have a baby, right?"

"I can't."

There is no talking to her. And now the tears come, just like that. Where have all the happy, well-adjusted women gone? Every one I talk to these days is one wrong word away from a crying fit.

"Alice . . ." I have no idea what to say anymore.

"No," she says, sniffling. "You're right. I'm sorry." She wipes her tears with her wrist and shakes her head. "I put you in a terrible position. I understand that. I just need to know that things are okay between us."

At this point, I just want her out of here. "They're not, but they will be."

"You promise?"

"Sure."

"Thank you." She stands up, still crying, and gives me a hug. I accept it, but my hands stay firmly at my waist, keeping my towel up.

"Okay. I guess I'd better let you put some clothing on."

"That would be great."

"Thanks for understanding, Judd," she says, and she must be joking, because, Alice, honey, I would travel to the ends of the earth, kill or die, just to find one single thing that I could understand.

Chapter 44

10:15 a.m.

You never saw a sorrier bunch of mourners. Paul's arm is tied up in a sling. The back of Phillip's hand is black and blue and looks like an inflated glove, to the point that his knuckles have disappeared. My lip is swollen and split. Picture us there in the living room, crouched uncomfortably in our low chairs on this sixth day of shiva, hungover and fuzzy from the prescription painkillers Mom doled out like candy this morning. We squint in the daylight, which seems aggressive and spitefully bright today. Wendy is exhausted because Serena hasn't slept through the night since she got here, and Mom is ragged and moody. There's been no sign of Linda since their argument yesterday.

According to the informational pamphlet Boner left on the piano, this is the last full day of shiva. Tomorrow morning he will come and lead us in a small closing ceremony, snuff out the shiva candle, and then we'll part ways, back to the flaming wrecks of our individual lives. In my case, I have no idea what that even means. My rented basement feels to me like a bad movie I saw and forgot.

None of us makes eye contact. We have pretty much had it with each other. We are injured and angry, scared and sad. Some families, like some couples, become toxic to each other after prolonged exposure.

Mom runs three weekly postpartum therapy groups in her living room, where young mothers come to share tips on colic remedies and

toilet training while venting their frustration about lack of sleep, worthless husbands, and how the last bits of pregnancy fat have taken up permanent residency in their asses. When we were kids, we called these
women the Sad Mommies and viewed them with a mixture of awe and
pity, spying from the top rungs of the staircase to watch actual grown-
ups cry. Some of those ladies could really wail, in a way that sent us
scurrying back to our bedrooms to laugh hysterically into our pillows.
Today, through a phone chain, or, more likely, through a Sad Mommies
e-mail distribution, a number of them have all arranged to come pay
their respects at the same time. This happens a lot, I've noticed. People
form shiva alliances, arriving together to eliminate the risk of a one-on-
one with the bereaved. Some of the Sad Mommies sit with infants
strapped to their milk-laden chests in little knapsacks, vibrating uncon-
sciously in their seats to keep the kids asleep.

"Don't rock them," Mom insists hoarsely. "You rock them now, you'll
be rocking them for the next four years. You're robbing them of their
natural ability to put themselves to sleep." This is why they pay Mom the
big bucks.

"Did you rock us?" Wendy says.

"Just you," Mom says. "I learned the hard way. The rest of you learned
to put yourselves to sleep."

"I'd like to go practice right now," Phillip says, resting his head on my
shoulder. I think of Tracy and shrug it off maybe a little more violently
than I meant to, and Phillip practically falls off his chair.

"What the hell?" he demands under his breath.

"Sorry."

There are seven mothers, three of whom have left their babies home
with the help. They are making a day of it. Brunch, shiva call, pedicures,
and then a quick trip to the mall. "Good for you," Mom says. "Any excuse
to take care of yourself is a good one."

An ad hoc therapy session breaks out. Paul, Phillip, and I listen in amazement as the women speak of all the injustices they endure, the sacrifices they make to propagate our species. Mom eggs them on, offers suggestions, wisdom, and absolution, which, when you get right down to it, is what they're really paying for. Among Mom's gems:

"Children crave discipline."

"Don't shield your child from anger; this business of saying 'Mommy is sad' when you're angry is just a bunch of new age crap. If he pissed you off, let him know it."

"One way or another, start having orgasms again. Restore your balance as a woman."

"Love them to pieces, but demand their respect."

The Sad Mommies share stories and offer harried grins, looking tired and put-upon as they discuss their marriages. One of them, bone-thin with the sad eyes of a puppy, says, "Having kids changes everything."

"Not having kids changes everything too," I say. The mommies look at me with guarded respect, as if I've just said something complex and profound. Mom beams and nods, proud of her emotionally damaged son.

A blond mommy with dark roots and a floral skirt casually unbuttons her blouse and unsheathes a large, pendulous breast to feed her baby. Her belligerent gaze darts around the room like sonar, daring anyone to have a problem with it. I've never fully understood the agenda of angry breast-feeders.

"That was once a tit," Phillip mutters.

Wendy smacks the back of his head, but without any real conviction.

11:30 a.m.

SAY WHAT YOU will about the Sad Mommies, but they don't overstay their welcome. They have schedules to keep, nap times and feedings to coordinate, manicure/pedicure appointments, and grocery shopping to get done. They rise as one, pulling up the low-riding jeans they really shouldn't be wearing at this particular juncture, offering harried condolences as they shoulder their designer diaper bags, fumbling for minivan keys, thoughtlessly slipping orthodontic pacifiers like corks into the mouths of their restive babies. Their heels click down the hall like jazz rim shots, leaving a palpable silence in their perfumed wake.

A number of the regulars are back, women mostly, friends and neighbors who have to have their morning coffee somewhere anyway, and those husbands who are retired. Peter Applebaum is back again, and you have to admire his tenacity. He's playing it a bit cooler this time, but he watches Mom intently, waiting for the right moment to pounce. I feel a surge of empathy for him. You can do everything right and still end up alone, watching time run off the clock.

Horry comes by to bring Paul some papers he requested. He shows no ill effects from this morning's seizure, taking a seat in front of Wendy to talk to her. They run out of conversation pretty quickly, self-conscious around the rest of us, but he makes no move to leave, and she seems happy to have him there.

The women are talking about a dangerous intersection in town. There's a short light and no left-turn lane, and there was another crash there just last week. Someone should do something about it. This leads to car crash stories, to speeding tickets, to the Paleys' lawsuit against the city over the maple tree that fell through their roof in the last rainstorm, to the new, ostentatious houses that are being built around the neighborhood in defiance of the zoning laws, to the Elmsbrook courthouse, to the mall they were building behind the courthouse but the project stalled when the bottom fell out of the real estate market and now it's a hangout for skateboarders and drug dealers, and someone should do something about it. The conversation unfurls through endless random associations, never lingering for very long on any one subject. No one asks questions or really even listens to anyone else, but just waits for them to finish so they can jump in with their own entry to the canon.

And it is right in the middle of this conversational jamboree that Mom suddenly stands up and looks over the crowd of visitors toward the front hall. We follow her gaze to see Linda closing the front door behind her, rubbing her shoes vigorously on the mat. Mom's smile is small and tentative, completely out of character for her. Linda looks up at Mom and grins a wry apology. Mom moves through the chairs, picking up speed as she goes, hits the hall at a slow jog, and runs into Linda's arms. They embrace fiercely for a moment and then press their foreheads together, whispering to each other, tears flowing. Mom takes Linda's face in her hands and, with great tenderness, plants a soft, lingering kiss on her mouth. Then she takes her by the arm and they walk out the front door, leaving the rest of us to figure out how to breathe in a room in which the oxygen supply has suddenly, inexplicably been depleted.

Peter Applebaum is the first to react. He clears his throat and rises to his feet. "Well," he says. "That was unexpected." He turns and walks sadly to the door, his head bowed in defeat. He was up for the challenge, maybe even invigorated by it, but this . . . he is too old for this. I get up and catch him at the front door.

"Mr. Applebaum."

He turns around, surprised. "Peter."

"Peter. You didn't need that kind of headache anyway."

He shakes his head and smiles faintly. "I'm seventy-two years old. I drink my coffee alone every morning, and I fall asleep with the TV on every night." He smiles. "There are headaches, and there are headaches."

"There will be other widows. I mean, have you seen some of these husbands?"

He has clear blue eyes and the wry smile of a much younger man. "Your mouth to God's ear."

"They'll be dropping like flies, I'm telling you."

He laughs a little, then pats my cheek. "Don't get old, kid. That was where I went wrong." I watch him as he heads somberly down the street. At seventy-two years old, women can still run roughshod over your heart. That's something that never occurred to me, and I find it terrifying, but oddly reassuring.

Chapter 45

My parents had an active and noisy sex life. Years of Dad's puttering in our walls had rendered them porous and poorly insulated, and we could hear them, as we lay in our beds at night: the steady bump of their headboard, Dad's low grunts, Mom's over-the-top porn star cries. We tuned it out like all the other noises a house makes: the clanging of the old steam radiators, the creak of the stairs, the hum of the refrigerator compressor, the plumbing gurgling in the walls. Dad never talked to us about sex. I guess he figured we'd pick it up through osmosis.

I was six years old when I walked in on them. I had woken up with a headache and padded down the hall to their room, the attached slippers of my pajamas whispering against the wood floor. Mom was on top, her back to me, rocking up and down, and I thought she must be exercising. Sometimes she exercised in front of the television, in tights and leg warmers that made her look like a cat. "I'm trying to look as good as her," she explained, nodding her head at the woman on the screen, who, like Mom, was on all fours, raising her leg behind her like a dog about to pee.

"She looks like a dog," I said.

"That's Jane Fonda, and she is no dog."

Jane Fonda had her hair piled up in a headband, which made her look like Mrs. Davenport, my kindergarten teacher. Mom, in her high ponytail and sports bra, looked like the genie in *I Dream of Jeannie,* whom I considered to be the most beautiful woman on the planet and whom I intended to marry one day. We would live in her blue bottle, which would stay on a shelf in Mom's kitchen, so we could emerge in a funnel of smoke every evening to have dinner with my family. When we were done Jeannie would blink and all the dishes would be done.

"You're prettier than Jane Fonda," I told Mom.

"Of course I am, sugar," she said, grunting as she lifted her leg. "But she has a better butt."

I laughed at the notion of a better butt. "But no one can see your butt."

"Women like to have nice butts even if no one sees them."

"That's silly."

"Isn't it?"

On the TV, Jane lifted her other leg. When it became apparent that she wasn't going to pee, I lost interest.

Mom was moving up and down on her bed, but there was no Jane Fonda on the television, just a steady panting. Also, she was naked. I looked at her butt and wondered if it was as nice as Jane Fonda's.

"Mommy?"

When she turned to see me, I saw my father's disembodied head, crammed awkwardly against the headboard, his hair mussed, his forehead dripping with sweat. He looked like he'd been buried up to his neck in the sand.

"Hey, Judd," Mom said, still rocking slightly, each breast bouncing lightly to a different rhythm.

"Are you exercising?"

"No, sweetie. We're making love."

"Jesus, Hill," my father said, trying to get her to cover up.

"My head hurts."

"Okay. Go back to your bed. I'll bring you some water and a drink in a little while."

"Can I come in bed with you?"

Dad said, "Jesus Christ," and pulled up their comforter, while Mom laughed the way she did sometimes at things I didn't intend to be funny. Normally I didn't mind—it felt good to make her laugh—but tonight I had a headache and I wasn't in the mood. So I padded back down the hall to my bed and promptly blocked out the entire event, the way you do.

11:50 a.m.

You can see your parents have sex, you can see your wife in bed with your boss, and still, none of it packs quite the same surreal punch as seeing your mother kiss another woman. Wendy ushers out the shiva callers—*"Thank you all for coming. We hope to see you again under happier circumstances"*—while Phillip handles the stragglers and those who can't quite take a hint somewhat less tactfully: *"Okay there, Mr. and Mrs. Cooper. Don't let the door hit you where the good lord split you."* And then it is just us, Wendy, Phillip, Paul, Horry, Alice, Tracy, and me, sitting in the living room, coming to terms with the new reality.

Paul opens the discussion. "What the fuck?"

"You didn't know?" Me.

"What do you mean? You did?"

"We had our suspicions." Wendy.

"So Mom's a lesbian now? Cool." Phillip.

"Don't trivialize it," Tracy says. "That was actually a very moving thing to witness."

"She can't be a lesbian," Paul says. "She was married for forty years."

"Well, it's a little late in life for her experimental phase, don't you think?" Wendy.

"I think they prefer the term 'bisexual,'" Horry says.

We all turn to look at him.

"And you know this because . . . ?" Paul says.

Horry shrugs, blushing slightly.

"How long?" Wendy demands.

"How Long is a Chinaman?" Phillip says, mechanically repeating an old childhood joke.

"Run and play, Phillip, the adults are talking," Wendy says. "How long, Horry?"

"I don't really know."

"Ballpark it."

"I think they should tell you themselves."

"Holy shit!" Paul says. "Mom is a lesbian."

"A bisexual."

"Whatever."

"Well, whatever, then," Horry says. "Mine is too."

"I think it's wonderful," Alice says. "I mean, they've been best friends since forever. What a deep bond they must have."

"Jesus Christ, Alice! My father's body is still warm!" Paul shakes his head. "Am I the only one who is having a problem with this?"

"A problem is something to solve," Phillip says. "If there's no solution, it's not a problem, so stop treating it like one."

We all turn to look at Phillip.

"That actually almost makes sense," Wendy says.

"It's something I learned from Tracy," Phillip says. "Isn't she something?" He leans forward to kiss her, and she turns away from his kiss.

"What's wrong, baby?"

"Not here."

"I just complimented you. What are you getting all pissy about?"

"I said not here."

"And I said, what are you getting all pissy about?"

"This isn't the appropriate time or place."

"My mother just stuck her tongue down her best friend's throat in front of her children and half the neighborhood. In case you've missed it, we don't really do appropriate here."

"I'm leaving," Tracy says, getting to her feet.

"Since when do you walk away from a discussion? You live for discussions. That's all you ever want to do is discuss the shit out of everything."

She looks down at him and shakes her head slowly. "You are such an asshole." Then she turns and heads back toward the den.

"But I'm engaging here, honey!" he calls angrily after her. "I'm taking ownership of my feelings." He watches her go, then shrugs and turns back to us. "Don't ever date a shrink," he grumbles. "It's like trying to read Chinese."

Chapter 46

1:45 p.m.

Jen has checked out of the Marriott. I make the drive to Kingston in just over ninety minutes and pull into my driveway, like I have a thousand times before. Her white Jeep is parked, as usual, too close to the center, and I have to open my door gently against the stone retaining wall to squeeze out of mine.

She comes to the door in her college boxers and an old concert T-shirt of mine. Elvis Costello and the Attractions. We went to see him play a few times. When I have a cold, I can sing "Almost Blue" and sound just like him. It never fails to crack her up. We have history, Jen and I, a mess of artifacts strewn haphazardly in our wake. Her hair is down, longer than I'm used to, and she is pale and tired, her eyes swollen from crying, and she looks for all the world like she can use a hug. So I give her one and she breaks down, sobbing violently into my neck, her body convulsing to the point that I worry about the pregnancy.

The bedroom smells of Jen. She lies down horizontally across the bed and closes her eyes. *We'll have to throw out the bed,* I think to myself. *There's a lot we'll have to throw out.*

"Run me a bath?" she says.

She lies in the tub, in the slanted shadows of the afternoon sun through the blinds, while I sit on the edge, tracing letters in the surface of the water. We talk for a long time, long enough for her to have to add hot water twice. I don't know what we talk about—the baby, the past, college, our honeymoon. She cries when she speaks briefly about Wade, not because she misses him, but because she's humiliated. I remember what Tracy said about gathering up what's left of her dignity. These are the facts: I am drawn to women like Jen, who are drawn to men like Wade, and it's not healthy for any of us, but that's just the way it is. The Tracys of this world will always fall for the Phillips, who can always be counted on to fuck the Chelseas. And round and round we'll go, doing our pathetic little dance, denying our own true natures in the name of love, or something we can pass off in its place. I can feel myself getting angry again. I'm not sure at whom. I've been angry for so long it's like a reflex now.

When Jen stands up in the tub, I watch the water cascade down her back. It's a sight to behold, and one I can't recall seeing before. We must have taken baths together, but I guess there's always something new to see. Back in our bedroom, she collapses onto the bed, wrapped in a towel. "Judd."

"Yes."

"Will you lie with me?"

This is my bedroom. This is my bed. This is my wife. When I was a kid, I would flex my eyeballs to make everything go blurry. If I can just do that with my brain for a little while, flex until certain thoughts become blurred, this can be my life again. I strip off the sheets on my side of the bed and lie down on the bare mattress. Jen watches me and understands, then turns away, pulling my arms around her, wearing me like a cape.

"Do you think it can ever be the same?" she says. She is fading, her voice thinning out like the voice of a little girl.

"I don't know."

"Or maybe not the same. Something different, but good."

"Maybe."

She sighs and then shudders, pressing her back against my front as her breathing slows. I press my lips to her bare shoulder and take in the familiar smell of her. I slide my hands over her chest and then down past her navel, to where her belly is hardening, just above her groin. She takes my hands and slides them down a bit lower, just above the pelvic bone, pressing them into one spot on her belly then another.

"There she is," she whispers. She leans her head back, her cheek lightly brushing mine.

"She?"

"Yes. It's a girl."

There is no reason I can think of that this should make me cry. Jen rolls over and wraps her arms around me, her damp hair falling over my face like a tent, and she rocks me back and forth, exactly like Mom will tell her not to rock the baby, or she'll be rocking her to sleep until she's five years old. She kisses my eyes. My cheek. My chin. My mouth, softly and with great tenderness. I can taste my tears on her lips. Sleep falls down on us like a heavy curtain.

4:40 p.m.

I WAKE UP with a start. The room is bathed in dusky shadows, and I am momentarily disoriented. I take a minute to sift through the facts and determine which are real and which the residue of dreams. I am in my house, in my bed, with Jen sleeping beside me. Just like that, the nightmare is over, the curse broken. Jen is snoring lightly. She never believed me that she snored, and I always threatened to record her, but, of course, never did. It was one of those playful arguments that we would carry with us unresolved into old age. I look up at the familiar brown swirl of water damage on the ceiling. If it is possible to feel affection for water damage, then that's what I feel for that little brown swirl.

Jen's towel has come unraveled in her sleep, and a lone breast peeks out like a sentry, standing guard. I run my finger gently across her collarbone, around her shoulder, and down her arm. The years fall away from her in her sleep, her brow smooth, her mouth slightly open, like a little girl watching a magic trick. I have loved her for so long. Our past trails behind us like a comet's tail, the future stretched out before us like the universe. Things happen. People get lost and love breaks.

I want to forgive her, and I think I can, but it's not like issuing a certificate. I'll have to keep forgiving her until it takes, and knowing me and knowing her, that's not always going to come easy. But at this moment, as she lies beside me, growing our baby girl inside of her, I can forgive her. I lean down to kiss her on the spot where her cheekbone meets her temple and let my lips rest there for a moment, inhaling the clean smell of her scalp. Then I whisper to her, my lips grazing the soft flesh of her earlobe. I hover in the doorway like a ghost, half-lit by the hallway lights, watching her sleep. Then I'm running, down the hall and then the stairs, which creak in all the familiar spots, and out the front door, where the cool evening air fills my nostrils like a drug.

Chapter 47

6:30 p.m.

Phillip is up on the roof. Not on the wide area we sometimes sit on, but on the topmost gable above the attic, perched like a gargoyle. There's a black Town Car parked in the driveway, its trunk open like a gaping mouth. A portly driver in a black suit leans against the car having a smoke. I jump out of my car and join Paul, Alice, Horry, and Wendy at the edge of the lawn. Serena, slung over Wendy's shoulder, sucks happily on a pacifier. Tracy stands in the middle of the lawn, looking up at Phillip.

"Please get down!" she calls up to him. "You'll kill yourself!"

"That's the general idea," Phillip shouts back. He stands up, one foot on either side of the gable, and spreads his arms out for balance. "Send the limo away."

"What's going on?" I say.

"Phillip proposed to Tracy," Wendy says. "In front of us all."

"And what did Tracy say?"

Wendy smirks at me. "Where have you been?"

"I went to see Jen."

"Really? How'd that go?"

I look up at Phillip, trembling on the roof, arms spread like Christ. "Everything's relative, I guess."

"He's taking it like a man," Paul says.

"I swear to God, if you get in that car I'll jump!"

Tracy turns to us. "You don't think he'd really jump, do you?"

Wendy looks up at Phillip and shakes her head. "Only one way to find out, I guess."

"I love you!" Phillip shouts.

"You're being childish and manipulative!"

"Whatever works."

Mom and Linda come running up from across the street. "What in the world is going on?" Linda says.

"Tracy's not going to marry Phillip," I say.

"Tracy's not a fool," Mom says. She steps out onto the lawn and faces Tracy. "There's only one way to treat a tantrum and that is to ignore it."

"Ignore it?"

"Yes."

"But he's not a four-year-old."

"Honey, we're all four-year-olds."

Tracy appears conflicted. "What if he jumps?"

"Then I'll have to rethink my thesis."

Tracy looks at Mom for a long moment, her eyes growing wet. "You must think I'm such an idiot."

Mom looks at her with great tenderness. "You're no idiot. You're not the first woman who wanted to believe in Phillip. But you're far and away the best one, and I'm very sorry to see you go." She steps forward and pulls Tracy into a warm hug.

"What's going on?" Phillip shouts from above.

Tracy looks up to him. "I'm going to leave now."

"Please don't."

Tracy turns to us and smiles. "Well, it was very nice to have met you all. I'm very sorry if my being here caused any problems." She steps over to me and gives me a hug. "Let me know how it all turns out," she whispers.

"Don't go!" Phillip shouts.

But Tracy goes. She casts a last regretful look back up at Phillip and then climbs gracefully into the car. The driver tosses his cigarette to take her bag and slams the trunk. We watch the car drive slowly down Knob's End and then turn back to the roof, where Phillip is now sitting dejectedly. "I can't believe she really left," he says.

"Will you come down now?" Mom says.

"I guess so."

But when he stands up to pull his leg back over the gable, his pants catch on one of the snow guards. He loses his footing and slides down the side of the roof, scrambling in vain to grab on to the slate shingles. There is time for him to gasp, "Fuck me!" as he slides down the roof and then over the gutter. He is briefly airborne, arms flailing, before landing hard in the hedges that line the side of the house. We all run around the corner of the house to find him lying flat on his back atop a crushed bush, looking up at the sky like he's stoned.

"Philly!" Mom shouts, falling to her knees in front of him. "Don't try to move."

"You ever notice how much closer the sky looks when you're lying down?" he says.

"Can you move your legs?" Wendy says.

"If I feel like it." He closes his eyes for a second. "That really hurt," he says.

"I'm going to call 911," Mom says.

He opens his eyes and looks at her. "Mom."

"Yes, honey."

"So what, you're like, a lesbian now?"

7:30 p.m.

MOM WAS TAKING care of Dad around the clock. When the stairs became a problem, they had a hospital bed installed in the den. Mom
would put him to sleep and then go upstairs to sleep alone in their bed.
She was tired and bereft and so Linda started spending the nights with
her. One night, more as a distraction than anything else, Linda con-
fessed to Mom that she'd had numerous female lovers in the years since
her husband had died. Mom had never kissed another woman, a fact of
which she was instantly ashamed. What kind of celebrity shrink hasn't
experimented? She owed it to her readers. "We were both sad and lonely
and sexually deprived, and within minutes we.were making out like a
couple of high school kids."

No one really wants to hear the detailed story of how their mother
became a lesbian, do they? That's not bigotry. I never wanted to hear the
details of her heterosexual sex life either. But Mom is ready to unload.
She perches herself on one fat arm of the leather easy chair in the living
room and tells us her story. Linda sits on the other arm, for purposes of
symmetry. They have clearly imagined this moment before.

"It started out as something purely surreal and physical." Mom
speaks in her TV voice, like she's narrating the documentary of her bisexual awakening. "But Linda and I have been so close for so long. It was
only natural that a physical relationship would evolve into something
more."

"You make it all sound so perfectly normal," Paul says.

"Well, yes. That's how it felt, I suppose."

"Except for the part where you were cheating on your dying
husband."

"Paul," Alice says.

"No, it's okay," Mom says. "He knew."

"Dad knew?" I say.

"Your father was a very enlightened man, sexually speaking."

"Our father?" Phillip.

"Let me tell you a story about your father."

"Please don't." Wendy.

Linda clears her throat. "Your father was always so good to Horry and me. He accepted us as family, he took care of our finances. When Horry was injured, and I was paying for all of his care, your father made our mortgage payments for a full year, so we wouldn't lose the house. I would never have betrayed him. Hillary was the love of his life, and he died knowing she wouldn't be alone. He told me that many times toward the end."

"So Dad was cool with it," Phillip says.

"He said he'd always sensed something there," Mom says.

"So why didn't you tell us?" I say. "You've always been so open about your sex life."

"I didn't want to complicate your grief. Mort was a generous and loving husband. He was a good father to all of you. He deserved to be mourned without any distractions."

Something occurs to me. "It wasn't Dad who wanted us to sit shiva, was it?"

Mom blushes and looks down at her lap. "Smart boy."

There are exclamations and groans of dismay from my siblings.

"Oh, come on!" Mom says. "You knew how your father felt about religion. Or, rather, didn't feel. I'm just surprised you all went along with it for so long."

"We thought it was his dying request!" Paul says. "Jesus Christ, Mom! What were you thinking?"

"Do you have any idea how hard it is to get the four of you to stay in the same place for more than a few hours? My husband, your father, had died. I needed you. And you needed each other, even if you still don't know it."

"Boner lied for you," I say.

Mom shrugs. "Charlie knows where his bread is buttered."

"Tracy wouldn't have dumped me if we hadn't come here," Phillip says, shaking his head.

"You're welcome, honey."

"You ruined my life."

"Oh, Phillip," Mom says fondly. "I may have overmothered you and screwed you up in ways large and small, but I think it's time you took some measure of responsibility for where you choose to put your own penis."

"You see? Right there. Please don't talk about my penis. It's out of your jurisdiction. Mothers do not sit around talking about their grown sons' penises."

"So grow up and I'll stop."

"You lied to us," Wendy says softly.

"Yes. I did."

"But you never lie to us. That's your thing."

"I never made love to a woman either," Mom says proudly. "People can change. Not often, and not often for the better, but it does happen." Mom, it should be pointed out, is loving this. Her children are shocked and mortified and hanging on her every word. There's our childhood in a nutshell. It's like we never left.

Phillip rolls off the couch, wincing in pain as he does, and stands up. "Okay. I forgive you for your lying and your treachery." He walks over to Mom and Linda and pulls them into a group hug. "I'm happy for you guys." Then he collapses onto the chair between them. "Anyone have any codeine? I think I'm bleeding internally."

Chapter 48

8:15 p.m.

Mom and Linda are over at Linda's house celebrating their official coming out. Paul and Alice are in my old bedroom behind closed doors, procreating under my poster of The Cure. Good luck and Godspeed. I give Cole and Ryan baths while Wendy puts Serena to bed. This entails standing outside her bedroom door and listening to her wail. I towel off Ryan while Cole splashes around in the tub, playing wildly with rubber dolphins that squirt water when you squeeze them. "Dawphins," he says.

"Don't be an ass, Cole," Ryan says.

"Hey!"

"It means 'donkey,'" Ryan says, giggling.

"Stop being a wise-donkey," I say.

He gives the matter some thought. "You're a donkey-hole," he says.

"You watch your mouth or I'll kick your donkey."

It takes him a second and then he laughs so hard I can see his ribs vibrating in his torso.

"Kick your donkey," Cole repeats in the tub. He raises the dolphins up above his head and brings them crashing down into the water, splashing us. "Fucker!"

"Cole!" Wendy hisses from the doorway. She offers me a pained smile. "We're working on that," she says to me.

"It sounds like he's got the hang of it."

"Fucker dawphin!" Cole says happily.

I am going to be a father, I think to myself.

8:45 p.m.

"IT FEELS LIKE the last day of camp," Wendy says. She is sitting on the edge of Cole's bed and I am sitting on the edge of Ryan's in what used to be Wendy's bedroom. "Tomorrow we all go our separate ways."

"You going to be okay on the plane alone with these three?" I say. Deflect emotions with logistics. It's what we do. Dad lives on in all of us. Our parents can continue to screw us up even after they die, and in this way, they're never really gone. My siblings and I will always struggle trying to confront an honest emotion. We'll succeed, to varying degrees, with outsiders, but fail consistently, sometimes spectacularly, with each other. The hardwiring simply runs too deep, like behind the walls of this house; circuit breakers on hair triggers.

"I'll be fine."

"And what about Barry?"

"What about him?"

"Nothing. Never mind."

Wendy sighs and looks down at her sleeping boy, her face a complex amalgam of love and pain and fear. I don't know that feeling yet, but I will soon enough.

"I have a very nice life, with a good man," Wendy says. "I love him for who he is. Sometimes who he is isn't enough for me, but most of the time, it is. There are women who would leave to find something better. I envy them, but I also know I'm not one of them. And how many of those women truly end up with a better man?" She shrugs. "No studies have been done."

"And Horry?"

"There is no Horry. Horry is a fantasy. And that's all I am to him. Time travel. We slept together as a favor to the kids we once were, not because there's really anything there besides history and some completely useless love."

She gets off the bed and onto her knees to kiss the forehead of each sleeping boy. Wendy taught me to curse, matched my clothing, brushed my hair before school, and let me sleep in bed with her when bad dreams woke me up. She fell in love often, and with great fanfare, throwing herself into each romance with the focus of an Olympic athlete. Now she's a mother and a wife, who tries to get her screaming baby to sleep through the night, tries to stop her boys from learning curse words, and calls romantic love useless. Sometimes it's heartbreaking to see your siblings as the people they've become. Maybe that's why we all stay away from each other as a matter of course.

8:55 p.m.

I COME DOWN the basement stairs to find Phillip sitting on my bed, holding my duffel bag full of cash. "This is a lot of money," he says.

"Yeah."

"Can I have some?"

"Define 'some.'"

Phillip thinks about it for a moment. "A grand?"

"Are you going to gamble it?"

"No."

"Are you going to buy drugs?"

"Jesus, Judd." He tosses the bag onto the floor and heads for the stairs. "Forget I asked."

"Phillip."

He turns around. "I have nothing, Judd. No home, no job, nothing. I've been waiting tables and sponging off Tracy for the last year. I'm just looking for a fresh start here. The plan was to work with Paul, but he's being a real dick about it."

"Well, maybe you have to work for him for a while, before you work with him."

He thinks about it for a moment and then hoists himself up to sit on the Ping-Pong table. "I could probably be persuaded to do that."

"I'll talk to Paul," I say.

"Yeah, because you guys are tight like that."

"People can change."

Phillip laughs and sits back down on the bed. "It's been nice here, this last week, being brothers again."

"We never stopped being brothers."

"It felt like we did."

"Yeah. I guess it did."

"Well, I'll have to stay more local to see my new nephew, huh?"

"Niece. It's a girl."

Phillip smiles. "A baby girl. That's nice."

"Yeah."

"I'm making a concerted effort to be considerably less fucked-up."

"I know."

He pulls himself off the Ping-Pong table and heads for the stairs. "Well, I'll let you get some sleep."

"Phillip."

"Yeah."

"Take a grand." Sixteen grand in a shopping bag feels like much more than sixteen grand in the bank.

"Thanks, man." He starts up the stairs.

"I'm serious. Come take it."

Phillip grins and pats the back pocket of his jeans, which I now see has a slight rectangular bulge. "Way ahead of you, big brother."

Chapter 49

9:25 p.m.

Penny opens the door brushing her teeth, dressed in leggings and a tank top.

"Hey," I say.

"Hey."

"I hope it's not too late."

"Too late for what?"

"Right. Good question. Well, for an apology, first of all."

Penny looks at me like she's peering through fog. I catch a glimpse of her lonely, cluttered apartment behind her. It feels like my fault.

"It's not too late," she says.

"I'm glad."

"Was that it?"

"What do you mean?"

"Was that your apology? I wasn't sure. Sometimes people say 'I want to apologize,' and then that's supposed to be their apology, when in fact, by saying they want to apologize, they manage to avoid the actual apology."

"Oh."

She shrugs. "I've been apologized to a lot."

"Penny."

"Is there something you want to say to me, Judd? Then just say it. You'll never have a less threatening audience."

"I didn't really think it out," I say. "I just came."

"Well, there's no danger of sounding too rehearsed then."

There's a small chunk of white toothpaste lodged in the corner of her mouth. I consider reaching forward to rub it off and decide against it.

"I'm really very sorry for leaving you at Wonderland."

She shakes her head. "That's not what you're sorry for."

"It's not?"

"You're sorry for not telling me that Jen was pregnant. That you were horrifically conflicted about it, that you're still in love with her, and that you were probably the worst possible guy for me to climb into bed with."

"Yes. I'm very sorry about that. Ashamed, really. It took me ten minutes to work up the nerve to ring your buzzer."

"I know. I was watching from the window."

"I really am sorry. You deserved better."

"I forgive you."

"Really? Just like that?"

"Yes, just like that."

"You still sound angry."

"I sound distant. Because I am. Because as much as I appreciate your coming over here, I have spent the last day building a big old wall between you and me, and I'm going to stay back here on my side of it."

"I guess I understand that."

"It's nothing personal."

We stand there in silence for a moment. I don't know what I expected.

"So, the shiva is over?"

"Yeah. I guess. Tomorrow morning."

"Then what?"

I shake my head. "I don't really know."

"Well, there's no law against taking your time to figure it out."

"I guess not."

"Baby steps," she says, and then grins joylessly. "Sorry. Bad choice of words."

"It's okay."

"Well," Penny says. "We're back to awkward again, and you know I don't do awkward. So I'm going to give you a hug . . ." She steps forward and hugs me. She is warm and light in my arms, and I am filled with a deep sense of regret as her hair tickles my fingers. "And now you should get going."

"Good-bye, Penny. I hope I see you again."

Her smile is at half strength but somehow genuine. "Take care, Judd Foxman."

9:35 p.m.

I'M WALKING TO my car when I hear footsteps behind me. "Judd."

I turn around and she launches herself into my arms, becoming airborne just before impact, squeezing the breath out of me. Her legs wrap around me, and I hold her there while she hugs me. When she pulls back, she is smiling brightly through her tears. "I was never good at walls," she says.

"No you weren't."

"I want you to know that I'm still going to hold you to our pact."

"Yeah?"

"Yeah. We've each got five years to come up with a better plan. If not, it's you and me, babe."

I nod. "You and me."

"You good with that?"

"I'm good with that."

And then, because we are lit like a movie in the glow of the streetlight above us, and because at that moment I love her as much as I've ever loved anyone, I pull her into me and I kiss her lips. When she opens her mouth, I can taste the toothpaste on her tongue.

"Minty fresh," I say.

She laughs in musical peals, like small tolling bells, the kind of laugh that can make a man feel just a little more whole.

Tuesday

Chapter 50

8:15 a.m.

Boner comes over to officially end the shiva. His left temple is still fairly swollen where Paul's pitch hit him, and he doesn't look terribly happy to be seeing any of us again. In the week we've been here, we've trashed his temple, resurrected his embarrassing nickname, and inflicted bodily harm. He asks all of the immediate mourners to sit down in our low chairs one last time. Once he has us all seated, he sits down on one of the folding chairs and speaks as if he's reading from a script.

"For the last week, this has been a house of mourning," he says. "You've taken solace from each other, and from the community. Of course, your grief doesn't end with the shiva. In fact, the harder part is ahead: going back to your regular lives, to a world without your husband and father. And just as you have comforted each other here this week, you must continue to look in on each other, especially your mother, to talk about Mort, to keep his memory alive, to know you're not alone."

Boner stands. "The following two passages are from the book of Isaiah: *'No more will your sun set, nor your moon be darkened, for God will be an eternal light for you and your days of mourning shall end. Like a man whose mother consoles him, so shall I console you, and you shall be consoled in Jerusalem.'"*

"It would be so nice to believe in God," Phillip murmurs to no one in particular.

We all look at Boner expectantly, like graduates waiting to throw their caps.

"Now," he says, grinning away the formality. "Please stand up."

We all stand up, and the shiva is over. We are glad that it's over but sorry to see it go. We love each other but can't handle being around each other for very long. It's a small miracle we made it through these seven days intact. And even now, we smile at each other, but our smiles are awkward and eye contact is fleeting. Already, we are coming apart again.

"It's now customary for all of the immediate family to leave the house together," Boner says.

"And go where?" Paul.

"Just take a walk around the block."

"What for?" Me.

"For the last seven days, you have been apart from the world, focusing on death. Taking a walk outside reestablishes your connection to the living."

"So, just walk around the block?"

"Yes," Boner says, annoyed. "That would be great."

It's cooler than expected outside, bright and blustery, the first winds of autumn whispering through the leaves. Mom walks between Phillip and Wendy, lacing her arms through theirs, adding a procession-like quality to our stroll. Paul and I fall awkwardly into step behind them, our hands jammed into our pockets for warmth.

"So," Paul says. "What's next for you?"

"I don't really know."

"Well, if there's anything I can do . . ." His voice trails off.

I keep my eyes straight ahead. "What about Phillip?"

"What about him?"

"He needs a job."

"You need a job."

"I'll sign over my share if you hire him."

Paul looks sharply at me and then sighs. "I'm pretty sure Phillip hasn't screwed up his life for the last time."

"You're probably right."

We walk in silence for a bit. I kick a small stone ahead of us. When we reach it, Paul kicks it, keeping it in play. "Dad always had a soft spot for him, didn't he?"

I nod. "He was everything Dad wasn't."

"Crazy, you mean."

"Loud. Warm. Emotional. Dad liked us because we were kind of like him, and he liked Phillip because he wasn't anything like him."

Paul sighs. "So what are we talking about here?"

"Dad's gone," I say. "And along with the business, we inherit the business of bailing out Phillip."

He kicks the rock a little too hard, and it clatters off the sidewalk and into the street. "Okay. Here's the deal. You keep your share. I'll bring Phillip into the business on a trial basis. But when it comes to him screwing up, you and I are partners. Fifty-fifty. Deal?"

"Deal," I say. It feels good to be talking like this, like brothers. We turn the corner onto Lansing, a short, crescent-shaped street that jughandles back around to Knob's End.

Paul stops walking and clears his throat. "I want to say something else."

"Yeah?"

"What happened the other night. I said some things."

"We both did."

"Yeah, well, the point is, I've been pissed at you for a very long time and that didn't do either of us any good. I wasted a lot of time being angry, time I can't get back. And now I see you, so angry about what happened to your marriage, and I just want to tell you, at some point it doesn't matter who was right and who was wrong. At some point, being angry is just another bad habit, like smoking, and you keep poisoning yourself without thinking about it."

"I hear you. Thanks."

Paul slaps my back. "Do as I say, and not as I do, right?"

"Right. Thanks, Paul."

He starts walking again, a step ahead of me. "Don't mention it, little brother."

As far as rapprochements go, it's awkward and vague, but the advantage to being as emotionally inarticulate as we are is that it will do the trick. So we walk on, lighter than when we left, the staccato click of Mom's stiletto heels beating out a Morse code on the pavement as she leads us back home.

9:10 a.m.

MOM CRIES WHEN she kisses Wendy good-bye. She can be so over the top as a matter of routine that when normal emotions come into play, it almost feels unreal. But we are her children, and we're all leaving her again. I kiss my two nephews good-bye and strap them into their car seats. "You guys have fun on the plane. Be good."

"I live in California," Cole informs me solemnly.

"Yes you do."

"Good-bye, Uncle Judd," Ryan says.

The next time I see them, Cole will be speaking in full sentences and Ryan will be a sullen adolescent sports fan with the first dusting of hair on his legs. He probably won't let me kiss his cheek anymore. The thought fills me with sadness, and I give him a second kiss.

"Donkey-hole," he says, and we share a conspiratorial laugh. Cole's not sure what's funny, but he laughs along with us, because he's two and why the hell not.

Wendy hugs me. "Go have some fun while you still can," she says. "Have meaningless sex. Crush women like beer cans. A little misogyny will be good for you."

"Have a safe trip."

"You're a wuss, Judd. But I love you. I'll come in when you have the baby." She kisses me brusquely and then moves on to Phillip, then Paul and Alice, and then hoists up Serena, sleeping in her little car seat, and climbs into the back of the van. As the van drives down Knob's End, I see Horry standing on his porch, raising one still hand in farewell. The van lurches to a stop in front of his house, and Horry comes down the stairs. The windows are tinted and don't open. Horry puts his hand on the glass, peering intently in. I can't see inside the van, but I imagine Wendy placing her hand on the glass, lining her fingers up with his for a long moment, before leaning back and telling the van driver to floor it, because she has a flight to catch.

9:25 a.m.

IN THE TOP drawer of my father's ancient mahogany dresser is a clutter of mementos. An expired passport; his high school ring; a monogrammed Swiss Army knife; a worn-out wallet; some loose cuff links; the old Tag Heuer watch he always meant to get fixed; a stack of our creased report cards wrapped in rubber bands; assorted souvenir key chains; an expensive-looking fountain pen; a gold butane lighter—also monogrammed; an assortment of loose screws, bolts, and plastic wire connectors; a wire stripper; and, in a small silver frame, a black-and-white nude portrait of my mother in all her young glory, before kids and breast implants would change the topography of her body. She is slim and fresh-faced and there's something awkward in her pose, like she hasn't fully grown into herself yet. I can tell from her smile that it was my father behind the camera. The frame gleams without a hint of tarnish. Dad took care of this picture.

I'll leave the Swiss Army knife for Paul and the lighter for Phillip. I slip my Rolex off of my wrist and into my pocket, and I pick up Dad's old Tag Heuer. When I was a kid I would hold on to his wrist and turn the diving bezel, enjoying the way it clicked around the face of the watch. I give the bezel a few turns. The clicks feel different without his wrist anchoring the watch. I flip it over and see that the back of the case is engraved. YOU FOUND ME. My mother's words, her naked love cut into steel. It's hard to imagine her ever having felt lost, but it's impossible to know the people your parents were before they were your parents. They really did have something, though, my parents. I don't think I ever fully appreciated that until right now. At first the steel is cold against my wrist, but it warms quickly against my skin, like a living thing. I slide the drawer closed and sit on his side of the bed for a minute, looking down at the watch. My wrist isn't nearly as thick as his was, and I'll have to have some links removed from the band when I get the watch fixed. For now the hands are motionless on the white face—the watch stopped working years ago—but I don't have much of a schedule to keep to these days.

9:40 a.m.

MOM, PHILLIP, PAUL, Alice, and Horry are at the table, eating a lavish brunch comprised of shiva leftovers. Phillip is telling a story that has them alternately gasping and laughing. He has many stories that can do that, and some of them might even be true. I watch them for a moment, unseen from the hallway, and then step quietly down the hall to the front door. For reasons I don't fully understand, being at the center of another tangle of good-bye hugs and well-wishes is more than I can handle right now. Alice will be weird, Paul awkward, Phillip exuberant, and Mom will cry, which will make me cry, and I have cried enough.

"Making good your escape, I see."

I turn to see Linda, standing at the foot of the stairs, watching me.

"No. I was just—"

"It's okay," she says softly. "Seven days is a lot of togetherness. Come give me a hug." She wraps her arms around me and kisses me once on each cheek.

"I'm happy for you and Mom," I say.

"Really? It's not too weird for you?" She blushes a little, looking younger and suddenly vulnerable, and I can see her a little the way Mom does.

"It's a good weird."

"That was a perfect way to describe it," she says, hugging me again. "Thank you."

"So, are you going to move in?"

"We'll see," she says, offering up a small, wry smile. "We're taking it very slow. Your mom hasn't dated in such a long time. This is all very new to her."

"I would imagine it is."

"Oh. Well, yes, that too."

She looks me over fondly, appraising me. "You look better than when you first got here."

"Then I was a cuckolded husband. Now I'm an expecting father."

She grins. "Don't be a stranger, Judd."

"I won't."

Outside, the sun lights up the red leaves of the dogwoods, casting the yard in soft amber hues. Across the street, two gardeners with noisy leaf blowers send up a twister of multicolored leaves swirling off the lawn, blowing them in a slow, graceful procession to the curb. A cat suns itself in a picture window. A woman jogs by pushing a baby in a running stroller. It's amazing how harmless the world can sometimes seem.

9:55 a.m.

I SIT IDLING in a gas station just before the interstate junction, drawing maps in my head. I can be at the skating rink in ten minutes. I can be back in Kingston in ninety. According to the GPS, I can be in Maine in seven hours and seven minutes. My car doesn't have GPS, but Phillip's Porsche does, and that's what I'm driving. I left him a note with the keys to my car. This morning, on a hunch, I counted the money in my bag and found it light two grand, not one, so I figure a little collateral is in order.

Penny. Jen. Maine. None of the above. There are options, is my point.

The girl gassing up her blue Toyota has piles of kinky brown curls held off her face with a black headband. She has great skin and funky black glasses that convey a sexy intelligence. She's a magazine writer, or maybe a photographer. When she looks over at me looking over at her, I smile. She smiles back and I fall briefly, passionately in love with her.

Options.

I want very badly to be in love again, which is why I'm in no position to look for it. But I hope I'll know it when it comes. My father's watch jingles loosely on my wrist, my mother's words resting unseen on my skin. YOU FOUND ME. It gives me hope.

I pull onto the interstate, grinding the transmission once or twice on the way to fourth. Dad made us all learn on a manual, his massive forearms flexing as he worked the stick. *Clutch, shift, up, gas. Clutch, shift, up, gas.* I hear him in my head and smile. We can all drive stick.

We can all change a flat. We can all repress our feelings until they poison us. It's a complicated legacy.

I'm not a fan of country music, but there's no better music to drive to. Turn the right song up loud enough on the Porsche's sound system and it will swallow you whole. The past is prelude and the future is a black hole, but right now, hurtling north across state lines for no particular reason, I have to say, it feels pretty good to be me. Tonight I'll sleep in Maine. Tomorrow is anybody's guess. I've got a baby girl on the way, a borrowed Porsche, and fourteen grand in a shopping bag.

Anything can happen.

Acknowledgments

Thank You:

Lizzie, for your endless support and encouragement. Spencer, Emma, and Alexa, who continue to amaze and inspire me. Simon Lipskar, who, nine years and five novels later, continues to represent me with passion, wisdom, and just the right amount of profanity. Ben Sevier, my editor, who read numerous drafts of this book, providing sharp insight and helpful suggestions at every step along the way. Kassie Evashevski, Tobin Babst, Rebecca Ewing, Maja Nikolic, and Josh Getzler.

About the Author

Jonathan Tropper is the internationally bestselling, critically acclaimed author of *How to Talk to a Widower, Everything Changes, The Book of Joe,* and *Plan B.* He lives with his family in Westchester, New York, where he teaches writing at Manhattanville College.

He can be contacted through his website at www.jonathantropper.com.

PRAISE FOR NOVELS OF JONATHAN TROPPER

1. Claire Cook
2. *Publishers Weekly*
3. *People*
4. *Entertainment Weekly*
5. Augusten Burroughs
6. Jane Green
7. *Daily Mail*
8. *Daily Mail*
9. *USA Today*
10. *New York Daily News*
11. *Publishers Weekly*
12. Tom Perrotta
13. Sue Margolis
14. *Booklist*
15. Lolly Winston
16. *Publishers Weekly*
17. Haven Kimmel
18. Jane Green